THE
HANGING

LOTTE AND SØREN HAMMER are a sister and brother from Denmark. In 2004 they began writing crime novels together. To date, they have written five books in this series. *The Hanging* is the first and has been sold in twenty-one countries.

D0063358

asd

THE HANGING

LOTTE AND SØREN
HAMMER

BLOOMSBURY

LONDON · NEW DELHI · NEW YORK · SYDNEY

First published in Great Britain 2013
This paperback edition published 2014

Copyright © 2012 by Lotte Hammer Jakobsen and Søren Hammer Jacobsen
Translation © 2013 by Ebba Segerberg

First published in Denmark as *Svinehunde* by Gyldendal

The moral rights of the authors have been asserted

Bloomsbury Publishing Plc
50 Bedford Square
London
WC1B 3DP

www.bloomsbury.com

Bloomsbury Publishing, London, New Delhi, New York and Sydney
A CIP catalogue record for this book is available from the British Library

ISBN 978 1 4088 4320 8
10 9 8 7 6 5 4 3 2 1

Design by Steven Seighman
Printed and bound in Great Britain by CPI Group (UK) Ltd, Croydon CR0 4YY

MIX
Paper from
responsible sources
FSC® C020471

THE
HANGING

PROLOGUE

The man in the field tossed the last couple of logs into place. Then he straightened up, pressed the backs of his hands above his tailbone, and stretched a couple of times to counter the surprising tenderness he felt. He was accustomed to physical labor, so he didn't count the few hours he had spent filling the pit as anything special, and compared to what he had accomplished over the course of the day, a little soreness was immaterial. It merely surprised him.

Moving with some discomfort, he took the last of the gas cans and poured the contents out over the logs, the uppermost layer of which was level with the ground. There were approximately fifteen cubic meters of seasoned beech wood, mixed with a little elm, chestnut, and birch, as well as a young plum tree with reddish brown bark on the sunny side and greenish on the shadow side, as he had noticed with an expert's gaze. There were also thirty-one bags of coal, an amount that he had meticulously memorized before he started and then tallied sack for sack as he carried them into place, so that the work would feel less monotonous. He glanced at his watch and noted that its face was covered with dried blood and that neither hand was visible. Just as when he had checked it last.

He tore off the watch and tossed it into the fire, then looked up at the sky, which was beginning to grow dark. To the west, a low band of clouds was illuminated by the scarlet rays of the setting sun, and the lake below the field lay gray and hazy. A storm was brewing.

From his backpack he took out a clean set of clothes as well as a plastic bag with moist towelettes. He bared his sinewy upper body, and although he was shivering the wipes felt good against his skin as he methodically began to wash up. He was particularly thorough with his head and hands, where the coal dust had left tracks and would attract attention, which made him think about the fact that he ought to have brought a mirror along. He smiled into the dusk. He didn't normally care much about his reflection but today was special. Perhaps it was even possible for him on this day in this godforsaken field in Sjelland to feel a smidgen of pride; yes, perhaps even shed his stupid nickname. Everyone called him the Climber. Only a few— almost no one—knew his real name, the name he had once had back when someone cared about him and he cared for someone. Until . . . it wasn't like that anymore.

This thought of childhood did not go unpunished: the pain in his lumbar region spread down across his buttocks and thighs with a ferocious sting. He ignored it and concentrated on changing his clothes, tossing the old ones on the pile. When he was done, he felt the sweetness of revenge rush through him. Apart from one unforeseen situation that he had kept to himself and would have to solve later, he had followed his instructions down to the last letter. Now it was up to the others in the group.

He took out a lighter, bent down, and lit the bonfire. The gasoline caught fire at the first spark and the flames blossomed up toward him so vigorously that he shrank back a step with alarm. For a short while he stayed to warm himself but his deep discomfort with fire quickly won out.

A bolt of lightning rent the dusk and he turned calmly to look at the sky. The storm was approaching faster than he had expected. In the gully to his left, where the forest sloped down to the lake, a couple of black storm clouds were advancing on him, as if the earth had opened up and let loose the dark powers of the underworld. Another lightning bolt, and a third dark cloud charged up the gorge. Then came the rain. Large, aggressive drops, thousands of sharp arrows that ricocheted from the ground and dislodged pieces of earth on the stubby fields. Powerful, cleansing, just.

For a moment he gazed at the pyre with concern but the water wouldn't extinguish the fire. At worst it would hold the flames at bay. He turned and walked purposefully toward the woods without glancing back. Soon he was completely engulfed by the dark.

CHAPTER 1

Monday morning fog rolled in over the land in white woolly waves. The two children could hardly see a meter ahead of them as they crossed onto the school grounds. They had to find their way from memory and soon their steps became hesitant and searching. The boy was slightly behind the girl, his school bag in his arms. All of a sudden he stopped.

"Don't go on without me."

The girl stopped as well. The fog particles condensed in her hair, and she wiped the droplets from her brow as she patiently waited for her little brother, who was struggling to wrench his bag onto his back. He had spoken Turkish, which he rarely did, and never to her; now he was occupied with the straps and pulling harder on them, but it didn't help. When he was finally done, he grabbed her hand. She looked around to see if she could spy the other end of the field through the mist.

She said, "Now see what you've done."

"What have I done?"

He tightened his grip and sounded small.

"Nothing. You don't understand."

She picked a direction at random and took a few blind steps before she stopped short again. The boy pressed up against her.

"Have we gone astray?"

"Idiot."

"It was light at Mother's."

"In a little while it'll be light here too."

"What does it mean, *astray*?"

She didn't answer him, and tried to convince herself that there was nothing to be afraid of, that the school grounds weren't particularly large, that they should just keep going.

"We aren't allowed to go off with strangers. No matter what, we can't go off with strangers. Isn't that right?"

She could hear that he was on the verge of tears and she pulled him along behind her in a series of uncertain steps, until she suddenly saw a slight glow diagonally in front of her and steered toward it.

Shortly afterward they were in the corridor in front of the gymnasium. The girl was sitting on a bench, reading, and her brother came running with a ball in his arms.

"Do you want to play ball with me? You're so good at it."

"Have you hung your clothes up properly and set your bag down in its place?"

He nodded, wide-eyed, the embodiment of sincerity.

"Come on, go and do it."

He lumbered off without objection, but was soon back and repeated his desire to play.

"I have something I have to read first. You start and I'll be there in a bit."

He glanced skeptically at her book. It was thick.

"Promise you'll come soon?"

"As soon as I've finished this chapter. Go in and play on your own. It won't be long."

He ran into the gym and soon she heard the sounds of a bouncing ball. She kept reading. From time to time she closed her eyes and imagined she was a part of the story.

The boy interrupted her.

"There isn't room to play," he called out.

"Why not?"

"Because some men are hanging up in here."

"So go around them."

Suddenly he was in front of her. She hadn't heard him approach.

"I don't like the men."

The girl sniffed the air a couple of times.

"Have you farted?"

"No, but I don't like the dead men. They've been cut up."

She got up angrily and walked over to the doorway to the gymnasium, her brother at her heels.

Five people were hanging from the ceiling, each suspended by a single rope. They were naked and facing toward her.

"Aren't they gross?"

"Yes," she said and closed the door.

She put her arm around the boy.

"Can we play ball now?"

"No, we can't. We have to find an adult."

CHAPTER 2

Detective Inspector Konrad Simonsen was enjoying a vacation. He was sitting in a room with a view in the top story of a summer house and was busy having his fourth smoke of the morning and a cup of coffee. He stared out through the oversize windows at a couple of drifting stratus clouds, not thinking of anything in particular.

The athletic young woman who appeared—just back from her morning run—had removed her socks and shoes so he did not hear her steps as she entered the room, and he gave a start when she spoke. Moreover, he was used to being alone.

"For heaven's sake, Dad. The least you could do is crack a window."

Her outburst was directed at the cigarette smoke that hung heavy in the air; she opened the french doors all the way so that a fresh sea breeze rushed through the room and tossed her blond curls around, until she decided that the worst of the smell was gone and latched the doors. Then she flopped into one of the armchairs across from him without showing any concern for the fact that she thereby crushed the newspaper tucked into her sweatpants.

He said, "Good morning, have you been all the way to Blokhus? That must have been quite a run."

"Morning—it's almost afternoon, sleepyhead. Yes, I've been down to Blokhus, and it's actually not that far."

He pointed to the newspaper.

"Is that for me?"

She answered with irony, but without an edge, "And thank you, my lovely daughter, for making me coffee."

"And thank you, my sweet Anna Mia, for making me coffee."

She took out the newspaper, but then her gaze fell on the ashtray and her steely expression told him what was coming. With a gesture of accusation she pointed to the shutters and her Bornholm dialect grew stronger.

"Four cigarettes before breakfast!"

"You know, I'm on break right now, so it's a bit different than usual."

He could have saved himself the lie.

"You smoke far too much, you drink too much, your diet is terrible, and to call you overweight would be an act of kindness."

He defended himself halfheartedly: "I almost never smoke at work and only moderately in the evenings so surely I can relax occasionally."

"Well, except for the fact that you're lying, that sounds very reasonable."

He didn't know what to say. He glanced in the direction of the newspaper, which was now very far away. Her already serious voice grew even thornier.

"You know you owe me fifteen more years, don't you, Dad?"

The number stung his psyche, and awakened the familiar knowledge of having been a terrible parent. It had been lying dormant for three years, since a happy May evening when she suddenly appeared on his doorstep and explained that she had one week in Copenhagen, and that it seemed most practical and economical for her to stay with him. Said it as if nothing could be more natural. Then she invaded his apartment and his life—an unknown sixteen-year-old girl, pretty, vivacious, full of life . . . his daughter.

There was nothing to do but lie down on his shield and hope for mercy, but the words didn't really want to come. To apologize seemed silly, and to promise reform and a new, healthy lifestyle was easier said than done. To top it off, he was not the type who found it easy to share his emotions. He launched into a couple of vague promises, until she suddenly shook off her seriousness and changed the subject.

"Let's get back to that another time, Dad. Tell me, have you gotten used to the digs? This is quite a sophisticated little cottage Nathalie has."

This topic was also explosive, even though it was slightly less personal, and if he hadn't known better, he would have suspected that she'd brought it up deliberately now that he was on the defensive. But she wasn't like that. It was only he who thought of conversations as a form of strategic play with winners and losers—a bad habit that he dismissed somewhat too conveniently as a professional disease and the result of many interrogations. He tried not to let himself be provoked.

"Yes, this is magnificent."

"Why did you get so sulky the day before yesterday when we arrived?"

"Because the Countess is my subordinate, and the whole thing was somewhat overwhelming."

"But you knew it was hers."

"Yes, my lovely girl, I did, but the Lord only knows I was not clear on the standard. This luxury villa would get the euro signs spinning in the eyes of the most exclusive vacation renter, and the fact that we're getting it for small change is unethical and probably also illegal."

"She's rich. So what? Anyway, enough with the 'girl.'"

"And then the refrigerator is stuffed with enough food to see us through an atomic winter."

"But we won't be here for an atomic winter, we're only going to be here for two weeks. You can just cut back on eating, of course. It certainly wouldn't hurt you to draw on your reserves for a while."

"No food, no drink, no smoking; what's next?"

She heard him and continued her lecture.

"Did you know that the flagstones on the terrace are hand-painted Italian stone and that the marble in the entrance hall is called *Ølandsbrud*?"

"How do you know that?"

"From Nathalie, of course."

No one else referred to the Countess as Nathalie, and it sounded strange to his ears. Nathalie von Rosen was admittedly her given name, but everyone, including herself, referred to her as the Countess.

10

"Have you been here before?"

"As it happens, yes."

"This gets worse and worse."

"Then you'll think this is even worse, because I have brought a gift along for you."

"A gift? Who is it from?"

"From Nathalie, but I was going to wait a few days before giving it to you."

There was nothing feigned about his look of bewilderment.

"You know, Dad, sometimes you are simply incredibly dense. This isn't that hard to understand, and—if you ask me—she's got a thing for you, and if you just took the slightest care of yourself and dropped fifteen or twenty kilos, you could make a great couple."

The room filled with the small, sharp sounds of bare feet on the whitewashed Pomeranian pine, and she was gone, before he had a chance to comment on her absurd idea.

The gift from the Countess was brilliant. Like a parrot on its perch, Anna Mia settled onto the armrest of his chair (when she returned) and watched closely as he unwrapped it. Aron Nimzowitsch, *Mein System*, the first edition from 1925, with a dedication from the master himself—a treasure that transported him into a state akin to ecstasy. Meanwhile, Anna Mia managed to read over his shoulder.

"What does she mean, 'Thank you for your help'?"

He turned the card over, too late.

"Don't you have any manners? You don't read other people's letters, do you?"

"I do. What did you help her with?"

"That doesn't concern you!"

They sat for a while in silence, she on the armrest and he in the chair.

"Tell me, how well do you two know each other?" he asked.

11

"Who? Me and Nathalie?"

Her feigned nonchalance was laughable.

"Yes, of course."

"That doesn't concern you."

They were back to square one.

Shortly thereafter, she became more communicative.

"I don't know Nathalie particularly well, and we haven't gone behind your back. Not very much at any rate, and the fact that I have been here before is pure coincidence. We ran into each other in Skagen last summer, and she asked me to lunch. But I already know how you have helped her. It was during her divorce, wasn't it?"

He hesitated.

"We talked a little."

She stroked him over the crown of the head.

"I believe you've earned your book, Dad. So do me a favor and for once don't let's talk about price. Nathalie would never expect to get anything in return for her gifts, that's how she is and you know it."

"Yes, I do. But it is a matter of principle."

"Maybe you have the wrong principles."

She got up and walked over to one of the windows as he gingerly, almost devoutly turned the pages of his book.

"I'm taking a bath. In the meantime you can figure out what we should do today."

"Yes, yes, that's fine."

She had to call him twice before he stirred, and he did not notice that the mood had changed again. He was too far gone in his game of chess.

"Is your cell phone turned on?"

"No. The agreement was that the outside world should be excluded, I think you will recall. Why do you ask?"

He got up with a last long look at a game in the book, then

12

stared out the windows and let his gaze wander along the horizon. The undulating-dune landscape unfolded before him like irregular windswept hills, a shining white where the sun hit them, inky gray and dark on the other side, some invaded by rugosa rose, others anchored by wild rye. In the distance he could see the North Sea with its glittering white-crested waves and above that a flock of wild geese flying south along the coastline. Suddenly he became aware of Anna Mia's arm around him, and her head heavy against his back. A feeling of shyness and awe overcame him, as if her youthfulness was something sacred. But he remained as he was and after a few seconds of eternity she said softly, "They're coming to pick you up, Dad."

Only then did he see it. A disturbingly foreign body slowly snaking its way up along the twisty dune road: a police car.

CHAPTER 3

Some four hours later, Simonsen found himself at Langbæk School in Bagsværd, staring out at the rain that was falling, bleak and silent. A canine unit was working in the bushes behind the playground. The police officer directed the dog with hand signals and shouted commands, occasionally bringing it back to be petted and praised. A young woman with a plastic bag wrapped around her head as a makeshift scarf walked up to the officer and for a while she watched the officer's gestures before a gust of wind splattered the window with water and greatly reduced the visibility. He turned his gaze back to the corridor. The colors on the wall were bare and dirty, alternating between various shades of yellow. The linoleum floor was pock-marked and looked like an obstacle course. Somewhat-successful artistic creations hung scattered about. The nearest one employed a preponderance of wire and very dusty soda cans.

He made a gesture of futility. "Dammit, Countess."

The words were intended for the woman behind him, who was talking on a cell phone, and they were said without anger, simply to point out the absurdity of having been transported across the country like an express delivery, only to end up standing around staring out into the dreary October weather. Without knowing much about the investigation, he was expected to take charge, and yet he hadn't the faintest idea where he should go next.

The woman reacted to his outburst, placing one hand over the phone.

"Hello, Simon, sorry about your vacation, but at least you got a couple of days. I hope Anna Mia wasn't too upset. Arne will be here in one second, he'll brief you." She smiled and returned to her call before he was able to answer. He returned her smile without really wanting to, and thought to himself that she had fine teeth. He let his stomach relax and looked out the window again, where the view was still depressing. The Countess's conversation went on and on, which he took as a discomfiting sign that the homicide unit would be in excellent shape to continue without its current chief when the day came.

And yet, perhaps not. Simonsen had been half following the conversation—which he pressumed was with one of the forensic specialists—and suddenly he was struck with the thought that something wasn't right. A slightly elevated tone of voice and questions in which there was a certain discrepancy between the level of detail and the time gave her away. When she launched into a question almost identical to one she had already asked, he grabbed

14

her by the arm in which she held the phone and pulled gently. She hung up without saying goodbye.

"When did you last have something to eat?"

"I don't know; a while ago. What time is it?"

He was very familiar with this condition and also knew that it was temporary. From time to time, all investigators encountered things that were difficult to deal with and that got under their skin. Unpleasant images that became fixed in the back of the head and could not be erased. This was clearly one of those times for her. He himself found it hardest when the victims were children, but that was something he had in common with most police officers, and he had not yet been inside the gymnasium. He halted his train of thought and came back to the present.

"Drive into town and get yourself something to eat. Be back here in an hour."

"I'm not hungry."

"That's an order, Countess. And turn off your phone."

She nodded, as if she understood. But he saw in her eyes that she did not. Normally she was the personification of stability. She was the one who pulled back when everyone else was driving off the cliff. She turned around and the dim daylight fell onto her face. And he saw that her face had the same ashen tint as her hair.

"It's horrible, Simon. I don't think I've ever seen anything like it."

"No, I don't suppose either of us has."

"Arne and I peeked in from the door and . . . ugh, it was awful."

"I'm sure it was. Now off you go. I have other things to do than worry myself about you."

He accompanied his comment with a smile to take the edge off his words. She appeared not to notice it. She remained where she was and he wondered if he should embrace her or simply place a hand on her shoulder. But he did neither; he wasn't good at that sort of thing.

Finally she said, "I'll be fine in a bit."

"I know you will. See you."

And then she left.

The special-education clinic had been temporarily transformed into an investigation hub. There were two bookcases whose contents had been emptied onto the windowsill, and on the table in the middle of the room was a stack of paper as well as a box of pencils. A whiteboard stood in front of the dark green chalkboard, so that explanations could be given in marker rather than chalk, and a map of the school had been hung on one wall of the room. It had clearly been posted in haste, and the result was sadly haphazard.

Simonsen studied the plan with a tilted head, while Arne Pedersen used the time to wipe off his chair. His pants were already stained in two places and he did not wish to make matters worse.

"How was your trip?"

"Unpleasant."

"What about the vacation house? Can you get a refund?"

"Unlikely."

The chairs, which had seen better days, creaked alarmingly when the two men sat down.

Simonsen rested his elbows on the table and asked curtly, "How are you doing?"

Pedersen was not unsettled by the question, which was a good sign.

"Better, but it wasn't easy in the beginning. I broke down twice, and I haven't done that in years. On the whole, that is. Not once—or twice—for that matter."

"But you're okay now?"

"Usually it's just children—well, you know."

"Arne, answer my question. Are you okay now?"

Pedersen gazed back at him steadily.

"Yes, I'm fine now."

"Good. Then give me an update on chronology, resources, and status."

This came out sounding more abrupt and imperious than he had intended but his irritation at the wait was still with him and he wanted to get straight to the facts. His words were promptly obeyed. Pedersen went through the events exactingly, starting with the Turkish mother who had dropped her kids off at 6:15 A.M. by the bicycle shed to the right of the school entrance.

He went on. "It was the first day after fall break and the school was already unlocked. The children went to their respective classrooms and hung up their coats, after which they met by the gymnasium in building B in order to play soccer. Inside, they discovered five bodies. The big sister searched in vain for an adult but did not find one. She called 911 from the teachers' lounge and was transferred to the Gladsaxe police station. The call was clocked at six forty-one. The officer on duty . . . excuse me . . ."

He stopped and appeared to reflect on something.

Simonsen said, "The name is not particularly important. But tell me, those two children. Aren't they a little on the early side? I thought instruction began at eight o'clock."

"That's correct, and I wondered about that too, so I asked the headmaster. It turns out that the school has a handful of children that meet up long before lessons begin. All schools are familiar with the problem. For some parents it is simply a matter of wanting to save money on morning care, for others it is a pressure they face each day—"

"Okay, Okay, go on," Simonsen interrupted.

"Yes, of course . . . now where was I? . . . right. The officer on duty instructed the girl to wait until a teacher arrived, and she then contacted her mother's workplace in Gentofte. The mother could not be located immediately, but the owner—a Danish resident of Lebanese origins who is somewhat familiar with the girl—decided to drive out to her. He arrived at the school a little before seven A.M. At the gymnasium he chased off eight children who had gathered there. He also called the Gladsaxe police again and at seven thirty-eight A.M. a patrol unit arrived—"

"At seven thirty-eight!" Simonsen interrupted sharply.

Pedersen avoided his gaze and adjusted his tie, a movement that his boss was all too familiar with.

"Cough up that name and tell me what happened."

Additional delays were futile, and the name of the officer on duty was produced. Also the explanation.

"He said that the calls could be deprioritized . . . since it was clear that they were from 'Mujafa types.' Yes, unfortunately that is a direct quote."

Simonsen was genuinely incensed.

"Why are you protecting a thug like that? Do you know him?"

Pedersen had been blessed with a youthful appearance. Despite his forty years he resembled an overgrown youth, and now he blushed from ear to ear so that his complexion matched his fiery red hair.

"We were at the police academy together. He and I are in a betting pool together."

Simonsen frowned and closed his eyes, but decided not to ask further questions. Pedersen was a good investigator—creative as well as effective—and it was a distinct possibility that he would eventually become the next division chief. But his passion for gambling was well known and there was more than one story circulating about him. One day they would have to have a talk, but not now, and if Pedersen owed the thug some money, he did not want to know it.

"We'll drop it. Go on."

"The patrol officers called for backup, the school was sealed off, and the children were sent home. The staff were assembled in the teachers' lounge and we were contacted of course. I arrived around nine A.M. and sent for you, whereupon I informed the police chief as well as rounding up Troulsen, Pauline, and the Countess. Then I got the whole thing under way and called in anything that can crawl: investigators, technicians, forensic specialists, canine units—yes, even Elvang is here."

"Why the dogs? What are we looking for?"

"Ten hands, among other things."

"Bloody hell."

"Exactly."

"Have you been inside the gymnasium?"

"No, just the doorway. On two different occasions. The first time I felt sick, as I told you. They're running around in space suits and it looks like a science fiction film, and as soon as I as much as breathed in there I got long lectures about contamination of crime scenes. You can guess who from. It's completely hysterical."

"The head of our Criminal Forensics Division is paid to get hysterical like that. What about Elvang?"

"Yes, what about Elvang? Obviously he had to wait. And in addition . . ." He searched for the words.

"In addition?"

"He called me a slave to fashion, but that's not particularly relevant."

"No, apart from the fact that he evidently still has some spirit in him."

"You can laugh all you want, it'll be your turn in a minute. He is waiting for you, once we're done. The room is probably ready by now. But while we're on the topic, I know with certainty why he isn't retired yet. My brother's new girlfriend works at the Ministry of Education, which oversees the National Health Service. That should count for something, it's not just idle talk. Do you want to know why?"

Simonsen wondered silently if his subordinate had a surplus of anything but rigorous facts, but he answered with a smile, "I'd love to, when we have the time. How are our resources?"

"It's not quite clear yet, but looks promising. We're about to be reorganized into a special unit. They're making the organizational changes."

"That sounds ominous. Who are *they*?"

"I don't know. I tell you, Simon, the first hour was like a zoo—I've never experienced anything like it. The minister of justice called twice and asked to be briefed minute by minute."

"The minister of justice? Why on earth doesn't he keep to the proper channels?"

"No idea. I didn't ask him that."

"'Minute by minute,' did he really say that?"

"Yes, he did actually. Verbatim."

"Astounding."

"You can say that again."

"On top of that, the national police chief called a couple of times. To underscore the fact that the minister of justice was to be briefed. And the second time he threatened to come in person, but the Countess talked him out of it. Then there was the police director, but that is natural enough. The county commissioner has the mayor of Gladsaxe on his back, so he called in frequently too. Moreover, the attorney general got on the line, distinctly out of sorts."

"The attorney general? How in the world did he get in the picture?"

"Well, that was what he was asking me about. He didn't want

anything to do with the investigation, I believe he said. He is not completely easy to understand and I could never figure out who it was who involved him in the first place. And the Countess has had her hands full. Both with the chairman and vice chairperson of the parliamentary judiciary committee. Among others."

"For heaven's sake, what a mess."

"You can say that again, and there's more. Finally I received a call from the head at the Department of State, Helmer Hammer—yes, that is his name—and that was immediately after the minister of justice's second round, so I was impatient with all the interruptions at this point. I was also a bit shaken, which I can see now in hindsight. Well, I told him in fairly direct terms that unless we had some peace to do our work, there would be absolutely nothing to report on, regardless of whether the queen herself called. Then I hung up or whatever it is you do with a cell phone."

"Hm, was that wise? What happened after that?"

"He called back."

"Smart move. Are you going to be directing traffic now?"

"No, he's reasonable when it comes down to it. He doesn't know anything about police work, which is something thankfully he volunteered himself, but he promised to stop with the interruptions and he's kept his word. There have been no VIP calls since."

Pedersen looked relieved. Simonsen tried to get the conversation back on track without sounding too impatient.

"That all sounds quite positive, but does not actually explain the state of our resources."

"Yes it does, because he also said that you should take the lead on the investigation."

"I'm already doing that."

"Yes, I know. Let me explain. That is, you should lead the investigation and exclusively report back to him. No one else."

"The usual lines of communication are being silenced?"

"In a manner of speaking, but it gets better. You can proceed freely, and you have no resource constraints whether in regard to man-hours or financials. He will take care of any administrative hurdles so that your time can be completely devoted to investigating."

"That is quite something."

"Yes, he is not without power. However, he did make a point of saying that your official mandate has not yet been drawn up, but that is just a matter of paperwork. You should get in touch with him when you have a moment. I have his number. So the sum of all this, Simon, is that you are basically your own boss."

"Did he say that too?"

"No, that is my own conclusion."

"Hm, it doesn't really matter to me that the usual protocol is put aside."

"It's better than having all kinds of highly elevated men and women throw us around according to their whims."

"Maybe, but we'll have to see about that. Right now we have other things to think about."

Suddenly the bell went off, high-pitched and piercing. No one had thought about shutting it off since the children had been sent home. It caused Simonsen to jump, and his chair groaned. For a split second he lay outstretched on his desk. Pedersen, whose relationship to school bells was less troubled, waited quietly until the noise ceased, after which he completed his report.

"The current division of labor is that Pauline is trawling the neighbors and the outdoor areas of the school, the Countess is responsible for the interior of the school, Troulsen is debriefing the school staff, and I am free now that you're here. Our most pressing problem is that the dead are as yet unidentified, and that the janitor is missing. Per Clausen is his name and he was likely the one who unlocked the school this morning, but no one has seen him. It is possible that he's indisposed due to excessive alcohol consumption—apparently that happens from time to time. As for the task of identifying the victims, I have a dozen experienced people occupied with the task of finding out if the five men have been reported missing anywhere. There are not yet any results."

Simonsen reflected on this, then stood up, and Pedersen followed suit.

"We'll meet in half an hour, make sure the others get the message. You can come get me in the gymnasium, but I want to get Elvang alone first. Tell Troulsen that not so much as a flea leaves this place without my permission, and get Pauline inside before she starts to look like a drowned animal. I don't even know what the hell she's doing out there—helping the dogs?"

"For Pete's sake, she doesn't have much experience yet."

"And she won't get it simply by getting wet. Or get her some proper rain gear. The school patrol probably has one hanging on a hook somewhere. And one more thing. There have been ten schoolchildren in the gymnasium. Has a crisis counselor been called in? What about the parents—have they been informed?"

"Oh, no."

Pedersen banged his fist against the doorframe. He had two children of his own.

"Take care of it, but first lead me to Elvang and tell your story about him on the way. You've done a fine job, Arne. Very satisfactory."

The praise sounded hollow. As if learned in a management seminar.

CHAPTER 4

The graveyard was deserted and the lone man with the umbrella moved slowly, almost humbly, past the gravestones that seemed to sense that he did not fit in. Every step he took made a crunching sound in the pea gravel and sounded wrong in the wet silence of the place. At an unadorned grave at the edge of the cemetery he stopped and placed a folding chair on the ground. Before he sat down, he gently placed a bouquet on the grave. The rain freshened the flowers like a last caress from nature and caused the man, whose name was Erik Mørk, to smile.

"I brought flowers with me today, Dad, because today was quite a special day. One that I have been waiting for a long time. Perhaps ever since I was a child, even if that doesn't make any sense. According to the radio, those who were executed have been found and the rest of the day will doubtless be quite chaotic."

He stopped and looked down at the earth, and some minutes went by before he went on. Then he smiled, and the smile came from his heart, which did not happen very often. He loved sitting there in the quiet stillness far from the world, and he allowed the minutes to tick by as he chatted about this and that at his father's graveside. His work was extroverted, though he was the opposite by nature. Perhaps it was the secret of his professional success. A success toward which he was indifferent, and one he would have traded for anything if only he could have had his childhood back.

"I have been completely on edge since I got a letter from the Climber last Saturday with videos of the minivan and the gymnasium, so I knew it had been done, but . . ."

The sentence was never completed, and he jumped straight into another topic altogether.

"This morning I was at the office, where we had an evaluation with a client. The campaign is going very well and everyone is patting everyone's back. They're selling a lot of worthless girls' clothes, we can add a new success story to the others, and both parties make a bucketful of money. Not a soul mentioned the eight little girls who at this moment are offering themselves like candy on billboards all over the city. For the love of Christ, they've hardly gone through puberty and . . . yes, I know it seems hysterical, because I if anyone am responsible for this, but I couldn't deal with it very well and had to take the rest of the day off."

The rain was tapering off. He folded his umbrella, shook it, and laid it to the side of his chair before he resumed his monologue.

"It is obviously one of the advantages of owning one's business that one can come and go as one pleases, and today I left, without really knowing why. We have conducted so many similar campaigns, and this one is far from the worst, so perhaps it's because I am particularly sensitive right now."

The clock in the church tower rang the hour. He stood up, stretched his legs, and crouched by the gravestone, where he had noticed a couple of wet leaves clinging to its face. Then he let his finger slide across the etching, back and forth a couple of times. Arne Christian Mørk. 1934–1979. As he meticulously plucked a few weeds that the gardener had overlooked, he continued to speak.

"Yesterday I took a fond farewell of Per, you know Per Clausen, the janitor I was telling you about. He is a fantastic man, and I will miss him. First we ate breakfast, and after that we watched the video sequences I directed. He was full of praise, but I have to admit they did turn out very well. In particular there is one simple one from the minivan that is quite captivating, a satanic little pearl, that will shake public opinion and toughen our national soul. It may become absolutely decisive, you just wait and see. It was Per's idea to mount hidden cameras above each seat, which was devilishly difficult, but turned out to be worth every bit of trouble. Other than that, we talked about everything between heaven and earth, not just about the coming weeks, almost as if he was on a normal Sunday visit. It is hard to imagine that I'll never see him again."

A car drove past on the road behind the cemetery and a few isolated snatches of a car radio broke the peace for a moment or two. He waited until the quiet descended again.

"When Per said goodbye he said something that I have thought a lot about: 'goodbye, foam guy.' That was his last word to me: 'foam guy.' Said with that crooked little smile that is so typical of him. He was obviously referring to the fact that I used to chew on foam as a child because I thought it could absorb the darkness inside me. I had almost forgotten about it, I mean, that I had told him about it. How I used to pick little bits of foam from all manner of places: cushions and seats, balls from gym class, the sweat band in my riding helmet, yes I even tore little pieces from my mother's shoulder pads. When I speak of it, I can recall the taste, even though one wouldn't think foam tastes like anything. But it does. It tastes of wrongdoing, of wrongness and guilt."

He shook his head to rid himself of his thoughts, and added thoughtfully, "It is unpleasant to remember and . . . well, perhaps Per captured it perfectly. When everything is said and done, that is probably what I am—the foam guy."

CHAPTER 5

Professor, *medicus*, forensic pathologist, and medical examiner Arthur Elvang was a churlish man. Konrad Simonsen steeled himself, determined to keep his focus and not let himself be distracted by the professor's sharp tongue. They met in front of the gymnasium, where Elvang sat absorbed in a newspaper in approximately the same place where the little Turkish girl had been sitting some seven hours earlier, and he, too, was reluctant to give up his reading material. After an eternity, he laid the pages aside and returned his awareness to his surroundings as his small, peering eyes behind the tortoiseshell glasses flew critically up and down over Simonsen, as if he were taking measurements for a suit.

"You have enough fat stores to last you through the winter, my little Simon. Too bad about your vacation. Where were you then? At a halfway house?"

He stretched out a twisted hand, and Simonsen, who thought he wanted to underscore his observations by sticking a finger in his stomach, drew back.

"Now don't be sulky, give me a hand to get up."

Simonsen gingerly helped him to his feet.

"I'm not upset. My daughter is always commenting on my girth so I am used to it, but it is many years since anyone called me 'little Simon.' That stopped when Planck retired."

Planck had been the head of the Homicide Division before him.

"Yes, time flies. Have you told your daughter about your diabctcs?"

Simonsen stiffened.

"How in all the world do you know . . ."

He stopped and regained control of himself. The professor's medical expertise was legendary, although he might simply have been making a stab in the dark. A guess he had now unwittingly confirmed by his exclamation. He hurriedly left the subject.

"Is the room free?"

"Yes, the technicians left about a quarter of an hour ago, but keep away from the back entrance as well as the bathroom. I hear that you have free hands in this matter. Is that correct?"

"Apparently."

"Then you should bring Planck in, unless he is senile. The two of you bring out the best in each other. And as it happens, he is more talented than you."

"He is far from senile. Shall we go in?"

"Yes, of course. Good idea, little Simon."

The corpses of five men were strung up in the middle of the room, each with a noose of a sturdy blue nylon rope around the neck. The ends were fastened around sturdy hooks screwed into the beams about seven meters above. The men's feet were about half a meter from the floor, and the bodies had been placed at least two meters apart in such a way that the four outermost bodies formed a square, the sides of which ran parallel to the walls. All the bodies were missing hands but the lower arms were intact from the elbow down to the wrist. The faces had been disfigured to the point that most of the human elements were gone; also the genitals, which had either been mutilated beyond recognition or removed. Death and the injuries gave the men a similar look, as if their physical differences no longer existed. Simonsen recognized the phenomenon and knew that when he had studied the dead a little longer, their individuality would return.

"Chainsaw?"

Elvang confirmed this. That was one of his positive attributes. He wasn't afraid to express an immediate opinion, in direct contrast to most other pathologists that Simonsen knew, who seldom wanted even to confirm the sex of a corpse before it had undergone a CT scan. And physicians were even worse.

"While they were still alive?"

"No."

The answer was a relief; the whole thing was horrific enough as it was, even though he surprisingly did not react physically when he saw the bodies. Perhaps because the room had been aired out, or perhaps because he had had time to prepare himself for the sight, or perhaps because he was mentally desensitized and had already seen more than was good for him. Who could know what the reason was, and who cared? Not he, at any rate. He continued his slow circle around the men.

In view of the fact that each of them must have bled a great deal, there were not a lot of bloodstains. Under each of the dead was only a small, viscous pool about the diameter of a tennis ball. The neck, the top of the chest, and the thighs were bloody, and there were also red clumps in their hair. Otherwise there was no trace of blood, but he could clearly discern the sickly sweet smell of blood that mingled with the stronger stink of excrement and bodily fluids. The temperature, and the three open windows, kept the stench at a minimum. The yellow-white swollen bodies led his thoughts to hanging sides of pork on a slaughterhouse assembly line, a disrespectful image that, to his vexation, he was unable to shake.

He focused on the heads of the men as he slowly moved in among the bodies and examined each of them. The wounds varied from person to person. Three of them had had their entire faces sawed off. The blade had been drawn straight down from the crown of the head to the jaw so that brain, mouth cavity, and throat were exposed. The rest had been slashed in a crisscross manner with the blade held perpendicular to the face. Two had retained their tongues and some teeth. One had an almost-undamaged eye.

The same destructiveness had dominated the removal of the genitals. Two had lost their penises and testicles, two others only the penis. On one the cut was so deep that the bladder had fallen out and was hanging out over the crotch. The remaining victim had lost only the foreskin. The man in the middle had emptied his bowels; sticky black excrement covered his buttocks and the backs of his thighs, and a handful of flies had found their way there. The wounds at the wrists, however, were clean and precise. Simonsen could see the marrow in the two bones of the lower arm and started randomly wondering which one was the ulna and the other radius. But which was the large and which was the small he could not remember.

He started over and walked another round, this time looking for identifying markers. A rough estimate put the men's ages between forty and seventy years. One had a gold ring in his left ear as well as a faded eagle tattooed on the right shoulder, and two had scars from appendix or hernia operations. One was bald and had an unnaturally dark complexion, probably from a tanning salon. The corpse in the back left corner had long, unclipped toenails that were infected with fungus and resembled pork rinds. In the right ear canal was a tooth with a gold filling.

A last round was devoted to inspecting the ropes that had been hung with mathematical precision parallel to the walls. If he lined them up diagonally and looked down the series of ropes with one eye, he was unable to see the final one. That was true of both diagonals. Someone had gone to a great deal of trouble inserting the screws into the ceiling.

Simonsen concluded his inspection and walked back to

Elvang, who had displayed only a fleeting interest in the bodies and now looked extremely bored.

"Your initial assessment?"

The professor did not hesitate.

"Hanged here, weren't moved. Wednesday or Thursday. Look like ethnic Danes. But don't ask me how it was accomplished or why there isn't blood everywhere."

"When will you have something firm on the time of death?"

The old man sighed. He was no longer a spring chicken and the thought of the evening's work that awaited him held no pleasure.

"I've had to call for reinforcements. On overtime hours, which you are paying for."

"Absolutely. Bring in as many as you like."

"Call me after midnight."

"Roger that."

Simonsen had only one more question. It was, however, somewhat controversial. Strictly speaking, it also fell outside the professor's line of work, but in view of the man's enormous experience and preeminent expertise it was not an unreasonable question.

"Terrorism?"

It took a couple of seconds for Elvang to grasp his meaning, then he grew impish. He flapped his hands by the side of his head like a hysterical teenager and said sarcastically, "Ooooh, ooooh, the monsters are coming. And they're not coming out of the forest, they're coming from the water."

Simonsen ignored this odd outburst and said coldly, "Nine/eleven, Bali, Beslan, Madrid, London. Was that also paranoia, Professor?"

Their gazes locked, then the old man finally shrugged.

"If you are thinking of holy crusaders with curved sabres and dreams about the caliph, well, there isn't anything here that I can see that points to such an interpretation. But I don't know what that would be in any case. Your question is ill conceived."

"Perhaps, but it's a question I will have to answer for the rest of the day."

Elvang did not reply. He glanced at the bodies and shook his head thoughtfully. With his bald, age-spotted crown, his thin ruffled hair and sunken chest, he most of all resembled a baby bird. Then he said, "I was in Rwanda in 1995."

"I didn't think you liked to fly."

"I only do it in cases of genocide. For four months I traveled literally from one mass grave to another. There were so unbelievably many murdered people that it defies description, and I discovered a degree of depravity and excess that you could not imagine in your wildest nightmare. It was indescribably awful, but that wasn't the worst. The worst thing was to come back home and realize that no one was interested. The victims were simply the wrong color to sell news and to refer to the catastrophe was almost in bad taste, so I apologize if I have a somewhat cynical attitude to the concept of terrorism."

Simonsen felt empty.

"I don't know what to say."

"There's no one asking you to say anything. Forget it, everyone else does. But tell me, how do you know I don't like to fly?"

"That's just what I've heard."

"It wouldn't by any chance be from that story about how the city's hotel chains have pulled strings to keep me in my job as long as possible because my fear of flying has brought international conferences to Copenhagen?"

Simonsen felt a faint warmth in his cheeks.

"Something along those lines."

The door at one end of the gymnasium opened. Arne Pedersen, the Countess, and Pauline Berg walked in, immediately followed by Poul Troulsen.

"You are a fool. To think that the country supports a homicide chief who believes that kind of nonsense. It is frightening. Shame on you. Get a bucket while you're at it."

"What do you want with a bucket?"

"Your latest recruit has not yet learned to suppress her instinctual human reactions."

The observation came too late. One second later, Berg collapsed and vomited onto the floor without making use of the plastic bag that she had been holding in her hand for that very purpose. Pedersen glanced down at his vomit-spattered shoes and took out a handkerchief. It was made of raw silk and had been rather expensive. He managed to lift one foot before the Countess snatched the handkerchief and held it out to Berg, who looked gratefully up at him before she retched again.

CHAPTER 6

The corpses in the gymnasium were gone and all the windows were open, and yet it seemed to Pauline Berg, when she walked in the door, that the smell was unbearable. But it was most likely a deception of the senses and thus possible to verify. Konrad Simonsen was sitting in the middle of the floor, staring up at the ceiling. He reminded her of a monk in a pagoda and she had trouble guessing what he was up to.

"Arne said you wanted to talk to me."

She could hear that she sounded like a nervous exam taker. Normally she dealt well with men, who often found her

33

attractive and intelligent, but her boss was the exception that proved the rule, and apart from the fact that her choice of clothing was sometimes criticized by his puritanical gaze, he seemed mostly to ignore her. That is, on a personal level. She obeyed his gesture and sat down next to him.

"Did you see the bodies?"

"Yes, the sweet old doctor showed me around. I've forgotten what he is called but he carried on a running explanation of everything while we were looking and it wasn't so bad."

"The sweet old doctor is Arthur Elvang, and all of us have gotten sick from time to time. You are definitely not the only one who has thrown up today but you'll find that you toughen up over the years. I don't know if that is good or bad."

"It will definitely be more practical."

She tried a smile but did not set much of a response, and the situation struck her as strange. She shifted uncomfortably.

He must have noticed her restlessness, or else he read her thoughts. At any rate he said, "There is a reason why we are sitting here—I'll come to that later. Tell me how the janitor reacted when you found him."

"It was actually a canine unit that tracked him down, or rather, the dog. It was down by the shed for the athletic equipment by the soccer field, and he claimed he had only just woken up. I don't know . . . there's not much more to say. He mostly ignored me, apart from saying that he would tell my teacher about the rain poncho. Arne was very thoughtful . . ."

"Yes, I know. That was nice of Arne. Go on about the janitor."

"He said that about the rain poncho to needle me, but apart from that he was quite meek. We delivered him to the Countess. He was afraid of the dog so it was told to stay behind. Out in rain."

"What was your impression of him?"

"My first impression was that he seemed pathetic. He reeks

of beer and needs a bath. On the other hand . . . he is also . . . it's hard to explain."

"Take your time. I'm a patient man."

She paused for reflection, and Simonsen studied the ceiling.

"He isn't quite as much of a wreck as he seems, I'm sure of it. And he is somehow . . . present."

"Highly conscious and aware?"

"Yes. No. Not in that sense. It's just that it seems like he knows what's going on the whole time, even when his answers are completely loopy."

"You were present when he was being questioned?"

"Only in the beginning. It was Troulsen and the Countess who interrogated him and it was sort of an unspoken agreement that I would just listen, but I read the rest. The recording was sent to HS and after an hour we had a transcription. I can tell that we have reinforcements—I've never experienced anything quite like this."

Simonsen noted that she had started referring to headquarters as "HS," which was new for her. "HS" for "Head Square," as they said in the Homicide Division. He replied, "I haven't either. But you were only there at the beginning?"

"Yes, then they sent me away to find a TV and watched your press conference."

"To keep an eye on me and see if I made a spectacle of myself?"

"It wasn't my idea."

She paused, then proceeded carefully. "They said that it wasn't one of your areas of expertise. Press conferences, I mean."

"I see. They said that? And what do you think? Did I make a fool of myself?"

Although he was difficult to read, she tried to be somewhat honest.

"No, I don't think so. You didn't really say much. It was

mostly the others, but you clearly don't care much for the platinum blonde from *Dagbladet*."

"Her name is Anni Staal and she represents a regrettable turn in human evolution, but personally I have nothing against her except that she should be deported. Was it so obvious?"

"No, I don't think so. Only to someone who knows you."

"And you do?"

The exam-taking pupil was back in one stroke. But only for a fleeting visit. Simonsen took the edge off his words by patting her kindly on the knee.

"Enough of that. Tell me how you felt when Per Clausen teased you about your age."

Berg was bewildered. "How I felt?"

"Yes, how you felt."

"Is it important?"

"Maybe, maybe not. Try to answer."

She closed her eyes to recall the episode and therefore didn't see her boss nod appreciatively.

"It wasn't mean-spirited. He was looking at me almost as if we were friends. He wasn't being snotty about it, if you get me."

"I understand. What else?"

"It was the only time he really noticed me. He teased me, but in a nice way, as if he cared about me."

"And you like him?"

She opened her eyes.

"Yes, I do. Can you please tell me what this is all about?"

"Later, later. How old are you again?"

"Twenty-eight."

"Thank you. And now for my ceiling. How is your geometry?"

"Neither good nor bad, but I'm no mathematical genius."

"That's not necessary. If you look at the screw holes for the hooks that were holding the ropes, you'll see that they have been placed with precision. Both in relation to the center of the room and in relation to each other. I've been pondering those holes for a while now and have arrived at the fact that the placement can be determined from the length and breadth of the ceiling panels. It's not immediately obvious, but not so difficult either, once you've caught on to the idea. You don't need measuring tape. You can manage it with some string, a pencil, and a thumb in the right place. It would be simpler, easier, and much more accurate."

"I follow what you're saying. Broadly speaking."

"The details are not of much consequence. But do you know how the lines in the intersection between two circles looks like?"

"Yes, they are curved."

"Exactly, and from the placement and dimensions of the arcs you can estimate where the centers of the two circles must be."

Suddenly a light went on in Berg's head and she saw it.

"A thumb. Do you mean prints?"

"Unfortunately not. The technicians have checked and there are none. I just want to know if the one who put in the hooks did so in the way that I would have done. You are said to be strong and flexible, is that right?"

She reacted by getting to her feet, adjusting her pants, and effortlessly stretching a leg over her head.

"That was a convincing answer. Martial arts? Gymnastics?"

"Ballet. Would you like to see a pirouette?"

"Another time. I didn't know you could dance."

"My mother had big plans for me. I was going to be a soloist with the Royal Ballet Company, nothing less would do. Thank goodness I didn't make it past the entrance auditions because my arches were too weak, so my mother turned her attention over to my little sister instead and let me dance for pleasure instead of duty."

Word upon word tumbled out; dance was Berg's great passion. In the daily routine she did not belong to the division's epicenter, and the fact that she was a part of Simonsen's inner circle depended exclusively on her age, not her abilities. She was there to provide the younger generation's perspective. Now she was enjoying telling her boss about herself, until she noticed his distant expression and it occurred to her that it might not be the time and place for her autobiography. Nonetheless, the monologue had loosened her tongue.

"You stopped listening a long time ago. Isn't that so?"

It was correct. Simonsen was in his own world, far from physical aesthetics and symphonic choreography. In his thoughts he was trying to imagine what could drive a person to mutilate five human beings with a chainsaw and hang them naked in a school, of all places. Hate, mental illness, callousness, idealism? None of these fit well, each at best only a partial explanation.

She had to repeat her question before he replied.

"You're not listening, are you?"

"More or less, but don't make too much of it. When things are back to normal I would like to see you dance and hear your story. And then you will have my complete attention, I promise."

He pointed at the ceiling.

"We're going to go up and take a look at the two closest holes."

It was clear that by "we" he meant "you."

"You want to know if there are curved lines at each hole and which way the lines are pointing, correct?"

"Just as I described it to you, yes. But the school scaffolding has been removed for investigation, and although the technicians used a crane when they removed the bodies, they unfortunately took it with them."

"So what are you thinking? I'm fit but my flying abilities are a bit rusty."

Her cheeky remarks flew out without a second thought. Luckily for her, he smiled.

"Of course they are. But perhaps we could . . . do a little work with the ropes."

They pulled the ropes out. Berg looked them up and down measuringly and agreed that he was right. As long as one was unconcerned with safety, it was not an impossible undertaking.

"But we can't afford to fall down."

"On the contrary, we can fall all we like, we just have to fall here."

He pointed to a large blue foam mat that was propped up against a wall.

"Actually, that will be an order."

She removed her socks and shoes while he maneuvered the foam mat into place, which she appreciated.

"I'm going to lose the pants as well, they're too slippery for climbing."

"You'll do nothing of the sort. Go into one of the locker rooms and find a pair of gym shorts."

"What if they don't match my top?"

"Come on, off you go. We don't have all day, and you've already wasted half of it with your ballet talk."

She ran. And was happy.

CHAPTER 7

Stig Åge Thorsen sat in the cab of his tractor and tried in vain to control his thoughts. Two days ago he had returned home from a vacation, a twelve-day cruise in the Greek archipelago. The trip had turned into a catastrophe, and it haunted him however much he tried to push thoughts of it away. Unwelcome flashbacks, which he had no mastery over, flashed through his head. He let his gaze sweep mournfully over the autumn wooded landscape that crept down the hillside to the lakeshore and stood green, brown, and red-gold in the haze. The day was gray and the skies hung heavy with rain over the lake. It was somewhat chilly, with no hint of a breeze. His thoughts slid back to the cruise and he gave up trying to fight them. In Greece the fall had been warm, and the first day was calm. . . .

He kept to himself, enjoyed the rhythmic thud of the engine, and spent hours at the railing as he watched the fishing villages along the coast slide by in clear pastel colors and a predictable dullness. The food was unfamiliar but good. They had bungled his name. Stig Åge Thorsen had become Thor Åge Stigsen, which gave him problems in the restaurant. He corrected the error but the next day they had forgotten about it and he had to explain himself again. Knossos was an experience, and there he met Maja, who was freckled and full of laughter. Her red hair blew in the wind as she walked on the deck, and she smiled when she tossed pieces of bread to the gulls that surrounded her in a screeching mass. She smiled at him and that was bad. Later he explained about phosphorescence and pointed out constellations. Maja was from Randers, she smiled again, and he moved a little farther away.

The ship called into Samos, where the guide told them about the Greek mathematicians Pythagoras, Euclid, and Archimedes, who could lift the Earth with the help of a lever. She drew diagrams in the gravel with a stick while the group formed a circle around her. He himself had no confidence in the principle, for when the rod slipped out of one's small hands, Father's chest was crushed under the car, but he did not say this. Instead he asked if Archimedes knew that the Earth was round. The guide rubbed out her sketch and then he was frozen out. Even Maja was irritated at him.

They went swimming at the beach at Saloniki, and after that they lay in the sand and let themselves be dried in the sun. They were alone and for the first time he touched her and gently stroked her head. His fingers slid in among her wet curls and came together in a long caress of his hand through her hair. Then that happened that was bound to happen. Maja gave a satisfied sigh, and he heard his mother moan. Suddenly he noticed his mother's hair, his mother's white arms, tasted her salt cheeks, felt her skin. Smelled her sex.

He said words, ugly words, without wanting to.

Maja got up and put on her clothes while he tried to explain without success. About Little Bear land, where Little Bear's mother cried because Little Bear's father was bad and gone; about Little Bear's mother's tears that were Little Bear's fault; about Little Bear who had to kiss away Little Bear's mother's tears and Little Bear who had to cheer her up, and about the nights that were so dreadfully long.

Maja left.

He left also. Dressed only in swimming trunks, he left the beach as quickly as possible. He wandered aimlessly on lonely roads that glittered in the sun and made his way through the landscape until he couldn't go any farther. His feet were red and swollen. He plucked a thorn from a bush and punctured his blisters. It alleviated the pain but only the outer one. Inside he always had a thousand eyes that looked back at their own night, and he wanted to puncture them all one by one, but for this the thorns were useless. Nothing helped. There he sat, looking at a random road in a strange land, humiliated for his arrogance—for his fleeting belief that he could control his own life—while the cicadas sang and the mountains in the distance smiled at him.

* * *

The guttural cry of a raven rolled in over the fields from the forest, and brought him back into the now. Stig Åge shifted uncomfortably. Who knew what bad luck the bird foretold? Then he focused on his work. It was his job to keep the fire going that Climber had lit on his property while he had been sent on vacation. The bonfire contained a minivan that he had never seen before. In a practiced way, he backed the tractor up parallel to the pit so that he could unload the sacks of coal and wood directly into the flames.

The compressor had stalled. He poured in more gas and started it again. They had dug out air ducts under the pit, so now the fire blossomed up again and the flames flared. He pitched the contents of the flatbed over the edge. The heat became more intense and he sweated. Per Clausen's calculations placed the temperature at close to twenty-two hundred degrees Celsius. Iron melts at fifteen hundred, steel at eighteen hundred, so when the police arrived there would not be much left to find. But a calculation was one thing, and reality was another altogether. That lesson had been firmly hammered into him while he was abroad.

CHAPTER 8

Konrad Simonsen felt exhausted. These workdays with no end in sight were an affliction, and as he got older it was getting harder and harder for him to keep his focus whenever the hours grew longer than was reasonable. He, if anyone, was expected to retain an overview of the situation, to keep his eye on the big picture, but instead he sometimes felt the situation was a complete blur—a fact that he had trouble admitting even to himself. So instead he used a preposterous amount of mental energy to sound as if he did, to sound as if everything were painstakingly planned, to sound as if he knew exactly what it was that would take place in the next hour. Yes, even sound as if he could recall what he himself had said an hour ago. This acting made him irritable and short-fused. The truth was that he longed for his soft armchair, a good book, and a couple of tomato sandwiches before bed. Then he thought of the fact that he hadn't bought any groceries and would hardly have any time to. He suppressed a yawn and focused on the man in front of him.

Per Clausen's appearance was at first glance wretched, with his washed-out overalls over a filthy sweater and one of the shoulder straps attached with a small metal wire. He had short, straggly, dark-blond hair that was badly in need of washing. His face was marked by sharp features and prominent cheekbones; his skin was sallow and drawn. But Simonsen had seen enough decay in his life to agree with Pauline Berg that the man's disrepair was relative: his teeth were brushed, his undershirt clean—even if tinged with pink after careless laundering—and his nails had been clipped recently. Then there was his gaze, which met Simonsen's with unflinching calm. Without aggression, but also without fear.

"My name is Konrad Simonsen, and I am spearheading the investigation that is currently under way in connection with the five people that were found hanged this morning in the school gymnasium. You have already met Officer Berg."

He gestured to Berg, who was sitting at one end of the table. Neither of the men broke eye contact.

"I'm going to start on a positive note. I'm pleased that you have made time to come in. It is the third time that we trouble you today."

"Thank you, Chief Inspector, that was very kind."

"In passing, I should ask you how you know my title. Mr. Clausen—"

"Per; just call me Per. It feels more natural."

"Then that's what I'll do. Per, I am too tired to worry about the little questions, and you have given me enough of the big ones. You should know that this conversation will be different from the others. For example, we will not use a tape recorder; as you have probably noticed, it is primarily I who intend to speak this time. I have been acquainting myself thoroughly with your previous meetings with us, and I wish to inform you about the conclusions I have drawn. In addition, I wanted to meet you in person."

"As you like. It's your party."

"Yes, I guess one could call it that. Which fits very well with the rather absurd explanations and deliberate nonanswers that you have served us in large quantities ever since we located you. I have selected a few . . . passages, if you will, so that we are clear on what exactly I am referring to. Pauline, if you please."

Berg was ready. She read in a clear, impersonal voice:

"Why did you go to the equipment shed to sleep when the police arrived?"

"So I would be fresh for the interrogation."

"What led you to believe you would be interrogated?"

"Because I was sleeping in the shed."

"If you hadn't slept there, you would probably not have been."

"What is done is done."

She turned the pages quickly and continued.

"We've been talking for almost an hour now and you haven't yet asked us why the police are here. How do you explain that?"

"I'm not the one asking the questions. You are."

"You aren't curious?"

"I think you will tell me sooner or later of your own accord."

"This morning there were five dead men hanging from the ceiling in the gymnasium."

"Hold on. That just isn't true."

"Have you been in the gymnasium?"

"Many times."

"When the bodies were there, for heaven's sake."

"No, I don't think so. I would have noticed something."

Per Clausen's only comment to the reading was an ironic tug at the corners of his mouth, hardly noticeable, but nonetheless hugely irritating. Simonsen ignored it and said gently, "Your actions and your evasive answers simply strengthen the impression that you are trying to attract our attention. Perhaps you enjoy being in the spotlight, perhaps you find it diverting to waste our time. I've met plenty of both types. My first guess is that you had nothing to do with the murders. If that's not the case, then you must be very simple-minded, because only very naïve people imagine that they can get through an interrogation by being more quick-witted and clever in their answers than the officials who are conducting the session. They cannot. The power dynamic is far too uneven for that, and sooner or later everyone slips up. Every single time. It's only a question of time."

"That sounds about right."

"Yes, it is. Am I boring you?"

"No, this is very interesting. Go on."

"I will. We are going to talk a little about your untruths."

"I see."

"Many people think that it is illegal to lie to the police, but that is, to put it mildly, not a belief that you appear to share. Most people also find it embarrassing to be caught out in a lie, and in this case too you do not follow the norm. Pauline has an example . . ."

Berg again took up the post as reader. This time, the task was slightly different in that she combined two reports.

* * *

The first session:

"And you are a widower, you say. How long has that been the case?"

"Klara passed away one day nearly eight years ago when we were out shopping. She was struck on the sidewalk by a drunk driver. I was holding her hand but didn't get so much as a scratch. The young hooligan who was driving got four months and after half a year he killed someone else. This time a four-year-old, and also when he was drunk. Today he is vice president of a large health-care company."

Second session:

". . . It turns out that your wife, or rather ex-wife, is not dead at all. Her name is Klara Persson, she lives in Malmö, and is in good health. How do you explain this?"

"Surely an ex-wife can be considered a little dead."

"Why do you feed us this garbage?"

"I must have been swept up in the moment."

Simonsen took over.

"And this is just one of your tall tales. You have lied about blood clots in your legs, about your employment at the school since 1963, that you often visit your sister in Tarm, and about your three convictions for arson. You also claim to be an alcoholic. On this point I want to give you the benefit of the doubt for now, and I want to show the same consideration regarding your visit to your sister last week, even though it was the first time in eight years that you went to see her."

"My, my, how time does fly."

Simonsen took no notice of the irony.

"We are deeply interested in the trip you took on your vacation and you can be sure it will be scrutinized in great detail."

"An intercity train from the Central Station, Tuesday at eight A.M. The train was called the H. C. Andersen. A local train from Tarm Trinbræt, Friday at nine thirty-four. That train was called the Fætter Guf."

"Thank you, but we will manage without your assistance in this matter since your reliability is in question. That is not to say that your carelessness with the truth necessarily means anything at all. I would be the first to acknowledge that lying is a part of human nature, but if you scrape a little on the surface it turns out that most exaggerations stem from a disappointingly banal source. A made-up degree that the ego polishes a little, a gray life that is colored a little outside the bounds of reality, those kind of trivialities. Your lies tend more toward a kind of pathological lying—pseudologia fantastica—but if so, this is a disorder you seem to have acquired in honor of the occasion. The rest of the school staff do not characterize you as a compulsive liar, actually more the opposite, which brings me back to the question: Why? What are you gaining by this? If there is a good reason for it, it currently lies outside my capacity for understanding. Tomorrow I would like to speak with you again. You will meet us here at the school at two P.M., and we'll drive into Copenhagen together. In the meantime we will dig into your life and see if we can turn up a thing or two that may explain your behavior. Please make an effort to be sober. If not, I may have to commit you to a forced abstinence."

"Will you write out a card? Like at the dentist?"

"No, we don't do that. And unless you have anything relevant to add, I believe we are done."

"That was it? That was quick."

"As I said, the aim was mainly to meet you."

"I see. Well, in that case, thanks for the pizza."

"I didn't know that we had fed you, but you're welcome."

Simonsen got to his feet but kept his gaze fixed on Clausen.

"One more thing—a minor question. How is your geometry?"

Per Clausen answered without missing a beat.

"Do you mean classic plane geometry or analytic geometry?"

"I'm not sure that I know the difference. I don't have your expertise."

"There is a big difference. Take good old Gauss, for example. He worked with equations and algebra as opposed to lines and circles. I have always thought that it was a bit of cheating or at least less elegant, but you have to give it to the man that it yielded results. He proved that the equilateral heptadecagon can be constructed with a compass and ruler. The first contribution in over two thousand years to the regular polygons."

"Impressive."

"Decidedly, but not particularly practical. I only know of a single instance where a heptadecagon has had a real-world application. Would you like to hear it?"

"Yes, very much."

This answer was true, which it normally was not. There was so much else and so many more relevant aspects to discuss with this janitor, but Simonsen wanted very much to hear his story. The man was strangely fascinating.

Clausen explained, "In 1525, seventeen sailors in Portsmouth were convicted by the High Court of Admiralty for having whistled onboard the *Mary Rose,* the flagship of the English fleet. For this kind of serious offense, justice only knew one kind of punishment, and the gallows were prepared according to Gauss's principles so that all of them could hang in symmetry. The drawings have been preserved at the National Maritime Museum in London."

"That is a good story, exceptionally illustrative, I must say, and very convincing even though it lacks a couple of centuries to fall completely into place, but I think I followed the point. Now, get home safely and don't forget that we have an appointment tomorrow."

The janitor gestured in the air with one hand as if to

underscore that a little slippage in time did not have to mean the world.

"A little artistic license is allowed, surely."

They shook hands and Clausen left. He had barely made it out the door before Simonsen lit a cigarette. Berg took out a saucer from under a plant and placed it in front of him. Her boss looked so tired that she was worried for a moment.

"He was much more focused than when the Countess questioned him," she said.

"Yes, I could imagine that."

"What was that last bit about?"

"Hard to say. His behavior appears completely irrational, but we will probably get to the bottom of his life in the next couple of days and then we'll see."

"But I mean, his story with the gallows—wasn't that a cut-and-dried way to link him to the murders in some way?"

"In a way. In addition to being extremely arrogant and demanding, I have no good reading of him, but that will change."

"Maybe he wants to deflect our attention from something or someone else?"

"Who knows? But time is on our side, and good old-fashioned elbow grease normally yields more answers than guesses and suppositions."

His comment struck home. Berg blushed slightly and let the subject drop, saying instead, "You promised to tell me why you wanted me to participate."

Outwardly, Simonsen appeared more sure of the janitor than he really was. Perhaps it had been a mistake to release him. The man's odd behavior lay outside Simonsen's frame of reference, which was the real reason that he had let him go home. It would give him time to think it through. But as soon as Clausen was gone, doubt had started gnawing at him. He pushed the thought away.

"He has lost a daughter," he answered. "His only child. She

would have been around your age today so I thought he would have a vulnerable point and that you could possibly be . . . a point of departure, but I decided against it."

Berg felt slightly ill at ease.

"I'm glad you did."

Simonsen did not pay attention to her tone of voice.

"This isn't a case of a stolen bike. There's no place for that kind of sensitivity."

"I know that, it would just have been unpleasant. Why did you decide against it?"

"He wouldn't have taken the bait, so there was no point. Why don't you head over and check with Troulsen to make sure the surveillance is in place. If Per Clausen so much as owns a dog, I want its stud register in ten minutes flat."

"I'll check. For the fourth time. But he is one hundred percent covered: local and remote surveillance, doubled-up coverage, and they are all experts. You don't need to be the least bit nervous, Troulsen says."

"Do it, regardless of what Poul says. Did we get a court order on his phone?"

"Yes, but it was difficult and it is only good for three days."

Simonsen stubbed out his cigarette, and suddenly remembered what feeling he had had as he sat across from Per Clausen. He had been looking for it and now it was there. It was the same feeling that he had once felt when he encountered opponents in various chess tournaments. Respect and kinship, fellowship, mixed with a mental aggressiveness, as if one could differentiate between a person and his or her brain. Accompanying this was the creeping conviction that his opponent had studied him, had pinpointed his playing style and perhaps also his life and personality. He smiled tightly and allowed his inner images of the dead chase away any feeling of kinship with the janitor. Then he turned to Berg.

"What was that about pizza? Is there any more?"

"Lots. Should I get you one? They are laid out in the teachers' lounge."

"That would be nice, if you are willing, but only if you are willing. You haven't been appointed as my assistant."

"I'm willing. Anything in particular you want?"

"The two least-fattening—you decide."

"Is there anything else you would like?"

"Yes, a quarter of an hour of peace and quiet."

And he got it.

CHAPTER 9

Arne Pedersen spun the wheel of fortune that was well balanced and surprisingly functional, probably the pedagogical fruit of six months' worth of wood shop. He had emptied a container with sugar cubes onto a table, where they filled in as chips. The wheel landed on a sun; he reorganized his sugar cubes and spun again. The metallic clicks filled the teachers' lounge.

"Could you stop that? It's getting on my nerves."

The Countess was troubleshooting an unresponsive computer. Its display was projected onto a screen, and, without understanding any of it, Poul Troulsen followed her efforts with interest. A stack of papers lay on his lap, the thickness of which did not bode well for getting any sleep.

Pedersen did not reply, but soon the wheel clattered on its

way to a new meeting with chance. The Countess glanced pleadingly at Pauline Berg, who caught her drift, got up, and shortly returned leading Pedersen by the hand and with a lump of sugar in her mouth. She pressed him down into an armchair by Poul Troulsen's side, where he sat and grumbled for a while before he got a look at his companion's notes.

"Are you planning to go through all that?"

Poul Troulsen was rumored to be as conscientious in his presentations as he was in his work. He also appeared alarmingly fresh, even though he was the oldest of them. For once, Pedersen backed up the Countess.

"Arne has a point, Poul. You should speed it up. Everyone wants to go home."

"Amen, amen, and amen again. I am tired, I don't want to be here anymore, and I don't understand why this janitor can't wait until tomorrow. How the hell does Simon get to be off?"

"I'm here now, Arne. And perhaps you are right, perhaps we should wait, but I am the one who's in charge of this investigation and assigning duties. You can either accept it, or leave."

Simonsen had entered through the back door and no one had noticed him until he stood before them. Back at police headquarters there was talk that the chief of the Homicide Division had an uncanny as well as annoying habit of always becoming the point of focus once he entered a room. Often without saying very much. But this time it was too extreme. Pedersen had respect for his boss but he was not afraid of him, and the admonishment was out of proportion. He sat back in his chair with a noise of frustration and an angry gesture. Simonsen came to his senses.

"Okay, okay, sorry. But you aren't the only one who is tired. We're going at this hard so that we can get home sooner. Let me start by going over the events of the day."

He then proceeded to do so, adding that he did not want them to put too much stock into their temporary organization and to flat out ignore the massive interest shown by the press. No one except Pauline Berg really listened, but all appreciated the fact that their chief seemed to have a good grasp of the situation, and the Countess thought to herself that her boss—standing there so strong and mighty—was a born leader. For everyone except himself. Only Berg had a question.

"If we ignore the reporters completely, don't we risk them becoming . . . what shall I say . . . negatively focused? I mean, the coverage hasn't focused on anything else all day, and even the international stations—"

"There are daily press conferences at headquarters, and it's not our job to sell newspapers or television fodder," Simonsen broke in.

There were no dissenting opinions, so that line was drawn. They could move on.

The Countess quickly dispatched with the topic of neighbors as no one had registered anything unusual, whereafter it was Poul Troulsen's turn. He stood up. The unnecessary gesture caused some of them to roll their eyes, but unfairly as it would turn out, as he took less than ten minutes to give an overview of the day's meager harvest. Troulsen had managed an impressive bit of research, which had turned out to be tedious, dull, unsuccessful, and at times difficult. Some teachers had acted impulsively and tried to leave, and one had actually escaped out a window, claiming that he had a legal right to his day off whatever was going on. He was now holed up at Gladsaxe police station, where he had been arrested for damaging public property, owing to the dirty boot prints on the windowsill. After that episode, no one left the school before they had given both oral and written accounts of their vacation travels. With the exception of two lovers who had spent the time together in Paris and who tried to conceal this from the police as they had concealed it from their spouses, there was nothing to dig into. No one had a past that indicated a predilection for mass murder. All in all, the school staff were law-abiding and the labors of the day resulted in nothing.

Or almost nothing, except for an incident that Poul Troulsen concluded with.

"The school counselor, Ditte Lubert. She is impossible. I interrogated her twice, if you can even call it that. She is . . . I can't describe it exactly. I actually think she is trying to hide something, but I have no idea what, so either someone else should take over or I need permission to hit her. Preferably both."

If one didn't know Poul Troulsen one could be fooled by his kindly and trustworthy appearance: an amiable, gray-bearded grandfather. Simonsen, who knew that his kindness had limits, reacted promptly at the suggestion of violence.

"Countess, haven't you—"

"I'll talk to Mrs. Lubert tomorrow," Berg interrupted.

Everyone turned to her with astonishment. Their new colleague was apparently a woman with some self-confidence, perhaps a stroke too much. Simonsen grunted his consent and after a couple of seconds Troulsen realized that he had been relieved of his duty.

"From the bottom of my heart, thank you. You have no idea what you are walking into, but good luck . . . and for heaven's sake, don't ask any leading questions or you won't hear the end of it."

Then it was done, and the miracle complete. Troulsen sat down.

Simonsen resumed the proceedings. He had pumped the Countess as well as Arne Pedersen about the janitor. Neither of them had made any objections but he knew they were wondering what he was up to. For others, the work and the presentations could well have waited until the morning, as Pedersen had so correctly observed, but Simonsen had insisted.

"On to Per Clausen. The fact that I didn't detain him is

nagging at me. Perhaps it was a mistake, and although I know all too well that you believe I am attaching too great an importance to him, I think you are wrong. Time will tell. Our main priorities right now are clear: to establish the identities of the victims, how they ended up at the school, and why they were hanged. Nonetheless, Clausen is our best angle for the moment. Arne, Countess: you have done some fine work, and much faster than I believed could be accomplished."

Pedersen commented, "It is because we don't have to wait, regardless of whom we ask for what. Overtime at headquarters will increase exponentially if this goes on."

"Which is not your problem, so forget about it. I see that you have prepared a complete little sideshow. We're all waiting with bated breath."

The Countess took over, but surprisingly did not start with Clausen's life.

"Tomorrow I will get some computer assistance from a new co-worker. That is to say, our student intern. His name is Malte Borup. Be nice to him."

She parried Simonsen's evident surprise rather elegantly.

"As you recall, I was given permission to recruit him. Now he has been freed of his other duties so we should all be happy. He is an IT genius and you'll love him, although he is a little rough around the edges."

She beamed like a little girl at having gotten her student. It was something she had been working on for a long time.

Simonsen introduced a sour note into her happiness. "If he doesn't fit in, he'll be out the door before you can say 'fatal error.' Now tell us about Per Clausen."

"Per Monrad Clausen was born in 1941 in Copenhagen," the Countess began. "His parents were Anette and Hans Clausen. His father was a carpenter and later a master carpenter, his mother a housewife. In 1947 the family moved from

Bispebjerg to Charlottenlund, where Per Clausen grew up, and in 1948 his little sister, Alma Clausen, was born. The family had no other children. Clausen did very well in school and his father was convinced to let him go on in his studies. He passed his university entrance in 1959, the same year that his father was made master carpenter. The family finances were in good order. After his examinations, Clausen worked in his father's workshop for one year and then matriculated at the Statistical Institute at Copenhagen University in 1960. The following year, in 1961, he was given a scholarship spot at the Valkendorf College in downtown Copenhagen, which is only afforded the most gifted students. Clausen graduated in 1965 with high honors, tending toward the exceptional. He received the university's gold medal for his thesis on spatial statistics and the distribution of prime numbers."

While she was speaking, Pedersen supported her presentation with images or bullet points on the computer screen. The Countess took a sip of water, then went on.

"From 1965 to 1969, Clausen worked at Boston University in Massachusetts, but in the fall of 1969 he returned to Denmark, where he was employed by the insurance company Union. He married Klara Persson in 1973. She is Swedish. She became a Danish citizen at the time of her marriage and was able to work as a dental hygienist. The couple settled in Bagsværd at Clausen's current address and in 1977 they had their only child, Helene Clausen. Clausen's salary increased steeply and was soon among the top fifteen percent in the nation. In 1987 the marriage collapsed because Klara Clausen fell in love with a childhood sweetheart. The divorce was difficult and characterized by bitterness. Mother and daughter moved to Sweden the same year; Clausen remained in Bagsværd. In 1988 his parents died and Clausen and his sister inherited almost nine hundred thousand kroner each. The following year he become embroiled in a controversy with the tax authorities as he donated half a million dollars to charitable organizations and wanted to be able to deduct the entire donation. In 1992 he was ticketed for speeding on the Hillerød motorway. In January 1993 Helene Clausen moved back in with her father and starteded ninth grade at the Tranehøj secondary school in Gentofte, and half a year later she started the Auregaard grammar school, also in Gentofte. In the summer of 1994, Helene Clausen drowned in a swimming accident at Bellevue Beach in Klampenborg."

"Where is she buried?" Simonsen interrupted.

The Countess glanced at Pedersen, who shook his head, whereafter she shrugged apologetically.

"At this time Clausen was fifty-three years old, and after the death of his daughter his personal life and his social standing both took a turn for the worse. In 1996 he changed jobs from chief statistician at Union to janitor at the Langebæk School. The job came through some assistance from his boss at Union, who knew the school superintendent in Gladsaxe. Clausen was a problem by this time: he drank copiously, behaved badly, and stopped taking care of his personal hygiene. However, despite misgivings, he managed this job better than expected, even if he ended up taking the occasional sick day and was occasionally indisposed due to alcohol abuse. He is generally well liked, but keeps to himself most of the time and never speaks of his private life. The last few years he appears to have gained a reasonable control over his alcohol consumption. Half a year ago he told the headmaster that he suffered from colon cancer and was given time off to receive sixteen doses of treatment at the Gentofte Hospital. He was often gone for one or two times per day but the hospital has no record of this treatment."

Simonsen got up and stood for a long time staring at the whiteboard as if he wanted to draw out additional details from the Countess's keywords. No one said anything; only the soft hum of the computer's internal fan could be heard. Finally their boss came back to life.

"I thought we were the only ones he was lying to. Where is he now?"

"At the pub. Surprise, surprise," Troulsen answered.

"Do we have any officers there?"

"Two inside, and two outside. Stop worrying, Simon."

Simonsen shifted his thoughts from the janitor and said, "One more thing. I've talked Kasper Planck into helping us with this thing."

He looked around. All four of them nodded and no one made any further comment.

The Countess drove Simonsen and Troulsen home. She listened to the latest news update, her boss dozed, and Troulsen talked about pizzas. The two others let him talk.

When the radio news was over, the Countess turned it off and poked Simonsen, who was sitting in the front passenger seat.

"Why have you posted guards? Isn't that overkill?"

"If you mean the officer in front of the school, he's there to learn."

"To learn what? That it's cold at night in October?"

"To treat people nicely."

Troulsen elbowed his way between them from the backseat.

"Look, you two, you've got to listen to me. If none of us ordered the pizzas and none of the teachers did, then who was it? Someone must have done it. They were all paid for and the bill was over two thousand kroner. You have to agree it's a bit mysterious."

The Countess tried to placate him by agreeing that it was strange. She wanted to hear more about the guard.

"Listen, the pizzas were apparently ordered for a party, and we sure wouldn't have ordered them for a party. The staff doesn't know about any party either. The school secretary was sure about that."

Simonsen suddenly became alert and almost shouted, "A party, you say. When was the order placed?"

"Well, at first I assumed it was sometime today but the delivery boy said they were out of pineapple, so three of the pizzas were different than ordered, and that indicates that they were ordered earlier. Otherwise they would have had to choose something other than pineapple when the initial order was placed."

"Look into it, Poul. You, personally. Find the pizzeria, where it is, when they open."

Troulsen had been struggling all evening to get his pizzas taken seriously, and now they were being taken almost too seriously. He answered meekly, "Okay, Simon. I will."

The Countess wasn't on board.

"What's all this about?"

"About criminal foresight, I believe. But let's wait for further discussion until the morning."

Which made no one the wiser.

CHAPTER 10

Helle Smidt Jørgensen doesn't scream. It doesn't help any.
Instead she whimpers like an abused puppy, a soft little Labrador with black fur; she buries her face in the fur to hide; the dog sleeps with her; the dog always sleeps with her, it's

her dog; she dreams that she wakes up; she's drenched in sweat and her nightgown is damp; she tosses the pillow aside, she has no use for it; one Sunday in summer, a family breakfast in the community garden; the table is set outside in the beautiful weather; the flag is raised; everyone is happy except her, her and the dog; they have to wake up and go; they have to get out of bed and find the pills; psychopharmaceuticals; fear is a normal reaction; Uncle Bernhard is sitting at one end of the table; the children are playing on the grass; she is not playing; she is grown-up; fifty-three years old, a fully trained nurse, nurse Helle Smidt Jørgensen, that's what it says on the name tag; anxiolytika; fear is made up of psychic, bodily, and behavioral symptoms; she hunches over and smiles because she is an adult, a grown-up nurse; Uncle Bernhard is assistant mayor, a grown-up assistant mayor; the dog lies down next to her; the dog is hers; you can bury your face in a dog; benzodiazepine; fear is an important survival mechanism when the organism is faced with danger; she is not in danger; she has the rest of the group; Stig Åge Thorsen and Erik Mørk protect her; Per Clausen slays fear; the Climber murders the night; Grandfather suggests that they sing, everyone loves to sing; she tells Grandfather that he is dead; and Uncle Bernhard is dead; and the dog is dead; her dog who sleeps next to her; and everyone is enjoying themselves; and Uncle Bernhard gets the banjo; Lexotan; anxiety disorders can be mitigated with psychopharmaceutical treatment.

They sing; Uncle Bernhard sings baritone; everyone likes Uncle Bernhard; Uncle Bernhard sings beautifully; Uncle Bernhard becomes mayor; Uncle Bernhard is handsome; everyone knows that Uncle Bernhard is handsome; three milligrams three times a day; she wakes up, goes out into the kitchen, the glass is on the shelf, she has to have three milligrams, three times three milligrams, three times three times three hundred milligrams, now! quickly, as soon as she wakes up; before the singing, she has to get up before the singing; everyone is quiet; everyone is looking at her; Uncle Bernhard is smiling, Uncle Bernhard smiles sweetly; Uncle Bernhard is nice when he smiles; Uncle Bernhard sings her song; it is a foreign song; only she and her uncle Bernhard understand foreign; Uncle Bernhard sings her foreign song; only she and Uncle Bernhard understand her song.

Be my life's companion and you'll never grow old.
She is grown. Fifty-three years old.
I'll love you so much that you'll never grow old.
She is a nurse. She is strong.
When there's joy in living you just never grow old.
She doesn't need to be afraid. She has pills.
You've got to stay young, 'cause you'll never grow old.

The song reaches out for her; the song embraces her; the daughters of the night rage in the sunlight; the song drives the dream away; the sun disappears, and the flag, the table, Grandfather, everything disappears; the bed is gone; the nurse is gone; it is dark; it is quiet; there is fear; she hides her face in the dog; she hears steps; she is so little and the steps are so heavy; panic can be mitigated with psychiatric or psychotherapeutic treatment.

Therapy chases away the anxiety; Uncle Bernhard chases away the dog.

She feels his moist breath on her neck; she can smell his brilliantine.

She hears him panting; she feels his fingers open her.

Helle Smidt Jørgensen doesn't scream. It doesn't help.

CHAPTER 11

The young man's fingers flew over the keys so fast that it sounded like a strip of cardboard in the spokes of a child's bicycle wheel. The Countess looked up from her reading and watched him surreptitiously as he worked. He was a curly-haired youth with blue eyes and an open face; he had a slender build, with a fashion sense that she could characterize only as unique. His downy upper lip held the beginnings of a mustache, but when he smiled it was difficult to suppress an urge to stroke his curls and want to rescue him from a cruel world that at best offered him only minimal chances for survival. Or so it seemed to her.

Malte Borup looked up as if he felt her gaze, and his hands hovered above the keyboard.

"That good-looking one, is she also a cop?"

"Her name is Pauline, and yes she is. As she told you."

"That's true, she did. I was using my eyes more than my ears."

"You're not the only one."

"What about the other one? The one with . . . well, the other one."

"She is a psychologist who will be participating in the discussion."

"What's she done?"

"Nothing. How is my laptop doing?"

"It'll be ready soon. I've sent a text message to the one with the beard. The strange one . . . one moment . . . I've got him here."

Her address book popped up on the screen. The computer worked as a natural extension of his thoughts.

"Poul Troulsen. I'll have to learn these names. He went to McDonald's, isn't that right?"

"A pizzeria. What did you write?"

"I just asked if he wanted to bring a couple of sodas back with him. Was that bad? I'll pay him back."

"No, that's all right, but I don't think he reads his text messages."

He glanced at the screen, realized there was no help to be had there, and shrugged.

"We'll go back to HS tomorrow. There's a canteen there where you can buy soda."

"Sweet. Will I meet the boss? That fat guy. I saw him on TV."

"You'll meet him today, but don't call him fat."

"Not fat. I meant slightly overweight."

"Don't call him fat, and don't call him overweight."

"Okay."

"His name is Konrad Simonsen and he's in the gymnasium with a guest. Maybe we can catch him before he heads back to the city."

Malte Borup stiffened. Like a frozen computer screen.

"I'd rather not see any corpses. I really don't want to, unless it's absolutely necessary."

"And you won't. The bodies were transported to lab a long time ago."

"Cool."

"Yes, I suppose you could say that."

* * *

63

It turned out that it was a matter of opinion if the dead were completely gone. A woman who turned up in a taxi brought a whole new perspective on the matter.

Simonsen was stubbing out his cigarette in an ugly black streak on the exterior wall of the gymnasium when he saw the car. He was on edge, almost irritable. The night had been too short and his head was about to run over with information that he was expected to handle. Big and small all mixed in together and every time something left his hands something new turned up to take its place. It was always that way in the beginning of a case, especially something of this nature, which was, mildly put, a high-profile case, but knowing this was hardly a consolation. On top of this, he had forgotten to call Anna Mia yesterday although he had gone to great lengths to promise her, and he had forgotten to thank the Countess for the chess book, which he had gone to great lengths to promise himself. But he had not been able to remember either of these, and as if that were not enough, he had, in a fit of terrible dietary planning, decided to subsist on a bowl of yogurt for breakfast, so now he was also famished. He tried on a smile that was far from genuine and walked up to meet his guest.

She was a weathered little woman who blended into the asphalt. They greeted each other formally. Her voice was dry as talc and without inflection as she started to dissect his current desires—and as if it were the most natural thing in the world.

"I sense a strong attraction to fish filets."

He knew she was teasing him. Sometimes she used her special abilities to stir up his rational world, just because. He had been through it before.

"Thoughts don't make you fat. That's just how it is."

Simonsen was a rational man. He did not believe in the Klabautermann, in the power of crystals or of earth power lines, and his window box had to make it through the winter without iron as a precaution against supernatural creatures, so when he nevertheless incorporated the little woman's talents into his regulated universe it was because she regularly produced precise, correct, and relevant facts that lay miles beyond what simple guesswork could have produced. However, from time to time she was wrong and at other times she had nothing to say. How she came by her information he had long since given up trying to understand.

They usually met in her home in Høje-Taastrup, where she and her husband managed a lucrative but discreet consulting business. Her husband called himself Stephan Stemme and produced strange stories for online advertising. Once in a while Simonsen received an e-mail with an audio clip from him. He usually deleted these. When he consulted with the woman he always brought an object related in some way to the case in which he was seeking assistance. That was crucial. Like a police dog, she had to have some material to work from, but in this forensic investigation he had no physical objects to present to her. The agreement was that she would simply walk around the scene and see if the spirits were willing.

It turned out that the spirits not only were willing, they were lining up to have a chance to speak.

The second after she stepped into the gymnasium she tentatively stretched out her hand and glanced alternately at the ceiling and the floor, as if it were raining. Whatever it was she saw, it contorted her face.

"A man has been castrated by his own son. There are drops of blood on the floor."

Suddenly she jumped back and was about to fall on top of Simonsen.

"Thank you. Who are they?"

Then it took hold of her. She stared in desperation down the length of the room, her hands pressed to her head, without words, apart from the occasional exclamation, but her gestures and facial expressions reflected an intense and unpleasant scene. The visions went on for quite a while. From time to time she covered her eyes, at other times her ears, and once she put her palms together and pressed her fingertips against her chin as if she was listening or praying. On one occasion she turned away in disgust.

Then all at once it stopped and she was left staring vacantly into space.

Simonsen was tense but remained silent even when one minute followed another and she stood there without sharing what she had seen. The first move had to be hers. Her response turned out to be as disappointing as it was surprising. That it was also a lie, was something he had no power over. The shadow world could not be consulted.

"Unfortunately I'm not getting anything else, and I would like to go home."

CHAPTER 12

The face was fleshy and pale with tiny beady eyes, and the thin girlish mouth looked painted on. The gaze was directed downward and the features crumpled into wrinkles as many people have the habit of doing when difficult decisions need to be made. A sour fish-face.

The head filled two-thirds of the frame, and the headrest, decorated with the Danish flag, made up the rest.

For a brief second nothing happened, then the face broke into a grin while an eager tongue tip flicked out a couple of times and moistened the red lips.

Something was said, whereafter the video sequence froze and caught the man in an unflattering grimace.

Anni Staal—reporter at the *Dagbladet*, whom Simonsen preferred to see banned from the country—was disgusted. The flag and the man made her feel unclean even though she did not know who he was or hear what he was talking about. She half-heartedly looked around for her headset and realized that as usual someone had taken it. At which point she gave up. The message accompanying the video had been anonymous. The sender was only noted as "Chelsea," which she didn't know what to make of. Anonymous messages were nothing new. She received several every day, so she shouldn't really be wasting more time on a single one.

The telephone rang. She grabbed the receiver and smiled when she recognized the well-known voice. After a short while she said, "I certainly remember Kasper Planck and that will be a sensation, so you'll get two thousand if we have a feature on him tomorrow."

She gave a time and a place and added, "All right, we'll say twenty-five hundred, but tell me something while I have you on the line. Arne Pedersen—you know, Konrad Simonsen's right hand—there's a rumor that he has gambling debts. Do you know anything about that?"

Again she listened, though not for as long this time, then she said, "I know, I know. With regard to Kasper Planck, do you think that I can get a comment from either Simonsen or Planck himself?"

While she listened to her answer, she deleted the e-mail and read the next one. She received two new messages before she wrapped up the call.

"I think I've got the right little Lolita-Anita for the job. The girl has such high morals she should be studying to become a minister rather than journalist, so she meets both of your criteria. And for God's sake, call me back soon."

She hung up and called out into the editorial cubicle area, "Anita!"

CHAPTER 13

There was nothing charming about the Pathology Institute in Copenhagen but through the years there had been many times when Simonsen had felt a certain relief upon entering the place. Perhaps it was the ubiquitous smell of rodalon that stung the palate and nostrils, but that nonetheless did not manage to conceal the heavy odors, or else it was the strange mix of hypermodern machines and gray-white organs in holding jars from an earlier era that appealed to him. The institute was a locked world where only a few insiders belonged, and he was not one of them.

Arthur Elvang went through the preliminary autopsy results. The board was soon covered and in a little while he would wipe it clean for the fourth time. Simonsen glanced at Arne Pedersen and Pauline Berg, who were sitting at his side and were following the professor's discourse with great concentration, in contrast to the head of Criminal Forensics, on his other side, who was sleeping. His name was Kurt Melsing and he was respected for his abilities. In contrast to the professor, he was a likable man. From time to time he nodded or gave a little snort, waking for a brief period of time, after which he soon fell back asleep. He had been up all night and none of the others wanted to interfere with his nap.

The presentation had lasted almost an hour and nothing indicated that Arthur Elvang was nearing his conclusion. Unfortunately, the information offered did not contribute significantly to making a breakthrough in the investigation. The lengthy explanation was caused mainly by the number of dead, but each individual relationship was useful. First, the time of death had been established to Wednesday, between twelve thirty and two o'clock. The cause of death had also been established: four men had died by hanging and the last by strangulation. The latter had probably fainted when the noose was fastened around his neck. Apart from that, there was almost nothing that cast any light on the identity of the dead, nor had they discovered any shared characteristics among the men apart from their mutilated sex organs. The ages ranged from forty-five years to approximately sixty-five, and the muscle mass of two of the victims indicated regular physical activity and therefore manual labor, which was not true of the other three.

But there was one glimmer of light. Arthur Elvang was working with a provisional set of names for the men, which Simonsen intended to borrow. The professor had established that looking from the main door to the back wall of the gymnasium was due north, whereby he came up with the following names for the dead: Mr. Northeast, Mr. Northwest, Mr. Southwest, and Mr. Southeast. The last person was called Mr. Middle.

When the lecture came to an end at long last, the three police officers had a chance to ask detailed questions and Arne Pedersen was the quickest off the mark.

"Could you repeat what you said about the use of anesthetic?"

The professor repeated himself. Simonsen noted that his

choice of words was basically identical to the first time, only spoken somewhat slower.

"All five men were partly anesthetized with Stesolid about two hours before they died. Stesolid is a tranquilizer or sedative. Depending on the amount used, it can cause either unconsciousness or drowsiness. The medication is administered by intravenous injection. All five bodies have a prick mark on the left or right arms and there are also marks on their upper arms most likely resulting from a tourniquet. The concentration of Stesolid in their blood is identical almost down to the decimal point, which indicates that they have received individually calculated doses determined by their body weight. The doses have been calculated and administered by a professional. One can deduce this if only because of the fact that all five injections hit a vein on the first attempt. My assumption is that a physician or nurse or the equivalent has handled the injections."

Pedersen followed up. "You said partly anesthetized."

"Yes, the concentration was not particularly strong, and its effects will have been limited. I assume that the aim was to make the men cooperative. Easily manipulated, if you will."

"You mean passive?"

"Something like that. Slow and dull for a couple of hours is more precise."

"You say that their body weight has been taken into account; were they weighed?"

"Not necessary. A competent assessment of their weight from their height and build is more likely."

Then it was Simonsen's turn. He had jotted down a couple of questions on his pad and now discovered that he could neither read nor recall the first. The odd pause caused the others to give him quizzical looks, and Kurt Melsing briefly woke up in the ensuing silence. Simonsen went to his second question.

"In regards to the identification, is it correct to assume that we have a partly intact dental impression?"

"From Mr. Northwest, yes, with an emphasis on *partly*. But combined with his approximate age it should be enough to establish an identification, if you can locate his dentist."

"You said that Mr. Northeast had a pacemaker inserted about forty years ago, when he must have been in his early twenties. Is that something that can be traced?"

Arthur Elvang paused before he replied, "He may have suffered from rheumatic fever. I'll give one eye that this is one of our homegrown surgeries. A Danish hospital inserts a pacemaker on a man, nineteen to perhaps twenty-five, sometime between 1961 and 1968. He was given a blood thinner. Marevan or Marcoumar. We'll analyze that later. Much speaks for the fact that he would have had his INR values measured quarterly in order to monitor his status and most likely at a hospital. That's not a bad point of departure for an identification. There can't have been many such operations at the time."

Pedersen interjected, "Will you help us?"

It was a rational thought since the professor was the ideal man for such a task, but given the work that still lay before him, it was unrealistic. In view of the man's age, which one often forgot, the question became unreasonable.

Simonsen modified it: ". . . To find someone that we can work with on this?"

Arthur Elvang looked in confusion from one to the other.

"Stop with the Donald Duck talk. Who is asking what?"

They both dropped the request.

The time was now ripe to put Kurt Melsing back into action, and they got some life back in the man, who was soon in the middle of an enthusiastic monologue on the subject of one hundred kinds of bloodstains, with a focus on arterial spurts and splatters. As opposed to the professor, his level of eloquence was relatively low and relatively disjointed, and apart from what Simonsen had noticed—that the floor in the gymnasium had been covered in plastic and signs—he offered nothing useful. That the man knew about blood was nothing new. Finally, it was too much even for Arthur Elvang.

"No one wants to hear about your bloodstains, Kurt," he interrupted. "Let's hear your conclusion. That is something they are more interested in."

Kurt Melsing redirected himself cheerfully and took out a piece of paper from which he read, in an admission to his evident limitations in expressing himself off-the-cuff.

"Our measurements of interfaces and angles as well as blood-stains on the corpses show that the chainsaw was operated from right to left at an angle of about sixty degrees to the ground. The person who used the saw was located about one meter higher than the body he was cutting. It is also evident that the men were standing on a raised platform of some kind before they were hanged. It is also clear that the spray of blood has often been intercepted by a flat surface. Taken together, this informa-tion leads us to believe that a kind of podium of about one and a half meters above the floor was erected. A scene with five trapdoors. Nothing short of an execution ceremony."

"Damn."

That was Pedersen. His tone was muted but it spoke for them all. For a moment all was quiet, as if angles, rotational speed, intestinal residue, and dental records retreated to the background and the full impact of five people's horrendous death hit them. Arthur Elvang broke the silence.

"Yes, it certainly can't have been very pleasant. The victims were transported to the gymnasium and up onto the podium in a more-or-less advanced state of sedation. Their clothes were removed. Where and how we don't know. Naked, with hands bound behind their backs and legs tied, they were placed apart

72

from each other, a noose around their necks. We have found traces of glue on their ankles and in several cases on their underarms, most likely from strong tape. Then they were hanged, and immediately after the hanging but before the next person was killed, the victim's hands were cut off. There are also a number of slashes made on the person's face. The bloodstains and angles of the wounds are the grounds for the forensic conclusion we have already mentioned. We can only offer an educated guess as to the order of executions. We think it was Mr. Southwest, Mr. Northwest, and Mr. Southeast. As previously mentioned, Mr. Northeast is an exception, and Mr. Middle was last. The mutilation of the victims' genitals occurred only after the podium had been dismantled."

As if by previous agreement, they all waited for Konrad Simonsen, who, despite the pressure of their silence, took his time to gather his thoughts. Finally he said quietly, "Plastic on the floor, newspapers above to absorb the blood, then a whole podium that is erected for the occasion and then dismantled and taken away?"

It was a question and it was of acute significance. Pauline Berg said, "It fits nicely that the janitor's father was a master carpenter—"

Simonsen interrupted her: "One moment, Pauline. Kurt?"

Kurt Melsing was as soft-spoken as Konrad Simonsen, but there was no hesitation in his answer.

"That is what happened, Simon. I know that it sounds sick, but it happened that way."

"There's no room for doubt?"

"No."

The Criminal Forensics Division had produced a visual re-creation of the events in which stick figures enacted the tableau that Arthur Elvang described. The sequence lasted two minutes, with occasional close-ups for details of particular interest. The animation was done in three dimensions, and though it did not appear particularly lifelike it depicted a stylized gruesomeness that gripped its audience and depressed the atmosphere further.

They watched it twice.

Melsing made a single comment: "We have used two perpetrators. It could have been one or, for that matter, five. We don't know and don't have a way to make a reasonable determination."

When the meeting came to an end, Simonsen lingered. First, however, he took the lead on psychologist Ditte Lubert, from Berg, who had made no headway with her. He would let the Countess or Pedersen—whichever one had the time—take a stab at it.

After the two others had left, he asked Elvang, "Can you give me a short lesson in craniofacial reconstruction?"

The old man beamed. It would be his pleasure, he said, and without any further need for reflection he launched into an explanation.

"The method is used for the purpose of obtaining an identification. It is not used here in Denmark, where forensic law enforcement in tandem with a well-functioning dental service with orderly files constitute a better, cheaper, and more secure method for establishing an identity. But it is employed to some extent in England, for example, and in the USA, where people are less documented, and in these places there are trained professionals. 'Forensic anthropologist' is what the Americans call them. The idea is that one models a face from an unidentified cranium, and the method is based on a combination of anatomy and statistics. In area upon area, one builds up single muscles or muscle groups once small custom-made pins are applied to the cranium. These anchors are placed in predetermined reference points and are trimmed in relation to the average soft-tissue thickness at a given location. The facial construction is often done with clay, and it is beneficial if the anthropologist has an artistic vein, a little like a translator, but an exact reconstruction of the face is impossible. For example, one can never replicate the ears."

He paused, then added thoughtfully, "Implicit in your question is of course the question of whether this method can be applied in this case."

"Yes, that was my thought. An identification is crucial. The odds that we will make it another way are good, but the teeth from Mr. Northwest and the pacemaker from Mr. Northeast can take a long time and do not of course guarantee success. If you can get me some photographs that more or less resemble the victims, I would like for you to start that now, rather than in a week. It is my only recourse if I am still empty-handed, and, as you know, money is no object for once."

"No, I've heard that and that's good, because it's expensive. Unbelievably expensive."

He stared straight out into the air, grunted something unintelligible, and said, "Come on, let's go take a look."

Melsing and Simonsen followed him.

The room they stepped into was light and clean. There was a terrazzo floor and walls covered in white tile, as in a bathroom from the fifties. The floor bulged slightly in the middle and sloped down to a trench that ran along the perimeter of the room, so that the entire area was easy to hose down. A couple of large stainless-steel sinks were placed between the windows, one for hands, the other for internal organs. Four stretchers were placed in the middle of the floor at least two meters apart, and a corpse lay on each. The sounds in the room were unpleasant and metallic as in a public swimming pool.

Arthur Elvang studied the facial remains on three of the bodies critically while his two companions remained silent. When he spoke, his words were directed mainly to himself.

"It doesn't have to be an anthropologist. There is a great deal of information here and no maggots, so perhaps a skilled facial surgeon. That could be interesting, putting together a team and getting them to use each other's knowledge. Perhaps a funeral director; a mortuary makeup artist from the States."

He reached a conclusion but continued his train of thought, now turned to the others.

"Back here we just pop them in coffins and advise the survivors not to open the lid. They aren't to be looked at here."

The chief of Criminal Forensics had been listening intently and was fired up about the idea. "I have just the photographer," he said. "She's a pure genius with her camera and in developing the pictures."

Elvang received this positively: "Yes, yes, good idea. I'd like to have her on the team as well."

The decision had been made. Simonsen's nighttime Internet research that lay behind his question had born fruit and he felt a measure of pride, although he could not know if the results had been the same had he been ignorant. He delicately inquired about a possible time frame and received—as expected—a rather gruff reply from the professor about how that could not be determined here and now. For the first time this Tuesday, Simonsen was finally in a good mood. Podium or not.

His good mood lasted less than ten minutes. When the meeting was over but before he had left the building, his cell phone rang. The Countess's message was brief and to the point, in direct contrast to his exclamation, which echoed in the institute's corridors.

"That is a lie; that is a damned lie."

But it wasn't.

CHAPTER 14

The Climber sized up the tree that stood in the square in Allerslev, a small provincial town outside Odense. It was a European beech; he estimated that it was about one hundred years old. The trunk was at least one meter in diameter and the canopy stretched out far above his head like an enormous red-violet bell; a couple of branches had been pruned here and there but on the whole it had been allowed to grow as it liked. It was not really in proportion to the square—it was simply too tall—but it had probably been there before most of the shops that lined the square were built. He let his gaze travel around and concluded with some satisfaction that there were no residential buildings nearby, which was key, because however carefully he tried to proceed, some noise was inevitable.

Coolly and soberly, he then surveyed the nearest hot-dog stand. The construction quality was low and the materials were cheap. Chips of concrete had crumbled onto the floor, the sliding door and the window to the right were Plexiglas, and white-painted plywood covered the counter under the window as well as the three outer walls. The lumber was simple pieces of pine hardly thicker than five-by-ten centimeters and the insulation was nothing to write home about—a single layer of rock wool held in place with faux tiles in hard Masonite. The roof was flat and sloped to a plastic gutter behind the building. One-half consisted of charcoal-colored roofing tiles, most likely fastened directly onto inexpensive veneer, and the other half—where the customers stood—was covered with translucent corrugated panels littered with leaves and insects and in rather desperate need of cleaning.

From the bench where he sat he could see the hands of the staff as they worked and from time to time also a face, reflected in a stainless-steel panel. White-yellow like a bulging abscess, bloodless, with dull eyes, as repulsive as a cadaver. Unfortunately, he would have to kill him first or else his chances of survival would be too great. There was also the matter of the tree—he had known that as soon as he saw it, even though it would make the work more difficult. Perhaps an unnecessary complication, but the symbolic value it would carry for the chosen was magnificent, and would certainly provide a couple of days of nervous stomach for the many regulars of the hot-dog stand. And a beech was so fitting . . . so wonderfully fitting.

He again turned to the tree with an expert's gaze and felled it in his thoughts. The hot-dog vendor had a side job delivering newspapers and started his days at an ungodly hour. It gave him a golden opportunity—he could work on the tree all night. If he set the chainsaw on low so that the blade ran as slowly as possible, the noise would be reduced to an acceptable minimum. The slow speed would mean his work would take longer but he had time. First a Humboldt fore cut. The blade on his chainsaw was shorter than the diameter of the tree, so he would have to work from both sides. Then the felling cut, parallel to the fore cut, sawn with an alternately pulling and pushing motion. A pair of sturdy plastic wedges were placed so that the blade would not get stuck, and then finally the heart cut, which he would do only at the very end. Twenty seconds more at a regular speed and then the tree would fall.

He glanced up one last time into the branches and then at the hot-dog stand, then he smiled and said a single word into the air: "Bam."

CHAPTER 15

Poul Troulsen walked into the reading clinic at the Langebæk School in high spirits, and the Countess used his entrance as a welcome opportunity for a break. She was in the middle of her second review of the failed interrogation session with Miss Lubert earlier that morning. This time, the woman had brought along her own lawyer—a well-meaning, competent, and most likely highly stressed fellow, since he was her brother-in-law. The Countess knew him well and she hoped for his sake that the sisters were very different. He deserved as much. Not that anyone deserved Ditte Lubert. Despite Pauline Berg's insistent questions and the lawyer's indirect assistance, the session turned into one long march in place, where every single word was turned, measured, defined, and redefined eight times by the psychologist until no one remembered the original question and no reasonable answer was possible. After almost one hour of this, Berg threw in the towel.

"What are you doing?"

"A lot of things at the same time. I have six teams going around the school rooms, plus two with neighbors. Mostly the teams take care of themselves, of course, apart from the fact that they call in every once in a while to say that they have nothing to report. At the same time, I've been gathering information on Per Clausen. Our operations leader calls me every half hour, so that is also something I have to contend with."

"Where is he now?"

"Right now he's shopping at a local grocery store."

"What's that? Our friend Lubert?" He pointed to the tape recorder in front of the Countess.

"Yes, good guess. Pauline didn't get anywhere. She's also a bit of a mouthful."

Troulsen grinned. "Play some for me."

The Countess rewound the tape.

"You're pretty debonair now that she's no longer your problem." She started the tape and turned up the volume. School psychologist Ditte Lubert's scathing voice filled the room.

"I'm sure I had some work to do."

"You have told us that you were on vacation last week. Isn't that correct?"

"One of you already asked me that once. You really should coordinate your information."

"But is that correct?"

"If I was on vacation or if I said that I was on vacation?"

"If you were on vacation."

"If I said I was on vacation, then I was."

"So you were, then."

"Is this really relevant in any way?"

"I don't know, Ditte."

The Countess pushed the Pause button and briefly explained: "She came in dragging a lawyer. He's an otherwise reasonable man who has the misfortune of being married to her sister."

"What did you do on your vacation?"

"Should I answer that? Do the police need to know what I did on my vacation?"

"No, you don't have to answer anything. We've been through this, Ditte."

"Does she actually have the right to ask me how I spend my time?"

"Yes, she has that right. But, as we've established, you don't have to answer."

The Countess rewound further and played another short bit.

"*. . . It may improve the communications if you tell her.*" The legal council's voice was tired.

"*I agree with that.*" Pauline Berg's voice was even more tired.

"*Then first she has to define exactly what she means by 'unusual.'*" Ditte Lubert sounded well rested.

The Countess sighed and turned it off. She said, "And it goes on and on and on. I have seen many extraordinary witnesses but she takes the cake. She's worse than the janitor."

"What do you think about her?"

"What I think? I think that Ditte Lubert is looking for a bit of a ride. Single mother, a kitchen-sink existence, envious of her colleagues' successes, querulous and puffed up, but I agree with you, if you push all that rubbish aside there is something she's hiding. Right now I just don't want to think about her. Tell me how things have been going for you. Have you found the happy pizza-delivery person?"

Troulsen sat down on the table next to her, ready to tell. The Countess sniffed a couple of times when he was closer.

"You smell terrible."

"There's a reason for that. I've been standing in pizza garbage up to my ankles for an eternity. But listen. When the joint opened this morning I was on the spot and had a long chat with the pizza mama herself. At first she didn't understand a single thing and when she answered it was eighty percent Italian. I'm telling you, it was hard work, but then luckily her son came out and after that it turned out that the woman actually spoke reasonable Danish but was hiding behind a fake language barrier as a defense mechanism when she realized she was dealing with the public authorities. The son managed to talk her into a more reasonable state of mind and after some back and forth they agreed that the pizzas had been ordered last Monday, by a man, whose order was specified on a note."

"Interesting. So, you were right."

"Yes, I guess so. Next time we'll try to get her to describe the man, something that was completely impossible today. After endless variations of the same five questions we concluded that the customer had been between the ages of twenty and eighty, was most likely neither a dwarf nor someone confined to a wheelchair and who was most definitely male. At that point I actually believed she was the victim of an undiagnosed dementia. In hindsight, this is clearly an unfair assessment but under the circumstances it was unfortunately more than justified."

"You searched the garbage for the note?"

"Of course. We turned three containers upside down in the back and started right in. The son helped me, while the woman directed, which was a joke. Finally we found it—a small, light-blue Post-it, where the delivery date and the number of pizzas were elegantly written in a strikingly rounded hand. A graphological gift, even if most of it was numbers. Everyone was happy and they gave me a coffee on the house so the whole thing ended on a nice note. Until I accidentally happened to glance above the counter where the various orders in the restaurant were hanging, written in—well, take a guess."

"A strikingly rounded hand."

"Bingo! It was just bad luck and the son was as annoyed as I was. He apologized for his mother's faulty memory but it was too much for his mother and she flew into a state. She poured out the worst vindictives over our sinful heads—a fine mixture of Danish and Italian—and in the middle of this abuse she calls out to us why we don't just go and ask the man himself. We just sit there gaping until the son pulls himself together and demands an explanation: does she know him or not? But no, she doesn't know anyone. He and his father are always the ones who get out and meet people, while she has to stand there selling pizzas. She just knows that the man is a janitor at her son's old school."

"That's a lie."

"Apparently not. She distinguished between knowing someone and knowing who someone is, which you have to admit is not a crazy thing. She claimed that was where her description got hung up, because she thought we meant his personality and not his appearance."

The Countess nodded thoughtfully.

"God only knows how Per Clausen will explain the order. It'll be an interesting afternoon. Won't you call Simon right away? He's probably done with Forensics by now."

"Can't you do it? I have to use the restroom and I also have to deliver these before they get too warm. Where is the new guy?"

Poul Troulsen proudly pulled two sodas out of his briefcase.

"Impressive. I really didn't think you could manage the whole texting thing."

"If the truth be told, I got some help."

"Malte is programming in the next room. He wants to set up a cross-referencing system for our reports. It was his own idea, and don't bother asking him for any details."

Malte Borup gratefully received his sodas. While he was digging for his money, Troulsen at first glanced idly at his work, but took a closer look when something caught his eye.

"Tell me, what are you doing exactly?"

"A cross-referencing system. It'll save you a lot of time. Automatic free text searching for connections. Inductive and asynchronic. I found a great AI-class library online. For starters I'm integrating with hospitals and telecommunications. Am done with the big hospitals with the exception of Herlev. They're a hard nut to crack but I'll try again this evening."

His listener did not look like someone who could appreciate the depth of this information so he added helpfully, "AI means 'artificial intelligence.'"

Troulsen laid a heavy hand on his shoulder and said calmly, "Maybe you should try to express yourself in sentences as opposed to acronyms. I'm having trouble understanding what you're saying—tell me, don't you know that it's illegal to break into other people's computer systems?"

Borup didn't reply.

"Aren't we the police, for God's sake?"

Troulsen's large mass so close-by made him nervous and when the subject changed he felt completely spun around.

"Malte, who is the prime minister of Denmark?"

He thought hard while his fingers scratched at the keyboard. The question could be answered by Google in a split second, but that would probably be cheating.

"Isn't it someone from Jutland?"

"It's always someone from Jutland. Give me more."

He crossed his fingers and took a guess.

"From Århus?"

Troulsen decided to postpone his bathroom visit. The last thing they needed was a first page headline about a police hacker. He returned to the Countess, recounted the situation, and ordered her to give her protégé a lesson in social studies, starting with the laws of the land. Not that the boy seemed to have any objections to any of it, but it appeared that he took the relationship much less seriously than seemed suitable.

"Okay, I'll have to talk to him. In the meantime you should see how well you remember your geography. Or you can take out a map of Denmark."

"What do you mean?"

"Simon wants one of us to go to Tarm and talk to the janitor's sister, and if I remember correctly I was the one who . . ."

She let the sentence hang in the air unfinished and he capitulated at once.

"I'll go. Can I take your car?"

The Countess's phone rang, so she simply nodded. The message was brief but serious, which she confirmed upon hanging up.

"Per Clausen has given us the slip."

"That can't be true. It's a joke."

"In that case a very bad one."

Tarm suddenly seemed extremely appealing.

CHAPTER 16

It was now sixteen days after nurse Helle Smidt Jørgensen had medicated the men in the minivan. Six unpleasant days and two horrible nights with Uncle Bernhard over her. She was particularly tense today, since tabloids and posters screamed of the mass murder and the entire hospital was talking about the news. It was almost impossible to think about anything else, and although her part at the rest stop last Wednesday had been over in ten minutes, images from the episode kept popping up in her mind's eye like an unwelcome movie. Unfamiliar faces with fearful, pleading eyes and hands that were shaking uncontrollably and the metallic clang of the handcuffs when they hit the back of the railing. The desperation of the men when she stood there in the van with the syringe raised like a torch and the tourniquet slung around her neck like a venomous snake. They roared like bulls and howled like dogs until the Climber came at them with a pocket knife and compelled them to quiet down. *Be quiet or you'll lose an eye, my dear Pelle . . . how about it,*

Frank, same for you, Thor, and you as well . . . was it *Peter?* She could not remember the names, only the Climber's witty and frighteningly honest voice.

"It's hard not being able to talk to anyone. Harder than I thought."

The old woman on the bathing stool smiled uncomprehendingly and Helle Smidt Jørgensen stroked her gently on the head. The touch brought a fleeting glimpse of presence into the vacant eyes, then she retreated into her own land.

"Is it Thursday today? That's the day my daughter comes by."

The woman took an evident pleasure in the water spilling over her emaciated, wrinkled body and Jørgensen gently soaped her up. She let the water run for the sake of warmth.

"I was playing cops and robbers, me, an old woman. So I got to try that too." She glanced at her patient and it occurred to her that "*old*" was relative.

"Not that I'm as old as all that, of course, but there I was with a hood, a gun, and the whole shebang. A real-life pistol or a revolver—what do I know? Even if it wasn't loaded. And then a whole bag of handcuffs."

"My daughter's coming today. Is it Thursday today?"

The towels were stacked in the warming closet and they were a pleasant temperature. She wrapped them around the old woman and gently rubbed her dry.

"I pointed the pistol at the Climber without saying anything. He begged for mercy while he was locking them all up and it just so happened that no one protested before it was too late. Yes, I'm sure they all believed it was a mugging and that the Climber, being the driver, was also a victim, and the truth only dawned on them when all five of them were handcuffed."

A tremble shot through the old woman. She must have raised her voice.

"My daughter is coming. My daughter is coming now."

"There, there."

She gave her a hug and stroked her back. The woman calmed down. After that she let the wet towels fall to the floor and started to rub lotion onto her in soothing circular motions. The old woman opened her eyes and hummed softly, and she continued the rubbing a little longer than strictly necessary.

"We have to remember to brush your teeth and make sure that it doesn't end up like last week."

She deftly grasped the woman's upper dentures and pulled on them. The last time she had bathed her the old woman had lost her teeth and she had become very anxious—not that she needed much to set her off. She brushed the set in hand soap while the old one rinsed her mouth.

"My daughter is coming to visit me. Is it Thursday today?"

"It is Tuesday today. Your daughter is coming over the weekend. It's a long time until then," she snapped without wanting to.

The woman reacted immediately.

"Call my daughter. She should come now. Is it Thursday today?"

"Shut up, you senile old fool."

The old one wept heartrendingly.

Jørgensen couldn't recall having struck a patient before. Never ever, not even a light slap like the one just now. She needed something to calm herself down, a pill or a drink or both. This was a stressful time.

CHAPTER 17

rne Pedersen and Pauline Berg strolled along the sidewalk. They got along well with each other and liked to break off alone when given the chance, as in this case, although they were very busy. Berg was in a bad mood so there wasn't much conversation but they did stroll. Perhaps it had become a habit.

In contrast, Pedersen's mood was wonderful. The meeting at Forensic Pathology had given the investigation if not a full-blown breakthrough then at least a new dimension, and on top of it he was a cheerful sort. He differed in this way from his companion, who walked half a step in front of him and looked like a scolded child. All his experience with women told him that it was best not to talk to her and to let time work on her mood instead of trying to intervene. Sooner or later she would be back to normal, that was almost always the way, so in the absence of conversation he took the opportunity to admire her backside. It was not such a bad alternative and he slowed down a little more.

When they reached the corner, where Berg's car was parked, they found a ticket on the windshield and, what was worse, the citation officer. He stood a couple of cars ahead of them, making note of a new offense. Pedersen decided to study the price list in the window of a laundromat, already firm in his decision not to get mixed up in the situation—a position he abandoned when Berg's objections quickly escalated from a discussion to a disagreement, and the color of her face indicated a continued escalation. He forced her away from the parking officer, managed to get the keys from her after some work, and hastily drove them away.

For a time neither said anything. She was the one who finally broke the silence.

"Thank you."

"You're welcome. Do you want to drive?"

"No, it's fine."

They continued a bit farther in silence, then Pedersen reached for the newspaper between them. He propped it up on the steering wheel and said, "Listen to what that journalist Staal says about Simon."

Berg looked disapprovingly at him. To read while driving did not seem a sensible combination.

"I would like to arrive in one piece."

He let her finish, then read, "Chief Detective Inspector Konrad Simonsen was more for decoration than substance at the press conference. He had clearly been muzzled. The leader of the investigation sat as meekly as a lamb on the outer—"

He got no further.

"Stop it, Arne. I feel terrible. It's like the whole thing's gone wrong and I feel like a complete failure."

He tossed the newspaper into the backseat with an attitude of defeat, then placed a hand on her thigh.

"Don't you think you just need a man?"

"Why do you behave like a simple swine when you're not?"

She sounded upset. He removed his hand and regretted his words. He tried something closer to the truth.

"Because you're silly, Pauline. Simon took the psychologist from you for the simple reason that you weren't managing her well enough. That's all. You're in a homicide unit, not a weekend trip with your girlfriends, and you may recall that Troulsen was missing, so it seems to me that you're making far too much of yourself by playing reprimanded or glum or whatever you are.

Whatever it is, Simon hasn't got time for your childish games. That is to say, if he knew you had them, but he doesn't because he's not a mind reader. And remember that in the situation you broke down completely and went along with his decision without protest although they hadn't helped you. But you chose to get upset afterwards and ten minutes ago you tried to reduce Denmark to a banana republic when you tried to use your police status to get out of a parking ticket. For heaven's sake, Pauline, what kind of society do you want to live in? And now you're blubbering as if you were thirteen and I was your dad, which I am not. So all in all, I'm more attracted to your body right now than your spirit."

She didn't answer, staring glumly into the traffic while she tried to shake off her bad mood. She had to admit that it wasn't the end of the world and after a couple of kilometers she had more or less collected herself. She thought about suggesting that they split the ticket—that would be fair—but on the other hand she knew he was always in financial straits so she decided against it. She smiled sweetly, which required effort. Then she made her voice an octave deeper and asked, "Do you want to know what I dreamed last night?"

Pedersen noted that she had regained her equilibrium, which was good, although the question was less so. Normally he was fairly honest but in this situation he did not dare tell her that there was hardly a man in possession of his senses who willingly listened to women tell their dreams—if one excepted therapists, who were, after all, paid.

"Yes, of course. But we're going to be there soon."

"Do you remember our summer party?"

He remembered it very well. Their unit threw parties with Narcotics, but unfortunately also with administration personnel and the executives. It was rarely much of a laugh. There were too many chiefs and too few Indians for that. At the last event they had rented space in the city. The party room was fancy and had high ceilings. Very high. The architect had indulged himself without paying any attention to maximizing usable space or taking heating efficiencies into consideration. Five floors had been taken out and replaced with glass, with gigantic inch-thick windows overlooking the water. A glass ceiling floated above them, which gave a clear view of the starry sky as the evening progressed. Unfortunately, he had to leave early as the twins were sick and he had promised not to be too late. It was a little frustrating. He had wanted to introduce Berg—completely new at that time—a bit more thoroughly to the rest of the unit. His noble intentions had to give way to familial duties. Later, he had introduced her during their trip to Skanderborg. Two times, in fact.

"Of course I do."

"In my dream I am dancing with you. It is about half past eleven, the party is at its peak, and we are one couple among many, twisting and turning around each other. Everyone is smiling and happy; some are wasted but not us. From the outside we look like all the other dancing couples but I have a plan, a plan you don't know about. Suddenly we find ourselves in front of the stairs. That is the plan, or to be more precise, part of it. I have deliberately, step by step, led us to it. Do you remember the stairs?"

He did. It was a broad, winding staircase placed in one corner, which was connected to a bridge running across the length of one wall right under the ceiling. A chain marked this as a closed area. He nodded and wondered where she was going with this.

"I take you by the hand and drag you up the stairs. At first you are skeptical at this idea but you follow along, and each time we go around we get farther and farther away from the others. The music gets weaker, we can talk without shouting.

91

I'm in my red Thai silk skirt—or, no, wait a minute, that's wrong—I have borrowed a cheeky little thing in a flippy bordello-colored velvet that shows a bit too much thigh but is nice and cool when I dance. Halfway up, I step out of my shoes. I'm not used to high heels. I bend over and set them aside."

He braked hard at a pedestrian crossing. She made no comment, but continued.

"From the top of the stairs we walk across the bridge where solid-glass panels are attached to the railing. That is a good thing because it's a long way down and I'm staying close to the wall. I can see and hear everyone down below. The music is old Gasoline and many of our colleagues are waving at us. Everyone is happy, with the exception of the little red-haired one from the secretarial pool—you've helped her out on a couple of occasions, she is sulky. I wave kindly to her but she doesn't acknowledge me. Perhaps she doesn't care for the food, even though she doesn't look like someone who is picky."

She stole a glance at him and saw that he was still listening.

"At the end of the bridge I stop. The large glass panels are nailed to the bridge but are not attached at the wall, and between the closest wall and the last panel there is enough room to squeeze by. I put aside my shoes and slip in and now I am standing on a little ledge intended to secure the structure. It's not without danger because it is eighteen meters down. When for a brief moment I let go of the railing, you also press through and place a strong arm around my waist while holding firmly to the railing with the other. You are taking care of me, which I am grateful for. And here we are, just you and me, somewhere between heaven and earth."

She had closed her eyes and leaned her head back as if she was reliving the dream.

"Under there is light, music, socializing, and colors; over us, the eternally cold night sky. You show me Orion's Belt and explain to me that Venus is not a star, it just looks like one. You are so smart and strong. I lean my head in towards your face while I brush my hair aside and you kiss me tenderly on the ear, don't you?"

His answer came without hesitation.

"Yes, of course."

"Of course you do. Well, below us more and more people have noticed us standing on the ledge. Someone is pointing and others try to call up to us but we can't hear anything so after a while they lose interest. I send a kiss down to Troulsen, who is sitting where I left him, drinking beer. Next to him is my purse, which he has promised to watch for me because it would be embarrassing if anyone opened it. My cheeks turn red just thinking about what is lying uppermost inside the bag, and you know it too since I removed my shoes on the stairs. My panties."

He confirmed this knowledge, without her having asked him to do it.

"Then I slowly rub my buttocks over your crotch. Back and forth, side to side, and both of us notice how you gather strength. You protest, but I override you. You should know that when a man says no he always means yes and your virility proves me right. Without forcing it, I bring my hand to help. First simply a finger, then more. I loosen your belt and unzip your fly while my other hand is holding your pants up. From down below, everything looks proper. You have coaxed the new girl in the unit to a remote corner of the room, everyone has noticed that, but how far you have led her astray is hidden by my body. I drag the front of your underpants down until the elastic holds them up, then I turn my feet so that my thighs part before I pull up my dress a bit and push you up into me. You groan in my ear, warnings, but also sweet things and other words that simply don't exist. Your arm muscles tighten and your grip on me grows stronger but it is a just a start because now comes the fun."

She smiled brightly without opening her eyes.

"I tell you that I am going to let your pants fall and now you find yourself in a dilemma. You are holding on to the railing with one hand, the other is around me, and you don't have another one around to hold your pants up so that they don't end up around your ankles. In front of the eyes of all your superiors and all of your co-workers, who will talk about you for all time to come so that your reputation, your career, your modesty—all is at stake. When I let go of your pants you have already escaped me and I put my arms around your back as far as I can while I focus. I'm thinking about what I have learnt again and again in ballet class. *Flexibility, power, posture, control,* these are the four key words. I loosen my hold on you and slowly let my body glide around in tiny circles. You call out my name even though we are so close, though not as close as before. Our bodies parted. Almost. Now it is all or nothing. The rotation gets bigger and bigger. *Flexibility, power, posture, control.* I get braver and braver, centimeter by centimeter until at last I find the outermost unstable balance. Then I hold up my arms in triumph toward the stars while I alternate between stretching on my tippy-toes and falling back onto my feet."

She was speaking more loudly.

"*Flexibility,* up on my toes, *power,* down again, *posture,* up, *control,* down."

Suddenly she opened her eyes and her voice changed.

"Oh, we're there."

They had reached the parking lot in front of the Langebæk School. They had been there for quite a while.

She took her bag from the floor. Pedersen protested.

"No, wait a minute. What happened then?"

"Happened? Happened where?"

"Well, in your dream, of course."

"Oh, that. I can't remember exactly. I think I turned into an angel and flew away."

"An angel?"

"Yes, an angel. When I was little, my dad often used to called me angel and when I was naughty I was an angel with dirt on my wings—isn't that poetic? But it may also be that I woke up."

She released the buckle on the seat belt.

"Don't get mad, Arne darling, dreams can't last forever."

Without blushing she reached down between his legs.

"But I think you need your wife."

CHAPTER 18

The two men across from the Countess looked like what they were, namely shamefaced lugs, whose careers were hanging by a thread. In their defense, it had to be stated that they had not tried to make themselves look better and that they had related the facts of Per Clausen's disappearance precisely and without elaboration, just as they had not offered any stupid excuses. It was a sensible approach, as the Countess would have skewered them for the slightest attempt at such a thing. Now she'd been given no reason. She inspected them from head to toe as if she were about to grade their performance. Both hunched under her gaze but said nothing and then she let mercy go before right.

"If you hurry up, you'll be able to get away before a very large and very angry man comes in, someone you absolutely do not want to meet."

To her surprise, they didn't move. She waited a couple of

seconds for a question that never came. Then she held her thumb and pointer finger in front of her eye and said, "I see in my crystal ball two colleagues sorting through the lost-and-found because they did not get to safety in time."

That helped.

Simonsen did not share the Countess's penchant for mercy and his enthusiasm was limited when he had to settle for hearing the story secondhand. In the absence of a better alternative, however, he sat down in a chair, ready to listen.

The Countess looked down at her notes and then related the distressing news.

"At about twelve o'clock Per Clausen was buying groceries at the local supermarket, where he filled his cart with everyday items as well as wine. After checking out he put his items back into the cart and started walking down toward Bagsværd's main street. At another shop he bought four sandwiches and two beers that he also placed in his cart, and at the kiosk he bought a box of cigarettes. Before he goes into these shops he covers his cart each time with his raincoat so that passersby can't easily view his purchases. The next stop is the hardware store at Bagsværd Hovedgade 266A. The business is located in the ground floor of a residential building with three floors and eight entrances. At this point he is under surveillance by five officers as well as a backup unit in a car."

Arne Pedersen and Pauline Berg entered the room and Simonsen shot them a sour look. They handily avoided making any eye contact; it was very clear to them that the boss was in a foul mood and that it was best to mind their own business. The Countess filled them in quickly before she continued.

"At the hardware store he inspects some shelves at the very back, then he suddenly walks into a back room and slams the door shut, having first stuck a match into the lock. From the store there is an exit to a parking lot behind the building but also—by way of a staircase—access to a storeroom in the basement, and before he heads down he jams the door shut with a wedge. The storeroom has an emergency exit to the basement corridor under the building and he walks through the basement, which, as I mentioned, is connected to eight different entrances. At the very end of the corridor there is a bicycle room where he has planted a stroller with a change of clothes, a kind of black, Muslim whole-body covering, easy to throw on over his regular outfit."

"Shit."

Simonsen sighed.

"Simple, but effective. With a stroller and his new outfit—I think it is called a niqab or a chador—he walks around the building and past the noses of his pursuers. Many of them remember him very well. Then he walks calmly up the main street and turns down toward the Bagsværd Station. With the stroller, he takes the S-train at twelve thirty-nine toward Copenhagen, but he gets off at Buddinge Station. He leaves the outfit and the stroller in an elevator and from the taxi stand he gets a ride to the Ballerup mall. Here we lose all trace of him."

Simonsen hit the flat of his hand against the wall and said, "I should have held him yesterday; his behavior was so odd that it was irresponsible to let him go. And even more irresponsible to turn him over to a couple of chumps who can't manage a simple job."

The Countess, who still feared the worst, watched him apprehensively.

Pedersen tried to be constructive: "We should be able to get a search warrant to his home."

His boss latched on to this with a spark of hope in his voice: "That's true. The pizzas and his disappearance are enough. Follow up on it, Arne. Go!"

But the Countess extinguished all light: "Unfortunately, his house is in flames. A fire truck is on the scene but can't quell it.

I got the news ten minutes ago. You can see the fire from the window, if you like."

No one did. The atmosphere was dark and depressed; Simonsen appeared almost groggy and said nothing. Again it was Pedersen who rallied. He tried to gather up the remnants: "At the very least we can put out an alert for him for suspected arson."

Berg picked up this thread, trying to sound optimistic. "With the kind of press coverage we're getting at the moment, we're sure to be able to get his picture in the papers."

Pedersen said, "That's right. He doesn't have a lot of chances if we keep surveillance at the airport and the major stations, because I think we can safely assume he's not going home again."

The Countess raised her palms into the air. "Just a moment. Unfortunately, there's one more thing."

They grew silent and let the bearer of bad news have the word.

"He left a message for us in the stroller. Or rather, to you, Simon."

The envelope was the kind that accompanies bouquets, and on the front it simply read "Konrad." The card inside was white without additional decoration. Simonsen read aloud, " *The little children who weep, give them light and songs of joy.*' What does that mean?"

The Countess answered sadly, "I'm not entirely sure but I have a bad feeling about it."

"And that is?"

"The line is from a Grundtvig psalm called 'Evening Sighs, Night Tears.'"

Simonsen pressed the note into the table like a weak playing card that had to capitulate to a higher trump and thereby unconsciously mimicking the Countess's note of alarm even before she came out with it.

"It is a funeral psalm. I don't believe we will ever see Per Clausen again."

CHAPTER 19

Per Clausen burrowed deep into the cushions and smiled sadly up to the ceiling while he let his whole body relax. It had been a delightful day. First there had been some unexpected work to take care of. The reasons behind Konrad Simonsen's having brought a young woman to his interrogation session the day before instead of a seasoned colleague was not so easy to interpret, and he intended to repay in kind. He had purchased a camera and been successful in capturing his subject without a significant wait. He printed the pictures at a library and sent the papers with instructions to the Climber. The rest of the day he had been able to devote to himself.

He had been home. He had visited his childhood one last time.

Much had changed, but for those eyes that could really see, the street was the same as fifty years ago. The asphalt was still smooth and flat, and the coating just a little bit finer than anywhere else in the world, which is why it had always been the preferred gathering place whenever there was going to be a game of marbles or hazing. Kids of all ages came wandering from near and far and in the light summer evenings it had swarmed with life. A horde of children shouting and yelling, winning and losing, smiling and crying, as they quarreled over the rules or formed fleeting alliances. Boys in knickerbockers and long harlequin-patterned stockings, crewcuts with dirty ears and eternally runny noses, the girls in plaid skirts with elastic waistbands that could be pulled down to reveal their pink underpants.

He crouched down with his left knee against the ground and his right leg sticking out behind him, and ran his fingers along the street in a long, sweeping motion one last time.

For a while he kept his eye out for a cat; just one little straggly kitten to help him relive the past, but he didn't see one. Back in his day the apartment buildings had been swarming with cats. In the daytime they sat on garbage cans or lay on steps lapping up the sun as they patiently kept watch for the cat mother, who turned up faithfully three times a week with sweet words and fish scraps. In the night they rent the silence with their mating yowls and territorial fights. When the cat catcher was on the street, all animosity fell away and everyone knew their role. The girls gathered together in small groups and chased the cats away; the boys attacked them with blow straws and slingshots. The little kids ran from apartment to apartment and called for assistance, while others peeled celluloid from handlebars and used their magnifying glasses to light stinking fires under the animal catcher's car. He usually left with unfinished business. Furious and cursing but without a catch in the back of his vehicle.

The last window on the second floor of the yellow building was his mother's. From it, she called goodbye to him when he went to school in the morning and called him up in the evenings when it was time for bed. The glass in the window was cracked and only his mother knew why. He had been sitting in the window at the time. The cornice of the building was cracked with frost and posed a hazard, so a scaffolding was erected and a large, jolly plasterer got to work. He sang beautifully while he worked, sang the sad song of the wild duck as well as any street singer. Housewives rewarded him with coffee—some even with beer—served straight out of the window. He had stood there on the scaffolding, singing and swinging his mortar and trowel, and caught sight of his mother in the window. He had made a cheeky comment about how the prettiest woman in the building deserved some extra mortar. The clump clung to the window and slid down over the glass pane. She had scolded him for his foolishness and secretly thrilled at the traces of it for the rest of her life.

He stood there for a long time, his mind attuned to the past, his reflection in his mother's window, before he quietly returned to his starting point.

Now he was at journey's end.

He removed his belt and tightened it around his left arm so that his veins stood out. He took the syringe out of his inner pocket, attached the needle, and filled it from two ampules. There wasn't much light—he was grateful for that, slid the needle in between the thumb and pointer finger, the student's comfort. He calmly pressed the plunger, loosened the belt, and closed his eyes.

He noticed with a tinge of irritation that someone had entered the room and he was a bit surprised that he could see the door from his vantage point under the cushions. Then he heard her voice and forgot everything else. She was wearing the pretty, white ruffled skirt he had bought for her when she was six years old and that he liked so much. She stood before him shining, happy, full of health, and he felt the tears stream down his cheeks; then he spread out his arms and ran over to meet her. She had been away from him for so many years and now he held her in his arms again. His wonderful little girl.

CHAPTER 20

Alma Clausen had been pigeonholed ahead of time by her guest. Widow of a farmer, a woman in her midfifties. Pious and from Tarm—all data that in Poul Troulsen's view stank of the cowshed, thickened sauces, narrow-mindedness, and plenty of room for intellectual improvement. Reality, however, proved quite different.

His expectations were initially met, however, in that Alma Clausen was a kindly, unassuming person, short and with a clothing style that he could describe only as drab. Her home was modest and nondescript. Flowery wallpaper, embroidered bell strings, and Amager shelves with porcelain figurines from Salzburg. Liver-pâté-colored mediocrity. Only at an embarrassingly late stage did Troulsen finally realize that the woman was incredibly sharp. This as he slowly and loudly asked her about her life.

"I thought you had received a report about me. Haven't you had a chance to read it?"

Haven't had a chance was the polite version; *haven't bothered* would be more accurate.

"What leads you to believe that we have a report about you?"

Her answer came without sarcasm: "Among other things because I spent an hour on the phone last night with the detective from Ringkøbing who was supposed to write it."

"I am trying to get these facts straight from you."

He could hear himself how unconvincing his explanation sounded. She glanced at his bag, then looked him in the eye and caught him out as if he were a child who had not done his homework.

"It *is* straight from me. Now I will get us something to eat. You can have a cup of coffee while you read."

And so it went.

Alma Clausen graduated in 1972 from Copenhagen University with a degree in theoretical physics and was accepted by the Niels Bohr Institute in Copenhagen. In 1977 she defended her doctoral dissertation. That same year she gave up her academic career for a life as farmer's wife in Ådum. She and her husband eventually celebrated their silver anniversary. When he died, she sold the farm and moved to Tarm. There she read up on the latest research in her discipline and was now an online instructor for the universities of Copenhagen, Berlin, and Stockholm. She had no children.

She called out to him from the kitchen, almost to the second when he was done reading.

"Come out and help me with the salad and I'll tell you about my work."

"I'm not sure I'll be able to follow you."

"Nonsense. Everyone understands it to some extent. No one understands it completely. That's what's so interesting about physics."

She was right, it was genuinely interesting. He sliced away and listened with fascination.

It was almost four o'clock before he got to the heart of his errand, which was Per Clausen's personality. By that time he had long ago turned off the tape recorder, which had appeared to irritate her. In turn she made every effort to answer his questions, as if one favor deserved another.

"How well did you really know your brother?"

"That's difficult to say. We don't see each other so often, and when we do, I'm almost always the one who comes to him, that is, except for last week. We sometimes e-mail and we call from time to time, often in regard to a mathematical problem."

"You help him with mathematics?"

"Unfortunately, no. It's always the other way around. He helps me. Per is the brains in the family."

"And when you communicate, is it only about science?"

"You could say that. Mathematics, physics, and statistics mainly, but we also discuss other areas such as religion, for example."

"Religion? Is your brother religious?"

"No, quite the opposite. I am, he is not."

"What about relationship matters? Do you talk about that?"

She didn't answer directly but continued to elaborate.

"It's only these past few years that Per has started to show an interest in spirituality, and that should be understood very broadly. Not in Christianity, that is, more precisely in questions of faith, morality, hate, love, compassion, and judgment . . . those kind of things."

"That strikes me as very lofty. No, that's the wrong word. 'Theoretical' is more what I mean."

"I wouldn't say that. Per is always very practical. Would you like an example?"

"Yes, please."

"Last Thursday we talked about demonization, about public morality and humanity. Per took as his starting point the large numbers of German refugees that Denmark was forced to accept at the end of the war in 1945—that is to say, mainly people who were fleeing from the advancing red armies in the east. After liberation, the authorities refused to grant these people medical care, and this was not because there was a shortage of medical care, or because there was no need for it, but simply because they were German. This resulted in a number of deaths, especially among children, who could have been saved."

She recited, "'If you hammer in the idea of an "us" and a "them" into the national consciousness, then the majority of the population will passively accept anything. Especially in these times when there is no common moral denominator to be found.'"

"That is your brother's claim?"

"To the extent that I can remember it, yes, but I think I do. Naturally I disagree with him, I have to."

"It sounds a bit fascist to my ears."

"Per is no fascist. I don't believe he has any political orientation whatsoever, and if he has one, he is a confirmed cynic."

"We see him as a bit of a provocateur, if that is the right word. What do you say to that?"

"That it's true. Per does like to tease people but it is seldom mean-spirited, and if he runs circles around you it's just to show that he can."

"What does he get out of it?"

"Nothing except a crooked little smile."

She smiled to herself.

"Hm, interesting. Back to the question of relationships—do you talk about them?"

"Not exactly."

"Then what?"

"If we do, it's always with a kind of agreement."

"I'm not sure I understand. Can you elaborate a little further?"

She reflected on this for a while before replying.

"As you must know, there was a period when Per drank a great deal. He was an alcoholic, no doubt about it. We never talked about it but after a couple of years when he got more control over his alcohol abuse we did sometimes talk about it, that he was beginning to live a healthier lifestyle."

"A kind of code?"

"You could call it that, but 'indirect little comments' covers it better. Of course it is a silly way to communicate. You can never know if both people mean the same things with the same words, but that's how it went. And it certainly doesn't happen very often that we touch on personal matters."

"So you are not very close to your brother?"

"I don't think anyone is. I'm no exception."

"You say that he used to drink. It began when your niece drowned?"

"Yes, it did. It was intense and very self-destructive; I think Per was trying to punish himself."

"Did he feel guilty about his daughter's death?"

"Yes, of course, and on top of that he was desperately unhappy."

"How was their relationship?"

"I don't know except that he loved her very much. Helene was a delightful child."

"Tell me about her. What was she like?"

"Fragile. Fragile and gifted. She had inherited her father's intellect, but not his robustness. She was also quite pretty. Probably took after her mother; that kind of thing doesn't exist in our side of the family."

Troulsen asked further questions about the girl. Simonsen had discussed the interview with him by phone the whole way from Nyborg to Odense, and Helene Clausen's fate was one of the subjects he was expected to clarify. But the girl's aunt was unable to shed much light; beyond the fact that the girl had had a nervous temperament, nothing of interest was revealed. He focused on the topic of her death.

"Do you know the details of the circumstances that led to her death?"

"Not really. She drowned but you already know that. It was a summer evening in 1994 at a Bellevue Beach with her school friends. More than that I don't know."

"You say that he felt guilty about her death. Why is that?"

"It's hard to explain. Perhaps he felt he hadn't watched carefully enough over her."

"Do you think he didn't?"

This time she waited so long before speaking that he thought she was not going to answer. When she finally said something, the result was not in proportion to the time taken to prepare it.

"I don't know."

He tested the waters gingerly: "Do you want to tell me what you think?"

Again a pause, as long as before.

"I think that Per came to say goodbye this last week. I think that my brother intends to do away with himself. I believe that Helene was a mental wreck when she returned from Sweden. And I believe that he was involved in the terrible things that happened at the school where he worked."

Troulsen felt blown away in his chair.

"That was something."

"Yes, I know, but it won't help you to ask more questions. I have nothing concrete to give you and what I just said is based on vague feelings and may be completely wrong."

She was right once more. He probed and probed for almost two hours before he gave up, after which she—despite his halfhearted protests—showed him up to the guest room.

CHAPTER 21

Konrad Simonsen and Kasper Planck were playing chess. From time to time they discussed the case and at other times one or other's comments simply hovered unanswered in the air. One of the advantages of a chess game was that there was no need to observe social niceties in conversation. As opponents the two men were well matched, perhaps because their strengths were so different. Planck's strength lay in tactics and combinations, while Simonsen was best at theory and strategy, and although he was exhausted after an all-too-long day he had—as usual—gotten off to the better start. This evening he would have preferred to skip the chess game, but whenever he was with his former boss it was the latter who called the shots. His vague hints about only discussing the case were summarily ignored and the old man went to get the chess set and the cognac. Tradition was going to be observed, mass murder be damned.

Simonsen focused on his opponent. Planck was a stately old man with a slim, sinewy body and gray-white hair that fanned out in great swirls around his tanned face. His clear green gaze swept the board.

As a boss he had been hard, a leader of the old school. At the same time, he was respected and—in his last years—almost loved. But what had made him into a legend in his own time was neither his leadership abilities nor his success rate at solving cases, for that matter. His status as a living legend stemmed primarily from the fact that he was able to handle the press, which reciprocated by making him into an icon. His revolutionary approach consisted of treating journalists as if they were people. An art that he had not necessarily been able to pass on to his successor.

Planck moved a pawn in the center without further reflection.

"What's the real reason you have gotten me involved in your mass murder, Simon?"

"You've assisted in other cases before since you retired. This is nothing new."

"Bullshit. You have never asked for my help before at the outset like this. And definitely never officially."

"Elvang thought it would be a good idea."

"That's neither here nor there."

A more truthful answer would have been that Planck was in possession of exactly those attributes for which Simonsen had the most pressing need in this case that was so different from anything else he had experienced. Time after time his predecessor had demonstrated an almost terrifying intuition in the course of an investigation. He was able to pick up and interpret very simple pieces of information differently and often more precisely than others, and if there was such a thing as a sixth sense, he was without doubt in possession of one. But at the heart of it, this ability was probably due mostly to the fact that the old man's mind always let one or more parallel possibilities remain open, in contrast to the systematic approach that characterized traditional police work.

They played a couple of moves, then Simonsen said, "When they carried the bodies out of the gymnasium, it was like back in the first couple of months after your retirement, and . . ."

He paused and the pause grew too long.

Planck commented sarcastically, "Take your time, the night is young."

"I would like to have had a strong conviction, something

edifying, if you understand. For example, the confidence that I will be able to track the perpetrators down no matter what. But I imagine that mostly I just felt alone and it has not gotten better today, to put it mildly."

"Well."

Simonsen thought that it had been too long since they had last worked together. Now he remembered again—his former boss had never been particularly warm. Nor was he himself, for that matter. Nonetheless, he had been hoping for some support. He asked with some trepidation, "Did that sound stupid?"

"Yes, extremely so."

"But for God's sake, man, who in the world builds a podium in order to execute five people? And at a school of all places."

Planck nodded slowly. "That's what we're going to find out."

Planck's use of the plural warmed Simonsen's heart. That was what he had been angling for. He took a sip of his cognac. That warmed, too. Then he refocused on the game.

In the middle of the match, when their positions were as good as even, Planck casually injected, "Turns out, I made a new female acquaintance today."

"I see, and who would that be?"

"I think you'll be more interested in what she is."

"And what is she?"

"A reporter at the *Dagbladet*; she was here for three hours this afternoon. You and I might make the front page tomorrow if we're lucky."

Simonsen dropped the piece he had just won and had to leave his chair in order to pick it up. The interruption muted his immediate reaction and he reined in his irritation.

"I wish you would communicate with me before you talked to the press."

"I would never dream of it."

"I know, but you should. So who is she and why is she interesting?"

"Anita Dahlgren, a student reporter under—well, take a guess."

"Oh no, you don't mean what I think you do."

"It may comfort you to know that she cares as little for Anni Staal as you do. Perhaps even less."

"That's not possible. But why did she come here in the first place?"

"Her boss knows that you've dusted me off. She wants to do a story about it."

Simonsen sighed. It wasn't hard to guess the angle the article would take, but he would get over it. What was worse was that his department was apparently as open as a sieve. He said, sourly, "She certainly has her sources, that Staal woman."

"Yes, and she is always working on acquiring more."

"What do you mean by that?"

"Anita said that she was preparing a proposition for that young guy, Pedersen, about some tax-free bonus money in exchange for a first page smacker now and then."

"Are you talking about Arne Pedersen?"

"Yes, Arne Pedersen. Rumor has it that he could do with a little extra income."

Simonsen shook his head. "She'll get nothing out of him."

"Maybe, maybe not."

"You're wrong. Arne isn't like that. But what else did you talk about, you and the girl?"

"Everything between heaven and earth. She liked being here."

"What gives you that impression?"

"It was obvious."

Simonsen did not look convinced.

Planck took a long, dramatic pause before he went on: "And

because she told me so. In fact, she's going to come back and see me again in a couple of days."

He smiled from ear to ear; his opponent grunted.

"Keep telling yourself that, you vain old rascal."

The game neared its end. Simonsen was down by a page but improved his position step by step, minimized his disadvantage, then recovered the lead and waved away his opponent's suggestion of a rematch.

For a while Planck let the game be.

"I have been reading, have looked at pictures, talked with Arthur Elvang, and there is one thing that I'm starting to feel sure of and that is that the people behind these executions are media hounds, as we called them in my day. Today it's called a *compulsion of self-exhibition*, but the essence is that they want to tell a story. It's warm and cold at the same time; logic and passion."

"So your little cub reporter is well planted, Meister Jakel?"

"She came to me, not the other way around. So in the best-case scenario I'm just taking advantage of a bit of good luck and you should too."

"How do you mean?"

"Perhaps Pedersen could be convinced to be a little less principled."

Simonsen answered hesitatingly, "Up front it sounds like a terrible idea."

"I see it differently."

It was not a bad argument.

"Let me think it over. You were going to say something else."

"They want to tell a story, I said. And you're overlooking the obvious, Simon."

Planck fell silent and Simonsen reflected on this. He disliked Planck's affinity for riddles.

"Can I help you with what this story may consist of?"

He hid his irritation behind silence.

"Of words."

"And words are important. Isn't there a word that you've stumbled over? Because there should be. It was used in today's press conference without anyone reacting to it. Twice, even, and the media is using it relentlessly. I think it is exactly what our horrible men wish, so this word is a key. Forget the identities, the transportation, the platform; you'll find out all of this sooner or later, but think about this word. I have used it many times this evening without hearing any objection from you. And recently."

Planck's eyes were shining. Simonsen was at a loss; he didn't speak and could not come up with anything. His opponent struck like a snake: one move and his pawn structure was shattered. The game was lost. He resigned to his fate and gave up.

"Devil. Tell me, what's the word?"

"Figure it out for yourself. You youngsters always think you get things for free in this world. Do you want to play again?"

"No, thanks all the same. One word, you say—do you mean 'execution'?"

"Good work, Simon. A little slow but good. Even though it cost you a game of chess."

CHAPTER 22

The wood shop at the Langebæk School was not a romantic place, and Pauline Berg eyed the row of work benches critically. At the very back of the room there was a band saw.

She shook her head firmly and pushed Arne Pedersen away, which gave her only a brief respite. His fingers soon wandered wayward again. Her storytelling in the car was apparently weighing on his mind, and having made her bed she now had to lie in it. Or so she thought and gave in to his persistence.

"Let's at least go up to that classroom with all the cushions."

Her suggestion was accepted.

They walked hand in hand through the hallways. Outside, the wind was gusting in the late-autumn evening and they had to raise their voices to talk to each other. Pedersen asked, "How was the house?"

Pauline Berg shook her head in exasperation. What kind of question to ask was that? He could have chosen a more romantic topic, given the situation. She thought back. The scene of the fire had been a depressing sight. Only the outer walls remained. The roof had caved in and blackened structural beams lay in disarray like a multidimensional game of mikado. A putrid stench of soot and smoke hung like a thick pillow over the place and she had coughed up phlegm. She answered him, half sourly.

"Horrible, I couldn't stand being out there. They were still working on the final stages of extinguishing the fire and a couple of times the walls collapsed with a bang like a pistol shot. It was unpleasant."

"What did the fire-forensics team say?"

"That it was arson and that no one was inside. He had poured gasoline in all the rooms and then placed the can on a stove plate and set the timer. Do you think we'll find him?"

"I don't know. In any case we have an enormous net out there. I talked to the Countess. She is leading the investigation from headquarters and he's the top priority for every single patrol unit this evening and night. Even the cemetery where his daughter is buried is under surveillance, as well as the beach where she drowned. We've also got the word out in the media with pictures and everything, but, as I said, I don't really know."

"Where is Simon?"

"With Kasper Planck."

"Did he call?"

"Yes, I talked to him before you arrived."

"Did he say anything interesting?"

Pedersen paused. The conversation had mostly concerned Anni Staal from *Folkets Formiddag* and had been completely perplexing. It had also involved his personal affairs, although Simonsen had been tactfully oblique. He answered her in a somewhat cryptic way: "He sent greetings from Kasper Planck. Tell me, did you spend three hours at the house?"

"No, luckily only a quarter of an hour. But we may have found a witness. Two little boys were in the vicinity of the school on Wednesday. The kids were running around collecting the little metal tops on beer and soda bottles. Whatever it is they're called. But one of the boys is in a preschool class at the school. Unfortunately he is somewhat developmentally delayed so we got nothing out of him, but his friend who is his cousin is fairly normal. He's five years old and lives in Roskilde. I'm going to talk to him this evening."

"That sounds more promising than my day. Simon is sending me to Sweden."

"Per Clausen's daughter?"

"Yes, and I agree that it's sensible to take a closer look at her, but why I can't take care of it over the phone, I don't know. That's one of Simon's weaknesses—to send us out without it being completely necessary. If you ask me, that is."

Berg squeezed his hand.

"Have you found out anything about that platform?"

"The school had one on hand for performances and that kind of thing. Something that could be set up and taken down. Now it's gone—the one they used—but we've known that for a while."

"Then what have you been doing?"

"Killing time. That is, until now."

"Downtime is a part of work. How many times have I heard you say that? But maybe that applies to other people's time?"

"Yes, of course it does. This school is nothing but a pain in my neck. If Per Clausen inserted the trapdoors in the podium at this location he certainly cleaned up well after himself. I'm happy that we're based primarily out of headquarters as of tomorrow because today has been a bit of a trial. Four hours in the gymnasium, the janitor's room, and the woodwork room, where I am expected to discover what someone or other may have overlooked."

"And have you?"

"Have I what?"

"Discovered anything?"

"Not a damn thing."

As soon as they were in the classroom, Pedersen started to disrobe methodically, placing each item of clothing neatly folded in a stack on a desk. He even folded his socks. Pauline Berg fell back into the pillows.

"Aren't you going to take your clothes off?"

"Does that mean that we're skipping the foreplay?"

She sounded more sulky than sarcastic; then she pulled her shirt off.

"Ouch, what was that?"

Something had jabbed into her elbow and at first she thought, despite the time of year, that it was a wasp. Then she moved a pillow and found—for the second time in the span of twenty-four hours—Per Clausen.

CHAPTER 23

It was one o'clock in the morning before the technicians were done and Per Clausen's body could be removed.

Simonsen had sent Arne Pedersen and Pauline Berg home when he arrived. There was no reason for them to stay, and he wanted them to go. In addition, Pedersen had been significantly shaken over their find, which surprisingly did not apply to Berg. He did not give any thought to the fact that he himself was also superfluous and would serve the investigation best by catching up on some sleep. Instead, he sat down behind the desk far enough away so that no technician felt compelled to order him out of the room. And then he waited patiently for the body to be ready to be removed. From time to time he nodded off and dozed for some brief moments. In front of him on the table was a receipt for a Canon SX100 camera, which was the only thing of interest that he had found in the dead man's wallet. It had been bought that same day—or more precisely, yesterday—at a photo shop in downtown Copenhagen. It had cost 2,450 kroner. Where the camera was he did not know, nor did he know what it had been used to photograph. The only thing he felt relatively sure of was that Per Clausen had not retained the receipt by accident. He had intended it to be found.

At one point he must have dozed off again because he was startled when a female technician gingerly touched him on the shoulder and said, "So are we good to go? May I call the ambulance staff?"

A couple of seconds went by before he pulled himself together and said, "No, I want to take a look at him."

"But the people are tired; everyone wants to go home."

Simonsen stood up and cut her off: "You asked me a question and you got your answer. I want to have him to myself now, but it won't be more than ten minutes."

"Okay, fair enough. Will you come out when you're ready?"

The question was foolish. He swallowed his sarcastic reply about whether she really thought he wanted to spend the night in there, and said only, "Yes, of course."

She left and locked the door behind her. He rolled his chair over next to Per Clausen's body. Then he sat down and studied the dead man for a long time, as if this would help him penetrate his secrets. The eyes and mouth were open, so the rotten teeth and dull pupils smiled grotesquely up at him—a final taunting grin from the other side.

When he had been sitting for a while he said, "You are a strange man, Per. You make everything that could be simple as difficult and complicated as possible. You could have taken your life yesterday morning at home in peace and quiet, but that was too easy for a man of your caliber. You wanted to show me what you went for first. Pizzas, arson, your absurd interrogation, your carefully planned disappearance, and now, here, your suicide in a room of pillows. And I'm not even sure I'm remembering everything."

He stooped and closed the dead man's eyes.

CHAPTER 24

FIVE PEDOPHILES MURDERED EXECUTION-STYLE IN DENMARK. The title of the e-mail message cut straight to the chase and the contents were an unholy mess of facts and fiction. First, that the Danish state was apparently hiding the fact that the five murdered men in Copenhagen were pedophiles, in order to protect the country's export of child pornography, which aligned rather nicely with the fact that Denmark allowed and supported pedophilic associations and Web sites and steadfastly refused to collaborate with the police in other member states of the European Union. Moreover, the legal consequences for the sexual abuse of children were ridiculously minimal and functioned largely as an official sanction of the phenomenon. Two concrete examples were then cited and analyzed. In conclusion, the recipient was urged to forward the message to others and also to write a letter of protest addressed to the Danish embassy in Washington, D.C.

Half a million letters were sent to various American post-office addresses on Tuesday night. The choice of destination had been Per Clausen's, and his arguments had not invited any objections. It had been a spring day in May, and the group was enjoying the sun and a glass of white wine on Erik Mørk's terrace as they planned the e-mail campaign.

Per Clausen said, "The United States is the locus of conspiracy theories par excellence and has a long history of being a breeding ground for bizarre theories. Aliens from

Roswell; manipulated moon landings; not to speak of the country's intelligence service, which—as everyone knows— is constantly popping off presidents, movie stars, and famous musicians, when they can spare the time away from their substantive LSD production. We can be certain that hundreds of warped minds or strange groups will forward the message, and naturally from their own perspective as the incontestable truth, which can only be doubted by complete idiots or dubious state-sanctioned leaders."

The Climber, Erik Mørk, Stig Åge Thorsen, and Helle Smidt Jørgensen nodded comprehendingly. None of the others felt compelled to go along with Per Clausen. Nonetheless, he continued to bang on the door that was already open.

"And Danes look up to the United States. They may not want to admit it, but what happens in the USA sets the agenda in our media, and whatever garbled rumors have taken hold there will be much more long-lived than fifty thousand pieces of junk mail in Danish letter boxes. Whether it is the truth or a lie or—as in our case—a little of both, is beside the point. If there is a discussion on the matter in the United States, it will rub off on Denmark."

It was Stig Åge Thorsen who ended Per Clausen's monologue. He said haltingly, "You know, Per, that's all very well and fine to send e-mails to the USA, but . . . uh . . . I saw a show about the moon landing that they claimed took place and . . ."

Per Clausen smiled broadly. Erik Mørk waved his arms and said, "We all get your point. How many e-mail addresses would you say I should get a hold of?"

"Half a million. It's a big country."

The first real hit of the campaign turned out to be in Baltimore, where a disgruntled systems analyst uncritically took over the message as his own. As luck would have it, the man had been fired after nine years of employment with Ericsson, the Swedish communications giant. The reason was corporate downsizing, which he found deeply unjust and took very personally. At the same time, he was not particularly proficient in his knowledge of geography and firmly maintained that Denmark was a large Swedish province. To him it was evident that the e-mail was telling the truth. The lack of morality in Stockholm was well known and it did not surprise him that things were even worse in the provinces. As revenge for his dismissal and as a kind of noble gesture he forwarded the e-mail to all sixty thousand employees at the company. In addition, he created his own abbreviated version that he sent to a quarter of a million Vodafone customers via his SMS-server in London, well aware of the fact that he could be fired only once.

Many e-mails died by the Delete button or got caught in spam filters, but a few came through intact and hit their mark. This was the case with a lumber baron and business owner from Knoxville, Tennessee.

The lumber baron was a ninety-three-year-old man who had emigrated as a child with his parents from Onsild in Himmerland, after which he had never set foot in Denmark again. But he remembered very well the old country with its golden, rippling fields of grain and idyllic little farms where the hollyhocks banged against the crooked windows while the sun sank and the people lit candle stumps. If they didn't simply pull on their nightcaps and creep into the hay, exhausted after a day's battle with weeds. When the old Danish emigrant read the e-mail he flew into a blinding rage—something he was accustomed to doing and a habit that had not grown milder through the years.

He had fared well in the USA—very well, even. He was the sole owner of eighty lumber retailers spread across the state. It had started as a local lumber emporium, which he had built up and steered with a hard but sure hand throughout his adult life. A few years ago he had been forced to retreat from the day-to-day affairs and after that he settled with overseeing his many markets as chairman, which meant that he involved himself in everything and made life hell on a daily basis for a handful of managers who had to jump and dance according to the old man's whims. Even now.

The old man's frail body trembled with anger at the fact that someone was accusing his native land of showing a despicable liberal softness toward child molesters, and two of the company's top officers were ordered to put everything else aside and, under his leadership, prepare an appropriate response to the offensive e-mail. The executives wrote a short memorandum that stated that in Denmark people were severely punished for any form of disorderly conduct or perversion. The rare sexual offenders that escaped the executioner's ax could look forward to years of labor in the royal quarries, for this was how the old man believed things worked. His two coauthors were very aware that this was at best a form of wishful thinking and at worst a form of dementia, but they both had families to support and neither of them wanted to lose his job over the state of the justice system in an inferior European nation. And by now they were accustomed to a little of everything.

The letter was posted on bulletin boards in sixty lumberyards, where no one read it except staff members who had great fun with the old codger's latest whim. Thus the rumor found its way into yet another of its dead ends, but in one of the stores there was a customer who had come in to get a key made. As host of the most popular radio show in Chattanooga, she was always on the lookout for stories with surprising angles and unexpected twists. She asked two clerks what they were smiling at.

On its way west, the campaign gathered momentum and in one of its many iterations the e-mail was transformed into a drawing. A drawing with a punch far stronger than Per Clausen's and Erik Mørk's studiously crafted words.

Two reasonably serious news agencies in Madison and Indianapolis had separately put out the story about the hanging of five Danish pedophiles and indicated that the national police were keeping the truth from the public. Both gave the Internet as a source, which was another way of saying that no one could vouch for the truthfulness of the information, but very few people took any notice of this. A middle-aged man in Tucson, Arizona, heard the news from his neighbor, who clearly enjoyed sharing it. Summary executions and subsequent mutilations were in her opinion the right kind of treatment for those kind of animals, which the state government could certainly learn from. The brief conversation across the fence energized and inspired him. He made his living as an artist who specialized in weeping children, and it was a good living. A great number of his unhappy faces hung in houses around the Midwest and his pictures were in demand. Maybe he wasn't a great artist. His repertoire was a bit too narrow for that and his talent insignificant. But few could—as he was able to—capture the helpless despair in the eyes of little boys who had been forgotten by God, but not the priest. Sharp cold twinges and short uncontrollable twitches appeared in his face, neck, and abdomen, which was normal when he worked. He said a fervent prayer before he went to his studio and began to work. Eight years at the Catholic Mercy School in Cleveland had left him with a fear of God in his soul and a fear of the world in his body.

CHAPTER 25

Toward Wednesday the investigation started to pick up steam. The morning had been slow and more or less without results, whereas the afternoon was fruitful. Konrad Simonsen stood for the official assessment of the day's work, which took place in his office at police headquarters in Copenhagen. He had nothing to relate himself, so he turned the meeting over to Poul Troulsen.

Malte Borup's cross-referencing program had proven its worth. The application was coded to reveal coincidences, as data was introduced. It was then up to a human brain to determine which of these were of interest and should be followed up. The majority of the output was indifferent: two instructors who had been in Oslo that fall, a neighbor with the same name as the school vice principal, but a bill from Bagsværd lumber was connected with a teacher's witness statement about the janitor's use of the woodshop equipment in the evenings.

Troulsen's visit to the lumberyard had yielded results. He said, "At the beginning of March, Per Clausen purchased the lumber necessary to construct the trapdoors in the podium in the gymnasium. It was a private transaction, in which the Langebæk's School account was charged. Possibly in order to get a discount, which in itself is neither out of the ordinary nor expressly forbidden, but the purchase speaks for itself."

He held out a green receipt so that everyone could see, then read aloud, "'Carriage bolt, leaf hinges, latches, swing hooks, toothed washers, and not least three rolls of plastic.' Clearly, this gives us at least a minimum time frame of the planning of the killings. In addition, in crucial ways this supports the technician's hypothesis of a scene in which—"

"Excellent work, Poul, but let's wait with the rest of your reflections," Simonsen cut in. "Unfortunately I have no time; the financial people are waiting for me."

"I thought you had free hands with regard to the financial considerations of this investigation."

"Free hands does not mean that expenses can run amok."

"And are they?"

Simonsen allowed himself a wry smile. "I don't know, but I'm certain that the three accountants who have asked to meet with me know a great deal on the matter. Arne, your turn."

Arne Pedersen had been in Malmö. His task had been to uncover Helene Clausen's life from 1987 to 1993. The trip itself turned out to be unnecessary since the Swedish police commissioner—who was contacted by telephone at Simonsen's request—could easily have managed the matter on his own. The Swedish police were extremely effective and gave high priority to the matter but no one had thought to involve Pedersen on the simple grounds that he was not needed, so he'd spent three interesting hours at Malmöhus Castle, where the city museum was located. Back at the police station in Kirseberg he received two reports, one in Swedish and one in English. Five closely written pages constituted a shining example of effective Nordic collaboration if one ignored the fact that the Swedes had done the whole thing.

His presentation was to the point.

"Everything points to Helene Clausen having been sexually molested by her stepfather while she lived in Sweden. Neither her mother nor her stepfather is prepared to speak on the subject but several independent sources have confirmed this. There is also the fact that after Helene Clausen grew up, her stepfather found other victims. He was cited on two counts of sexual molestation of a minor in 1992. These cases were never prosecuted due to a lack of evidence."

He patted the reports.

"These documents also contain an explicit report from a psychologist who no longer found it necessary to observe her doctor-patient confidentiality. She was also the one who recommended that Helene Clausen move back to Denmark."

The Countess took the opportunity to ask a question: "What about Helene Clausen herself? Didn't she confide in anyone?"

"It appears not, at least not directly to the psychologist. Apparently she blocked out her memories and tried to forget, which is not uncommon. On the other hand, we don't know what happened during the years she was in Denmark."

Simonsen hurried them along again: "That's something we need to take a look at. Get a couple of officers going on it. Anything else, Arne?"

There actually was one other thing. The Swedish colleagues had asked him delicately, on two occasions, if the Danish police were concealing the sexual orientation of the victims, whatever that meant. He had denied this but it was evident that they did not believe him. He would have liked to share these episodes if Simonsen's timetable had allowed for a discussion of minor matters. But apparently this was not the case, so he shook his head. But it still struck him as strange.

Berg's trip to Roskilde had also been strange but not without results. The boy, who had played with his cousin at the Langebæk School last Wednesday, had turned out to be a sweet and bright little thing with white-blond hair, prominent ears, freckles, and an appealingly frank and direct way with adults. With the mother's help, she had been able to get the child to recall surprisingly quickly that day during the autumn holiday when he and his playmate had gathered bottle caps. In order to further stimulate his memory, the three of them had enacted this activity in the living room and this tactic had had the intended effect. The boy suddenly remembered that he had been chased away at one point by a man who looked like Buller's father. Buller turned out to be another playmate. Berg's heart skipped at this. The mother, who had grown alert to the fact that the information could turn out to be significant, did what she could to get the boy to elaborate on his description by going back over it step by step. But here they ran into a hurdle because although Buller's father was dissected from top to bottom, there was nothing particular about him that apparently matched the unknown man at the school.

At this point the phone rang and the mother left them. Then the boy explained very secretively that the unknown man reminded him of Buller's father because he drove a bus. He recognized the words *bus driver*. This piece of information was critical and unleashed further questions, which Berg, however, chose to wait with until she was joined by his parent. But when the mother returned, she had coldly and abruptly asked her to leave, without any additional explanation and without further comments. So from one minute to the next Borg had found herself outside the door, which slammed shut behind her.

Simonsen asked her, "That was rather strange. And you have no idea why?"

"No, none at all. I was thrown out. What should I do about it?"

"Leave, just as you did. You couldn't do otherwise. That happens. You can't be the hero every time."

Berg blushed. Pedersen gazed up at the ceiling. Simonsen went on, unaffected.

"This reminds me of the fact that Per Clausen's suicide was caused by a potassium solution. The pathologist called. I have canceled additional technical studies, as they simply will be a waste of time and resources. There must have been dozens of people who—"

The Countess cut him off and got his attention. No one else interrupted the boss.

"Simon, I can verify the van. Do you want to hear it?"

"Of course, of course. I am done anyway."

Earlier in the day there had been a miracle when the school psychologist, Ditte Lubert—under great pressure—let her defenses fall and finally cooperated with the authorities. The Countess related, "At Gladsaxe town hall they have performed their own little bit of sleuthing by going over the past ten years of accounts at the Langebæk School with a magnifying glass. A clerk reacted to three telephone calls to Pretoria in South Africa and he contacted the telecommunications company to find out if there had been any similar calls last fall vacation, which indeed turned out to be the case. Thereafter he informed me."

Troulsen predicted the course of events, outraged at the psychologist: "So her recalcitrance was based on a simple case of telephone abuse?"

"Yes. I called the number and got an answering machine that said Ingrid Lubert was not available at the moment. Then I contacted her brother-in-law to share this turn of events with him. You know, the lawyer, he was extremely cooperative. In part he confirmed that his other sister-in-law was stationed in South Africa for Danida, and in part he promised to have yet another talk with Ditte Lubert, but then there was apparently some atmospheric disturbance on the line."

She formed her hand like a cell phone and cleverly mimed a bad connection. Then she smiled briefly.

"When I went through everything one more time, he wanted to be sure that he had understood me correctly, that what I had said was that this kind of unauthorized use of county telecommunications could mean that his sister-in-law could be demoted from senior to junior school counselor unless she rectified the situation by cooperating fully with the police, which I could find no fault with. Ditte Lubert turned up twenty minutes later. Without the lawyer."

Troulsen commented again: "Very entertaining."

"Like a dentist appointment. She was sulky enough but she came crawling back on her knees and admitted that she called her sister last Wednesday. To save money, she walked over to the school and used the speech therapist's office phone to cover her tracks. The call ran from one twenty-one to one fifty-four, which we know from the account invoice, and on her way home she saw a white van that was turning out from the school's back entrance. It was around two o'clock but unfortunately that is all that she saw. No matter how hard I pressed her after that, she was unable to elaborate on her answers. This time there was no resistance, she simply had nothing more to contribute."

Pedersen asked, "But is she sure that it was a minivan?"

"Completely sure. Unfortunately, that hardly narrows down the field. The smallest are eight-passenger but they range all the way up to twenty for the largest. I'm sending a vehicle expert to her home tomorrow, but I doubt it will give us anything."

Simonsen took over.

"At least now we know how the victims were transported to the school. Who they are, why they were killed, and why no one misses them are still unknown. Of course, there have been numerous inquiries, but as yet none that we can use. The best guess is that they are all thought to be on vacation and won't be missed until later. Countess, can you organize a new door-to-door round regarding the white minivan? Ideally this evening. Sorry."

The Countess agreed, and Berg also volunteered. She felt she owed something.

The meeting was over and Simonsen stood up and paused in

the middle of the floor. His co-workers followed him with their eyes as he swayed from side to side for a moment as he gathered his thoughts. Then he took a deep breath and took on Kasper Planck's role of posing questions of his co-workers, although he hated being in that position.

"What is the difference between an execution and a murder?"

No one made a motion to answer, as the question appeared rhetorical.

"An execution is legal, a murder illegal. The state retains the right to kill its citizens. Citizens do not have that right in relation to each other. The act itself is fairly similar and for the person who is affected the difference is negligible. For the victim, the outcome is the same if an executioner cuts his throat or if he is strangled by his neighbor, but from a judicial and sociological viewpoint there is a world of difference. The executioner maintains the social order. The murdering neighbor breaks it down. *Order* is the key word in this context."

His words grew many and the point was oversold. Perhaps because he was a man who cared about right angles and logical relationships. When he finally finished, none of his listeners could have had any doubts about the social-order-building aspect of executions.

The Countess summed it up in a friendly way: "The execution ceremony sets this act apart from a mass murder. But . . ."

She hesitated, and Simonsen took over again.

"No buts. It is the difference that's interesting. But let me take the opportunity to remind you not to use the word *execution* in this context. And then on to our big question: why the mutilation? It doesn't fit the pattern. It goes against everything I've mentioned, so either I'm mistaken with regard to the words and the legitimacy or else this step has been so desperately necessary that the perpetrators have had to accept it as a kind of sloppy side effect."

"Identification?" the Countess chimed in.

"Yes, that is the most obvious explanation, but the ones who are behind this must know that we will secure the identities of the victims sooner or later, however much they have mutilated the bodies."

This time Pedersen jumped in: "They've given themselves time."

"Yes, that may be. In any case it raises a number of interesting questions. If you are right, why do the perpetrators need time? And anyway—it is logical to destroy the men's faces and to remove their clothes, but why remove their hands? It would only be necessary if their fingerprints were registered, that is to say, if they had a history with law enforcement. And what about their genitals, which have no role in identification at all? Think this over, discuss it among yourselves in your free time, and let me know if you think you have found an answer or—which is of equal importance—if you have found any good questions."

Over the course of the last few words, Simonsen had moved toward the door. His intention was to slip away as soon as he was done with his little lecture. But this backfired completely. Malte Borup was standing outside with a piece of paper. He had been standing there for a while without daring to interrupt, and his waiting time only increased when Pedersen rushed over and waved him away.

Simonsen snapped, "Can it wait, Arne?"

The question was ignored and thus received its answer.

"She called me about an hour ago. Just as you predicted."

"Who called?"

"Anni Staal from the *Dagbladet*."

"And what did she say?"

"Well, it took a while. She was very careful and naturally I played along and was guarded . . . yes, it was a bit of theater—"

"And what was the conclusion?" Simonsen interrupted.

"That I will pass along any news when I have any, and she . . . what shall I say . . . will compensate me for my troubles. Dammit, Simon. It's like a bad American TV series; this kind of thing isn't like you at all. And what will I do with the mon—"

Again Simonsen interrupted, this time with his palms raised defensively in front of him. "That last bit—I don't know anything about that."

"Okay, okay, I get it. It was Planck's idea, wasn't it?"

"Yes, for the most part."

"It's illogical, almost amateurish."

"He has a feeling it may come in handy."

"Illogical. Dare I say, idiotic."

Finally, Simonsen allowed himself some time to talk. He said quietly, but intently, "You are right, but I have worked with Kasper Planck for over twenty years, and as I stand here I can give you at least two occasions when his illogical and perhaps silly feelings have saved a person's life. Not to mention the many times these illogical and silly feelings have solved a case. But you are naturally welcome to back out of the arrangement, if you don't—"

This time it was Pedersen's turn to interrupt. He wrapped up the conversation in a conciliatory way: "No, it's fine. I just wanted to let you know."

Pedersen stepped aside; Malte Borup was next in line. The young man hurried up to his boss as soon as he saw that the coast was clear.

Simonsen unfolded the piece of paper he handed him, scrutinized it, and then asked, "What do I do with this?"

"It is everywhere, and it's spreading as we speak. Blogs, newsgroups, sites, even the really big ones. Fox TV has it as a top story, as well as MTV. It's like a supervirus but people are taking it home themselves and sending it on, and you can already buy T-shirts from . . ."

He fell silent, looking at his new boss's face, and wrapped things up with a "that is, maybe."

Simonsen listened with forced patience. Impatience was a bad habit with him when he was involved in a big case, but in opposition to the rest of his staff, this young man read him poorly. In any case, he was convinced that he was up in the red-alert area, sure that what he had to tell was urgent. For his part, Simonsen lacked the command of the details in this matter to determine its urgency. He glanced at the paper again. It was hard to let it be.

The sketch was disarmingly simple with its few striking black lines. The artist had captured a dark, relentless gravity with sureness. The perspective followed the line of sight that one of the final victims might have had, immediately before the trap-door opened. The viewer of the sketch looked, so to speak, through the eyes of the victim. Slightly ahead and to the side one could see the backs of the heads of his already executed companions. Some bars drawn on the right indicated that the events were taking place in a gymnasium, but what primarily drew one's interest were the spectators. At the top was a judge enthroned as a slightly moth-eaten heavenly father, half god, half clown, with a dusty accoutrements next to his limp hand. The law book, a thunderbolt, and scales. A tragicomic relic from the storeroom of antiquity with a vacant stare and dead flies sprinkled in his wig. Below him were children of all ages sitting on the floor, staring with sad eyes at the convicted; present in the moment, as dozens of small alternatives. Patient, just, without mercy. One could almost feel the rope tightening around his neck, and Simonsen shivered. The title was "Too Late."

CHAPTER 26

"Even though many of you know me well, there are significant events in my life that you do not know anything about and that unfortunately continue to haunt me. I will never be able to shake free of them even if I were to live to a hundred."

Erik Mørk was nervous. His beginning faltered and lacked conviction, and he felt an unfamiliar lack of control. Despite his low voice, he had had the full attention of his audience from his very first words. Most of them were employees in his small business and a handful were his personal friends. The remainder were strangers that Per Clausen had rallied. From where and how he did not know, only that they were one hundred percent loyal. And it was in a long look by one of these unknowns that he found the support to continue—an unusually pretty girl with blond curls and supportive blue eyes. He raised his voice slightly and launched into what he had to say.

"When I was five years old, my father died, and my stepfather moved in. From that day forward until I went to an orphanage at age ten, I was raped three, four, or five times a week. Summer and winter, weekend and weekday, morning and evening, year after year after year. Sexual abuse became such an integral part of my childhood that I believed for a long time that it was the way things were, that all kids went through what I did. It was simply not something one talked about, in the same way we don't talk about shitting. We do it, but we rarely mention it. As an adult I realized that I had been both right and wrong.

Right in that this is not something we talk about, wrong in thinking that the rape of a child is normal. It is rather more common than most people imagine, or rather bother to imagine, but it is not, of course, completely normal either."

He avoided cliché-laden words such as *taboo* and *a sense of guilt*. The connections were simple and immediately understandable. To bring psychology into it would be a mistake.

"As a ten-year-old I tried to murder my mother, which was illogical since in my eyes my childhood had been normal. Why I did not target my stepfather is another question. He was my tormentor, not her. In fact she warned me when he was on his way—by screwing up the volume on the television. I tried to crush her skull with a cast-iron pot that I threw from the window of my room one day when she was in the yard with the laundry. We lived on the third floor and I missed the mark by several meters but the intention was unmistakable so I ended up at the Kejserstræde Home for Children. The first day I was there I was beaten up. Everyone received that welcome. When I crawled into bed that evening—black-and-blue like one giant bruise—I was the happiest child alive."

He looked out at his audience. The atmosphere was intense. No one drank or ate or looked at one another. Everyone was following him intently—motionless, with bated breath, as he confided in them. He felt tears pressing at the back of his throat. Not because of his childhood but because they were listening and giving him respect, solidarity. His voice remained steady when he spoke again.

"Many people other than me have been abused and perhaps I belong to the lucky ones, however damaged I have been. A more tragic example is my little sister. She replaced me when I went to the children's home, but unfortunately she was more frail than I and she never got over her wounds. One morning she sat down on the coastal railway line, a cloth over her head.

She was twenty-two years old. The train driver was granted early retirement. He only lasted three years. Evil metastasizes."

He regretted the expression as soon as it left his lips. It was too medical and the image too stilted. It had sounded good in his head. He continued, somewhat irritated.

"I've often wondered what she was thinking about when she heard the train come screeching, its brakes on full. My stepfather? Nothing? Herself? Me? I will never get an answer but I keep asking the question, and the day she died I promised her that when I got the opportunity I would write her obituary. Not by telling her story—it is too banal and will be forgotten—but by asking a string of questions. Today I have the financial means and I intend to use them. The moment is right. The five executed men in Bagsværd were all active pedophiles, each with numerous abuses on their conscience. As you know, the rumors have been swirling for a while and my source in the homicide unit tells me that the police will confirm them in the next few days but that the information is being temporarily withheld. There is subsequently no doubt that the sexual abuse of children will soon become a dominant topic in the media. My questions will line up in the wind, show another truth, give another perspective."

He turned on the projector with rehearsed timing to avoid too much of a focus on the dead men, and everyone naturally looked up at the image.

"This advertisement was in all the papers this morning, big and small."

He gave them a minute while they read with amazement, then he tossed out his calculation.

"It is, of course, an unverified number, but many researchers estimate that between one and two percent of the population has been sexually abused in their childhood, which is to say, that around five thousand children between the ages of five and ten years are at this time being victimized. I myself was raped some eight hundred times as a child, but perhaps I was an unlucky outlier among the unfortunate. I place the estimate of average rapes for the average abused child in this age group at two hundred. Each of you can now try to make these calculations on your own but I'll spare you the trouble. My guess is that every single day around five hundred children are abused in Denmark. If I am right, then tell me, what is the biggest problem in our society? The day cares? Schools? Freeways? Or is it the five hundred children who will be raped tomorrow?"

He paused. The statistics created a certain distance, as statistics always did, and the intense silence from earlier was gone. It was time to come in for the landing.

"As the ad says, I want to try to get people to make their own assessment and I want your help to do this but you have to decide if you will do so or not. Those of you who are my co-workers also have a choice. You can take the next three weeks off fully paid and without using your vacation, or you can stay here and help me. If you feel that you can't engage with this, then I would rather that you stay away. Now I want you to get up for a while. Walk around and talk to each other, think it over—and then report back what choice you have made."

He turned off the projector.

"Let me end by telling you that I once knew a wise man who has unfortunately passed away. He asked me if I believed that the world could be changed by a handful of people fighting for a new order and he gave me the answer himself, which is as ordinary as it is true, that the world has always been changed in that way."

Erik Mørk waited eagerly for any preliminary indications. In the scenarios he spun out at night he had imagined a string of different reactions, but none of them matched up with reality. The woman straight ahead of him was apparently speaking for many, and in advance he had written off her as too analytical, unmoved by emotions. But he was wrong.

"I don't need more time. Just tell me what to do."

CHAPTER 27

The night was cold and the Climber was freezing on the square in Allerslev.

From time to time he slapped his arms around himself, but it didn't help much. Through his work he was used to being exposed to the elements and he had years of experience in dressing for the weather. Despite all this, he had underestimated the cold of the night and his sinewy body did not carry much in the way of extra padding as in-built protection for the chilly north wind that was sweeping over the square with increasing intensity.

A gust of wind—a little stronger than he cared for—caused him to look up into the crown of the tree he was standing under. The upper branches were illuminated both by the streetlamps and by the clear white moon. The tree was ready to be felled and could not take too much wind. He narrowed his eyes and concluded that there was no immediate danger of the tree coming down on its own. In a short time his victim would be arriving for work. It was now more than half an hour since the morning papers had been delivered, tossed helter-skelter in front of the hot-dog stand. He shook himself again and jumped back behind the tree trunk for shelter.

Suddenly he noticed a man with a bottle in his hand unsteadily making his way across the square, aiming directly for him. He retreated farther into the shadows. Shortly thereafter, urine ran out on both sides of him and he heard the man mumbling, without being able to make out his words. He carefully pulled his cap visor down in order to conceal his face lest he be discovered. Then he mouthed into the night, "Not this time, Allan, no one is that lucky."

The words were directed to the hot-dog vendor. At that moment, the light in the stand went on. The darkness gave way and for the next couple of seconds the Climber held his breath until he heard the man on the other side of the tree leave. He peeked out hesitantly and followed the drunk with his eyes until he turned a corner. Then he took his stick and crossed the square to the hot-dog stand.

The vendor was bent over the newspaper bundles and did not immediately realize that he had a visitor. It was the voice, that well-known voice that he could never mistake, that made him look up with a start.

"Good morning, Allan. Give my regards to your brother."

With his solid beech stick the Climber rammed the man in the skull. His body collapsed in a limp heap, while his head landed neatly on a bundle of newspapers. Blood flowed from his nose out over the latest news. The examiner took a step to the left and put all his strength behind the next blow. He was skilled with an ax and had no trouble striking his victim right on the neck. Ten seconds later he was back at his tree, where he paid no heed to the noise and started up his saw.

An earsplitting crash rent the morning asunder. The sound wave thundered down the street, bouncing off the building walls, shaking the earth, and rousing the town from its slumber.

The Climber smiled out into the dark and gave himself time to savor the sight of his handiwork before he disappeared.

CHAPTER 28

On the square in Allerslev where the Climber had felled his tree some five hours earlier, a police photographer picked up a newspaper. An ad had caught her gaze. The wind tugged in the paper and she smoothed down the sides to reveal the advertisement. She read, disgusted, but could not tear her eyes from the questions. An emergency technician came up behind her and laid a hand on her shoulder.

"I think you should move back, little lady."

The phrase pissed her off and she turned angrily, but discovered that she knew the man. He grinned.

"You'll have to excuse me, but when I saw that it was you I couldn't help myself. And you really are too close. There's a great deal of power in this kind of tree, and unpredictable tensions. Haven't you ever heard of trees felled by the wind? A heavy branch could squash you like a little bird and that would be unfortunate. One death is enough."

He nodded in the direction of the trunk and she followed his gaze. The gigantic tree filled most of the square. Five people were busy working around the top of the tree, all men. They were working intently but gently with their small chainsaws in toward the crushed hot-dog stand. She moved back and let the newspaper flutter away in the wind. The entire area was awash in papers and one more or less wouldn't matter. The EMT walked with her.

"You look tired," he said.

"I am. I've worked all night and should be in bed. How long do you think it'll be take before I can get started?"

"Ten minutes at most, then we'll be in. Where were you working tonight?"

"At the Pathology Institute in Copenhagen. It's really tough, pretty morbid, but superinteresting. I'm part of a team of facial surgeons, artists, pathologists, and computer experts. Some of them international. All of us under the direction of a single lovable, dictatorial old man who unfortunately doesn't hold sleep in high regard. I only made it back to Odense at ten, and was called out here after that."

"Is it the pedophiles from Bagsværd?"

"Yes. That is, not that I know for sure if they were pedophiles. It's hard to tell when people are dead."

A police technician called out to her. He pointed to a half-empty bottle of beer at the foot of the tree. She looked questioningly at the emergency medical technician and stepped forward only when he indicated with a nod that she could safely approach. She prepared her camera. The brand of beer was Elephant. She crouched in front of it and noticed the pungent stench of urine. She zoomed in on the bottle and got to work without allowing herself to be distracted by the smell. Only when she was finished did she wrinkle up her nose and tilt up her head to take a blessedly deep breath. At almost exactly the same time, there came a call that an entry had been created.

The same technician who had pointed out the bottle led her to the corpse. The man had been knocked to the ground and he lay on his stomach, his head turned toward her, nailed to the floor. He was impaled by a thick branch that entered at the base of his spine and exited through his belly, as if a vengeful arrow had been fired in heavenly fury. Even at first glance she started with surprise, which her colleague misread. He wrapped a reassuring arm around her. She pushed him away and stared in disbelief at the dead man. There was no doubt in her mind.

She had photographed his face earlier that evening.

CHAPTER 29

The ad filled half a newspaper page. It was in full color and had been expensive.

At the top was a photograph of an eight-year-old boy. The grainy quality and the boy's long, blond hair, which grew past his ears, indicated that he had been captured for posterity in the seventies or eighties. Apart from that there was nothing special about him. He was smiling self-consciously into the camera and it was not hard to imagine that he wished the picture taking would be over soon so that he could get out and play soccer. At the very bottom of the ad was another portrait, this time of a presentable man in his midthirties who stared straight at the reader. His gaze was steady and decisive, his expression serious, except for the smile, but also angry. It was tempting to compare the two faces, but for the trained gaze there was not much of a likeness.

The text between the two pictures was in an old-fashioned-typewriter font that emphasized the raw and immediate message. Four short paragraphs written in the first person declared that the boy had been sexually abused. That those who should have been his protectors had failed him and that the man had always felt shame and kept his childhood story secret. Until now. The final paragraph was made up of a series of questions: How many children are growing up like this? How many children in Denmark will be raped this evening? Ten? One hundred? Five hundred? A thousand? What is your guess? Or don't you care?

At the Roskildevej County secondary school, class 3Y was reading the notice. One of the students in the class had passed around a photocopy of it as a precursor to something she wanted to tell. Now she was standing next to the teacher's desk and waiting patiently while the teacher sat on a chair in the corner of the room. The girl was one of his star students and it had not taken many pretty smiles to persuade him to let her have the first ten minutes of the lesson for her own purposes. Apart from being clever, she was also unusually attractive, and he looked her up and down stealthily with a gaze that contained more than pedagogical interest.

When everyone was done reading, the girl told them calmly about her childhood. Without hatred or pathos. She was gripping, and never before had 3Y been so quiet. Each word soared, every sentence perfectly formed, and she affected them like no one before her had done, with a story that could coax tears from a stone. Her issue. Their issue. Everyone's issue. Every one of them felt it—for the first time in his or her life.

What none of them knew was that the girl had spent a long time preparing her speech. She had known that the notice would one day appear, and that she would then stand ready with her own story. Many, many times she had stood in front of the mirror and rehearsed until everything had been perfected: her tone, phrasing, the lump in her throat, the spontaneous blush—even the curl of hair that accidentally fell over one eye at a certain moment. Inside she felt nothing except a glowing vanity at living up to her role as fire starter. Even though she knew that this was only the rehearsal and that a bigger scene was waiting for her.

She was done in ten minutes. She ended her speech with a tear glittering in the corner of her eye, pleading with her classmates to help her spread her story. Just like the man in the ad, apart from the fact that she could not afford expensive media interventions. Seconds later, her request had been fulfilled as her classmates' thumbs hammered like drumsticks over their cell phone keys and sent her story into circulation. Two friends who were gifted in practical matters talked briefly and found that they were on the same page. The shopping trip was canceled. The Diesel pants could wait. Without further ado, they piled money on the desk, as a way of speaking for the less affluent. And others also consulted their wallets.

And the spark caught. Like a fire in a haystack, the confessional narrative spread among Danish secondary-school students.

CHAPTER 30

Konrad Simonsen was looking at Helmer Hammer's house. It was a pretty villa in its original condition with tall mahogany paneling and ornate crown moldings. The floors had been sanded smooth and polished white with pipe clay. He peered out the window until he caught sight of a jogger his own size making his way around the lake, which gave him a bad conscience. He left the window and inspected the pictures on the opposite wall. They were four original lithographs of Hans Scherfig's naivistic elephants. They were striking and fit very well into the decor.

"You know, of course, that he was a communist?"

He turned in surprise. A girl was standing behind him. She was around sixteen years of age with black matted hair, worn jeans, a ring in her nose, and peeling nail polish in a vibrant shade of red. Her sweater was unraveling on one arm and she was wearing two different, extremely worn sneakers. There were no laces in one and the ones on the other were undone. Her clear eyes shone with intelligence.

"Dad has all of his books, even the yearbooks from *Land and Folk*. He collected them in his Red Period."

Simonsen did not really know what to say, and decided on an affable smile.

"Is he still with you?"

"He was called in, apparently something important. It's like that all the time. It's always very important and extremely irritating. Are you the one who is supposed to find the ones who killed the five men in Bagsværd?"

"Yes, me and a whole lot of other people."

"I hope you don't find them."

She said this without aggression, more as a considered opinion that should naturally be respected. Against his better judgment, Simonsen found himself impressed with her self-confidence.

"And why is that?"

"Because the five men were child molesters, of course."

He had denied this rumor at least ten times in the past twenty-four hours. He had even gone so far as to issue a press release, which, as far as he knew, was unprecedented. The dead men had still not been identified, so their sexual predilections could belong only to the realm of speculation, even though the information he had uncovered lately surprisingly enough seemed to speak for there being truth to the rumors. He could not bear to start the day, however, where he had stopped it last night and definitely not before breakfast, so he decided not to correct her. Nor was it particularly likely that she would allow her opinions to be derailed by mere facts. Why would she, when no one else did? He chose another line of argumentation, and looked her straight in the eye.

"Last time I looked in the law books, there was nothing in it about the right to kill pedophiles."

She returned his gaze without faltering. Her voice was friendly, albeit with a note of mockery, as if she were explaining something to a sweet but not overly bright younger brother: "If you are looking for things that are allowed, the *law* book is a bad place to start."

Piqued, he shifted his gaze.

He was rescued by her father, who was finally finished with his call.

"And if you don't get your backpack and get going, you can start looking for a paper route for your pocket money."

Helmer Hammer's show of anger was unnecessary. He was clearly proud of his offspring, for which one could hardly blame him.

"Yes, Daddy dear."

She kissed him quickly on the cheek and left. Almost. She turned to them in the doorway and her smile could have melted an icicle. Her final words were aimed at Simonsen: "Dad always speaks nicely about you, he likes you, he just doesn't show it. That's one of his weaknesses. You're welcome."

Her shoelace dragged on the floor behind her as she walked away.

Breakfast was excellent and the subsequent conversation disheartening. Simonsen had both good and bad news from the medical examiner's office. He started with the positive: "Today I'll get likenesses of at least two of the victims and supposedly they are lifelike enough to be published in the media. That will almost certainly lead to an identification."

"Sounds good. I allowed myself to place a call to the professor yesterday, but . . . eh . . . ." The police chief hesitated. "He claimed that I was an illusion. That I simply wasn't aware of it myself."

"He can be a little odd at times."

"Yes, you could say that."

"You should come with me sometime. I'm good at handling the old codger."

That was a lie. No one was good at handling Arthur Elvang and least of all Simonsen. He was simply more accustomed to embarrassment and therefore more prepared than most.

Hammer nodded and left the subject.

"In my line of work there isn't anything called sin or shame. You either deliver the goods or you don't. I was supposed to set the agenda, reassure the public, give you time to work in peace, and I haven't managed very well with any of it. If at all."

He was silent for a couple of seconds, then continued: "If there is a thing that politicians hate, it is getting relevant questions that they have no idea how to answer. I understand that all too well."

"You're no wizard," Simonsen interrupted. "How are you supposed to control all the possible and impossible allegations? When most of them are untrue and some out-and-out ridiculous?"

Hammer listened to Simonsen's support, then continued in the same defeated vein: "The minister of foreign affairs talks of a veritable bombardment of e-mails to our embassies, all of them maintaining that the Danish authorities are deliberately withholding the fact that the five slain men were pedophiles. The media is indulging in wild speculations on the same topic. On top of this, we have all these campaigns and protests against the so-called laissez-faire attitude of our society toward the sexual abuse of children piling up like a pyramid scheme. Mainly at secondary schools and institutes for adult education. At this point. And to top it all off, the minister of justice appears to have gone into hiding, which I haven't quite decided if I should take as an advantage or disadvantage."

Simonsen got the conversation back on track, effectively if a little inelegantly: "I'm afraid that it's going to get worse."

"You're not serious."

"Unfortunately, I am."

He told him how Elvang had contacted him the evening before and—neighing with laughter—told him that Mr. Middle had been killed twice. The facial features of the hot-dog vendor in Fyn and the victim from the gymnasium were so similar that it could not be sheer coincidence. He kept silent about the old man's amusement, however.

Hammer looked pained. "Another murder?"

"It looks that way, I'm afraid. The professor is almost never mistaken but we'll get a firm answer today. I'll call, of course."

"There's more, I can tell."

"Yes, there is. The vendor's name was Allan Ditlevsen and he was forty-nine years old. He had been convicted of two sexual crimes. One for sexual misconduct with a twelve-year-old boy, the other for sexual abuse of an eight-year-old girl who the father apparently lent out when he did not abuse her himself. That put him in jail for eighteen months."

"The pedophile pattern."

"That's right, if one can call it that, and perhaps one can at this point because now there is yet another event to support it. A woman from Århus turned to the local police yesterday and said that her husband, Jens Allan Karlsen, had been murdered in Bagsværd. Or so she declared. The man was supposed to be on vacation in Thailand but has not called home as expected. We have a positive photographic match of an ear from a family photo and that of Mr. Southwest. The technicians have no doubt, but some DNA material from the man's brother will give us an answer today."

"And Jens Allan Karlsen was a pedophile."

"Jens Allan liked to have sex with children. That is a direct quote from his wife, who was forbidden to involve herself in his affairs. Now he is dead and so she decided she might as well turn to the police in case she could be of assistance. The woman is completely believable. I have spoken to her myself on the telephone."

He avoided any mention of Helene Clausen's upbringing in Sweden. Additional speculation was of little use.

"So what you're telling me is that the pedophile rumors are true."

Simonsen gave himself time to think before he replied. There were many reservations and unknown factors to be raised, but he skipped over them all and spoke clearly when he finally answered, "Yes."

From his expression, it was evident that this answer weighed heavily on Hammer.

"Do you have a cigarette?"

"No."

"You're lying."

"Yes, but you won't get one."

They grinned at each other. The teasing gave them a feeling of release, a moment of respite from the storm. Hammer's voice was a notch lighter when he continued.

"It's going to seem like a concession if you are right. As if we were pressed to let out the truth. That's worrisome, not least for you."

"For me?" Simonsen was genuinely surprised.

"You've met my daughter. She is a fairly normal girl, even though she does everything she can not to be, and you heard yourself what she thinks of the investigation. Imagine her attitude becoming widespread, which is what she and her classmates are working on day and night at the moment."

"No one in their right mind believes that we can abolish the sexual abuse of children by killing all pedophiles."

"No, not anything so drastic. But a tacit public acceptance of what has already occurred. How will that affect your work?"

"It would naturally be devastating."

"That it will be. Do you think it's planned?"

Simonsen noticed that he was beginning to sweat. Not because of the conversation but because his inner thermostat sometimes malfunctioned, particularly these past few months. He loosened his tie and dabbed his forehead with a napkin. It helped a little. Then he asked, "Planned?"

"As in planned, orchestrated, manipulated. You know what I'm saying."

"Who would do that?"

"I don't know. But if the pedophile e-mails are telling the truth, they can't simply be dismissed as slander. Someone may have been in on this from the start. You can't guess your way to these things. I'm sure you've already put some thought into this."

He had, and then rejected the idea. Speculation was a waste of time when what he needed was something firm. Until this evening he had had a great deal of time, but yesterday's murder and the chief's alarming picture of a hostile public had changed things. Which really struck him only at this moment.

Simonsen stuck his hand into his pocket and pulled out his cigarettes.

CHAPTER 31

The church looked striking in the low autumn sun. The whitewashed stone dazzled and the quartz in the foundation glittered like thousands of drops of water.

Erik Mørk put one hand up to shield himself from the sun while he gazed at the building. The transept and nave were distinctly Romanesque, with rounded windows, ornamental stonework, and finely detailed cornices. The tower, porch, and vestry were constructed of granite and brick, late Gothic outbuildings added some couple of hundred years later. The church wall could be dated back to the Middle Ages, and the tower clock was a construction from the eighteenth century, made of black-painted wrought iron.

Mørk was hardly an architecture maven. But he had arrived early enough to have plenty of time to gather his impressions of the neighborhood and possible police activity. It was easily done, and then he had spent some time at the reading room of the local library, which turned out to be located next to the church. There he read what he could about the parish, the congregation, and the history of the church, which seemed a fitting way for him to pass the time.

Now he was sitting in the shelter at a bus stop, a comfortable distance from the authorities and with a fine vantage point. It was as close as he dared to get. The Climber sat beside him, sulking because he was not taking part inside the church. Mørk had pulled him into a shed when he happened to discover him, which he found somewhat frightening. But strictly speaking, neither one was in a position to chide the other. They had both disobeyed Per Clausen's orders about not attending his funeral.

The Climber was still having trouble making peace with their location.

"It's a strange way to say goodbye, just looking at the outside of the church. Are you sure there are police photographers?"

"Yes, and a lot of other photographers from the papers, and that's almost as bad. We shouldn't even be here. Neither one of us, and definitely not both of us. This is as good as it gets. We're not getting any closer. That would be insane."

The Climber unwillingly accepted this. "I don't have to like it." He added, chuckling, "Per would go nuts if he saw us. We would never have dared to do this if he were still alive." He sounded like a naughty schoolboy, savoring his own audacity.

Mørk felt a sting of irritation. He secretly wanted the Climber as far away as possible, out of the country, even. He had done what was needed—magnificent—but now he was superfluous and a walking security risk.

"You're right. His influence around here has gone way down since he died."

The sarcasm was wasted.

"Why do you say that? That's obvious."

Mørk regretted his words and halfheartedly offered an explanation. He felt uncomfortable with the Climber and would much rather have been alone. The situation had brought them together but they were hardly on the same wave length—anything but. It was imperative not to start a disagreement.

Nonetheless, there was something that Mørk wanted to know, now that he had this unexpected opportunity. After some harmless small talk, he gathered himself.

"I read in the paper that you didn't just cut their hands and faces, you made short work of their privates. Is that true?"

"Yes," the Climber said.

"That wasn't part of the deal. Why did you do that?"

"It seemed like a good idea at the time."

Mørk had trouble holding back a sneer. "Perhaps you can clarify."

"It was only a few slices."

"A few slices? With a chainsaw!"

"Yes."

"All of them?"

"Sure."

"Why?"

"The truth is probably that the chainsaw took over. Once I started it was hard to stop and then I wanted to show Frank what was going to happen with him after he died. If you understand."

It was not completely true. He had performed the last mutilation long after he had disassembled the scaffolding and carried it out to the van, before he had cleaned the floor.

Mørk accepted the explanation without digging deeper. It was what he had imagined, and in any case, done was done. From a marketing standpoint it was of course incredibly unfortunate—that kind of thing was hard to sell—but there was nothing to do about it now. He therefore simply nodded, and the Climber elaborated.

"I had the most intense desire to flay his crotch before he died."

"But you didn't do it?"

"No, strangely enough."

"I'm glad to hear it."

They didn't have anything else to talk about. The Climber did not ask about the campaign, and Erik Mørk preferred to remain ignorant of the other details of the murders.

People arrived to the church in a steady stream, either by themselves or in small clusters. Many were young. Some of them dropped off bouquets of flowers, then left again. Some of them placed their bouquets on the church steps and a few lit candles they had brought with them from home. There was still some time to go before the actual ceremony.

Mørk tried to fill the time.

"Four hundred years ago they burned witches in this country," he said.

The Climber did not reply. Instead, he stared at the tree by the church entrance. He squinted because of the sun. It was a horse chestnut, and a few brown spiky capsules still clung to the upper branches, waiting to fall to earth.

Mørk went on: "They took the farmer's children in the night and flew them to the witches' sabbath. After the rack, their confessions corroborated each other's so there was no question of their guilt. But the minister appealed on their behalf and called for the gallows as opposed to the stake. That almost cost him his frock and his life because the masses went ballistic. And they got the stake. In front of this very church, in the year 1613. I find it uplifting to think about."

The Climber turned his head and became alert. "You are a strange man, Erik. What about those poor women?"

"Yes, yes, of course, but I'm not thinking of the women. I'm thinking of how everyone came together in a unified front against evil. What common fear and rage can lead to."

The conversation ran out because the Climber didn't respond. Soon the church bells started to ring and the guests went into the church. There were many of them.

Mørk commented on it: "I don't think that any of our five will get as fine a funeral."

"Six."

"Six? What do you mean?"

"There are six now. There's been an addition to the group."

It took a second for Mørk to understand, but when he finally grasped the meaning he jumped up. He screamed. Without thinking about discretion. A couple of latecomers who were trotting hastily up to the church cast concerned glances in his direction.

"Tell me, have you gone completely mad? You're completely sick in the head."

The Climber remained calm. "Take it easy. There's a perfectly reasonably explanation and I would have tried to find you to tell you personally if we hadn't met up here. It's the reason I'm here at all. I came to this funeral on a whim, since I was out in these parts anyway."

Mørk wasn't listening. "You can't just go around killing people," he said.

The Climber smiled and said softly, "Allan Ditlevsen, you know, the hot-dog guy, came down with gallstones the night before our event. Frank—Allan's older brother—found a replacement. But when the younger brother found out that his sibling was going to hell and not to heaven, the police wanted to . . . Well, you can figure it out for yourself."

Mørk regained control over himself and nodded curtly, and the Climber told him about the hot-dog vendor from Allerslev who no longer was. Then he asked, "And Allan Ditlevsen never had any suspicions?"

"I don't know about that, but it's well known that he was not the sharpest tool in the shed and he also wasn't one to stay out of the way of the cops. I called him at the hospital and asked about his health. Talked about summer, cheap drinks, kids, and sent greetings from his brother, who unfortunately couldn't come to the phone, and that last part was true."

"Why didn't you tell us?"

"I was afraid that Per would call the whole thing off."

"Hmmm. At least you're honest. And what was that business with the tree all about?"

"Believe me, it was the most fitting funeral bouquet he could have had."

"Can't you give me a real answer?"

"Yes. It was just my way of battling the forces of evil."

CHAPTER 32

The net was pulled tighter around the liars. The three women from the suburbs soon had enough evidence to ensure that justice was going to be served. He had sworn falsely when he took his Hippocratic oath and he deserved no mercy, regardless of what sex he was.

Pauline Berg devoured the end of the medical novel. The youngest member of the homicide unit had snuck away to spend her lunch break in her favorite café on Hovedbanegården. Like the others in the unit, she had a secret hideaway where she sometimes indulged in a half hour's retreat from death, murder, and the more bestial aspects of human nature. Or so she thought.

The Countess had appeared at her table and cleared her throat at least three times without being noticed. Now she laid a hand over the magazine.

"Hello, world calling Pauline. Are you completely gone?"

Finally Berg looked up and blushed ear to ear, caught in the act like a fat person digging into the pastries. She frantically folded up the magazine and stuffed it into her bag. It sounded as if the Countess had noticed neither her choice of reading material nor her red cheeks.

"You're going to Middelford, my dear."

"Alone?"

"No, with me. We have identified two of the men. Mr. Middle no longer exists. He has been replaced by Frank Ditlevsen, fifty-two, a systems analyst from Middelford. Mr. Southwest is very likely the retired manufacturer Jens Allan

156

Karlsen from Trøjborg in Århus. He was sixty-three years old. Arne is taking him on. Jens Allan Karlsen was identified twice over, as it happens. Only five minutes after we received the results of the DNA test, Skejby Hospital—where his heart was checked four times a year—called, just as Elvang had predicted.

"Five minutes too late to be of any use."

"Well, you can say that. By the way, are you the one who called Allan Ditlevsen 'Mr. Extra' on the notice board? If so, you are in for a lecture from Simon about respect."

"No, that was . . ." She caught herself midsentence. "That wasn't me."

"Good for you."

The sinner in this case was Arne Pedersen. Berg had seen him write it . . . and even worse, she had laughed. She quickly switched to a safer topic.

"Is Frank Ditlevsen brother to the hot-dog seller?"

"Yes. Frank is the older brother and the one in the gymnasium; Allan, the little brother, in the hot-dog stand."

"And he was killed by a tree?"

"Not exactly. The technicians are sure that he was killed with a branch shortly before the tree crashed on his head. But that's a minor detail. The fact is that someone went to great lengths to fell that tree and the felling itself was done with professional expertise. But it was not done to accomplish the killing itself since he was already dead."

"Why on earth?"

"I don't know."

"What does Simon say?"

"He says that you should finish your coffee already so we can get started. The brothers live—or rather, lived—at the same address in Middelford. Everyone is working like crazy to gather more information and we'll be kept briefed along the way."

"Good news. So we finally got our breakthrough."

"Seems like it, and there's more. We now have good photographs of Mr. Northwest and Mr. Northeast that will be broadcast in the media tonight unless we manage to identify them beforehand. In a gentler way."

"What do you mean?"

"Those are Simon's words. To get a picture like that shoved in your face by a TV screen without advance warning is pretty awful if you're next of kin, but we don't really have a choice. If there is a crazed killer on the loose picking off child molesters, time is of the essence."

The words were jarring in Berg's ear. There were people she felt more strongly about protecting.

"Yes, I see what you mean."

The Countess picked up on her tone of hesitation and reacted with unexpected vehemence.

"I assume that you're in complete agreement with me, otherwise you might as well stay home . . . and put in for a transfer while you're at it."

She had no formal authority but both women were very aware that there was real force behind her words. Berg quickly adjusted her attitude.

"Of course I agree with you, one hundred percent."

The Countess accepted this assurance and smiled.

Berg returned the smile and said, "So, we're on our way to Fyn?"

Their assignment did not come as a surprise to her. It was clear that as soon as they received certain identifications they would have to go out in the field and earn their daily bread regardless of where that might be. Already yesterday she had seen where things were heading and had asked a neighbor to look after her cat.

"Yes, we are, and as I mentioned, there is not a moment to lose. We'll drive by your place so that you can pick up some clothes. I assume you've already packed some?"

"Yes. Arne said that we would in all likelihood travel all around the country, wherever he got that from."

"It was an educated guess. But perhaps you're disappointed that you are paired with me and not with him?"

Her voice was cheery but there was a definite sober undertone. Berg chose to take the question at face value and answered honestly, "No, I'm not. The thing between us . . . I don't know that it's going to amount to much, nothing messy at any rate."

"If you say so."

"I mean, he's in a good situation already. With his kids and all."

"You'll have to ask him about that. If you can sleep with each other, you should be able to talk a little."

"But I'm asking you."

"You want my honest opinion?"

Berg nodded.

"Arne would never leave his children and he won't in this case and you shouldn't try to get him to. Nothing good will come of it. But we've got to get going now and I'm in a hurry."

Berg, who was familiar with the Countess's great disdain for parking tickets, did not let herself be chased off immediately with these words. Instead she calmly finished her coffee. She had confirmed something that she really had known all along, and although her colleague had not exactly minced her words it was still a relief to hear. She dropped the subject and asked, "How did you know where I was? And why didn't you call?"

"I did call. Four times, with no answer, so either your cell phone ringer is set too low or else you've turned it off, but Simon said you were most likely in here, reading women's magazines."

Color flooded back into Pauline Berg's cheeks. "How can he know that?"

The Countess smiled. Without much empathy. "How can I know it?"

Then she added in a more conciliatory tone, "Simon's network of contacts within the corps is extensive and you have chosen to hide in one of Denmark's most frequently patrolled neighborhoods, so I think you've been spotted. Probably by a male colleague. They tend to notice you. Do you come here frequently?"

Berg grabbed the straw and ignored the question and said, "Yes, someone must have blabbed. So damn typical of men."

The Countess nodded.

"Couldn't agree more. But let's get going. I'm going to tell you a cute little story on the way about how a mayor sent a psychologist to a psychologist."

CHAPTER 33

Anni Staal was sitting at her desk at the *Dagbladet* and waiting patiently for her cub reporter to be ready. Anita Dahlgren leafed through her papers without rushing, well aware that this glacial pace irritated her boss.

The relationship between the two had gone from bad to worse in the past couple of days and it was now clear to both of them that they could not stand each other. Reluctantly, however, each had to grant the other a fairly high level of professional competence. Anni Staal had been in the limelight ever since Monday, when the murders in Bagsværd were discovered. Her subject matter took up a large part of the paper and there were many indications that this pattern would continue for a while. Despite the considerable stress, she was thoroughly enjoying the situation. *Like a rat in a sewer,* Dahlgren thought, who also grudgingly admitted to herself that she could learn a great deal from her appointed mentor. If she discounted the woman's total cynicism and a disturbing lack of objectives other than advancing herself, her boss was a spectacular journalist.

For her part, Staal was not blind to the talents of her student. The girl was quick-witted, hardworking, intuitive, and above all she had some exceptionally creative approaches, all of which made her highly usable. That on a personal plane she appeared too soft to navigate the real world was less important. Staal had many co-workers with the opposite characteristics and she could live with the fact that the girl was churlish and unbearably didactic. Her shoulders were broad and she had encountered far worse.

The fact was that their work together was going very well.

Anita Dahlgren's timing was perfect and Anni Staal's words about getting her ass in gear stuck in her throat.

"You asked me for a report on the reaction from secondary schools around the country. Generally speaking, throughout the day there have been a multitude of examples of adult-education or secondary-school classes boycotting their regular instruction in favor of various studies that in one way or another relate to the sexual abuse of children. It's hard give you a firm estimate, but my tentative conclusion is that about one-third or half of the secondary schools in the country have been affected. There are, however, large regional differences. The phenomenon is strongest in Copenhagen and the larger cities. These activities will most likely continue on Monday, and intensify. Probably creeping into the upper classes of the middle schools. That has already happened in individual instances."

"What do they want to achieve? And who is behind all this?" Anita asked.

"Your last question is easy to answer. No one is behind it. It is spontaneous and spreads from one institution to the next, but there is no doubt that the abuse ad from yesterday set this whole thing off."

Anita nodded.

"As well as the rumors about the mass murder. But what the students are doing varies. In some places they are investigating the number of children that are abused on a daily basis, like the ad urged them to. In some places, children are telling others of their own abuse and in other places pedophilia is simply the agenda of the day. Their distribution channels vary: blogs, posters, or the community board at the local supermarket—you name it—flyers, happenings, letters to the editors, to name a few. There's a lot of creativity."

"They must have a goal, dammit."

"If so, it remains rather vague. One could say that the intention is to put a spotlight on child abuse—that is, to press society into taking stronger measures against abuse, something along those lines. But those are my words. I get varying explanations depending on whom I ask."

"All of us are against child abuse, there's nothing new there, so if there is a message it's one that's preaching to the choir."

Anita leafed through some more papers. This time without unnecessary slowness. She had written a couple of sentences that could later go into an article if she was asked to write one. She read aloud, "'Many young high-school students say that they have now found a common cause. In a world where they are indoctrinated on a daily basis about the unyielding demands of globalization in order to develop a competitive and competent intellect, and where the devil mercilessly harvests the mediocre, it is easy to understand that a comprehensible antimolestation message is a gift from the gods. Even higher is the Ministry of Education. The opposition to the adult world that for years has condoned the practice of child abuse is obvious and sparks a feeling of standing united with the same noble purpose, even as the real reason recedes into the distance.'"

Anni nodded thoughtfully. Then she said, "'Young high-school students' is redundant. Replace 'sparks' with 'gives rise to' and strike 'noble,' as well as the final clause. And then use a few more periods, for God's sake. I'm assuming you also have a few stories from a personal point of view."

"Of course. Among others, one about two sisters at Virum High School. Do you want to hear it?"

"Yes."

As Anita read the account aloud, Anni took the opportunity to sift through her mail. Normally, Anita would not have accepted such denigrating treatment, but she knew from experience that her boss belonged to that rare class of people who are capable of doing several things at once, not simply in word but in actuality. Unfortunately, she did not yet possess this capacity herself. She therefore went on as if nothing had happened and kept reading from her papers. It was only when she had the opportunity to focus on her listener that she discovered she wasn't listening. Anni sat with an expression of incredulity, staring at her computer screen.

"Tell me, are you the least bit interested in what I am saying?"

Anni turned her attention back to her young charge for a moment. She sounded slightly absentminded when she answered. But at least she was honest.

"No, not really. Do you have any earphones?"

"Do you mean headphones?"

Anita smiled with exaggerated sweetness. "Yes, that's what I mean. Will you please lend me some?"

That her response had not provoked so much as a snarl meant that the computer contained something very special, a fact that was underscored by Anni's next sentence: "Kiss my ass."

The words were sent straight out into the air without a final address. Anita leaned backward to take a look. But she couldn't. Anni might have been absorbed in her own affairs but she was not completely oblivious to the outside world. She quickly turned the screen, and this time she snarled.

The next few hours were hectic but also productive. Anni called her new police source, well aware of the fact that he would be exasperated. Only two days ago she had solemnly sworn that the contact would always go from him to her and never the reverse. This was a rule that was clearly important to him. Now she was breaking it at the very first opportunity. That would cost her, and she would pay eight thousand—a sum that was among the highest she had ever paid to an informant. Officially the *Dagbladet* did not pay for its news but almost all journalists made exceptions from time to time. Often in the form of a discreet hundred-kroner note or two, and preferably to the lowest members of society. A bit of grease that was later covered up in the books. But this time she had crossed over the limits of acceptability and was forced to charge the amount to her own account. A temporary measure, she hoped, unless the story was a hoax. It was a gamble and, in contrast to her source, she was not one to place bets.

Anni Staal and Arne Pedersen met in the arcade by the Rådhuspladsen. His envelope was brown, hers white, and they exchanged them. But she was the only one who said thank you. Pedersen let the money disappear into the inner pocket of his coat and said, "There are three pictures. Two of them will be made public this evening. You're paying for something that you will get for free in a couple of hours anyway."

He had said the same thing on the phone after she had talked him down in price. Anni Staal thought that in that way he showed integrity. He did not want to cheat her.

"Yes, I understand perfectly. Remember to call if you get more names. That's included in the price."

"I'll call, but you won't. Never again."

He turned his back to her and left before she could reply.

When she arrived back at the newsroom, the IT department had retrieved her deleted e-mail from Tuesday, just as she had demanded. All that remained was to go back and review, and the excitement shot her pulse up into the danger range. It quickly subsided again, however. There was no doubt that three of the men from her most recent e-mail matched the pictures in the envelope and one was also identical to the face from the first e-mail.

She had watched the Tuesday video with sound, which caused a spontaneous outburst: "Well, I have no pity for you. You got what you deserved—not that one can say that kind of thing aloud."

The culture-and-arts editor who sat nearby looked up from his paper and asked kindly, "Why are you doing that, Anni?"

Anni locked her computer and went straight to the editor in chief, hoping that she would be lucky enough to find him available. He was not. She was effectively stopped by a secretary who watched diligently over access to her lord and master.

She nodded toward the locked door at the very back of the room and asked, "When is he free?"

"It may take a long time. It's financial."

"Listen here, my love, why don't you go in there for a second and tell him that he has a meeting with me in Lokale Viggo at six o'clock, and then find the director and her new legal scam artist—"

"Senior legal counsel."

"Whatever. Make sure that they come along as well. At the

same time, arrange for a computer with speakers and an Internet connection. Oh, and some sandwiches, beer and water, of course."

"Do you understand what you're asking of me? What should I say this meeting is about?"

"Nothing. Now make sure that they're there regardless of what other plans they have. I know you can do this if you want."

"And why would I want to?"

"Look, I'm well aware that anything other than a damn good reason would have me strung up by my ears."

The secretary peered at her seriously over her gold-rimmed glasses. She was most comfortable when things proceeded in an orderly and predictable manner, which they never did. Nonetheless, she struggled day after day to establish a bare minimum of order in her boss's day. Anni Staal's highly irregular suggestion fit poorly in this context.

"Not just your ears, he'll have your whole hide, Anni."

"I know. Just make sure they come."

The secretary nodded halfheartedly. Then she added in an unfriendly tone, "You can get your food yourself. I'm not in the catering business. The technology is already in place. Tell me, don't you read your Internal mail?"

Anni Staal drew back, smiling broadly. She had not for a moment thought that the secretary would take on any of the practical arrangements, but in her experience difficult requests went down better if the other party had something to refuse.

CHAPTER 34

Konrad Simonsen sat at his desk and tried to make his way through the stack of reports that had accumulated in remarkable number over the past couple of days. The task was impossible but he tried as well as he could, skimming mostly and crossing his fingers that others would have a better eye for the details. After a couple of hours of intense work his eyes started to water, which added to the difficulties of his work and also made him feel old. He adjusted his desk lamp and tried to continue for a while without his glasses. Neither helped. Then he found a stack of tissues at the back of his desk drawer and continued to read, wiping away his tears at regular intervals and cursing his colleagues' inability to express themselves succinctly. In this way he managed to make his way through another five files and had just grabbed the sixth when there was a knock on the door and Arne Pedersen entered the room, almost before he had time to look up.

"Are you busy, Simon?"

"Yes, as you can see." He let a hand fall heavily onto the stack of reports, deliberately singling out the wrong stack, one he had already read but that was now taller than the one he had not yet read.

Arne Pedersen nodded indifferently and asked, "Why are you crying?"

"My eyes aren't what they once were. Tell me, does tissue paper have an expiration date? These are not very absorbent."

He gathered up the used tissues that lay scattered in crumpled wads around his desk and swept them into the trash.

Pedersen replied, "They can be good or poor quality but I don't think they have a sell-by date if that's what you are asking. Maybe you should consider getting stronger glasses. You should go to an optometrist and get a check-up."

"Thanks for the advice. What do you want? Is it important?"

"No, nothing special. I have something on that child-abuse e-mail that you asked me to take a look at, but I can send you my notes."

"No, thank you, spare me any more notes. Sit down and tell me about it. It'll be a good time for me to take a break."

Pedersen sat down while his boss stood up to stretch his legs. He paused by the window for a short time and looked down over the city. The sun was going down and there was a strong wind. He turned back to his place and trained his eyes on his subordinate with a grim expression.

"Now that you're here, there is one thing that we may as well get over and done with. One thing that I expect you to adhere to in future."

His tone was more telling than his words and indicated that Simonsen was wearing his boss's cap. Pedersen sat up in his chair.

"From now on I expect you to keep your amorous escapades separate from your work, and especially from my crime scenes, which you can define as the entire school building for now."

"But—"

"And you can put away your aggrieved attitude. I have much better things to do with my time than convince Kurt Melsing to . . . shall we say, refrain from certain forensic investigations surrounding Per Clausen's death."

He held a hand out as a stop sign while he continued.

"And I do not want to know whether it was necessary or not. What I do wish, however, is that I will not be placed in a similar situation. Do we understand each other?"

Pedersen's thin defenses collapsed. "Yes, we do. It won't happen again."

They sat in silence for a while, then Simonsen said, "So, what about that e-mail? What have you found out?"

"The server is German. Its physical location is in Hamburg and you can probably guess who accessed it. Or, rather, signed up for Web hosting on it."

"Per Clausen?"

"Naturally. He's had the account for a year and paid for it online with a credit card. The American e-mail addresses were uploaded there over the summer in several rounds from the library computer at the Langebæk School, so it is Per Clausen again, but the interesting thing is how the mail distribution was started. It was started from a cell phone that has been traced back to a transmitter erected where the Jyllingevej crosses Motorring 3, that is, in Rødovre. The IT nerds are writing a report right now that you'll get Monday at the latest."

"Cell phone, you say. What was the telephone number?"

"The SIM card in question was sold at a Statoil station—we don't know which one yet—but we're working on it. In addition, the mail addresses were purchased from one or several sites. There were around five hundred twenty thousand, so it can't have been cheap. There are a couple of folks working on that one as well."

"Okay, Arne. I'm making a note that the e-mail mailings are linked to the crime through Per Clausen, which naturally is of interest but is also what we would have guessed. Clausen has also been taken to Rødovre to . . . oops, no, of course he hasn't. For good reasons. I knew I was getting too old and tired for this job."

Pedersen smiled crookedly and concluded on his behalf, "So Rødovre is a place that we should keep in mind in case it pops up in another context."

"Yes, so far I'm with you. Anything else? Anything new with the identifications?"

"Not a thing. No one is missing these five, at least not yet, but Jens Allan Karlsen from Århus is of course about to get a visit. Also, the Countess and Pauline are in Middelford. Elvang's pictures have been released, so the three remaining victims will be identified within a short period of time, even if we have to deal with the usual."

"And what is the usual?"

"Yes, well, we have to assume we're going to get a flood of wrong information. It would not surprise me if we spend most of tomorrow separating the wheat from the chaff. There are many who don't want to see us clear this up."

"That part is slowly becoming clear to me. Have some people ready to check the names. There's not much else we can do. Did you find out why it was so urgent for Anni Staal to get the photographs a couple of hours before everybody else?"

"No, but maybe I can ask her this evening. I've promised to call her as soon as we can confirm a couple of the identifications."

"Try that. And what about Clausen's funeral?"

"Well, it was thoroughly photographed, as you know. But there were a lot of guests and we don't know who most of them are so without a comparative basis we have nothing to go on. I have put a halt to the task of identifying the attendees."

"With what motivation?"

"It requires too many resources in relation to the expected return. Not least because most of them can't be expected to be cooperative. But I e-mailed you about it yesterday."

"Hmm, I'm a little behind on my e-mail, but that sounds reasonable. Do you have anything else?"

"No, nothing of any significance."

The conversation was over and Pedersen should have made a move to leave but he did not. Instead he squirmed on his chair, preparing to utter words that never came.

When the silence became embarrassing, Simonsen said,

"Well, what is it? Come on, out with it, Arne. I don't have oceans of time and you don't either."

"No, I know that . . . it's just that . . . I've always thought it unpleasant to be reprimanded by you."

"That's the damn point. It should be unpleasant. But that's over now. What's your point? Hopefully not that I should feel sorry for you."

"No, of course not. Not like that. But I was thinking about Pauline . . . I mean, it's my responsibility . . . I mean, I was the one who led the way to the classroom where we found Clausen and—" He stopped short again.

"And what?"

Finally he came out with it: "And I would hope that you wouldn't feel the need to say anything to her. That is, I hope it's enough to have talked with me."

Simonsen had not even considered confronting Berg about the matter. Now he frowned and stared down at his folded hands and nodded thoughtfully like a stern but just father who in this matter should consider letting mercy go before justice. Unfortunately, his expression stayed intact only until he looked up at Pedersen. Then he broke into a grin.

"In the first place, it took me a long time to summon the nerve to discipline you and—whether or not equal treatment is called for—this is the extent of it. I'm not going to get involved in who is together with whom except for the fact that you have orders to treat Pauline decently because I like her. In contrast to some of the others you've thrown yourself over."

The atmosphere lightened; the boss was gone. Man-talk could resume. Pedersen said with relief, "I know it's bad, Simon. With my family and my kids and all that. But I'm kind of into her. It's like someone's given me a present that I didn't deserve."

"Hm, I think you've gotten a number of packages before Christmas, from my recollection . . ."

Simonsen never finished his sentence. Suddenly he was struck by the thought that he had received a present recently. A book on chess, a book he had never expressed any thanks for. He struck his hand against the table with irritation and flushed alarmingly.

Pedersen asked with curiosity, "What is it? Tell me."

But Simonsen did not obey this injunction. He pointed to the door.

"Absolutely not. It's a private matter. Go on, get going."

CHAPTER 35

The woman in the stairwell explained with barely suppressed fury, "The door doesn't lock. As you can see, the mechanism isn't working. He asked me to keep an eye on his place while he was gone, as if someone would wander up to the sixth floor for a burglary. But I said yes, I did, in order to be a good neighbor and I'm glad I did. I walked up the stairs twice to take a look and make sure everything was fine but the second time I heard sounds and went in and it turned out to be the television. He had forgotten to turn off his video. Go in and see what your friend was up to, that animal." A stern finger pointed at the door.

One of the men protested halfheartedly, "We don't know him that well, we can't just walk in."

"Look at his film first and you'll think the better of it. What about Angelina?"

A sudden gust of wind blew through the stairwell. The door behind the woman opened. The girl's black hair fluttered in the wind. Silently, without looking right or left, she glided past the men and pushed the neighbor's door open with her finger. Steadily, without words, she turned around and withdrew with singular dignity, taking her mother with her. The breeze ceased and the twins stared at the locked door. It said EA KOLT JESSEN. She was their cousin. Their at times very insistent and unceasingly demanding cousin, who had called and asked them to come. They entered the apartment without saying anything.

The woman was right. All their hesitation vanished when they saw the video. They sat down heavily on the sofa and waited in a mood of apprehension.

"Do you think Angelina was afraid of us? She didn't say hello or anything."

They were used to people being nervous at their appearance. They were both enormous and had powerful, coarse features. In addition, each of them had a droopy eyelid—something they'd had from birth—that gave them a menacing appearance. Then there was their dark biker-style leather clothing—a warm and practical choice for a professional sheep shearer on his way to work, but which was perhaps frightening to a four-year-old girl.

"I don't know. She didn't seem like it."

They sat for a while in silence.

"To hell with it, I can't stand it."

They had set the video on Pause but the frozen image was unpleasant enough.

The one brother stood up and pulled a cloth from the sofa table, causing a vase to tumble and smash against the floor. He draped the cloth over the television screen. There were two framed posters on the wall behind them. WELCOME TO DISNEY-LAND in large boisterous letters over a smiling Mickey Mouse, most likely a souvenir from a trip. The other was a reproduction of Edvard Munch's portrait of Friedrich Nietzsche with the philosopher's famous pronouncement GOD IS DEAD in black text over the art. The brother who was standing grabbed a chair and smashed it against one of the pictures. The glass splintered diagonally and a large piece fell to the floor while the actual poster remained intact. He cut a tear into it with the sharp edge of the glass and held up the result: half a mouse and the torn NEYLAND had no meaning, so he moved on to the next poster. His brother walked into the bedroom to relieve himself.

The owner of the apartment was not a small man and was in excellent condition but he didn't stand a chance. The brothers were simply too powerful.

Without allowing themselves to be derailed by his wild protests, they grabbed his head and forced him in front of the screen. The cover of the video had fallen to the floor. It claimed that the film was about the siege of Leningrad—false advertising unless one counted the introduction. His clothes were removed and a firm grip on his red hair made sure that he stared at the naked children.

"What is this? Can you answer me, you disgusting pervert?"

The unfortunate man answered as best he could but was not particularly convincing. In part because he had the handicap of the merciless grip on his neck.

"It's not my video. I borrowed it from one of my friends who's a cop. And I've never seen it before. Fuck, you *know* me."

His last remark was regrettable. Neither of the two men wished to be reminded of their acquaintance.

"A cop. Since when did the police start lending out child pornography?"

The distrust was massive and impossible to overcome.

"You like little kids? Then we have something in common. I do too, just not in your way."

A shockingly hard and brutal blow struck the man in the

174

region of his kidneys and he screamed in pain. A kick that was aimed at his groin missed its mark and hit his thigh. The next one was more precise. The neighbor who lived one floor below called the police.

CHAPTER 36

The meeting in Lokale Viggo at the *Dagbladet* was postponed three times. The editor in chief was a busy man and Anni Staal had no choice other than to accept the delays with irritation and a hope that the new arrangement would hold. It got very late before it finally took place.

Along with Anni Staal in the meeting room were the editor in chief and the new senior legal counsel. An overhead projector displayed the contents of a computer on a large screen at one end of the table, and in the bottom right-hand corner it indicated a time of 10:41 P.M. A tray of sandwiches struggling not to dry out was placed before the three participants, but no one felt tempted. The editor in chief pried the cap off his beer with a little *plop*. He used his lighter. Anni nodded approvingly and he opened one more, then slid it over to her. Then the door opened and a man in his early sixties rushed in. He—the publisher and executive editor—tossed his coat onto a chair and sat down. He greeted each of them as he grabbed a beer. In contrast to his colleagues, he took a plastic cup and inspected it against the light before he ponderously poured himself a glass. Only when the glass was filled did he begin.

"Sorry for the delay but it wasn't easy for me to get here. And, Anni, this had better be damn important. I can't remember when I last attended a meeting without knowing the agenda and definitely not at this time of day."

Anni Staal wasted no time.

"You can judge for yourself. This afternoon I received an anonymous e-mail from a sender by the name of Chelsea. I have no idea if this refers to the girl's name, the city, or the soccer club. There was a video file attached to the e-mail. The whole video lasts about ten minutes and consists of smaller segments spliced together. You don't have to be an expert to see that. On Monday I received another e-mail from the aforementioned Chelsea, also with an attached video file that I unfortunately at the time did not realize the significance of. We'll see the video from Monday first, it won't take long."

No one else said anything and Anni started the video.

A face with a measuring gaze and a too-red mouth filled the screen. Anni Staal said, "This is taken inside a vehicle, probably a van, and I don't think he knows he is being filmed."

A monotone voice floated out of the speakers: "Well, what's it going to be? Isn't there something that tickles the gentleman's fancy?"

The man's expression remained unaffected for a few seconds, then turned serene. He licked his lips and answered eagerly, "I think I'll take this one, this tasty little morsel, number three."

The video stopped but the words hung in the air and only dissipated slowly.

The publisher's plastic cup shattered. He had squeezed it beyond its breaking point. The beer spilled out over his arm and down one pant leg. He broke the tension for all of them by bursting out, "Jesus Christ—what the fuck?"

The lawyer sprang up with a bunch of napkins but was waved away. The outburst was not regarding the spilled beer and the executive editor didn't bother trying to dry his clothes. He simply moved to another chair. No one had heard him swear before.

The managing editor asked Anni softly, "Do you know what he's looking at?"

"No, but it isn't that hard to figure out."

"A menu of children," the publisher snarled. He waved at the screen, where the man's face was still frozen. "Get rid of him, Anni. I simply can't stand it."

"Then it's time to see what happened to him."

The projector displayed the man's face again. This time the camera was handheld and the quality poor, out of focus from time to time. Occasionally a diffuse white object covered the screen. When the camera pointed down, which it did once, one saw that the man was naked and apparently had his hands tied behind his back. There were bloodstains on his cheek and down across one shoulder, and around his neck was a sturdy blue rope. He spoke haltingly but clearly and with great intensity.

"No child shall be subjected to arbitrary or unlawful interference with his or her privacy, family, or correspondence, nor to . . ."

Anni paused the video on his face and distributed three packets of papers. On the first page was the same picture as that on the projected screen.

"His name is Thor Gran and he lived in Århus. The picture that I gave you is from the police. I got it this afternoon and then my informant gave me his name. The photograph was taken after his death, and after some specialists repaired his facial features. Thor Gran is one of the five murdered men from the Langebæk School in Bagsværd, and the film that we see is a record of the execution. It also shows three additional executions. I have two more positive matches that you can verify in a moment."

The managing editor's reaction was inarticulate and almost

sputtering. It was difficult to tell if he was angry or excited. "Are you completely out of your mind? For the love of God, this is . . . this is—"

The publisher interrupted sharply, "Be quiet and listen to what she has to say."

Anni Staal went on. "What we have here is an exclusive. None of our colleagues from other media—I have made inquiries—have received anything like it. Not even the police."

She resumed the video and the man on the screen continued his speech.

". . . Nor to unlawful attacks on his or her honor and reputation . . ." The camera angle changed abruptly. It was clearly a cut. "The child has the right to the protection of the law against such interference or attacks."

The publisher asked Anni Staal, "What is he talking about?"

She paused the video again and explained, "He is reading excerpts from the United Nations Convention on the Rights of the Child. I believe that the photographer is holding a piece of paper that he is reading from. From time to time it crosses in front of the camera but not here. By the way, this information has cost me twelve thousand kroner."

The publisher did not hesitate for a second. "Granted, go on," he said.

"A child has the right to be protected from all forms of physical or mental violence, injury or abuse, neglect or negligent treatment, maltreatment . . ." The man's chin quivered as if he was cold, and tears streamed from his eyes. There was another cut. ". . . Or exploitation, including sexual abuse, while in the care of parents, legal guardians or any other person who has the care of the child."

An audible click followed, then the face disappeared from the frame and was replaced by the blue rope. The camera panned down. Thor Gran looked surprised as he swung back and forth, the image coming into focus only every other second. Anni Staal paused the video once more and set the counter to zero.

"There are three more that you are going to see."

CHAPTER 37

The pub was three-quarters full, the air dense and thick. People were drinking beer but no one was boisterously drunk. Cigarette smoke swirled like playful blue snakes under the low ceiling, where it was caught in the spotlight that illuminated the woman on the stage. She was singing and playing guitar. Her voice was deep and raw with a rousing quality all its own, which easily reached the back of the room and the audience. Most of the patrons were listening and even the bartender behind his shiny bar was showing some interest. She was singing "The Crying Game," from the film of the same name—a tragic number that suited her voice—and she interpreted the song with great feeling and a fitting amount of anguish.

Pauline Berg rubbed her eyes, which were irritated by the smoke. She sipped her beer and looked at the Countess, who sat beside her, absorbed in the song. This was the first time that they were working together on a major task and the Countess had revealed aspects of herself during the day that Pauline had not seen before. Her colleague could be a very dominating person when the situation called for it. As happened that afternoon when they arrived at the brothers' residence on the outskirts of Middelford.

The house was a stately two-story affair with a full basement and an attic as well as a gazebo and a shed. Allan Ditlevsen had lived on the upper floor, his brother Frank below. Seven police officers were ransacking the place. On the Countess's orders, she and Pauline started with a quick tour to get an initial impression, first upstairs and then downstairs. They ended in Frank Ditlevsen's kitchen, where the leader of the operation was waiting for them. He was a taciturn man in his early fifties.

The Countess began, mainly addressing Pauline Berg, "Two well-kept homes and a high standard of quality with a pocketbook generous enough to accommodate all reasonable requests. Perhaps a bit more decorative than comfortable, but that is my taste."

"Agree. Everything here is nice and expensive, nothing is old. That is, no heirlooms. You know, mahogany sideboards, china cabinets, Amager shelves, that type of thing."

The Countess nodded appreciatively.

Pauline Berg enjoyed the nonverbal praise and tried to follow up her success with a preliminary question to the leader of the operation: "Frank Ditlevsen was a consultant and had a good income, but what about Allan Ditlevsen? How much does one make as a hot-dog vendor in Middelford?"

"Allerslev, not Middelford, six kilometers from Odense, and he also had a paper-delivery route there. Allan Ditlevsen made two hundred fifty thousand and Frank Ditlevsen half a million as reported on their income tax returns this past year. An expert in *information management* with courses and companies bringing in the money. The guys in Fredericia are preparing a report that you will be able to read when ready."

The two women exchanged glances. The operations leader was clearly no master of the spoken language and the content of his message was also rather unremarkable. Nonetheless, he looked pleased.

The Countess took over.

"You have seven men under your command. That is not enough. Are there more on the way?"

"Eight. One is away picking up a child but he'll be back once his wife gets home. But my people would really like to get home, for the weekend and such. Some of them are also saying that the case is . . . well, it's just that they want to get home. You understand."

"Frank Ditlevsen owned this house and his younger brother lived with him. They did not have shared finances, we've looked at the bills. His mail is in a packet on the kitchen table, probably gathered by the other. Copenhagen said that we should look for travel brochures or receipts or money transfers from the bank, and there's nothing like any of that. And Frank Ditlevsen's passport is gone. For now."

He took a deep breath, then picked up and went on just as haphazardly.

"Allan Ditlevsen has been apprehended twice, once for the grave sexual abuse of a minor. We are looking into whether his older brother is also a pervert, that's important. Illegal pictures and that sort of thing. Both brothers had lots and lots of videos, tapes and diskettes, so that's been divvied up between my team members—the ones who had the time. But my list shows who got what and so I can cross it off and keep track of it. There are war films and action films according to the covers but no one knows what's on the inside. That's what we're going to have a look at."

The Countess stuck her cell phone in her inner pocket, and now the narrative became slightly more coherent.

"We're also taking a look at the computer. Allan Ditlevsen doesn't have one. We are very careful as one should be and a specialist will soon be arriving. But there's nothing illegal on that computer as far as we can tell. Just letters and that kind of thing. No pictures. And I've interrogated Frank Ditlevsen's ex-wife about his pedophilia but there's nothing much to be had there because she doesn't want to cooperate in any way and the daughter is gone."

Then he was finished and the Countess thanked him coldly, whereafter she left and let Berg remain with the him in uncomfortable silence.

Twenty minutes later, eight men were either sitting or standing in Frank Ditlevsen's living room, staring at the Countess's backside. The atmosphere was tense and the two women from the capital would not have won many votes had it been a popularity contest. But that was not their job. Nonetheless, they reacted in very different ways to the negative vibrations. Berg smiled apologetically at every opportunity and wished herself far, far away. The Countess simply worked.

She was on her knees on the floor with a screwdriver, and at her side was Frank Ditlevsen's dismantled computer. A mess of wires hung from the bookshelf. The computer had been connected to a video machine, and an external CD burner and a forty-two-inch wide-screen LCD television commanded attention from the middle of the room. With a couple of strong sidelong blows she loosened the computer chassis, wedged it open, then lit a miniature flashlight and methodically inspected the electronic bowels. Her cell phone rang and she handed it over her shoulder to the operations leader without a word. He took the call and left the room.

When he returned, she stood up and delivered her orders in a clear voice.

"A detective inspector from Århus will be here in an hour and he will take over command. No one should do anything else before he arrives. Twenty-five additional officers are also on their way from various locations in Glostrup and Århus. They will join us as soon as they're able."

A younger officer was lounging on a sofa with a mug of coffee and clearly had an attitude problem. He protested, "So, lady, we're supposed to lie around staring at nothing for an hour?"

The Countess turned ferociously in his direction, but the soon-to-be-deposed leader was faster. Perhaps he would never be a great lecturer and perhaps his investigation methods were not world class, but he knew how to protect his people. He whispered something inaudible and the officer stood up and apologized, even as if he meant it. The Countess generously let the matter drop. She waved a couple of electronic gadgets in the air.

"The big one is a hard drive, the little one is called a reborn card. Is there anyone who found anything like these when they were searching?"

The men looked and shook their heads.

"Then you know what you're looking for. Somewhere in this house there will be a hard drive. Find it when you get back to work."

"Excuse me, but how can you know that?" It was the young man again, who this time was on his feet.

"Dust—or rather, the lack thereof. Frank Ditlevsen habitually changed out his hard drive. That is also the best and simplest way to maintain privacy on one's computer."

She looked around for additional questions but there were none.

"I'm leaving now but will be back this evening, so we'll all see each other again. And I mean all of you."

She swept out of the room. The men started to mumble to one another, clearly antagonized by her authoritarian manner. Berg smiled meekly and shuffled off in the Countess's wake.

The two women used the next two hours to track down Frank Ditlevsen's daughter, which eventually led them to the inn where they now sat. At this point it became clear to the Countess and

Berg that truculent colleagues were the least of their problems. Officers who put in only superficial effort were one thing, an uncooperative community was something else entirely.

Many people clapped when the singer finished. During the applause a man walked up onto the stage and handed her a note. She read it and excused herself into the mike, then jumped down with some agility while soft, nondescript music seeped out of concealed loudspeakers.

The Countess and Berg praised the singer when she sat down at their table. She thanked them in a reserved manner. The bartender brought her a glass of juice and she took a sip while the Countess began her line of questioning.

"You are Frank Ditlevsen's daughter?"

"Yes, I am." The voice that had seemed sensual in song now sounded raw. Harsh and spent.

"My name is Nathalie and this is Pauline. We're from the police. Would you like to see our badges?"

"No, that's okay."

"And you know what's happened?"

"My father and uncle are dead? Yes, I know that. The whole country does."

"They were killed."

"Yes, that's what you say." The woman tried to appear indifferent but her voice quavered.

Pauline jumped in: "Your mother said that you were on vacation. Why did she do that?"

"I don't know."

"She lied?"

"I'm not responsible for my mother. You'll have to talk to her about that."

Berg thought to herself that she had to agree. The problem was that it was difficult to extract a single word out of her mother and the few that came out were patently untrue. Like her claim that her

184

daughter was in London, or Birmingham, or was it Liverpool? The mother hadn't even bothered to hide her fabrication.

The Countess changed the subject. "Aren't you sorry that your father is dead?" It was a question.

"I didn't see him much."

"Why not?"

"That's just how it was."

"How old were you when your parents split up?"

"Nine."

"Nine years old. That must have been a shock."

Tiny beads of sweat appeared on the woman's upper lip and forehead. Onstage she was attractive, up close like this almost ugly, and her self-control was close to cracking. Even if the questions were not unreasonable, just hard.

"I don't know. Can't you let me be? I don't know anything, I didn't see either my dad or my uncle, okay?"

Berg was not without sympathy. "Your father and uncle were murdered. We can't let you be," she said.

"I haven't killed anyone." She was having trouble getting the words out.

The Countess shook her head and for a moment she considered waiting until the morning. The location was the worst possible for an intimate conversation but she pushed this thought aside. They had been in Allerslev right before coming to the inn, and the shattered hot-dog stand was an argument against giving anyone extra time. Whoever it was who was on a rampage out there could return to strike again at any time.

"I am aware of that, but I have to ask you this: did your father abuse you as a child?"

It was the last straw. The answer was a cry of desperation: "Why are you doing this to me?"

People turned, and their sympathy was not with the police. The woman was crying quietly.

185

A muscular bouncer got up from a neighboring table. He placed a protective hand on the singer's shoulder and said softly, "Perhaps you should leave."

The Countess took out her badge and held it out under his nose. "Is that a threat?"

The man remained calm. "No, it's not a threat. I'm not stupid enough to mess with the police but perhaps you should leave anyway. She doesn't want to talk to you and if you stay here she won't be able to talk to you. And anyway, you already got your answer. Look at her, for fuck's sake. Can't you put it together for yourselves?"

The women looked at each other. Then they got to their feet. The Countess pulled out a card and laid it on the table. She nodded toward the weeping singer.

"In case she changes her mind, or if anyone else can help."

The bouncer still remained calm. "I don't think so. We can't stand child molesters in this town."

People clapped as they made their way to the exit.

CHAPTER 38

In Kregme, at Arresø, Stig Åge Thorsen was following the police car with his eyes as if slowly crawling up the country lane and he smiled when he saw it stop at the fire. He used the extra time to review his instructions once again.

Avoid long answers, only answer when you are asked a direct question. Don't say anything if there's any doubt in your mind.

Don't say anything if you are confused and ignore any kind of a threat. Silence is your friend, these lines are your message.

He could almost hear Per Clausen's voice and his smile widened. He wasn't nervous, which surprised him a little, and he walked out into the yard to greet them. A pale afternoon sun emerged from the heavy skies. It was chilly and he shivered.

The patrol car rolled into the driveway. He nodded to the driver and watched as he parked the car parallel to the farmhouse, close to the stone wall as if anything but ninety-degree angles and straight lines were an insult. To his annoyance, he realized that he knew the officer. It was an old classmate. Or had he been in another class in the same year? He couldn't remember but would have preferred it otherwise, it would have been easier. The policeman stepped out of the car and walked over to him. He was in uniform.

"Hey there, Stig Åge."

"Hello."

"I'd like to talk to you about that bonfire of yours out in the field. We've had a complaint."

It wasn't a question, so he remained silent.

The policeman glanced uncertainly at him when it became clear that no answer was coming, and he retreated almost imperceptibly before he tried again: "What is it you're burning out there?"

"A stranger turned up and gave me twenty thousand so he could dig a hole on my property. He wanted to set fire to his minivan. I dug the hole and made sure there was a good oxygen supply. Drove out the fuel, sacks of coal, wood and kerosene, before I went on holiday. When I came back, I tended to the fire twice a day. That was the deal."

He said his piece loud and clear without trying to conceal that he had prepared it ahead of time.

The policeman took another step back and stared at him with skepticism. The word *minivan* had triggered something and he was thinking hard—apparently in vain—while he scratched the back of the head as if he wanted to scratch it out. Finally he said, "What is it you've gotten yourself involved in, Stig Åge? Is this the minivan they're looking for in Bagsværd?"

"A stranger turned up. . . ." The piece was delivered exactly as before.

"You're coming down to the station with me."

"Am I under arrest?"

"Nah, no, I was thinking you could come of your own accord."

"Absolutely not."

The policeman scratched himself so hard that one would have thought he had fleas. "Can you repeat that part about the bonfire?"

Just as before, he recited the piece word-for-word, and the officer got into his car while Stig Åge Thorsen waited patiently. Through the window he saw that the man was talking. A certain amount of time went by, then the car window was lowered.

"Stig Åge, I'm placing you under arrest. It is Saturday, the twenty-eighth of October, and the time is two fifty-three P.M. Please be so kind as to get in." He scratched his head again, then added, "Up here next to the driver's side."

Stig Åge Thorsen obeyed, without saying a word.

CHAPTER 39

The Countess was awakened at quarter past five Saturday morning, when the night receptionist called and announced unceremoniously that the police were at the front desk with mail for her. The time of day was most clearly a little act of revenge from all the people that she had whipped into working overtime the day before, which she couldn't really hold against them. She therefore did not complain when she staggered downstairs and received the envelope from the motorcycle officer. Otherwise she might have questioned the fact that the packet was addressed to her while Berg was allowed to sleep.

The report was exhaustive and extremely detailed, almost sixty pages about the Ditlevsen brothers' lives, so there was some work in separating the wheat from the chaff. A bath rid her of sleepiness and two packets of peanuts stilled the worst of her hunger. She sat down to read.

A couple of hours later, in the car, her head start was massive. Berg sat beside her, in the passenger seat, and skimmed the material.

"Good work, don't you think? Are you almost done?" the Countess teased her.

"Done? Are you out of your mind? It's impossible to absorb all this in fifteen minutes."

"Oh, I don't think it's so hard. Just concentrate on the essentials and forget the rest."

Berg nodded and leafed defeatedly through the papers.

The Countess came to her aid: "Should I go over it with you? Then you can follow along at the same time."

"Can you remember it?"

"Of course not, only the main points."

"How can you? I just don't understand."

"I had peace and quiet to concentrate before you came down to breakfast. You'll pick it up along the way."

"You mean, if I supplement my magazine reading with a trip to the library now and then."

The Countess shrugged, somewhat uncertain of where the conversation was headed. Her colleague's confession was not part of the plan. Nonetheless, she kept her three hours of work to herself and hurried on.

"It wouldn't hurt you, but all right, let's get started. Frank Ditlevsen was born in 1952 in the village of Ullerløse in Odsherred and his younger brother three years later. They had no other siblings. The mother left the family in the summer of 1956. She emigrated to start a new life in Leeds, in England, where she had a childhood friend. Perhaps she was fleeing from the father. It's not clear."

Berg confirmed this. She was following along in the papers and felt inadequate.

"Life in the home was austere. The father, Palle Ditlevsen, supported himself as a worker, a hired hand, if you will. Did some work under the table here, some small things here, seasonal harvesting, temporary positions for the county. Repaired bicycles, once also selling them—stolen bicycles. There are two police reports but no prison sentence or fines, so matters were probably settled amicably. The boys are neglected and occasionally the father enjoys the bottle too much. The county checks up on the family and things are not good. The file is brutal reading, there are five reports. The first from 1962, the last one from 1967. The boys ought to have been removed, but the need of the children takes second place to that of the taxpayers. The county takes their time and the brothers grow up."

The Countess gave her passenger time to confirm the details. Berg turned the page and read, this time purposefully. When she had finished, she said, "That is all correct, go on."

"Frank Ditlevsen gets an apprenticeship position and in 1971 he is a full-fledged lithographic printer. His life appears stable. The same employer until 1986, when the business might as well hang up the keys as new technology is devastating the industry. Ten years earlier, Frank Ditlevsen got married. The bride was a housecleaner from Rørvig. The couple's only child was born later that same year. That was our singer from yesterday. Allan Ditlevsen follows his father's footsteps, if I can call it that, apart from the fact that he doesn't drink. From 1971 to 1993 he has records at the tax authorities with no less than forty-six different employers. Unfortunately, positions such as 'teaching aide' and 'day-care assistant' are on the list."

"Smashing—that's it, almost word-for-word. You are amazing."

"The father dies in 1985. That same year, Frank Ditlevsen becomes an independent instructor and earns a degree in languages in record time, namely the time it takes him to falsify his educational credentials. He builds a solid little enterprise with a firm client base within larger companies in the Copenhagen area. No one questions his background."

"Right. As far as I can tell, it's only come out now during the course of the investigation."

"Yes, his clients did not doubt him, or else they were simply satisfied. He appears to have been good at his job. Now, on with the report. In 1994, Frank Ditlevsen buys the house in Middelford and two years later he gets divorced. Mother and daughter move away. After he gets out of prison, Allan Ditlevsen gains more stability in his professional life by getting a job selling hot dogs and delivering newspapers in Allerslev, and the past few years there is not much to report. People who knew the brothers all describe a quiet life, but we haven't been able to track down any close friends as of yet. They may not have had any."

The Countess stepped abruptly on the brake and a fox barely escaped with its life. It disappeared into a thicket.

Berg had finally put two and two together. She asked skeptically, "When did you get this report?"

"At five this morning. I've had it for three hours, so you don't have to feel stupid."

"It's impressive regardless of whether you've had time to prepare. I mean, you remember all those dates."

"Perhaps I don't. You can't check everything."

"Why didn't you call me?"

"And wake you up? Why should I? But listen to this. We'll be there soon."

"Okay, shoot."

"If you disregard Allan's two charges and Frank's unfortunate predilection for acquiring borrowed feathers, the brothers appear to be a genuine social-success story. Their start in life was far from promising, but little by little they got on solid financial ground and stable employment. The only red flag is that the two men's finances don't quite add up. Three experienced accountants have compared the contents of the house and the brothers' bank statements with the household incomes. Going by Danish tax laws, the accounts make more sense if the two of them had additional income that the income tax authorities knew nothing about. But this is guesswork. We don't have any concrete evidence."

The assumptions about black-market activity were strongly supported during the course of the afternoon, when the search of the house revealed one hundred sixty thousand kroner in cash. The officer who had discovered the money proudly displayed it to Pauline Berg and said, "The bills were stored in four boxes of frozen ground fish, stuffed into the very back of the freezer. The ground fish didn't fit in with the rest of the contents, which could all go straight into the oven. The money lay at the very bottom of the boxes in packets of forty-one-thousand-kroner bills. The top layer was frozen fish and the cartons were carefully glued back together. The fish cartons were without a doubt selected because their width so perfectly fits the length of the bills."

Pauline Berg wasn't sure if she was expected to praise him.

The officer was twice as old as she was, so it felt strange. She looked in vain for the Countess.

"That's clever, very clever."

She felt ridiculous, but the man's face lit up and he said, "This find, combined with the fact that most of the videos contain child pornography, makes the case obvious."

"Yes, completely obvious."

"If you ask me, they got what they deserved."

But Berg was not asking. She set about counting out the money, until he left. The bills were freezing.

The next development in the investigation came that afternoon, and as fate would have it, the two women from Copenhagen were responsible for them both, which was extremely unfair to the horde of hardworking officers, but the great detective in the sky clearly did not feel in the mood to reward classic police work this time around.

Most of the credit had to be attributed to the Countess in that her discovery came from a series of excellent conclusions. There was hardly any doubt that the brothers sold child pornography. The amount of cash in the freezer, their videos, Frank Ditlevsen's electronic equipment, and the charges filed against Allan Ditlevsen all pointed in this direction, and the most promising channel of distribution was the Internet. A brief but skilled examination of Frank Ditlevsen's Internet transactions, however, eliminated the possibility of the electronic distribution of illegal material. The brothers must have used a more traditional method of sale that would have been slower but more secure, and in this light the hot-dog stand emerged as a three-star disguise.

The Countess assigned four officers to the matter and they drove to Allerslev, where the remains of the stand had been tossed into containers. With the ground-fish cartons in mind, she told the men to look for objects that had earlier been stored in the commercial freezer and two black plastic bags were recovered and opened. The Countess was pleased. She encouraged the men with a short pep talk and then removed herself from the smell. The upshot was uplifting—almost thirty foul-smelling CD-ROMs.

Pauline Berg's contribution to the investigation was an itch and felt like a complete accident. When the Countess drove to Allerslev, Berg felt superfluous. That she was expected to discover this or that was a given, she just didn't know how. In the absence of a more brilliant idea she walked around the garden without discovering anything except a persistent itch under her boot in a particular place. She tried to mitigate the situation by kicking herself in the heel a couple of times but to no avail except that the irritation claimed more of her attention and soon appeared unbearable. On her way up the stairs to the main entrance she stopped and pulled her zipper down with one hand while with the other she leaned against the mailbox, bolted into the wall to the left of the door. It was awkward but better than sitting down on the wet stone steps. After having scratched herself thoroughly she realized that the bottom of the mailbox felt wrong. The mailbox was constructed so that the sides extended a few centimeters past the bottom. She bent down and peered up at it. A special holder was glued to each end to enable the convenient concealment of two hard-disk drives.

CHAPTER 40

Saturday became a frustrating day for Konrad Simonsen and his investigation. Arne Pedersen's pessimistic prophecy about a flood of false information, in reaction to the publication of Arthur Elvang's posthumous photographs of the victims of the mass murder in Bagsværd came true to an unfortunate degree.

Already on Friday evening the calls had started to pour in to police stations around the country, especially to the police headquarters in Copenhagen. The majority were from people who tried to impress on their listeners all kinds of nonsense about the murder victims. Many were easy to weed out, but not all, so the work of identifying the deceased went on. The exception was Mr. Northwest, who was confirmed as Thor Gran, a fifty-four-year-old architect from Århus. Two architecture students had walked into the Lyngby police station with a newsletter, *The Architect*, from April 1999 with an article about landmark buildings and restoration techniques by Thor Gran. Even a layman could have established a connection between the picture in the newsletter and Arthur Elvang's facial re-creation. With the identification of Mr. Northwest, all that was missing were the names for Mr. Northeast and Mr. Southeast. Simonsen had gone home convinced that both of these would be established by the time they met the following day. This optimism was perhaps justified since he did not know that the two architecture students had been rejected three times and that only their determination had secured the investigation's results.

Simonsen was back at work at eleven on Saturday morning, since he had used the morning to address a series of personal matters that he had been putting off because of his workload. Once he arrived at his office, armed with a cup of coffee and a bag of croissants, he sat down at his desk and started the day by calling his daughter. He and Anna Mia were going to the movies that evening and he wanted to find out where and when they should meet before he threw himself into the tasks of the day. His telephone was dead. He tapped on the switch a couple of times without hearing anything, then took his cell phone out of his inner coat pocket. It was turned off because he had received several calls from random people that night who apparently wanted nothing more than to wake him up, and he had forgotten to turn it on again in the morning, which was a mistake. He activated it, waited for a signal, and immediately received a call. A young woman or girl told him, giggling, that she had recognized her brother among the published photographs. He heard shouting and laughter in the background. He ended the call without reply, then immediately received another call. This time it was a man who claimed to have seen one of the victims during a soccer game at Brøndby Stadion. He turned off his cell phone again and went to Arne Pedersen's office, where a note on the door directed him to Poul Troulsen.

Troulsen's office was far and away the nicest at the Homicide Division. During a long career and with a sure eye for quality, he had obtained furnishings that made the office look more like a living room than a workplace. The pièce de résistance was a gigantic flat-screen TV that had originally been purchased as a digital information screen for the lunchroom but that had ended up in his office due to an unfortunate bureaucratic oversight. It was an arrangement pleasing to everyone since no one particularly cared to have his meals interrupted by inconsequential messages from police management. Instead, they now actually had a place to gather whenever there were sporting events of national significance. And a cozy place at that.

When Simonsen walked into the office, Troulsen was lying on his couch watching a cartoon while Arne Pedersen was lounging in an armchair eyeing a betting sheet. Neither one appeared in a hurry to interrupt his activities when the boss arrived.

Simonsen said, "What on earth is going on here?"

Troulsen turned off the TV and said, "Nothing, except I'm amazed at how bad cartoons have gotten since I was a child and it's a bleeding shame."

Pedersen put his sheet down and explained, "Half of the people in this country have gotten the misguided idea of calling the police. Our lines have gone down. You can't call in or out."

Simonsen was confused. "Why is that?'

"Well, our modern society is vulnerable like that. Half of the population may be an exaggeration, of course, you don't need more than a couple of thousand and you've maxed out our capabilities. And now I'm talking about the whole country and not just here at HS. We've just seen a telecommunications expert on the news, which of course will get even more people to call."

"Are you telling me that lines are down at other police stations?"

"More or less. There is some variation but no one has a good grasp of the situation."

"What about management? Have they been informed?"

Troulsen sat up on the couch. He commented ironically, "Yes, we've been down to the mailbox with a letter."

Simonsen shot him a disapproving look.

Pedersen said, "The national chief of police is at a conference in London. His second-in-command is at a golden wedding anniversary in Falster."

"So no one is trying to put a stop to this nonsense?"

"Don't think so. It's only in the last half an hour that it's gotten really bad. Three-quarters of an hour ago the telephones were still working but the wait for incoming calls was absurdly long. We were down at the exchange—"

"The call center," Troulsen interrupted. "Remember it's called the call center now. It was the exchange in the olden days, back in the stone ages when the things actually worked."

Simonsen reprimanded him impatiently: "Stop it, Poul. If you don't have anything constructive to add to the conversation, you should just go home. Go on, Arne."

"Sure, but unfortunately there's not much more to say. Except perhaps the fact that one or more of our colleagues must have added fuel to the fire by posting our private cell phone numbers and direct work lines on the Internet, but you must already have discovered that. You and I are on the list, but Poul, the Countess, and Pauline have unlisted numbers. Do you want to see one of the pages where our numbers are published?"

Simonsen shook his head.

Troulsen broke in, this time with a positive contribution: "I've gone out and bought twelve cell phone start-up packages. They're in Arne's office. Just put your SIM card in one of them and write your new number on the board."

"Good thinking but it'll have to wait. Did they say anything at the exchange? Is there any point in going down there?"

"Not in the least. They're running around like chickens with their heads cut off and speaking in technical tongues, but the reality is that they are as powerless as the rest of us. It'll only get better when people stop calling."

"And when will that be?"

Troulsen shrugged. Simonsen looked over at Pedersen. He, too, had a blank expression; he held his arms out and shook his head.

"So we just wait it out?"

It was a rhetorical question. Neither of the two men answered but both avoided his gaze. Simonsen stood there silently for a while, then left suddenly without saying anything else.

He came back to the office an hour later. The atmosphere in the room had not changed significantly since he'd left. Troulsen was idly leafing through some reports and Pedersen had turned back to his betting sheet.

Simonsen managed to get life into them by saying, "The situation has been as good as resolved. We can count on having normal communications within the span of an hour or two. Let us use this time to find out how we should proceed with gathering information about Mr. Northeast and Mr. Southeast when the serious calls resume. We should probably assume it will take an extra day before we get it sorted out. I also want to know how far we have come with Thor Gran. And last but not least, you can put your SIM cards back in your regular phones."

Pedersen asked with some astonishment, "What's happened? Why has it stopped?"

"It hasn't stopped completely yet, but there has been a significant reduction. Shall we get to work?"

Troulsen ignored this and turned on his television. He found the news channel, where a picture of Simonsen in his younger days filled half the screen. A slightly lisping female announcer's voice asked, "But doesn't this cast the police in a less-flattering light, that the public can even think of engaging in something like this?"

The static-filled telephone connection only partly concealed Simonsen's profound irritation as he said, "Don't you understand what I'm telling you? I couldn't care less how it casts the police. Tell me what you're going to do if you're attacked on the way home."

"I'm the one who's asking the questions."

"No, you're not. You're the one who's had a burglary. It's your child who's been abducted. It's your car that's been plowed into by a drunk driver. And what do you want then?"

The hesitation was two seconds longer than it should have been. Two seconds only magnified by the fact that Simonsen had hung up and thereby ended the interview.

CHAPTER 41

O n Sunday, all hell broke loose.

The five doomed men stared at the reader from the front page of the *Dagbladet*. Each of them was pictured in his last few seconds except for one who was already dead. The thick blue nylon rope was clearly visible on all. Fear emanated from their eyes and sold more copies of the paper than the most notorious royal scandal ever had. No sympathy was to be found among the editorial staff. The headline clearly took a position against the victim and read succinctly, in thick black print, JUDGMENT DAY. The newspaper carried an insert of eight pages, a photo montage that displayed the film sequences Anni Staal had received almost frame by frame, so that none of the juicy details escaped the reading public.

Anni and the publisher were standing outside the main entrance of their workplace, waiting. It was nine o'clock and the street was deserted, misty, and gray in the cold morning.

Anni tried a third time: "Are you sure you don't want me to participate?"

Her most senior boss gave a huge yawn. It had been a long night and he was tired. "Yes, Anni, I'm sure. You should show yourself and then leave. They shouldn't think you're hiding. I don't want to risk them ordering a search for you or whatever it is they manage to think up. Tell me about the atmosphere."

"The atmosphere?"

"In the newsroom, among the people, around. They say you can hear the grass grow."

Anni Staal brushed the praise aside. It was laid on too thick. "They say so many things, but the links to our Web site are glowing red or whatever it is that links are. There have been one hundred thousand hits and that's just the beginning. The whole IT department has been called in to manage the situation. They have already boosted our server capacity in order to hold down the video-download time."

The director was uninterested in technology. "Smashing, smashing, but what are people thinking? I mean, when they have seen the videos. Is there support for our headline? Did we frame it correctly?"

"The film clip from the minivan with the one called Thor Gran hardens most hearts. You know, the one where he decides on his tasty little morsel—"

"Shush! I don't want to hear that phrase again. Never again."

"So you are typical. Almost everyone reacts like that."

The director said sharply, "Let's talk about something else."

Anni ignored this order and went on: "Thor Gran has taken your language, dirtied what was clean. Now you can't bear to use the words. You almost can't bear to think them."

"Now you're a psychologist?"

"No, but I've been talking with someone who is."

"Okay, you may be right. It still makes me sick."

"But it's also telling. People's immediate reaction of sympathy goes quickly down the drain. The next time they see the images from the execution, it is with hardened eyes and a silent acceptance, or something closer to actual approval. I have been getting some e-mails."

"Well, freedom of speech is there to be exercised, and there's nothing in the law books about having to condemn murder."

"And I can promise you that not many people will. Quite

the opposite. But of course it's the most outraged types who write. I tend to think that most people are not crying buckets over these victims. And I am sure that many people just like you have a sentence in the back of their heads that they don't want to say and would very much like to forget when they form their opinions."

The publisher smiled faintly. Then he glanced at his watch and thought longingly of his bed. He looked in vain down the street and saw nothing. They stood without speaking for a while, then he resumed the conversation.

"So keeping the news a secret worked?"

Anni hesitated before she answered, "Yes, I believe so. We took every precaution. Nighttime kiosk sales of the papers around Copenhagen were suspended and trusted people watched over the papers that were loaded on the night trains to the provinces. No employee was allowed to take any paper home with them, so the shock should have hit the country at about the same time. Were you afraid of a censure?"

"Not afraid exactly, but I feel you aren't being completely clear, Anni. Did the news get out despite our best efforts?"

"I don't really know. The police at least were taken by surprise and a number of officers on the periphery were openly puzzling over the fact that every time something significant happens in relation to the child-abuse murders, the state seems to be lagging far behind the events. Chief Inspector Simonsen doesn't appear to have his foot on the gas. And the minister of justice was most certainly not forewarned. I heard the news on the radio at nine, where he ran the gauntlet at the Christiansborg parliamentary palace between several vociferous reporters. He was talking nonsense."

"Poor man. First he is left behind, then slaughtered."

"There's an open season on politicians all year round and minister blood is one of the most dignified fluids one can press out of a story. It is something that results in personal prestige, and from time to time also a raise. Did you get any of that?"

"No, I'm tone-deaf when it comes to greedy scribblers. Tell me why you hesitated."

"Not for any real reason. It just seems to me that this meeting has been a little too easy to arrange. You shouldn't underestimate Helmer Hammer. He has powerful friends. Very powerful."

"I don't follow the connection."

"Perhaps there isn't one but we shouldn't be blind to the fact that there are, shall we say, differing strands of opinion. We have seen this the past couple of days, and from time to time have stepped on some tender toes. For example, there have been discussions of making the travel industry financially responsible for any holidays where tourists end up getting too close to local children."

The publisher was not impressed. "The travel industry. Give me a break."

"Or banks, for transactions on the Internet with regard to child pornography. That's also an idea that has been circulating and gaining in popularity. But look, your guests are here."

Anni Staal pointed to the taxi that was just turning the corner. She had to poke at him to get him to look.

Helmer Hammer also had to poke his listener, and Poul Troulsen got himself an admonishing shove for his words about a welcome committee of dubious quality. On top of it all, Hammer leaned forward and saw through the window of the taxi that his fellow passenger had been right. If two people could be called a committee. He rubbed his eyes and suppressed a yawn. Sunday had barely started and he had already been up for more than five hours.

The telephone had rung at four o'clock and a voice that was familiar but that belonged to someone who on no account was supposed to contact him at home made him wide awake at once. The woman who had awakened him had several names. One of these she used in her highly skilled work in finance, and the other was used for more social activities. He was one of the very few people who knew both. He also knew that if one was in possession of a small fortune and had the right connections, she could be rented on a daily basis and that she was worth every penny. He listened and silently prayed to higher authorities that there was a natural explanation for her call, which went against all business ethics. His prayer was heard. She had a copy of the *Dagbladet* for him. Her penthouse apartment was nearby and they met halfway between. He got his newspaper and a kiss on the cheek. That he thereby owed her a large favor, she was far too smart to mention.

The order of the day for the following three hours was damage control, and it was not much of a consolation that he was able to ruin the sleep of a large number of other people. With call after call he gradually started to get something of a grasp on the situation.

By the time he collected Poul Troulsen in the taxi Hammer was therefore in a reasonable mood and was able to handle the invective that the detective directed at him.

"I may as well say this straight off—if you're planning to slaughter Simon you can go to hell, I don't care how much power you have. But don't count on me for one second."

Mildly put, the man seemed to have no faith in the authorities.

Helmer Hammer answered calmly, "That's not what this is about. Quite the opposite, as I explained on the phone."

"I hate myself for going behind his back. What's with all this secrecy?"

"Your boss is brilliant at leading investigations and lousy at dealing with the press. The last thing I need right now is having him let loose on the *Dagbladet*. And the police business can be dealt with on a lower level, by which I mean you."

Poul Troulsen sensed that Hammer was telling the truth and relaxed a little.

"What is Simon doing right now? Where is he?"

"He's in bed, sleeping, which he deserves and has a great need for."

Poul Troulsen nodded. It was difficult not to like the man.

"How did you manage it?"

"I got lucky."

They drove for a while in silence. Then Troulsen asked, "Why me? I can't stand those filthy bastards either."

"Because you may feel that way but you don't bite. Because you know your place and you hold your tongue in a meeting. And because the one you call the Countess is in Odense."

Troulsen gave a strained smile. They drove another couple of streets. This time it was Helmer Hammer who broke the silence.

"What are you thinking about?"

"That honesty can be abused. Are you always this direct?"

The executive did not have to answer. The news came on the radio and they both listened. The high point was an interview with the minister of justice in which even his most exquisite and fluid formulations were not sufficient to mask the fact that he knew absolutely nothing.

"What a fool," Troulsen commented.

Hammer was less judgmental. The minister had been his only blunder, but that was what came from cutting himself off from the world.

"He is a survivor. Perhaps the most tenacious of them all."

The taxi arrived at the destination. Troulsen said provocatively, "Well, I'll be damned—a welcoming committee of the tabloid-press scavengers."

Hammer gave him a shove. Without any effect.

"I'll wring the teats off that stupid bitch."

"No, you won't. You'll keep your mouth shut. Diplomacy is not for the likes of you."

The taxi stopped. Hammer added, "And just so you know, bigger men than you have had to eat their words."

Then he put on his most charming face and got out.

The two men were escorted to the conference room where Anni Staal had presented her videos Friday night. A woman in her thirties sat at the handsomely laden table and waited. The chief legal counsel of the *Dagbladet* stood up and shook their hands as she introduced herself, then she sat back down expectantly. Troulsen immediately felt a kind of kinship with her. It was clear that she, too, had been assigned a secondary role. The two leads chatted as they helped themselves to refreshments. Each of the women poured herself a glass of juice; Troulsen had a cup of black coffee. After three rolls and a croissant, the publisher finally began the meeting.

"Since you are the ones who called for this discussion, I think it would be appropriate if you could tell us what we can assist you with."

Helmer responded with unexpected vehemence, "You can skip the pleasantries. Don't you think you owe us an explanation?"

Forgetting that he was supposed to keep his mouth shut, Troulsen fell in behind him: "This is a clear-cut case of withholding evidence, and you—"

Helmer Hammer stopped him with a hand movement, which he immediately obeyed, much to his own surprise. His sentence was left hanging in the air. But their host picked it up. He glanced invitingly at his accompanying employee.

"Perhaps we should discuss this matter of evidence first. Would you?"

His legal council wanted nothing more. For the next ten minutes she used lengthy legal phrases that no one listened to. She wrapped it up triumphantly: "And anyway we sent the video sequences with an accompanying letter to the Store Kongensgade police station on Saturday night. The material was delivered around two o'clock. In the letter it is made clear that the videos may have some bearing on the police investigation of the pedophile murders, which, for your information, we are not obligated to inform you of."

"Do you have a copy of this letter?"

Faster than anyone could say "pro forma," she found two copies in her file and handed them to her guests. Poul Troulsen and Helmer Hammer thanked her. The publisher smugly poured himself a cup of coffee and gallantly offered the coffee-pot to his lawyer, who declined with a shake of her head. The guests read the letter. It was long, ornate, and unnecessarily complicated. What it should have explained in eight lines was stretched out over three and a half pages and only on the middle of page 2 did the reader have a reasonable chance of gaining an impression of what the letter was really all about.

Helmer Hammer finished first, and said, "Yes, with this you could have been sure it got put at the bottom of the pile. You haven't even printed it on your own letterhead."

The lawyer was halfheartedly apologetic: "That was an oversight. It was late. But as I see it, we have followed the law to the letter."

"Perhaps you have and perhaps you haven't." Helmer Hammer answered her, but he was looking at the publisher. "To this point six people have been killed and we have no guarantee that this won't continue. If it turns out later that this . . . shall we call it a *delay*?—can reasonably be claimed to have cost a person his life, then I promise you that your actions will be tried in a court of law and that it will be a very long and drawn-out affair."

The publisher did not look like the kind of man who wanted a very long and drawn-out affair on his hands. He flinched uncomfortably. In direct contrast to his lawyer, who aired her chemically whitened teeth in a wide, expectant smile.

The next step belonged to Helmer Hammer. He took a piece of paper out of his coat pocket. Poul Troulsen saw that it was a handwritten note and not particularly long but could not read the contents.

The publisher read it, grew pale, and was silent for a moment. Then he asked, "What do you want?"

Helmer Hammer took his paper back and said quietly but directly, "A recorded transcript of the conversations Anni Staal has with the readers at twelve o'clock as well as access to the contact information for those people who have relevant information about the victims. In addition I would like Anni Staal's full and active cooperation with Poul Troulsen over the next few hours."

The publisher's face took on an unhealthy hue and his voice went up an octave as he replied, "That's completely out of the question. We do not give out the names of our . . ." He stopped when Helmer Hammer took out his cell phone and started dialing. He turned helplessly to his legal counsel and said, "Thank you very much. You've been a lot of help."

It took a moment before the woman realized that she was being asked to leave. When the penny finally dropped, she quickly stood, gathered her papers, and left the room with a sullen air and without saying goodbye. The men waited until she was gone.

As soon as the door banged shut, Helmer Hammer also got to his feet.

"I think I'll be going as well and I'll let you take care of implementing these arrangements. I'm certain that you will find a reasonable solution. Poul, can you call me in half an hour when you've come to an agreement?"

His sharp arrogance had effect. The publisher was absolutely not accustomed to being treated like one who implemented arrangements. In the absence of viable alternatives, however, he had no choice but to submit.

CHAPTER 42

Konrad Simonsen's contribution to the events of Sunday morning were exactly zero. He slept. Given the pace of his work the preceding week, no one could have held this against him, especially when one took his age into account. Which is exactly what his daughter, Anna Mia, did when she stole into his bedroom and turned off his alarm clock, which was set to six. The moon was shining outside the window and its reflected light fell on his face. She sat for a long time on the edge of his bed and looked at him. His breathing was alarming, heavy and panting. Occasionally he gasped for air. The sounds pained her and she promised herself she would take his diabetes treatment in hand. And his smoking. After a while he fell into a more peaceful sleep. She stroked him gently on the cheek and smoothed his pillow before she left.

It was past ten o'clock when the groggy and confused chief inspector walked into his living room, where his daughter and former boss were patiently waiting with breakfast.

The old man and the young woman had divvied up the roles between them beforehand and Anna Mia began, before her father had really even opened his eyes.

"A lot has happened this morning but we have banded

against you and let you sleep. That is to say, Kasper and that Hammer."

She handed him a cup of coffee and lit his cigarette. The latter had never happened before. Simonsen inhaled greedily while Kasper Planck carried on.

"The victims are now all identified with a one-hundred-percent degree of confidence. There has even been a press conference, but first read here."

Anna Mia laid the *Dagbladet* in front of him. She had been sitting on it. Simonsen stared, openmouthed. They gave him some time to read, knowing what his first question would be, knowing he was not yet fully awake.

"Why didn't I know anything about this?"

Kasper Planck explained without mincing his words, "You have been in temporary quarantine. Considered likely to make a fool of yourself; in short—you've been passed over, put in the corner."

"That's starting to become clear to me. What else?"

"Helmer Hammer called me this morning, or rather, it was still nighttime, and we agreed that it would be best for all parties concerned if you could concentrate on rest. You are going to have a long day. Then I called Anna Mia and was lucky enough to find her here. You went to the movies last night, I understand. I hope it was a good one."

Anna Mia was the one who answered.

"Yes, it was. I cried, and Dad slept."

Simonsen grunted and stood up.

"I want to see these videos."

"Shouldn't you eat something first, Dad? We've bought some poppy-seed buns for you."

But he refused.

When he returned to the table he did not comment on what he had seen, but the gravity of the contents was plain to read on his face. They ate, while Kasper Planck reiterated the events of the morning in greater detail. Simonsen listened without interrupting, and both his guests noted with relief that he smiled when he learned that Anna Mia had interfered with his alarm clock. They had not expected this reaction. When they heard him whistling in his bath a little while later they declared success and drank a toast with coffee. Anna Mia cleared the table. Kasper Planck sat down at the computer and played the videos one more time. He wasn't much use at cleaning up.

Anna Mia said goodbye when Simonsen returned fully clothed. Both men got a kiss and Kasper Planck insisted on giving her a coupon for a taxi from a booklet he had picked up at the accounting department at police headquarters because in his opinion the usual patrol cars did not live up to the standards of old.

When the two men were alone, they sat back down at the table.

"You've taken this very well, Simon."

Simonsen did not reply at once. He looked out the window, upward, as far as the eye could see. A dark gray mass from the west was gobbling up the blue sky on top of him. It would rain soon. He thought that for the first time in a long while he was looking forward to the workday. Sleep was a good thing. Then he focused on his uninvited guest.

"I like Helmer Hammer," he said, "but you two have not exactly given me many chances. As far as I can figure out, you also have several hours' head start on me."

"Yes, I guess so. But enough of that. What do you think of the videos?"

"I have many thoughts but the first is that they should never have been published. They are in every way shape and form disgusting."

"That's an adjective I've encountered a couple of times now. As well as related terms such as *detestable, perverse, abominable, nauseating, repulsive,* to name just a few."

"Encountered where?"

"In comments from readers. There are hundreds already."

"Most people don't care for murder. That shouldn't surprise you. What's your point?"

"That the outrage is not directed at the murders but almost exclusively at Thor Gran for his . . . selection of the third child. Even your daughter had that reaction."

Simonsen nodded doubtfully and felt helpless. As the leader of the investigation he could hardly be responsible for the reaction of the public, and what could he put up against a collective distortion of perspective other than hope that it would correct itself? Or else just get to work. He said simply, "Well, that's horrible to hear."

Kasper Planck dropped the subject and said optimistically, "Well, now we finally have something concrete to work with, so let's get go down to the HS. My honest opinion is that you've run a superb investigation so far, even if the coming days are the ones where you will have to show what you really go for."

"I'm not planning to show anything of the kind, and now that I've been kept in the dark all morning, another half an hour will hardly make a difference. You can spend this next bit of time by telling me what you get out of drinking beer at the immigrant kiosk on Bagsværd's main street. One can hardly claim that you have been particularly communicative, and the few times I've had time to call you've sounded halfway drunk. But you probably didn't want to spend so many hours out there unless there was something to be had, I assume. I've wanted to ask you this for a long time and now is probably as good a time as any."

Planck nodded respectfully.

"You are getting better and better, but I haven't brought my notes with me and my memory is not what it once was."

"And you get worse and worse. You can save that nonsense for the kids. Just start talking. I'm not expecting you to solve this crime on your own."

The old man screwed his eyes shut and smiled slyly. Then he began making strange sounds. Some time went by before Simonsen realized that he was humming. It was not an enjoyable experience.

"Stop it, that's horrible. What's wrong?"

"'Lady in Red,' by Chris de Burgh. I thought you knew something about music?"

"I also have ears and they obey their maker. Can't you express yourself like a normal human being? Tell me about the woman in red if she is relevant but at least use words, please."

Planck started to talk in a monotone.

"The kiosk is on the Bagsværd main street, and the owner is called Farshad Bakhtîshû. I just call him Farshad. He is at least sixty years old and born in Shiraz, in Iran. He has a doctorate in astrophysics and taught at Teheran University until he fled Ayatollah Khomeini's regime in 1984. Denmark apparently had no use for his education, which he realized after a couple of years. In 1988 he married woman who was also a refugee from Iran. Farshad is a friendly and intelligent man who for the past twenty years has mainly used his intellectual gifts to find ways of cutting corners with the tax authorities so that the citizens of Gladsaxe can keep buying their discounted soda water and so his family gets by. He has three sons and a daughter, and he is also the closest thing to a friend of Per Clausen that we have been able to find."

He paused for a moment to reflect. Simonsen waited without saying anything.

"They became friends, the janitor and the kiosk owner. Among other things they share an interest in mathematics. Per Clausen visits the shop once or twice a week, where he ends up sitting in the back room talking with his friend. Especially in the evenings, when there are almost no customers around but the shop stays open until midnight. Clausen is usually drunk, but mostly sober as of the past year, and Farshad doesn't drink. Their friendship stretches back some seven years. Many of their conversations are of no interest to us, but not all. For example, the two men discuss revenge a couple of times, revenge for the daughter's suicide and the man who abused her. This is mainly Per Clausen's preoccupation, but Farshad has also been hit hard. Two sisters and a brother have fallen into the claws of the Islamic Revolutionary Guard— terrible fates—I'll skip over the depressing details. The two friends weep together, light candles on the birthdays of their dearly departed, the anniversaries of their death, sometimes locking up the shop."

Simonsen was about to interrupt. The narrative had become more than a little disjointed, but suddenly Planck changed direction of his own accord.

"But last spring the conversations about Helene Clausen and Farshad's family come to an end. Per Clausen avoids talking about them and changes the topic if they come up. Farshad doesn't understand why but he is a sensitive person—a very fine person all around—and respects these new signals from his friend. At the same time there is a striking physical transformation in Per Clausen. He cuts back significantly on his drinking. For a while he is almost always sober, then he starts drinking again, but much less severely than before. The transformation is quite abrupt and according to Farshad it stems from an event in February or March of last year."

"The woman in red?"

"Good guess, Simon. She had to come in somewhere. And she does. Literally. Into the shop around ten o'clock one evening, where Per Clausen is lying indisposed in the back room. Farshad remembers him as unusually intoxicated. Incoherent, even.

When this happens, he is allowed to sleep on a cot until Farshad can coax him out at closing time. The woman is in her thirties, wealthy and good-looking according to Farshad, and also polite, focused, and friendly. She wakes up Per Clausen and takes him with her in her car without a single protest. The car is a silver-gray Porsche and she is dressed in an eye-catching crimson suit. She gives him a note with her name, address, and phone number and tells him that he can call her if the janitor is ever in a similar condition. Unfortunately the note has been lost. Per Clausen never mentions her but he is picked up by her one more time, also in the Porsche. This time he is not drunk and it seems as if he has made previous arrangements. In addition, Farroukh Bakhtîshû, one of Farshad's sons, has seen Per Clausen driving with her on another occasion but the time unfortunately was not determined."

Planck drew out his final sentence, as if wondering if he had covered everything. Apparently he had.

"That's all of it, in broad strokes anyhow. I wish I could assure you that it is important but I can't. Farshad is a cooperative type of person who is happy to help the police but only with facts. He is not interested in jumping into speculation about his late friend's suspected involvement in the murders."

Simonsen reflected on this. Then he said, "She sounds interesting. We want to talk to her. Keep going with Farshad if you think there is more to be had there. Get someone to find out how many silver-colored Porsches there are in the city and if it's possible to trace her that way. Put a couple of men on the neighbors and the school people and ask about the car and the woman."

"I've already done that last part, without results. But I wouldn't say no to another round with Farshad even though I don't expect to turn up anything more. We can drive in to the

HS together so I'll get an overview first of how far we have come. Then I'll head to Bagsværd."

"That's exactly what we can do," Simonsen said and got to his feet, feeling energetic and rested.

CHAPTER 43

The Countess had borrowed an office at the police station in Odense Midtby.

Someone banged on the door and was told to enter. An unusually large man in his early thirties was led into the room and placed in front of her. One of his eyelids drooped, which gave him an unsettling, almost pleading look, a comic touch. The officer left the room and she let the man sweat in silence for a while before she began the interrogation.

"My name is Nathalie von Rosen and I've been sent here by the Crime Division in Copenhagen. And you are in some deep shit. That goes for your brother too."

The man's upper lip trembled and his reply came haltingly: "I've been thinking it over, and I'm pretty sure I want a lawyer."

"Well, I can understand that, and you'll certainly have use for one. I've come straight from the hospital, where I listened to your victim talk, or whatever it is one should call what he did in order to make himself understood. You know, it's hard to talk properly with a broken jaw."

"That was an accident."

"Yes, you could say that. And a serious one at that. A broken wrist, two broken ribs, a broken nose, the broken jaw I already mentioned, blows and kicks all over his body, and I'm sure I'm not remembering half of it. Then there is the other accident that transformed his apartment into a dump."

The giant was fighting back tears, the lawyer forgotten.

"We didn't know that it wasn't his video."

"And if it had been, it would have been perfectly all right to beat him to a pulp?"

"We can't stand people like that."

"No, that appears to be a trend these days, but in the eyes of the law there is no difference who the owner of the offending video was. What may make a difference is the fact that your abused friend does not wish to press charges. He claims that he understands you, and I have to say that he must be an unusually tolerant person."

A small spark of hope was lit in the man's eye.

"He doesn't want to press charges?"

"He doesn't, no. He is hoping that you can come to an agreement about a reasonable restitution for the damages his home has suffered, but don't get too excited. Your prayers won't help you because if he isn't willing to press charges, I will. That is to say, formally it will be the public prosecutor but practically speaking he will act on my orders. And I may as well add this— you will be regarded as lost cause. We are talking about an extreme act of violence that was premeditated and took place in the victim's own home, which will count as strongly incriminating. My educated guess is that you stand to get at least six years in prison but that will be up to the judge. Perhaps you'll be lucky and get away with five."

The prediction was wildly exaggerated. She pressumed the man to be fairly ignorant of the law and she was right. Her talk about six years hit him like a ton of bricks. Pleading and confused, he managed to get out, "But when the charges have been dropped, why do you want to put us in prison? You know it was an accident. You know we aren't thugs."

She got up and walked behind him, satisfied with the way things were going.

"Why do I want to press charges? What I should give you right now is a speech about justice and vigilantism and that kind of thing. But truth be told, it's because I'm in a bad mood."

"Because you're in a bad mood?"

"You heard me. When my mood is bad, I get very unpleasant. If *I'm* not feeling good, I don't want others to. That may strike you as small-minded but such is life and it is awfully unfair that I should have to be in a bad mood, don't you think?"

"Yes, of course, but . . . but . . ."

"You haven't even asked me *why* I'm in such a bad mood."

"Oh no, sorry. Why are you in such a bad mood?"

"It's thoughtful of you to ask and I will tell you why I feel this way. Yesterday I interrogated a woman who as a child was sexually abused by her own father. It was a stinky job but someone had to do it, and it fell to me. In addition, I'm in a foul mood because of the newspapers. I can't stand what they write. And last but not least, I'm in a terrible mood about the fact that I can't go home and relax because I'm tied to a big case that I wrestle with day and night. Don't you feel sorry for me?"

"Yes, of course. I feel bad for you."

The big man looked more like someone who felt sorry for himself.

The Countess sat down in her chair and continued. "This morning I thought I had a good idea that would make me happy again. Namely, I've got a lead on a . . . gentleman, shall we say. He is from Fredericia and in contrast to your poor friend his sexual preferences are clearly directed at the younger age bracket. Much younger, when he can manage it. If he wishes, there is no doubt that he could help me and tell me things that would otherwise take me a very long time to find out. So I've requested some reports on him: name, pictures, and such."

She allowed her hand to fall on a dossier that lay on the table between them.

"Actually I had been planning to go out to the Gudme Sports Complex to see if I couldn't get somewhere with him. There's a youth-wrestling tournament and he's planning to be in the audience, but I've given it up. The problem is that whatever I ask him, and even though it is in his best interest to cooperate with me, I know that he will not help me one bit. He will clam up like an oyster and just wait for me to give up and leave. What I want is for him to get a stroke of inspiration. That he would suddenly realize that he ought to do his duty as a citizen and give me information from his . . . environment. That would make me happy."

Her listener was somewhat slow on the uptake. "That would make you happy?"

"Yes, you can bet it would. Simply the thought that there is someone who might be able to convince him to meet with me puts me in a decidedly better mood."

"So you want us to—"

She interrupted him sharply: "I have nothing to do with the specifics of who talks to whom. But, as I said, it would make me happy if he—unharmed and unmolested—were to be enticed to have a little chat. Please make a special note of that phrase: '*unharmed and unmolested.*'"

"*Unharmed and unmolested.* Sure, I get it, as gentle as a lamb. We won't hit him. Never again, never ever again."

"That sounds very sensible, but oh my goodness—look at the time. I really don't have time to sit here chatting with you. Wait until you see the *Dagbladet* and then you'll understand what I am up against. And tonight the GOG women are playing against Randers with a home-court advantage. That's a game I simply have to see now that I'm in Odense. First handball and then a cup of coffee in the cafeteria after the game. From a quarter past ten."

The Countess stood up.

"I'm going to go and ask if the guardsman is ready to release you. During this conversation I have come to realize that I would like to think a little more about this matter before I decide to press charges. Now, remember not to look in this file while I'm gone."

She locked the door behind her and mumbled, "Lucky bastard."

CHAPTER 44

The police station in Copenhagen was a powerful and monumental building. From the outside it appeared hard and forbidding, with its gray, dirty walls of rough plaster and mortar and its lack of adornment, if one didn't count the entrance, where two solid iron cages flanked the colonnades. Striking and heavy-handed symbols that were covered with oversize golden morning stars in case there was any doubt about the symbolism. The rest of the building ran in straight lines along the streets with window after window that all opened inward in order not to break the strength of the facade.

Kasper Planck set the pace across the courtyard and Simonsen slowed his steps, which gave him time to enjoy the architecture. He had always liked the HS's sober style, which in his eyes was harmonious and appealingly restrained. The interior, however, struck him as confused and nonfunctional—a Spanish monastery with mock bourgeois ornamentation and art deco lighting in the bathrooms; the famous round interior courtyard with its many faux-antique double columns and its redundant third-floor balustrade, which he found outright ugly. The circular yard had the unfortunate side effect of creating curved hallways of differing lengths that made orientation for newcomers a near impossibility.

Simonsen moved through his place of work with familiar ease. On the way, he lost Planck, who bumped into an old colleague. Soon he was at the Division of Criminal Investigations, where he banged on the door to Arne Pedersen's office and walked in without waiting for an answer.

Pedersen stood at the back of the room. He was talking on the phone but interrupted himself when his boss entered. Simonsen tossed his jacket onto the coat rack in the corner.

"Give me an update, Arne."

"We have now secured the identities of the five victims, and more information is streaming in."

Pedersen gestured to the notice boards behind him and added with a boyish grin, "What about you? I hear you are well rested."

Simonsen ignored the comment and turned around. There was a big piece of paper on the middle board, fastened with pins in each corner, which hung slightly askew. Simonsen took his time to point this out, then he took a step back and concentrated on the content.

Thor Gran	**Palle Huldgård**
(Mr. Northwest)	(Mr. Northeast)
Unmarried	Widower
Architect	Office manager
54 years	63 years
Århus	Århus

Frank Ditlevsen
(Mr. Middle)
Divorced
Consultant
52 years
Middelford

Jens Allan Karlsen	**Peder Jacobsen**
(Mr. Southwest)	(Mr. Southeast)
Married	Divorced
Retired	Shoemaker
69 years	44 years
Århus	Vejle

Over each name was a photograph of the deceased. In two cases it was possible to discern the panic-stricken expressions of the faces from the videos, while the three others were normal, smiling portraits.

Pedersen commented, "Elvang and his team of experts slaved away for days to re-create their faces and then we get the whole thing given to us in a matter of hours."

Simonsen shrugged. "That's how it goes. And don't forget that we found three of the names ourselves."

"And we were only sure of one."

"Yes, yes, but that's beside the point now. Anything else?"

"Yes, lots. New information is streaming in constantly. There are about ten officers for each victim, with the exception of Frank Ditlevsen, of course. All teams have a sponsor here at HS and the local police chief is the coordinator, but you should feel free to reorganize as you like."

"No, that sounds fine. Any prior record of pedophilia or other kinds of sexual abuse directed at children? I want that confirmed today. Or unconfirmed, if possible. For all of them."

"Peder Jacobsen was charged but then the case was dropped and that's twelve years ago. For the others we still don't have anything but we'll get it by the end of the day. All the teams are focused on that issue."

Simonsen grabbed a marker and put a thick red mark by Frank Ditlevsen's name.

"Remember Jens Allan Karlsen? His wife told us all about his hobby, that is, sleeping with children."

Simonsen began to make another mark, then decided to hold off. "It's not enough. I want something from his wife. The same goes for Peder Jacobsen. Dropped charges are not enough."

"Okay, I'm sure it's coming. What about me? Should I go to Århus?"

"No; in fact I'd like the Countess back from Middelford by tomorrow at the latest. Pauline can stay where she is, if she likes. That is, if the Countess agrees. You'll take care of that. Have we found out if the victims were planning to go on vacation? And if so, have we confirmed where they were headed?"

"We know that they were going on vacation. We know that they were headed overseas and we know that the trip was going to last three weeks and that it was most likely they were traveling to Thailand, but no travel brochure or anything like that has been found in their homes. We're assuming that their holiday started in the minivan early Wednesday from a place in Århus and we're guessing that they were headed to Kastrup International Airport. But there are no booked plane tickets that went unused, at least as far as we can tell."

"Assumptions and guesses—we've been doing that for

almost a week. What about the Great Belt Bridge? I'm assuming you've put a team on investigating what they have from last Wednesday morning."

"Yes, naturally. Two experienced guys from Korsør, but . . . well, there's some . . ." He was searching for his words, which was unusual for him in a work-related context. "Maybe I should start at the other end. Did you see the opinion poll on the home page of the *Dagbladet*?"

Simonsen tried his best to conceal his irritation. He had been in sore need of sleep, he now realized. That he was not yet fully brought up-to-date on every last detail was an unavoidable consequence. He said sourly, "I have been sleeping, you know. And sleep gets in the way of my reading."

Pedersen caught the sarcasm and said, "It asks people if they would want to help the police in their investigation of the pedophile murders—they're calling them that. That is, assuming they had valuable information. Sixty-four percent said that they would not." He raised his voice a notch. "Fucking sixty-four percent, Simon. It's outrageous. And then there's a link to a lecturer at the law school who gives pointers for how to withhold information from us, the simplest and most effective of which is not to remember anything, however brain damaged, feeble-minded, and untrustworthy one might appear."

"And what does this apparent desire to return to the laws of the jungle have to do with the Great Belt Bridge?"

"I'm afraid that it isn't just the *Dagbladet* readers who are turning a blind eye. And that videotaped scene with . . . you know the one where he chooses the boy . . . I mean, that hasn't exactly made things better. Haven't you seen it?"

"Yes, I have. And the Great Belt Bridge?"

"Yes, right. All of the recordings that track traffic across the bridge in the time frame that we're interested in have mysteriously been misplaced or possibly erased by mistake. Then there's the issue that all of the employees at the bridge have had a collective memory lapse. Most of them, at any rate. No one can apparently remember a single thing."

Simonsen reflected darkly on this and then pushed his thoughts away. The scope of this phenomenon was unclear and therefore meaningless to speculate about further.

"We'll take it as it comes. Troulsen says that Anni Staal received two short videos from the minivan that were not uploaded to the Web. What about them?"

"That's correct. I wouldn't exactly call them videos, more like picture sequences. Each image lasts no longer than a second and is taken from the inside of the vehicle through a window. Technicians have established these as authentic, without any image manipulation or the like. The first one shows the back side of the gymnasium but we don't know where the other one was shot. You can see a bare field and a sliver of forest in the background."

"God knows what that's all about. Some kind of message?"

"I've wondered about that, but don't have a good take on it. Not that I've had a free minute to think about it. There's just been no time. Reports have been welling in. The volume of paperwork related to the case is increasing precipitously and no one has time to even skim the information. My overview is sporadic at best."

"Better than no information."

"I guess that's right."

"You take the minivan, Arne. The departure from Århus, the exact time and place, the vehicle type and registration, the location of the other video, et cetera. I will take over responsibility for the units in Jylland."

"Then this may be something for Arne."

They both turned.

Planck had snuck in. He was holding a cell phone.

"You must be the most difficult man in Denmark to reach at the moment, Simon. They've created a special access for you where one has to dial three different numbers before you even come on the line."

"It's to separate the fools from the idiots. Otherwise I wouldn't do anything except talk on the phone. It's bad enough as it is."

"Well, this man is neither a fool nor an idiot and he was turned away nine times."

Simonsen waved his arms in a theatrical gesture. "I wish you would respect the systems. He gets one minute. Tell him that."

Planck introduced him: "The chief inspector is ready for you now. Take your time." Then he held out the phone.

Simonsen took the phone, grunted his name, and listened. One minute grew to five. From time to time he asked a short question. Pedersen tried unsuccessfully to decode the conversation since it was obviously important. He did not, however, get further than a guess. Simonsen placed the cell phone on a desk without turning it off.

"I believe that the final destination of our minivan has been found." He pointed to the phone. "Take him along with you, Arne. You're going to Frederiksværk. And you've got your hands full."

CHAPTER 45

Simonsen's orders that any criminal records of the victims, specifically charges of child molestation, should be uncovered as quickly as possible spread like rings in the water across the nation, and despite the loud objections of many officers regarding the weekend work, the police machinery worked smoothly and yielded results. Troulsen gathered the threads together. Just back from the *Dagbladet,* he had a good knowledge of the victims. When he felt there was enough evidence to establish a sexual orientation toward children, he went to his boss. Simonsen waited in his office, where the poster of the victims now hung, stolen from Pedersen. The next red checkmark went to Jens Allan Karlsen from Århus, alias Mr. Southwest.

Troulsen explained, "Bags of videos in the crawlspace under the house, several diskettes with fingerprints belonging to Allan Ditlevsen—that is, the hot-dog vendor from Middelford. He was also active on KidsOnTheLine.dk. At least four meetings with young virtual friends and unfortunately very real meetings. Also, he was thrown out of the Danish Boy Scouts. Would you like that story?"

Simonsen shook his head and hung up.

Peder Jacobsen—Mr. Southeast—was much more difficult to pin down as a child molester. The matter was inherently sensitive and none of the man's friends could or would put this label on him. In his personal effects there was also nothing that pointed to a sexual attraction to children. The police worked hard and long without results and finally the matter was resolved in a hamburger joint in Brabrand.

A fourteen-year-old boy and a man in his forties were sitting at a table by the window. Two plainclothes policemen walked over to them and one of them stuck his police badge under the nose of the man.

"Scram."

The other grabbed the man's coat and pushed it into his lap. He added, "Now!"

The man left without protest and the two officers sat down.

"When did you last get something to eat, Tommy?" The snarl in the officer's voice was gone.

"Think it was yesterday."

"What would you like?"

"A cheeseburger would be good."

"We'll buy you two, once we leave."

The officer who was sitting next to the boy took out a photograph from his jacket. It was rolled up into a cylinder and he had to smooth it out against the edge of the table a couple of times before it lay flat.

"Do you know this guy?"

The boy glanced at the picture. "That's one of the guys who got murdered, isn't it? I saw it in the paper. Is it true what they say?"

"Yes, it's true. Do you know him?"

"A couple of years ago. I'm too old now. He preferred the younger ones. Try talking to Jørgen or Kasper. Maybe Snot-Sophie."

"Perverse? Violent?"

"No, not at all. Straightforward. In and out, done."

The officers nodded to each other. That was enough. The older one looked sadly at the boy. His son was the same age. He played video games, was a goalie in soccer, and blushed if you asked him about girls.

"Do you have somewhere to sleep tonight?"

"No, you lot have seen to that."

"What if I drive you home to your mother? I'm sure she'd be happy to see you. If only for a few days."

The boy considered this proposal, unused to kindness offered without a hook. "No, thanks, but it was nice of you to ask." He did not explain himself.

The two officers got up to leave, and on their way out one of them bought two cheeseburgers and a glass of juice.

Ten minutes later, Simonsen placed a red checkmark against Peder Jacobsen.

Palle Huldgård—Mr. Northeast—also liked boys. A female officer was responsible for that particular breakthrough. The man that she consulted was a psychologist in private practice. But he was free on Sundays, like most people. Looking him up was her idea and it had seemed like a good one—if a little unconventional—at the time. Now she was no longer sure. The psychologist was suspicious and curt, as if he had already guessed what she was after.

She laid her cards on the table: "I'm part of the team investigating Palle Huldgård. He was killed ten days ago at the Langebæk School in Bagsværd and we know that both of his daughters consulted you. Their names are Pia and Eva Huldgård."

She looked him in the eyes without seeing much reaction, only a slowly kindling anger. She laid aside her friendly tone and grew sharp. "There are twenty of us turning Palle Huldgård's life upside down. We are supposed to find out if he was a child molester and we have several witnesses who have told us that he molested his daughters when they were little. Severe incest over a period of many years. They also told us about you."

"Severe incest—you could call it that. I've never heard of the other kind. Go on."

"There isn't anything else to say. You've already guessed what I want. Either you confirm the molestation to the extent that you are able or else we go after the daughters."

She did not mention that they both seemed to have been swallowed up by the earth, which was the real reason for her visit. She was making a virtue out of necessity.

"Clearly that's something both they and I would rather avoid, at least as far as I can tell. I can imagine how unpleasant such a conversation would be."

"I doubt that. There are only a few people who can, thank God."

She tried to entice him: "It will stay between you and me. Your name will not appear anywhere."

He thought for a long time as she waited. "If I don't break

229

my ethical rules," he said, "it will be at Pia and Eva's expense. Is that how it is?"

"Yes, unfortunately."

"Then you have your confirmation. Please leave."

And she did. But she was happy to come away with a result.

In Copenhagen, Palle Huldgård got his checkmark.

At the end of the afternoon, a clear picture was emerging. Troulsen summed it up to Simonsen: "I have had several double confirmations, sometimes triple confirmations, that is to say, independent sources. It's bubbling up like gas in a slurry tank. Want to hear more?"

"Definitely not. What about Thor Gran?"

Thor Gran was Mr. Northwest and he was the last one without a checkmark.

"Apart from the infamous clip in the minivan, he appears to fall outside of the regular pattern. In his home he had a good number of photographs, where a suspicious number depict naked children, but in an artistic way without sexual situations, which makes the material aesthetic rather than pornography from a legal as well as an ethical standpoint."

"Yes, of course. We can't use that for anything. Isn't there anything else?"

"Five or six times a year he took a short vacation. The trips lasted about a week and took him to the kind of places where children could very well have been the main attraction. So perhaps he kept his preferences in check at home and let loose when he was abroad. But that is just a thought. The fact is that his life has been gone over with a fine-toothed comb but we have found nothing."

* * *

Pauline Berg and the Countess were having a bite to eat in Middelford when the call from Simonsen came in. The Countess left the restaurant during the conversation. Berg stayed behind with her meal but she didn't like it and preferred to risk getting a little hungry later rather than force it down. The Countess quickly returned. She placed a ticket in front of her colleague before she sat down again.

"You are going to a handball game, sweetheart, and unfortunately I am going to Århus. There are problems with one of the victims. That is, establishing if he was a child molester or not. I don't know if I can make a difference but Simon is obsessed with getting this cleared up today."

"You mean I'm going to have to take over your contact? Can't you put it off?"

"Why should we? You can handle him, I have no doubt about that. And when I have time I'll tell you how this meeting came about. It was a little bit special."

"All right, I'll do it, but can't we finish our conversation about the videos?"

The Countess stared into the air for a few seconds and said slowly, "The answer to your question is that it is definitely relevant for you to see one of the videos. It's been a couple of years since I saw anything like that—and I'm glad I did. It puts things into perspective. We can drive by the house and take a video and a portable player to the hotel, but I'm warning you, it's not particularly nice. In fact, it's worse than one would think."

Berg nodded gravely. Then she jumped to another subject: "What about handball? Do I really have to see the game? Can't I just use the ticket to go upstairs to the café? I'm not that interested in sports."

The Countess smiled. "If you can watch child pornography to develop your professional capacities you can also stand to go to a handball game."

And so it was.

Three hours later, the Countess wished fervently that their roles were reversed. While Pauline Berg was watching a game of handball that by all rights was hers, she was sitting in Århus with a colleague from the local police force, groaning inwardly in irritation over a political fossil of a witness who had to be well into her nineties and who, according to her home nurse, could tell some mean stories about Thor Gran in his younger days. And perhaps she could, too—the old bat's mind was certainly sharp enough—she just didn't.

The woman was a communist and had been so for more than seventy-five years. "Stalin-Sally" or "Russian-Sally," as she was called back in the day, were nicknames she wore proudly. She was even more proud of the fact that she had once heard Beria speak. Her voice was thin but clear: "Lavrentiy Beria himself. It was in Tbilisi in 1937 at a special party conference. I sat in the second row and listened to this famous man speak, how he revealed a whole serpent's nest of traitorous activities spread over the entire Transcaucasus and even in the Central Committee for Armenia. He could definitely get people to listen, that handsome Migrel. Everyone was cheering in the streets and demanding justice against the fascist criminals and Trotsky dissenters, so they made short work of it—if you understand."

She drew a wrinkled hand across her throat.

The Countess shook her head a little and asked for at least the fifth time, "But what about Thor Gran? You promised to tell us about Thor Gran. That is why we're here."

"I'm getting to him but these things hang together. Rest assured, I have a couple of juicy things to say about him, a few things I believe you can make use of."

Then she continued in the same irrelevant vein. A little later, when she was done praising Beria, she went on to Kollontai. The remarkable Alexandra Kollontai herself, whom she had met in Stockholm during the war. Later yet, it was Richard Jensen. The boiler man himself who had denounced the party president as a renegade, long before he displayed any signs of it.

After an hour of idle chatter and a review of the highlights of communism, the male detective tossed in the towel. He left with a muttered comment that he had been at the health insurance office with Vivi Bak, the famous Vivi Bak herself. Also he had once defecated in the same restroom as Prince Joachim, the very same restroom. He showed himself out.

The Countess stayed. She intended to trick the old woman, who was plainly a snob in her own red way. As it happened, the Countess had some ammunition up her sleeve. Especially if she—in good communist tradition—altered the truth a little. She interrupted loudly, "My grandfather knew Dimitrov."

The woman stopped her monologue and squinted suspiciously at her. "Dimitrov himself? The leader of the Comintern?"

"The one and the same. *The* Georgi Mikhaylov Dimitrov."

The Countess had heard the name ad nauseum. The apartment below hers was inhabited by refugees from Bulgaria, an older married couple who gave little girls sweets and lemonade and told stories from the other side of the world in a funny, broken kind of Danish. They had cursed Georgi Mikhaylov Dimitrov so often that his name stayed with her even forty years later. The old woman's interest was kindled.

"Well, then, out with it," she said.

"Not so fast. Something for something. You have to talk first. About Thor Gran, and only about Thor Gran, if you actually ever knew him. When you're done, I'll tell you all about the committee chairman."

The woman seemed to be turning this over in her mind, with evident mistrust.

"The Comintern's chairman. He was chairman of the Comintern."

"Yes, of course he was. Everyone knows that."

Finally, the woman started to tell her story.

"Well, I was a skilled needlewoman and in the early sixties I worked for Thor Gran's father, the shoe manufacturer and financial speculator. There I was a head seamstress and there must have been over a hundred employees, so that was something. His home was next to the factory and we watched his son grow up. A bad and arrogant child who had trouble keeping his fingers to himself when the time came. But that was neither here nor there. We knew how to deal with a puppy like him. It was worse for the gardener's little girls. That's the kind of thing you want to hear about, isn't it?"

The Countess confirmed this. She wasn't sure if the woman was making this up or wanted to assure herself that her story was living up to the expectations.

"It went on for a period of time until one day he was literally caught with his pants down, and then all hell broke loose. The gardener, who was very attached to his children, threatened to go to the police but the old man talked him out of it and they came to a financial arrangement. What was done was done and the girls were better off with a little sum of money, even if the perverted young man should have been put behind bars. I handled negotiations on behalf of the gardener. Do you follow?"

"Completely. Please go on."

"Well, the factory owner was an ugly capitalist of course, but he was also an honest enough person and he dug deep in his pockets. Eighty thousand kroner to each child and another twenty thousand for a new family home in Bornholm. It was a lot of money in those days but neither of the girls ever fully recovered from the events so I really don't know how much it helped. After a solid dose of fatherly caning the son was sent to boarding school in England. This punishment was part of the agreement but it was also the easiest path to take."

The Countess was far from impressed. In part because the incident lay over forty years in the past, in part because the trustworthiness of the old woman lay in a village in Russia, or rather the Soviet Union, and it would not be easy to have the story confirmed from other sources. At the same time, she perceived that the old woman was holding something back. She took a chance.

"But you spread this story in the Party. And when Thor Gran came back from England . . ." She let the sentence hang in the air.

The woman answered willingly, "Yes, he did some favors for us occasionally. That's true."

"And when the Party dissolved he continued to do favors for you?"

The old woman sputtered, "The Party lives. The Party will always live. And anyway, he had enough money, he owned an entire studio."

"How much?"

A little time went by before she answered, "It varied. Sometimes a few hundred or so when he was here."

The Countess concealed her astonishment.

"He came and visited you?"

The woman pointed to a vase that stood on a teak bookcase behind them. "Take that down."

The Countess fetched the vase. It was cheap, with a Grecian motif of three dancing women. She shook it and heard a metallic clanging noise.

"And what are your three graces guarding?"

The old woman snorted. "Graces! Do you think I care about graces? Turn it upside down."

The Countess obeyed this command and something fell out. "What now?" she asked.

"Under the bed. The large wooden chest with the latches. I can't get it out myself."

The Countess followed these instructions and eagerly opened the box. At the very top was an amateurly constructed brochure advertising a three-week vacation to Chiang Mai, Thailand. Two of the pages featured pictures of Asian children.

They had numbers.

The Countess's gaze lingered on the boy in the upper row on the right. He was hard to resist, although there was nothing really special about him compared to the others. A normal, smiling boy with white teeth and all-too-childish features.

The old lady turned her back to it and said, "I'm not the one who is responsible if he kept up his disgusting habits. Tell me about Dimitrov. How did your grandfather know him?"

"I can start by telling you about the treatment of prisoners in a Bulgarian prison in 1946. I've heard something about that, and later we'll talk more about this, but first I have to call someone."

Her hostess snarled, the Countess made her call, and Simonsen got his final checkmark.

CHAPTER 46

Pauline Berg was watching her first handball game ever. She had arrived in good time and had watched with some curiosity as the room gradually filled with excited hometown fans. Sports talk filled the air around her but even the videos of the day were discussed and snippets of disgust and anger swirled in the mix: *That kind has no pity; they got what they deserved;*

finally a solution for them; great to see the animals strung up; they should crush their balls next."

She felt out of place. She didn't belong in this aggressive audience. It was very different from the world of ballet and dance. The clothing alone was frightening. In the row immediately behind her were three women who had war paint on their faces and in their garish team shirts and scarves they looked more like goddesses of revenge than sports fans. The man to her left had a good-size belly and whitewashed overalls. From time to time he slapped his rolled-up program against his thigh in an ominous way, alternating from one to the other, apparently only for the sake of the sound. The seat on her right was empty for a long time but someone arrived at the last minute—a thin reed of a man who wound in and out among people and made his way down the row in a long, elegant slide that ended at her side. He greeted her with an insipid smile and a slight lisp. She nodded curtly and gave a cursory smile in return.

The umpire started the game and she tried to follow along. It was hard because the events transpired quickly and with a practiced ease. Then the audience exploded as one and gave a synchronized roar. Alarmed, she shrank down in her seat while the man to her left took the commotion as an opportunity to place a hand on her shoulder, and the commentator's voice came booming through the loudspeaker with a recitation of names. Her gaunt neighbor did not take part and she thought that perhaps he was preoccupied.

But bit by bit she became caught up in the atmosphere, picked up the basics of the game, not least from the insightful utterances of the supporters who interpreted the events on the court with expert ease, and soon she was enjoying the passionate outbursts and eye-catchingly synchronized movements of the crowd. Like the leaves on a tree, which elegantly fall in line with the wind. She carefully clapped along and rose out of her seat at a goal, howling at appropriate moments.

People restored themselves in the breaks, rested their voices and built up their resources. Popcorn, chocolate, apples, and bananas were sold, while outdated music filled the air. She smiled at her neighbor to the left and he slapped his rolled up program in friendly reply.

She was ready when the whistle blew for the second half. The whole hall was seething and bubbling, and she was as loud as anyone. A preliminary climax arrived when the home team finally drew even and the crowd exploded in roars of triumph and popcorn. She cheered and jumped. An apple came sailing toward her in a gentle arc, lost, not thrown. Her neighbor on the right caught it with an impressively quick reaction. He licked his lips and took possession of his catch. But his selfish action and his total lack of engagement provoked her, so she prodded him roughly and shouted, "Today we're going to win!"

A sigh rippling through the crowd must have drowned out her words because he misunderstood her comment and helpfully extended the piece of fruit. She grabbed his gift and tossed it indifferently into her bag to rid herself of his kindness.

The teams were neck and neck, creating excruciating tension as the clock ticked, and for a while it looked as if they were headed for a tie, but then came the decisive play. Five players in a counteroffensive before the ball finally landed in the opponent's net. The goal caused a spring to go off in her body and she flew up into the air, screaming in delight. Then she threw herself deliriously into the arms of her other neighbor, patted his round cheeks, and received his joyful drool on her neck. Then she jumped up onto the chair and leaned back with her arms outstretched in victory, confident that someone would catch her.

After the game she steered her course to the café. Adjusting to the world of work felt strange and she had to concentrate in order to chase the feelings of rapture from her body. She managed it completely only when she laid her eyes on the man who was sitting alone at the back of the room, easy to pick out. A nice-looking gentleman in his late forties, well groomed, elegantly dressed, and neatly trimmed. Berg did not shake his hand—that would have been unprofessional—but she gave him a quick nod in greeting before she sat down.

She began with a test, to see if he was lying: "Thanks for coming. Did Allan Ditelvsen sell illegal videos from his hot-dog stand?"

She had to wait for an answer. He stared at her throat and she struggled with a feeling of aversion.

"Don't bother with your games. I'm only here because of your gestapo methods and I see that on top of everything else you're a Christian. By this sign thou shalt conquer." He pointed to her necklace, which had fallen out of her shirt during her victorious rapture and was now visible. A prettily melded X and P in gold that she had been given a couple of years ago by a Greek boyfriend. It was their initials. "And you can't even acknowledge other people's views on love."

She quickly tucked her necklace inside her shirt. "Drop that bullshit; it makes me sick."

"The cultured veneer is thin, I see."

"Since you obviously want to know, then yes. You rape and violate children one day and call upon cultural values and the protection of the law the next. Sometimes I wish that society didn't give a damn about protecting the freedom of expression and human rights."

"That's a good start to this conversation, then."

The meeting had become completely derailed. Berg pulled herself together.

"Just answer my question and we'll both get this over and done with."

The man appeared to see reason. "Yes, Allan sold videos," he said.

Nothing else followed, even when Berg continued to wait.

"Better get your mouth going. I'm not going to drag every word out of you. Either you talk or we're done here."

The man elaborated sourly, "Allan sold videos from his stand and he had a lot of clients, especially from Jylland. He was very cautious and only did business with those he knew and always in cash. He was expensive but the quality was very high. Customers were supposed to buy three times a year or they were excluded but a lot of them came once a month. He had been in business for a long time, trading in cassette tapes before this. Those weren't so good. I think he changed suppliers about a year or two ago. The material came from Germany, I believe, and the brothers edited it into final form."

"Frank Ditlevsen was in on this?"

"Yes, Allan never did anything without Frank, and he was scared shitless by him. Frank was the brain. Allan was too stupid to manage that kind of enterprise on his own."

Berg took out a copy of the *Dagbladet* and placed it in front of him. She smiled briefly when she saw how he shrank back.

"How many of them did you know?"

"All of them."

"They had the same inclination toward children as you?"

"Yes."

"They were going on a trip?"

"Three weeks in Thailand. Frank arranged it. It was incredibly cheap, under ten thousand including luxury hotel accommodations, meals, and excursions."

"How did they find takers?"

"I don't know. Probably from the hot-dog counter, but the whole thing was hush-hush. That goes for everything that the brothers were involved in."

"You weren't invited?"

"I couldn't get the time off."

"What about Allan Ditlevsen? Couldn't he get the time off either?"

"He came down sick, with gallstones, so Frank must have found a replacement. I don't know who it was, but it must have been difficult."

"Did Frank Ditlevsen arrange the whole trip on his own?"

"I don't think so, but that's just a guess."

"So guess."

"Well, Frank had one of his old boys bring him the films from Germany and I got the impression that he was also involved in the trip but I have never seen him. Frank kept him close and Allan was not allowed to say anything. I am one of the few people who even knew he existed."

"*Old boy*, what do you mean?"

"One of the ones from where they used to live. In Sjælland, I don't remember where."

Berg was filled with happiness and pride. This information was giving her the most significant leads in the case so far. She kept questioning him but he did not have anything else to tell her.

"We'll stop here. Just one more thing and then you can go. I'm just curious how it can be that none of you have stepped forward voluntarily to help us now that you know that six of . . . your own have been murdered. We're trying to find the perpetrator, you know."

The man smiled a joyless smile.

"To find our killer? You are deeply naïve."

He stood up and hurried away.

Once she was back at the hotel, Berg took a long, hot bubble bath. The evening had been incredible, both the game and the interrogation, and she could hardly stand to wait until the Countess got back. *Old boy,* two small words that could mean a significant breakthrough in the case.

After the bath she sat on the bed naked and took her time with her lotion. Then she glanced at her laptop and decided that it was actually a good time to engage in ten minutes of unpleasant background information. She started the video completely unprepared and paid the price. It was extreme, and she stared in terror.

The boy was young, far too young, no one could be so evil. She screamed aloud in the room, wanted to stop, couldn't, and stared straight into hell. She cried. First, a silent weeping that turned to wailing. She folded the screen down with her foot and held her hands over her face but the images kept playing in her head and she rocked back and forth like a mental case. Her necklace became tangled in her wet hair and she struggled to get it loose, in order to focus on something else. Neither attempt was successful. Then suddenly her thoughts returned to the man in the café and an insane rage took over. *High-quality.* That was what the swine had called this assault. High-quality. She dried her eyes, first with her bare arm, then with a tissue from her bag, where she also had the apple from the game. She ate it, complete with seeds and all, while her rage slowly transformed into a controlled, glowing hatred.

The telephone rang and the display showed it was the Countess. She stood up. The necklace was still tangled in her curls and she tore it loose and flung it on the floor. Tufts of hair followed.

The fruit forced sucrose to her brain and she started to think clearly again, very clearly. She confronted her problem directly. Last Friday the Countess had threatened her into agreement and she had obeyed, had allowed herself to be dominated. Perhaps because she envied her colleague her talents and, if the whole truth be told, her summer villa. Which was actually a tax haven, a way in which to get even richer, but that was another story. These thoughts crowded her mind and she stole a little time.

242

"Wait a second, my battery is about to run out. I'll get a charger."

Working relationships were like marriages—if the disagreements became too large, one had to separate and find another bed partner. The fact was that she accepted the murders, and the Countess did not. Victims of incest hated their parents; society persecuted pedophiles. That was natural, the way it should be. Here she had slaved away all Sunday and a mean God in heaven had rewarded her with the rape of a child. Her belief in the compassion of others was gone, extinguished by the lost eyes of a five-year-old child, and another, more primitive truth was banging on the door. The right of the common man, the will of the people, good old-fashioned revenge.

She was ready. First, she listened: the Countess would be back in an hour, things had dragged on—then came her answer, which was delivered without hesitation.

"You know, I think I'll hit the hay. I'll see you tomorrow. That handball guy was a shyster. He didn't know anything."

They hung up. She smiled grimly and felt suddenly bashful in her nakedness.

CHAPTER 47

The two men strolled into the field, which was heavy with autumn and unfit for walking. Mud clung to Stig Åge Thorsen's rubber boots and Erik Mørk's shoes were destroyed. He was also wet far up along his trouser legs. Mørk had only himself to blame. In spite of the light rain and dull sky, he had insisted on going out into nature. Thorsen, the country boy, had followed him and allowed him to determine the route without objection.

"How did it go in Greece? Did you have a good trip?"

Stig Åge Thorsen paused before saying, "I mostly want to forget it. There was a woman, but . . . well, it just didn't work. Tell me how the campaign is going. I'd rather talk about that."

Mørk nodded, happy not to hear any more about the woman.

"We are very busy. Support is streaming in from all corners of the country. By telephone, e-mail, fax, text messages, or even in person sometimes. So much has happened . . . but the best thing is that we have created a pedophile database. It has been built with the help of sentences and the population register as well as the client list the Climber picked up in Middelford. Per Clausen must have started this work a long time ago with a professional archivist behind the construction. 'Recidivism-prone and Compulsive Sexual Deviants' is the name of his report. It's not exactly a bestseller but the result is excellent. In addition we've grown a superb network in record time. There isn't much that happens in the world of media or at Christiansborg without me hearing about it five minutes later.

"And this evening I have a meeting with a television producer. He is a legend among documentary filmmakers but I have promised not to mention his name. Per Clausen has put him in touch with a girl and she would be absolutely fantastic. She is one of our own and they are training her for an interview."

"That's great, but what are the regular people thinking? That's what I would like to know."

"Well, the videos in the *Dagbladet* this morning have been a tactical hit and the most effective is without a doubt Thor Gran's sexual self-disclosure."

". . . You know what I'm talking about, don't you?"

"Yes, of course. But don't remind me of it."

"No, I wouldn't dream of it. It certainly is a piece of pure gold and I tell you that I shouted aloud the first time I saw it. The expression with the little troll number three—it has etched itself into people's heads, and peaceful sorts who don't normally support violence are suddenly . . . what should I say? . . . more nuanced. One the one hand a murder is wrong of course, but . . . you know. It's like with terrorists and torture."

"I'm not sure I do, but I'm not sure I give a damn. How many have registered on the site?"

"Almost eight thousand at this point and we are guaranteed to reach twelve thousand today. People's generosity is surprisingly great. Many are prepared to do things that could cost them their jobs. Others want to give money. Among other things, I've had a meeting with a couple of nice gentlemen who represent three large American church organizations. Politically they are a good deal more to the right, but have great means. They want to support us financially, preferably anonymously, so we'll have them pay for a string of full-page ads in the papers later."

"What about the ones who just register?"

"We'll divide them into three categories. Most of them will be organized into local chapters and will join the activities there. Category two we will ask to help us. For example, we now have two lawyers who are preparing a comparison of sentences for pedophilia in Denmark and other countries. Their work will appear on the home page tomorrow and the report will be sent to all of our members. The problem is that soon we won't be able to take on more people. And then we have the third and final category: the ones who have a . . . how should I put it? . . . a fiery temperament, and there are quite a few of them, but we will handle them discreetly. And internally. Not all of my co-workers know that I am registering them. Understand?"

Stig Åge Thorsen nodded, although it seemed complicated

to him. He said searchingly, "So we are directing the war, if one can put it that way. Is that how it is?"

"We absolutely have an enormous base but to claim that we alone determine the image in the media would be a real exaggeration. There have also been backlashes. Not everything is rose-colored. Take a look at this."

Erik Mørk took a badge out of his pocket. It was oblong with black lettering on a yellow background. It read, "5, 6 . . . 7, 10, 20!"

"A couple of gymnasium students thought of it. That is, first five pedophiles have been killed, then six—and later on seven, ten, and twenty. But it's too extreme and pushes too many segments away. They're also writing the slogan as graffiti and people don't like that. Unfortunately we haven't quite managed to stop it. There's someone printing T-shirts with . . . well, take a guess . . ."

"Per Clausen."

"Exactly. Have you seen them?"

"Yes, after you published the article about my arrest on the Net, people make pilgrimages here. They bring all kinds of flammable material that they throw into the minivan pit, almost like a ritual. Often gasoline but other things too. Last night it was magnesium and it lit up like shooting stars. I went over there for a look this morning and there were a dozen people and one of them was wearing one of those Per Clausen tops. Without his windbreaker on, so you could really see it. The police have all kinds of problems with this fire. At first they just put up police tape around it but that was quickly torn down, so they put up one of those mobile fences and it took them all afternoon, but last night someone removed that too, so they may have to stand guard if they want to prevent sabotage."

They had reached the end of the field where a stone wall and a thicket of stunted nut trees and sloan bushes stood between them and a meadow leading down to the water. Both bored their way through this obstacle. Below this the autumn forest spread out in all its colorful splendor in front of a lake, that lay still and rain gray.

Mørk stopped on top of the wall and took in the scene. "It must be quite a pleasure to live here." He jumped down, enchanted, and took steps into the sank meadow.

The country man managed to stop him. It was impassable bogland. "Better than prison, of course. But you shouldn't go that way unless you want to risk me getting the tractor to pull you out of the mud."

Stig Åge Thorsen led them along an animal path that ran next to the stone wall. Mørk asked, "Well, how did your interrogation go? It's your turn to tell."

"I was under arrest for almost one day but not much happened the first few hours. From time to time they questioned me, always by someone different, but they did not manage to take me down."

"And how would they? Starting a bonfire on your own property?"

"No, that must be the conclusion they came to as well. On the other hand . . . there was no doubt that they would have liked to keep me there. And I was there for almost the full twenty-four hours they were allowed before they had to involve a judge. At the very end there was a policeman by the name of Arne Pedersen from Copenhagen. He was very nice while at the same somehow more dangerous than the others. His biggest interest was in what I had done with the money. The money I claimed that I was given by the stranger."

"What did you say to that?"

"That I had donated them to Sanlaap, and that part is actually true in a way. He didn't drill deeper into the issue but as you know I've been called in for another round of talks in Copenhagen tomorrow."

"Yes, and I will make sure there are reporters. It won't be difficult but you should maintain your silence, although you should feel free to mention your interview with me on Thursday."

"Go to WeHateThem.dk on Thursday evening if you want to know more." Stig Åge Thorsen grinned. Mørk did not. The advertisement was deadly serious.

"Yes, something like that. We'll also spread the word of course. High and low. Anything else?"

"No, not really. Well, actually—I've received a letter from Helle, a real letter. She wrote that she isn't doing very well. You know how she has trouble with thoughts of her uncle at night. So last night I drove to Hillerød and called her from a telephone booth. What should I say? She sounded almost intoxicated and extremely unhappy, but she wanted me to send you her greetings. And to the Climber of course, if I see him, though I hope I don't."

Mørk answered briskly, "And you won't. He will very soon be on his way to Germany. Most likely in a couple of days and at most by next weekend."

"Why hasn't he left already? I'm not the least bit comfortable with him, not after this business with the hot-dog stand. It was part of our agreement that he was supposed to leave as soon as it was over."

"And he will. Unfortunately, he thinks he is invincible because so many people are backing us, but I haven't been pressing the issue either, I should add. He's not a bad thing to have up one's sleeve. In a way he is my ultimate trump card with the media, even more than you, if you can see what I mean."

They walked for a while without speaking. The wind swept through the tops of the trees above their heads and drops showered down from the branches. Mørk slapped his arms across his chest to get warm, and Stig Åge Thorsen asked, "What now?"

"We'll build you up the next couple of days and then we'll do your online interview on Thursday. I'll introduce it this afternoon and then we'll call for a demonstration on Friday."

"What if they sentence and jail me?"

"They won't. They simply don't have enough evidence to hold you."

"And what about after that? What about our demands?"

"They will be made public immediately following the interview."

"They aren't up on the home page already?"

"No, until now there isn't anything up there except vague formulations about combating child abuse. No one can disagree with that. In the final analysis all this comes down to politics and here we will have some heavy hitters, but apart from the fact that the people's sentiment supports our populist-minded minister of justice, none of the others have shifted. They are leaning back, winning time, and hoping that things get back to normal in a couple of weeks. And of course that we will be found. Those are the ones we need to shake up, but believe me—they aren't losing any sleep over a couple of days of a school strike. That isn't enough to get them to act."

"Then they'll be indifferent to a demonstration and also to my interview."

"Of course they are. But the situation is in our favor. We're only missing the last little bit. Unfortunately, this bit will negatively influence public opinion. That can't be helped. So we'll have to create the illusion that public opinion hasn't changed and I think that is possible to a degree. At least for a couple of days and that is sufficient. It's mainly a question of angles and timing."

Stig Åge Thorsen stopped and put a hand on the shoulder of his comrade.

"I know that you and Per Clausen discussed these things in great detail but you sometimes forgot to inform the rest of us. You're talking as if I know what the next step is but I don't. To be perfectly honest, I don't always understand what you are talking about."

Mørk made a disarming gesture and said, "I'm sorry, I should have said as much, but the next step was taken this morning. The pedophile database has been distributed to our category-three members."

Stig Åge Thorsen's face showed that he was still not following. Mørk had to spell it out: "Violence."

CHAPTER 48

The entries in Erik Mørk's database fell hard over the country and created much unhappiness. Jylland was heavily overrepresented since the client base of the Ditlevsen brothers was a significant source.

Thus, a handful of people were gathered outside a property in Kvaglund in Esbjerg. They all stood with their heads tilted back and were looking antagonistically at a man on the fifth floor who was half sitting, half standing in a window far above them. In one hand he was holding on to the transom that separated the lower panes from the upper, and he was crying. From time to time he looked down in terror. A middle-aged woman whose blue-fox-fur coat indicated that she did not live in the neighborhood shouted, "Jump, you beast. Come on, get on with it, we don't have all day."

A younger man chimed in. He sat on a moped, slightly apart from the others. "Yes, come on, dammit. Get it over with, you sissy."

A kitchen window in the building opened and an agitated woman with dyed red hair and a checkered apron leaned out and looked up. The fur lady explained without prompting, "He's a child molester. He molested two small children in Nakskov eighteen years ago. It's outrageous that our children have been living with someone like him in their midst."

"*Our* children, you mean. I don't believe you have any children here."

The fur lady didn't reply but a comrade answered in her stead. His Danish was halting. "I have four children outside his door."

The woman gave the group the finger and slammed her window shut. The shouting continued. Shortly thereafter a patrol car pulled up and two officers got out, a man and a woman. After making their way through the crowd that had now swelled in number, they disappeared into the entrance. On the fifth floor, the door to the apartment was covered with slurs such as "animal dung," "child fucker," and "perverse shit." Above these was some Arabic writing that most likely did not contain the friendliest sentiments. The male officer enabled their entry with a well-directed kick that broke the door handle and forced the door open. The woman walked in. She stopped a couple of steps from the would-be suicide and after a little while her colleague turned up behind her.

The man in the window was clearly desperate. "If you get any closer, I'll let go."

The female officer grabbed a nearby chair and calmly sat down. Cries from the street flowed together into a rhythmic, roaring choir. *Jump, jump, jump.* The cry was picked up all along the block and the echo came rolling with a slight delay, like a distorted bass.

"We'll stay where we are, we just want to talk with you."

The man did not react.

"It's not worth it. Things can change and get better again."

The officer spoke slowly and persuasively but her words were drowned out by the chanting from the street, so she ordered her colleague to go down and put a stop to the shouting. The man in the window glanced pleadingly at her, as if she could eliminate the evil of the world, but in this he was severely mistaken. As soon as they were alone she abruptly changed her attitude. As a child she had been her father's little doll, until he drank himself to death. Little one, little doll—the last days had opened the door to a room inside her. She stood up and walked toward him.

"Jump or climb back in. It makes absolutely no difference to me."

He stared at her in disbelief for one long second before he relaxed his grip. Cries of jubilation from the crowd accompanied his fall.

The shop owner in Arnborg, south of Herning, was not jubilant, in fact he was concerned. Three of his regulars had come into his shop but none of them greeted him. Now each one was standing there silent and very serious, without a shopping basket. One of them was standing by the marmalades and jams, the other by the wine, and the last one by the counter. The silence was broken by the sound of shattering glass as a jar of jam broke against the stone floor of the shop.

"Oops, that was clumsy of me."

The shop owner reassured him, "That's all right, Karsten, these things happen."

"It's just—oops—it just happened again. And again, and again and look at this."

A crash punctuated each observation.

"Tell me, what the hell are you doing? Can you please leave my shop?"

The man by the wine section had carefully selected two bottles.

"These two look good, I think I'd like to have them tonight. Oh no, now I'm being clumsy too, what a mess."

The taciturn customer by the counter leaned forward and laid a hand on the shop owner's shoulder. The shop owner was large and strong, but the man by the counter was bigger.

"That tall guy from Sørvad works here, doesn't he?"

"No, not anymore. Is that why you're breaking my wares? I fired him this morning. I had no idea that he was . . . well, you know."

This piece of information brought a smile to all three gentlemen and one of them took out his wallet.

"Now that paints an entirely different picture. We heard that you intended to keep him on in spite of his behavior. I think we had five jars of marmalade, two bottles of red wine, and I'm going to have twenty King's. Plus we should have a round of cold ones in the next room.

The shop owner allowed himself to be placated when he saw the money and heard about the beer.

"Yes, why not."

He called out to the back room, "Magda, can you make yourself useful with a floor mop and a bucket of water?"

Then he turned to the men.

"Dammit, you could have asked me first, you know me."

They nodded somewhat sheepishly as what he said was right—they did know him.

CHAPTER 49

The lady in red is definitely an interesting factor in Per Clausen's life. The difference in age and social status alone shows that there was something special about their relationship. The problem is, of course, that we don't have any reasonable idea about where to look for her. The make of car, her red clothes, and two meetings in a certain location—and all this from over two years ago—is simply two thin a basis to work on."

Simonsen grunted impatiently but this did not affect Poul Troulsen. A good presentation took time.

"According to Kasper Planck, the kiosk owner, Farshad Bakhtîshû, and his sons now recall that that the woman in red had a slight limp."

"So what if she did?"

"It could be nothing, but there's something else, and this time it has to do with the piece of paper with the woman's name and address. One of the sons thought of a detail that struck him as unusual. The address that the woman wrote down was a street, so it ended in *vej*. That's of course too common to be helpful in itself but the unusual thing is the dot over the *j*, which was shaped like a heart."

"Which means?"

"Well, I grew up in Jægersborg and I know that in Gentofte County there is a distinctive detail in the street signs. If the street sign ends in *vej* then the dot over the *j* is printed as a little red heart. Other *j*s or *i*s for that matter are printed with a regular dot. This information is public but in practice it is only people from Gentofte who recognize the heart. Some find it so cute and appealing that they reproduce it in writing their addresses. My mother, for example, always wrote hearts over her *j* when sending a postcard. To this you can add the fact that the woman in red is most likely wealthy, which fits very well with the profile of that county."

"Okay, I'll give you that it seems reasonable to assume that our mysterious woman is from Gentofte. Go on."

"Per Clausen had two connections to Gentofte in his life. In part through his own childhood and in part through his daughter's schooling. The woman's age indicates that the connection between the two of them originated through his daughter."

"Sounds plausible enough, but now you are building a maybe on another maybe."

Poul Troulsen ignored the objection and continued: "After her return to Sweden in January 1993, Helene Clausen entered ninth grade at the Tranehøj School in Gentofte. The following school year she started the first year at Auregaard Gymnasium, which lies right next door. That she was admitted in a school in Gentofte County when she lived in Gladsaxe should immediately have raised questions. It isn't very common."

"I know the story as well as you," Simonsen interrupted.

Troulsen glanced skeptically at him. There were now hundreds of reports in the case files and he had realized the connections only yesterday. Simonsen caught his disbelief and said quickly and sourly, "We were inattentive, yes, but after a couple of days these connections were revealed by Arne's trip to Sweden. When Helene Clausen came back to Denmark she refused therapy. Her father did the next best thing. He had a colleague whose wife worked with traumatized children in Copenhagen and was also tied to the Tranehøj School as a psychologist. Per Clausen looked her up and she promised to help. She talked to a friend about cross-county flexibility regarding the girl's schooling. The friend was married to the mayor of Gentofte at the time. Unfortunately, Helene Clausen never received professional counseling. It may have cost eight people their lives. And in future, kindly refrain from doubting me when I say that I know."

"I'm sorry, I just figured that with the volume of paper . . ."

"Let's move on. Poul. Where do you want to start? We have had a team at the school and one at the gymnasium and they have done a reasonable bit of work. What can you add to the investigation?"

"Maybe nothing, but their task was primarily to shed light on whether or not Helene Clausen had been sexually abused during her time in Sweden as well as to clarify the circumstances surrounding her death. What they did not look into was any ties between Per Clausen and his daughter's classmates."

Simonsen nodded. "Hm, you have a point there."

"Exactly, and the work already done gives me an excellent point of departure. It is clear from the reports that the girls in room one-A, class of 1993, at Auregaard Gymnasium had an informal leader of sorts. Today she owns a small temp agency in Hellerup and I have an appointment with her."

Simonsen folded his hands and stared up at the ceiling. Then he made up his mind. "You are probably out hunting ghosts. Start with a renewed search for a silver-colored Porsche now that the area can be limited to Gentofte and then keep your cell phone on. Good luck."

CHAPTER 50

The investigation had been given a longish piece in the *Nyhedsjournalen*, which was positive. What was less positive was that Monday's preparatory meeting between the Homicide Division and the TV station almost stalled. Simonsen, Arne Pedersen, the Countess, and Pauline Berg were there from the police. The TV station sent a producer and producer's assistant. The work took place in the police headquarters in Copenhagen and everyone was tired and irritable.

The producer had signed off from the start. First he held an unnecessarily long-winded and partly incoherent introduction in which he stressed to the police investigators the importance of a clear message. After that he said almost nothing. He looked like someone after a long weekend of drinking, his breath had a foul smell of old beer, and both chairs on either side of him were vacant. His assistant concerned herself only with the keyboard on her laptop. She wrote down every word, which made the others self-conscious even though no one said anything.

Three reconstructed scenes had been prepared for the program, each of them about one minute in length. The first depicted the transportation of the victims, the second showed the murders, and the third, which was the shortest and most fabricated, showed the minivan on its way from the school to the field in Kregme at Arresø. The only thing lacking was narration. All the film clips were computer animated with puppets as actors, which lessened the realism but had the obvious advantage that the scenes could be easily modified. After each film scene the police had the opportunity to comment and ask for witnesses of the event to come forward. The problem was, what comments and witnesses to what.

Simonsen grabbed the remote and pointed it at the television. They were still on the first scene. "Should we watch it again?"

The three others protested in a rare show of unison. The producer looked relieved, the assistant kept typing. Everyone speculated about what to say. Arne Pedersen held steadily to his opinion.

"I'm leaning most to the woman. The film doesn't show that she's giving injections or measuring out doses of Stesolid according to the body weight of the victims. Her presumed medical background also doesn't emerge. Physician, nurse, nursing assistant, midwife, veterinarian, medical student—we should make sure to get that in."

It was nothing new, merely a rewrite of his own argumentation, version twenty. Or so the Countess thought, and injected, "I still think that the minivan is a better angle. Only six adult witnesses have come forward. There must be more, and maybe we can get a make, year, or even a license plate; I mean, that minivan had to come from somewhere. It must have been sold, bought, registered, and owned. The alternative is that we wait until the technicians come up with something from Kregme and we only just received a court order. It almost seems like sabotage."

Pauline Berg parroted the Countess's point but used twice as many words, as if she wanted to give innocent men a headache. Or so Arne Pedersen thought while he prepared to take up his own line of argumentation again.

Simonsen asked Pedersen, "How are things going with the minivan? When can we get a forensic report?"

Pedersen gave a pessimistic answer: "There have been

problems keeping people away. Someone is tossing all kinds of garbage down into the pit to get it to burn even longer but we're finally closer to getting a handle on that. The problem is that the technicians want the fire to die down of its own accord so that they don't destroy any more evidence. The earliest we can hope for is that in about three days they should be able to say if they will have something to say, if that makes sense. It could be weeks if not months before we get something usable and even that is uncertain. We have to assume it's been over a thousand degrees for a number of days down in that pit."

Simonsen shook his head as if he wanted to chase the bad news away. He was sweating, his legs ached, and he shuttled back and forth between the Countess's and Arne Pedersen's points of view. Now he tried to reach a compromise: "We'll mention the minivan and call for witnesses, but concentrate on the woman."

Everyone was satisfied, with the exception of the production assistant, who knew that she was destined for a glorious career in the media world. For a brief moment she abandoned her keyboard and involved herself in the debate. It was the first time she said something, so her thin voice attracted their undivided attention.

"Keep the messages simple."

And then they were back to the beginning.

Berg stared speculatively at her white throat and wanted to throttle her. Simonsen wiped his forehead with his handkerchief, the producer yawned openly, and Pedersen started yet another variant of his argument.

The work proceeded at a snail's pace. After a long time they finally agreed on the message that would follow the first video. The simple message. Simonsen had finally taken Pedersen's side: they would focus on the woman with the anesthesia. She had been observed climbing into the minivan when it paused at the outskirts of a rest stop on the freeway between Slagelse and Ringsted. The witness had later retracted his statement but no one put much stock in that. The next sequence was played back four times and a couple of smaller corrections were made, then they tackled the question of what the message should be.

The producer disappeared for a long time and the officers grew nervous that he had become lost in the building corridors. He returned, his face flushed. He had a seasonal beer with him that he'd picked up somewhere and that he unselfconsciously started to drink. The alcohol gave him strength to join in the fray, which turned out to be an advantage. If one could see past the man's foul smell and pedantic manner, he was a brilliant project leader. Everyone fell in line and agreed that the title should be "The Man with the Video Camera." This was as far as they could agree and everyone knew it.

Simonsen began, "Aka Frank Ditlevsen's secret friend? Aka the killer and tree feller from Allerslev? Aka Stig Åge Thorsen's stranger? Aka the driver of the minivan and the executioner from Bagsværd?"

It was a question. The Countess remained firm in her belief and was quick to answer, "Yes."

Pedersen again played devil's advocate: "Maybe, but very much a maybe. This is much too uncertain to put this out there. We risk derailing the whole investigation. Guesses and speculations—that's simply too thin." Simonsen nodded thoughtfully while Pedersen continued. "Particularly with respect to Stig Åge Thorsen's stranger, who we aren't sure even exists. It could be one man, it could be five or ten women for that matter. That country bumpkin is not the most reliable witness, to put it mildly, and his motives are unclear in every way. He'll probably turn out to be another media stunt. We don't even know if the remains of the minivan are at the bottom of his pit."

The Countess countered, "The technicians have established a match between the last film clip and the view seen from his land."

Pedersen replied, "A preliminary match, and even if it were

true it would not necessarily mean that the minivan ended up there."

Simonsen jumped in: "Let us take this from the beginning—that is, Frank Ditlevsen's secret friend. Pauline, give us a summary."

Berg would have preferred that he had turned to the Countess. Her secret knowledge that Frank Ditlevsen's secret friend was one of his so-called old boys stuck in her throat and today she would have a given a great deal for a do-over of yesterday. She sat straighter in her chair. The producer stared lustfully at her breasts and the production assistant tapped away at her keyboard.

"The only thing we have are the accounts of two neighbors, of which only one has any substance. The next-door neighbors have seen a man in his thirties visit the brothers on a few occasions over the past year. They say he has his own key. But the description is incomplete: light-haired, above average height, slender and well proportioned, always arriving on foot or by car with Frank Ditlevsen."

Simonsen suddenly interrupted: "Give me a summary of the murder of Allan Ditlevsen and focus on the tree felling."

His voice sounded unusually sharp and Berg looked at him in bewilderment. Neither of the two others said anything but she could tell from their expressions that they were as much at a loss as she was. She followed his order. Anything else would have been inconceivable when her boss was acting like this, but his shifts in mood were strange, almost bizarre. Luckily she knew the facts of the tree felling almost by heart.

"The perpetrator felled the tree in eight blows at around four to four fifty during the night between Wednesday and Thursday of last week, and the tree finally came down at five thirty-eight A.M.. Shortly before this, Allan Ditlevsen was killed by blunt trauma caused with a beech stick. The hot-dog stand was shattered by the tree. The perpetrator gathered up his things and disappeared into the front door of the building at Ved Torvet

18. Here he goes down into the basement and out through the back entrance to Garvergade. Traces of sawdust have been found all along this path but after this point we don't know where he went. Our best find is a series of four footprints from the stairwell in number 18. As it happens, the building has no residents. It is ready to be demolished."

The Countess finally got it. She stood up and left, while Berg continued her recap. She even managed an account of the forensic report without a manuscript. The Countess quickly returned with a disoriented Malte Borup in her wake.

Simonsen stopped Berg as abruptly as he had ordered her to start. Then he turned to the producer and said, "Your assistant is very hardworking. Tell me, what is she writing?"

The producer's surprised, somewhat puffy face removed any suspicion of conspiracy for the moment.

"I've been wondering that too. Why are you writing this all down, Marie?"

The movement on the keyboard stopped and Marie instantly reached for the mouse. The Countess gripped her wrist a couple of centimeters away from it; Borup took over her keyboard.

Pedersen was the first to comment on the situation.

"Dammit."

The meeting was adjourned and set for the following morning, at which time the producer promised to return with a new assistant. He was endowed with a truly professional spirit, and unless he was an excellent actor he had not prompted his assistant into these subversive activities. He had no idea whom she had been reporting to online. The feeling among the investigative team was depressed. It was not so much that the assistant had caused any real damage. It was of course unpleasant that their conversations were now circulating on the Internet but they could deal with that. What was so shattering was the firsthand demonstration that a part of the general public was simply working against the police. In case any of them had been harboring any doubts in this regard, they were finally set straight.

Simonsen tried to breathe some fire into his team: "The damage is negligible. The situation is constantly changing and if the media get a little more background information it isn't the whole world. In any case we have to keep working and forget this."

Unexpectedly, it was Malte Borup who spoke up.

"I don't think it's for the media, more likely to one of the many anticop pages that are constantly popping up on the Web. Some of the sites are pretty big."

The others stared at him in astonishment. Pauline Berg asked for them all, "Anticop pages? What do you mean?"

"You mean you aren't following this at all?" slipped out of him. He regretted it as soon as he'd said it, and apologized, slightly pink: "Sorry, I didn't mean it like that. Of course you follow. With everything else that is . . ."

Simonsen came to his aid: "No, Malte, I'm afraid that we aren't following at all but perhaps we should. Can't you give us a quick synopsis?"

"All right. There are sites like Pillory.dk and SeksSyvSytten .com and then of course the one who put an ad in the paper about being . . . abused as a child. He is far and away the biggest. That one is WeHateThem.dk."

He stopped. Oral reports were not his strong suit.

Berg helped him along: "What do they do, Malte? Can you tell me about that?"

"Well, you can join them as a supporter, and what they want is that it should be punishable to be . . . that is, to be . . . mean to children."

He blushed and stopped. Berg had an urge to grab his hand. After a brief pause he started up again of his own accord.

"That is, really punishable, like in the USA, where you really can't get away with it."

Now it was the Countess's turn.

"What else do they do, Malte?"

"Unfortunately, I don't know."

Pedersen appeared in the doorway. He was holding a stack of papers and radiated urgency. "What they're doing is making sure that defenseless people are assaulted or driven to their deaths. Twenty-three incidents, over the entire country. From Gedser to Skagen, and not as a figure of speech—completely literally."

He threw the papers down on the table and the others bent over to read them. Afterward, no one said anything except Borup.

"I can bomb their pages off the Internet if I—"

Berg laid her hand over his mouth and he blushed more than ever. Simonsen's cell phone rang.

He answered brusquely and listened. When he hung up, everyone was hoping it was not another piece of bad news. For once, their hopes were realized.

"Troulsen has found the woman in red and it sounds promising. They are both on their way here."

CHAPTER 51

The owner of the temp agency turned out to be a friendly woman. Poul Troulsen knew her age already, she was in her late twenties. But he was wrong in the rest of his expectations of her. His image of a polished, self-confident career woman was shattered by someone both jovial and plump who did not spend unnecessary resources on her appearance or the interiors of her establishment. She led him into a conference room that looked more like a homeless shelter, and without asking him she handed him a plastic cup of lukewarm coffee. He took it and thanked her politely. It tasted terrible.

"As you know, this is about Helene Clausen's high-school years. I have heard that you were one of the girls who was most engaged in what was going on in class."

"You could say that. I was a terrible bitch actually. At the class reunion there are still some girls who hate me but I can understand why. I was not particularly pleasant but you're right when you say that I was well informed."

"And you were in the same class as Helene Clausen for a year?"

"Yes, until she drowned, but I can't remember her very well and I have to think hard even to remember her—you know, conjure her up in my mind's eye. I can remember that when I first saw her I was on my guard. She was both pretty and smart so I spotted a potential rival." She shook her head. "Unfortunately, that was how I was. Well, I didn't need to have worried. Helene turned out not to be very social and after that I didn't pay much attention to her. I remember her death clearly of course. We made a lot of noise but forgot her almost immediately."

"I have a picture of her if that would help."

"No, that's okay. I'd rather not. But anyway, we weren't particularly tightly knit. Helen wasn't close to anyone in the class."

Troulsen thought that the observation was largely corroborated by the reports that he had read.

"You aren't the first to say that," he told her.

"No, she kept mostly to herself. That's why I almost called and canceled, because I didn't think I had anything to tell."

He pricked up his ears. "But you didn't?"

"No, I didn't, because maybe I can help after all. At least a little. You see, in those days I kept a diary, and after you called, I looked in my old journals. It was no pleasure and there wasn't much about Helene. Almost nothing. But it got my thoughts going and I suddenly remembered something. There was one time when Helene and I drove together. I can't remember what we were doing or if anyone else from the class was with us, only that she insisted that we both put our seat belts on. I must have asked about it, but in any case she told me about a girlfriend who had been in a car accident. A really bad one. It was interesting that she used the word *girlfriend*. But unfortunately that is all that I can contribute."

This did not trouble Troulsen.

"Don't be sorry," he said. "That may turn out to be an important piece of information."

"This is about the murders at Langebæk School?"

"Yes."

"I don't know if I want you to solve them."

"Well, you wouldn't be the only one. You're honest, at least."

Troulsen stood up. She remained seated.

"I think it's hard. On the one hand a crime has been committed, but on the other hand . . . it's complicated."

"I don't share that opinion, but thank you for your time and thank you for your help."

She followed him out.

Next, Troulsen drove to Helene Clausen's old school, whistling happily. The reports did not mention a girlfriend from elementary school so he must have gotten something.

The Tranehøj School was an institution of the classical style. A four-story block of a building with two wings and a blacktop playground, bells on the walls, and dismantled water receptacles for thirsty children of the past. Signs to the school office were prominently placed, and in the front office he found a woman in her late forties. She had earphones on and was typing. Troulsen had to clear his throat a couple of times to get her attention.

"Sorry, I didn't see you. Have you been here a long time? What can I help you with?"

"No, I've just turned up. Are you the school secretary?"

"The one and only."

He took out his badge. "Poul Troulsen, from the Crime Division."

She put the earpiece on the desk, where it kept burbling. "Well now, that sounds serious."

"Not really. I'm here to get some information about a former pupil."

"By the name of?"

"Well, you see, that's the problem. How long have you worked here?"

"Longer than I care to think. I'll be celebrating my twenty-fifth anniversary next year."

"That sounds perfect. Ninth grade in 1992–93 and it is a girl."

"We've had more than a couple of those. I hope you have a little more information."

She had a heartwarming smile. Troulsen smiled back in return.

"Yes, I do. She was in a car accident, apparently serious."

He was prepared to go on, to talk about the friendship with Helene Clausen, but the woman shut her eyes and held a finger up in the air. He waited.

Shortly thereafter, her face relaxed.

"Emilie. Her name was Emilie. Yes, it was a terrible accident. Both of the girls were hurt. It happened up by Helsingør, and it was Emilie's own fault. She was speeding and had been drinking. But in the end they both recovered."

267

Troulsen frowned. It didn't add up. Students in the ninth grade did not have their licenses, but the secretary explained the discrepancy before he spoke.

"That was the older sister. She was a fair bit older than the younger one, maybe four, five years or so, and she was the one I remember. She was here at a school-anniversary celebration and we chatted a little bit. I can't remember anything about the little sister, only that she was in the accident, and it was just after she had left the school."

"Last name?"

The secretary shook her head. "No, but she became a doctor, in case that helps. It's strange. I can see her so clearly but the little sister is completely gone. We should take a trip to the basement."

"The basement?"

"Yes. If you come along I'm sure we'll find her last name and whatever else we have on her. I keep the old yearbooks down there. I know it isn't exactly the National Archives but it's not uncommon that I can help track down former pupils. You know, for reunions and the like."

A deep, powerful voice interrupted them.

"Tell me, what's this all about?"

The principal was standing in the doorway to his office, broad-chested and imposing. Troulsen looked at him. His considerable belly stretched his red suspenders nearly to the breaking point. His face was fleshy and grim, and a pair of steel-rimmed glasses were pushed up on his bald head.

"I'm from the police and I'm trying to get some information about a—"

"I heard you," the principal broke in. "What are you going to use the information for?"

"What I'm going to use it for? I'm going to use it to solve a crime."

268

"What kind of crime?"

Poul Troulsen answered with some irritation, "That's not relevant."

"I think I know what kind of a crime it is. I've seen you on the Internet."

"And?"

"Do you have a warrant?"

"A warrant? Why on earth would I need a warrant?"

"There's no public access to our archives."

With a heavy hand he shoved the secretary, who had just stood up, back in her chair.

"I know that we disagree on this point but you will come to accept that I make the decisions around here. We don't give out personal information about our pupils without a legitimate reason."

The secretary's eyes flashed and she waved his hand away while she appealed to Troulsen. Unfortunately, there wasn't much he could do.

"Am I to understand that you're refusing to assist me in my work?"

"You work is of no concern to me. I am refusing to give you access to our personal files unless you have a search warrant or written permission from one of my superiors in the administration. Other than this I have nothing to discuss with you."

"Your personal files . . . that's preposterous. I only need one name."

"As I said, I have nothing more to discuss with you."

"Then I think I'll have to swing by the town hall and have a conversation with your boss."

If Troulsen had been hoping that the man could be intimidated, he was wrong.

"That's an excellent idea. The superintendent, the director of child and cultural affairs, the county director, or the mayor. Take your pick."

He sounded unsettlingly sure of the outcome, regardless of which person would review the matter.

"Thank you very much. I hope that we'll have a chance to speak again soon."

"I don't, but who knows?"

Troulsen fished out a card and held it out to the secretary without saying anything. It wasn't necessary. She took it in front of the principal and they both saw how his fingers twitched in readiness to prevent the exchange.

"Try anything and I'll arrest you on the spot. For obstruction of justice or for obesity, whichever suits me best."

The threat worked. The principal kept himself in check. Frustratingly enough.

"The superintendent, the director of child and cultural affairs, the county director, or the mayor," Troulsen said, reciting the hierarchical phrase that the school principal had given him.

The receptionist at the Gentofte city hall did not seem overwhelmed by the choices he gave her. She typed for a while, then looked at a screen. "Looks like it may have to be the director of child and cultural affairs. What should I say this is in regard to?" She emphasized the word *may*.

He showed her his police identification, which she examined suspiciously for an overly long period of time before she decided it was genuine. Then she gave him a little card with an office number and pointed him in the right direction with a long purple fingernail. He left without thanking her.

The director was a small man with a sleazy, indolent appearance. His handshake was limp and sticky like a ball of dough. He showed Troulsen a seat on the other side of his desk, for which the latter had to wait patiently while the man cleared his papers out of the way. Finally he sat down with his elbows on the table and his palms together with his head resting against the tips of his fingers, ready and receptive. Troulsen expressed the matter at hand in a concise way. The man across from him nodded thoughtfully during this explanation as if the connections were complicated and only the chosen could fully comprehend it. Afterward he continued nodding while he commented on the matter in a steady stream of polished nonsense.

Troulsen's phone rang in the middle of this speech and, mostly to irritate the director, he answered it, but it was good that he did because the woman he was looking for was on the other end. The school secretary had been busy, secretly checking the archives. The woman confirmed her visit to the kiosk in Bagsværd and was ready to see him within the hour. It could hardly have been better. He wrote down her name and number and hung up.

The interruption had lasted less than a minute, but it changed everything. His errand was suddenly superfluous and he told himself that he should leave, that he was too old for this, that he didn't need the extra grief, and nonetheless he stayed put.

The director had paused for the telephone call. His attitude remained unchanged, however, and as soon as he regained Troulsen's attention, he went on: "As I said, I am not a lawyer, so it is possible that there are some aspects of this case that I have not taken into account—"

Troulsen jumped in: "So your conclusion is that you don't wish to help me." His tone was sharp, impertinent. Once again his superego admonished him and told him to keep a check on himself, preferably to leave. It helped about as much as using a Band-Aid to treat hay fever.

"That is definitely not my conclusion, Officer Troulsen. You are getting ahead of yourself. The matter will be given a thorough consideration."

"And when do you anticipate reaching a conclusion?"

"I think we should be able to do so relatively quickly. It is of considerable importance that the Gentofte County School District be a cooperative partner to the other public entities, not least to the police."

"And by quickly you mean . . . ?"

"I would rather not commit myself to a certain time frame."

His mouth stretched upward by a couple of centimeters. It was a smile and Troulsen realized that the man was enjoying himself. He stood up.

"I would bet that when you were a child, you were one of the ones who ran straight out of the school yard as soon as there was a fight."

"I beg your pardon?"

"I said, I guarantee that you were scared shitless by fighting. Have you ever experienced any police brutality?"

The suggestion of physical violence sucked all confidence out of the director, who crumpled like a punctured balloon. He folded his arms across his chest and his voice shot up a couple of octaves.

"Are you threatening me?"

"It makes no difference if I am or not, and if you don't want anything to happen to your nose, you'd do best to keep still."

The man obeyed. Small beads of sweat broke out on his forehead and along his as-yet-unharmed nose. Troulsen's gaze fell on a pair of scissors that lay on the table and for a split second he thought about cutting off a tuft of his hair and forcing him to eat it. Then his common sense returned and he limited himself to giving the man a light slap on the back of the head.

"Before I go I can inform you of the procedure for filing a complaint with the police. You turn in your paperwork to the nearest police station and the zoom—within only a few years you will receive a rejection."

While he spoke he moved slowly to the door. He nodded a

goodbye, smiling, relieved that he had managed to control his temper to a reasonable degree.

CHAPTER 52

The episode at Gentofte's city hall had not vanquished Poul Troulsen's sense of humor. He was extremely satisfied with the day's developments so far and now all he hoped was that the woman in red would turn out to be cooperative, which their telephone conversation indicated she would be. He also, of course, hoped that she would have information that could advance the investigation. Preferably by a great big leap forward. They could certainly use the help.

Emilie Mosberg Floyd was an attractive woman in her early thirties. She had a well-proportioned and slender figure, her face was animated and pretty, her choice of clothes expensive and somewhat ill chosen. An orange-red shiny satin skirt, a short-sleeve cotton blouse in the same color, and a cropped jacket in a roughly woven wool that alternated between orange and purple in a stylized pattern with tulips. Her black shoes would have been appropriate if she were going hiking.

She greeted him at the door of her large brick house and showed him to the kitchen for a cup of coffee. The initial pleasantries were quickly dispatched. She was the first to change the subject.

"You want to know about Helene and Per Clausen. You'll have to excuse me switching to this so abruptly but I only have half an hour and then I have to be at work."

She smiled winningly. Her teeth were very even and the green watchful eyes were lively. Her words had a teasing charm.

"Yes, I do. You knew them both?"

"Yes, I did, but mostly Per. My relationship to Helene was secondary. She was friends with my little sister, not me. They were in the same year at school, but you know that."

The answer was a little surprising and sounded promising. Troulsen was definitely more interested in the father than the daughter and he was not without a sense of anticipation. However, he forced himself to proceed methodically.

"Perhaps you could tell me a little about your own background first?"

She nodded.

"That sounds reasonable. So, I was born and raised here in Gentofte. In 1992 I went to the university and began my medical studies. The following year my little sister and I had a bad accident in my father's car. I was half drunk and fell asleep at the wheel. It was during summer vacation. We were both badly hurt and our recovery took almost a year. But the psychological damage was the worst. When I resumed my studies, I was still not fully recovered. I had problems concentrating and frequent crying fits. One day I was visited by a psychiatrist by the name of Jeremy Floyd, who was the chief physician at the Sexology Clinic at the National Hospital. Even though my problems did not fall within his area of specialization, he had promised one of my instructors to give me fifteen minutes of his time, primarily to urge me to seek professional help. Four months later we were married and it changed my life. I bore and raised our two sons and studied at the same time. For a couple of years I worked constantly if I wasn't sleeping. In 2001 I graduated and was then employed at the National Hospital, where I am doing my residency in cardiology. Last year Jeremy died in an accident. His other great passion other than his family was mountain climbing, and it killed him. Aconcagua took him."

She glanced at him and Troulsen nodded. He assumed that Aconcagua was a mountain but did not want to interrupt her in order to ask. She went on, but only briefly: "The past few years I have been alone with the children, who right at this moment happen to be on a camping trip."

After giving him the information about her children's whereabouts she had apparently reached the end of her narrative. Her stressed expression was exaggerated when she checked her watch. Troulsen ignored it. Instead, he gave her a couple of key words: "Helene and Per Clausen?"

She emptied her coffee cup and refilled it, starting to talk again at a slightly faster clip.

"Helene Clausen was a friend of my little sister, as I mentioned. My sister's name is Katja, Katja Mosberg, and she lives in Austria. Her partner is a Norwegian who works for the foreign service—the Norwegian one, that is. Helene started in Katja's class in 1993. She came from Sweden, where she had lived for a few years with her mother and stepfather. Helene was shy and introverted but she and Katja got along well and they spent quite a bit of time together. Among other things they did their homework together and complemented each other well. Helene was uniquely gifted in mathematics, physics, and chemistry—anything to do with natural science. On the other hand, she was not so good at Danish, probably because of her many years in Sweden. Katja was just the opposite: good at Danish and bad at math. Unfortunately, the bad-math gene is something we share and you might say it's the reason that I got to know Per, because when Katja and Helene were in ninth grade I was in my first year of medical school and my worst subject by far was statistics. All my fellow students were sweating over anatomy or some of the more traditional medical classes, but statistics threatened to cut short my career before it had even begun. I simply didn't understand it and even today I start to feel ill if someone mentions regression analysis or significance level."

She smiled as if she wanted to apologize for her lack of statistical knowledge. Troulsen thought that if he ever developed heart problems he wouldn't care if his surgeon could handle probabilities. Again she glanced at her watch, this time without trying to hide it, and he knew they would have to wrap it up soon.

"Katja talked to Per about me. She has always been a busybody, making arrangements for other people, but in this case there was a good outcome. Per was very happy about Katja and Helene's friendship and he was also a sweet man who liked being helpful if he could. He started tutoring me. One or two evenings a week, for free. He didn't even want to hear the mention of money. My father was happy to pay for anything that had to do with his daughters' education. But back then Per was making a good salary himself."

She shook her head and corrected herself: "No, I take that back. He wouldn't have taken any money even if he had been as poor as a church mouse. He was like that. Always helpful."

Troulsen glimpsed a genuine tenderness in her for her old tutor and it wasn't the first time he had seen something like it. Per Clausen was apparently the kind of man who touched the people around him.

"Well, the end of this whole thing was that I got through my final examination with a perfectly respectable passing grade, which I had Per to thank for. That summer I had the accident and then Helene died, as you know. Katja and I were the only ones who knew her background, who knew that she was most likely committing suicide when she drowned. And Per, of course, but I only became sure of that a few years ago."

She looked up and met his eyes. "You know that Helene was abused by her stepfather?"

Troulsen confirmed this and she went on.

"The following years I didn't see Per. I thought of him from time to time and was planning to look in on him but it never happened. An excuse, however weak, is also that I had my hands full those years with two toddlers and medical-school studies. But before I get to how I met Per again I think I have to tell you a little about my late husband."

She paused until Troulsen indicated that he accepted this change in priorities. He nodded, which he would have done whatever she had proposed. She was a wonderful storyteller, the kind where all you had to do was lean back and listen.

"My husband's name as you know was Jeremy Floyd. His father was from Canada and his mother from Denmark. He spent the first years of his life in Quebec and then his family moved here. He received his medical training at Århus and after that he went on to specialize in psychiatry at the National Hospital. His greatest interest was in human sexual behavior, and after his doctorate in the psychology of sexual criminals he was appointed chief physician at the Sexology Clinic. In addition to his job at the hospital he had a private practice that he ran here from the house, where he would help victims of incest and later anyone who had suffered abuse as a child. In the beginning, taking on private patients was mainly a way for him to feed his scientific curiosity. By working with both perpetrators and their victims, he closed the circle, as he put it, but after a while the private practice took over and he ended up with long waiting lists. He also had trouble saying no and—I may as well just say this—he also liked the money."

She stretched her hand out for the thermos flask and shook it hopefully. It was empty. She got up and took a couple of cans of soda from the fridge, placing them on the table but strangely enough without opening them. Troulsen was not tempted. He didn't like cola.

"My sister's old ninth-grade class got together the fall of 2003. At the reunion, Katja happened to hear that Per had been doing badly ever since Helene's death. She heard he had lost his job, was drinking and generally falling apart. When she told me, I got serious about going to see him. Perhaps you could call it a repayment. He had helped me when I needed it, and now the time had come to pay him back. I think I visited him half a dozen times. He was often drunk or half drunk but always happy to see me. We talked mostly about Helene although there wasn't much to say so our talks became endless repetitions of the same sad themes, and if I can be completely honest I started to get a bit tired of the visits even though I was the one who initiated them. But then I had an idea. It was something close at hand, of course. I convinced Jeremy to take Per on as a patient. It was difficult, but I succeeded. In his own way Per was also a victim of abuse although he had not suffered it personally, so it took a great deal of pressure on my part to get Jeremy to try it out. It was even harder to get Per to accept the role of patient and at first I didn't think it would work. But Jeremy was clever and driven once he had become professionally involved, and I also think that Per realized after a while that he needed the help. At any rate they eventually embarked on a course of therapy, and there were only a few times when I had to go and get Per because he had missed an appointment. There were two times I had to put him through detox. He wouldn't hear of taking any Antabuse."

Troulsen observed, "There was one time you picked him up at a kiosk in Bagsværd Hovedgade?"

"Yes, that's right."

"You were driving a silver-colored Porsche?"

"Yes, that's also right. It's my dad's. I have an Audi myself."

Troulsen nodded. That made perfect sense.

"We've combed through hospital records for ambulatory

alcoholics. But Per Clausen was never admitted as far as we can tell."

She smiled somewhat sheepishly.

"Well, both Jeremy and I worked at the National Hospital. Let's just say that on a couple of occasions he got a spare bed. A little outside of the regular system."

Troulsen groaned inwardly. It was just this kind of thing that made an investigation so difficult.

"Anyway, there was more and more order in Per's life, the more he and Jeremy talked. The therapy helped. But there isn't much of a concrete nature that I know about the course of the therapy because Jeremy never discussed his patients. They demanded privacy and Jeremy was happy to give it to them. The patients had their own entrance and I was basically not even supposed to show myself in my own garden when they came or went. I did learn a little bit later on but paradoxically it was through Per. After a year of consultation he joined a self-help group."

She stopped. The word hung in the air. Also the small tremor in her voice when she said it. She was far from stupid and must have thought about the importance of her knowledge for a long time, and Troulsen noticed how his resentment of her suddenly grew explosively inside him. He had to exert a great deal of control to remain calm.

"Why haven't you contacted us?"

The question leaped straight over a great many things and she could easily have deflected it in the first round but she made no attempt to do so.

"I don't really know. Maybe I just hoped I wouldn't get involved. And I don't have any names of the people involved in the group. I'm not even sure how many there were." She stared straight out in front of her before she resumed. "There's no doubt in my opinion that it was wrong to kill those people.

279

Very wrong and Jeremy would also have thought so, but I'm not sure that it has anything to do with . . ." She didn't finish the sentence. Perhaps because she herself didn't believe it.

Troulsen said gravely, "You won't be able to go to work today. I have to take you in to the police headquarters in Copenhagen."

Emilie Mosberg Floyd realized immediately that she had no choice.

"I guess so." She nodded thoughtfully and repeated, "I guess so."

Troulsen could not have agreed more.

CHAPTER 53

Anita Dahlgren sat in the cafeteria at the *Dagbladet*. She was alone at her table, which was just as well because one of the many unwritten rules of the paper forbade cell phone conversations at lunch, and she was breaking that law. On the other hand, a higher authority mandated that employees get good news, so the dinner invitation she had just received from Kasper Planck compensated for her lawbreaking, she decided. At any rate, she ignored the irritated glances of her colleagues. The invitation was a surprise and at first she was both happy and flattered. But this delight wilted somewhat in light of the matters she discussed next.

"So are you telling me that I should buy the groceries myself and make the meal?" She listened. The old man's rudeness was outrageous. "Tell me why I'm not hanging up on you. I don't understand it myself."

A colleague at a nearby table shouted that it seemed like a really good idea. At the same time, Anni Staal appeared and sat down across from her, as if materializing out of thin air. It was an amazing feat given what she was carrying. In one hand she was expertly holding two bottles of beer with glasses set upside down over the top. Without interrupting, she pushed one beer across the table.

Anita wrapped things up: "Yes, I do know that you're a weak old man, but . . . and . . . I'll do what you say. I'll see you tomorrow at five."

The conversation was impossible with her boss sitting one meter away, which was why she capitulated—two minutes before it would probably have happened anyway. She aggressively turned her attention to Anni. Whatever was outwardly lost had to be conquered internally.

"I don't drink beer at this time of day. What do you want? I'm on break."

Anni smiled ironically. "I actually don't either."

"Then why did you buy them, for God's sake?"

"Because this is personal, and because we are Danish. We don't talk about personal things without beer, do we?"

Anita realized the logic of this. One had to honor one's cultural heritage. She gave in and took a swig, but without any kind of toast. That would have been too much. Anni also drank. Afterward, she wiped her mouth with the back of her hand.

"You don't like me, do you?"

It was a silly question. They both knew the answer and it came curtly: "No, I don't like you. You are good at what you do and I can learn from you but I don't like you."

"Well, you aren't the only one. I've learned to live with it over time."

"In the best, most arrogant way."

"If you say so. I didn't come here to quarrel with you."

"Then why?"

"You have a really good source in the Homicide Division, isn't that true?"

"Did you really think that I would answer that question?"

"Please note that I have not asked who it is, only if you have one. But, all right, it's fairly easy to guess who it is so you don't have to say anything. I'll assume that is how it is."

"You have your own sources."

"Let's put that aside for the moment. What is your opinion on the pedophilia murders?"

"You already know."

"Come on, don't be so contrary. Give me the quick rundown."

"Sure. My employer is setting a new record low in appealing to vigilantism and mob rule. This witch hunt for child molesters is disgusting and we don't stop at anything to help make it worse. The politicians are lining up to express themselves in a suitably diluted manner so that the real message doesn't miss even the most ignorant voter. Five, six . . . ten, twenty, two hundred, one thousand, they are animals, not people, let us exterminate them. Where is it I've heard this before?"

This angered Anni against her will and also hurt a bit, which was an unfamiliar emotion. But the girl's historical parallel pierced her otherwise impervious surface. She took care, however, not to sound too upset.

"I'm not advocating violence, but I also am not going to stand for the rape of children. And definitely not for children being ordered as if they were consumer goods. I don't think even you can ignore that video?"

Anita made a gesture of helplessness. The discussion was futile.

"And how do you think we make our living? Have you taken a look at the latest sales figures?"

"No, I haven't. I've been reading stories about beatings and bands of thugs from across the entire country, but we'll probably choose to downplay those in tomorrow's paper, on account of space restrictions."

Irritation oozed out of her.

"Tell me, why don't you find another job?"

"How do you know I'm not looking?"

"I don't. Have you seen our new opinion poll? It was posted on the Web site yesterday."

"No, luckily."

"Question: *Do you truly wish that the pedophile crimes will be solved?* Do you want to take a guess?"

"I'd rather not."

"Sixty-four percent no, twenty-eight percent don't know, eight percent yes. We're putting it on the front page."

"That I can well imagine. We're feeding the dog its own bile."

"What do you mean?"

Anita did not answer immediately. She finished her beer first. It had disappeared alarmingly fast. An occupational hazard at such a young age. The self-reproach was exaggerated and she smiled a joyless little smile.

"It doesn't matter. Why don't you tell me what you want from me?"

"Your help. I've been thinking that the biggest problem for the police right now is public opinion. The Homicide Division doesn't just have an investigation to perform, it also has a PR problem. To put it another way—if they can't change public opinion, their job will get harder and harder and sooner or later they will realize this."

"And where do I enter this picture?"

"I want an exclusive interview with Konrad Simonsen."

"*You* do?"

"Yes, me. And it has to be with him, not one of the people

he shoves to the front when the public needs to be informed about something. If we can overcome our personal antipathy, this arrangement could be mutually beneficial."

Anni underscored her logic by tapping a finger on the table. She didn't mention that the idea had come in the mail from a reader. A couple of borrowed feathers wouldn't hurt. Anita was thinking it over and coming to the conclusion that her boss was right.

"And this is something that you want me to pass along? Why so complicated? Why don't you just call and ask him?"

"I'll think about that."

"Rubbish. You think fast. Tell me if you're going to do it or not."

The answer was arrogant and dismissive: "Maybe, maybe not. You'll find out."

Anita stood up. "Thanks for the beer."

Anni watched her leave.

"You're welcome, you little bitch."

CHAPTER 54

Selfish bitch."

Poul Troulsen snarled at Emilie Mosberg Floyd. Arne Pedersen and Pauline Berg glanced at him, then exchanged looks. This reaction wasn't like him. Normally he was calm and balanced—at least when he was among his colleagues—but the woman had apparently gotten under his skin.

All three of them were sitting in a narrow cubicle behind interrogation room 4 at the police headquarters in Copenhagen. The pane of glass between the two rooms filled most of one wall. On the other side it looked like a mirror, a standard arrangement in police stations around the world that allowed others to participate in the sessions without being seen or heard. This was at least how it was envisioned, but the concealed speakers that carried the sound were from the Stone Age so the acoustics were terrible and the voices took on a metallic and highly irritating echo. From time to time they dropped out entirely. The Countess's voice in particular was distorted. She sounded like a cartoon character. Being deeper, Konrad Simonsen's voice came through more intact.

Troulsen did not turn his head when he asked, "Aren't you two going somewhere?"

Berg stood up as if she had been given an order.

Pedersen asked, "Why are you so angry with her?"

"I don't really know. Maybe because I don't think for a moment that she was planning to turn to us if we hadn't found her. Maybe because I'm dead tired of this halfhearted cooperation from the public. In the best case. If it were up to me, we would simply replace people with a newer and better model, as the poet so excellently suggested to the powers that be. I haven't had such a tough time in my job since I stood guard at the American embassy during the Vietnam demonstrations in 1967. And a couple of hours ago I took it out on a greasy little bureaucrat at the Gentofte city hall, which irritates me and will probably give us an unnecessary and silly complaint."

Pedersen fell into a similarly despondent mood and started thinking about his own troubles. "I know what you're saying. On Friday one of my boys was bullied by his classmates because of my job, and now we have to go to a meeting at the school because he gave one of his tormentors a bloody nose. Normally

I try to teach my kids to handle things without violence but this time I made an exception and told him I was proud of him. I wish the pride went both ways. Unfortunately that's not the case right now, even though he doesn't say anything directly."

He could have added that he was also thoroughly tired of having to deliver tasty morsels from the investigation to the *Dagbladet*, just because a retired old crank had a feeling. But he said nothing about any of that.

"Why don't you ask to be switched to . . ."

Berg's comment was kindly meant. She was having problems, too. But their faces brought her to silence.

"And leave him all alone with this shit?" Troulsen's sweeping gesture toward Simonsen was almost reverent.

Pedersen stood up and pushed Berg along in front of him. He excused her inwardly, she was from another generation. Maybe less masochistic, maybe just a little dumber.

On the other side of the glass, the interrogation of Emilie Mosberg Floyd was proceeding well. She was cooperative. Without complaining, she repeated what she had already explained to Troulsen. She took her time in the telling, and tried to convey feelings or mood when asked. From time to time—if she found a question difficult—she thought long and hard. But there was nothing painful about these silences, and both Simonsen and the Countess waited patiently. So they were doing at the moment, even though the pause was unusually long. In return, she gave an extensive report.

"I really don't think that it's particularly relevant if he stopped drinking. Per was an alcoholic when I found him, there was no doubt about that. He only barely managed his job and was indifferent to everything. His life went to pieces when he lost Helene and he punished himself by destroying his health and his psyche. But the conversations between him and Jeremy had an effect. As I mentioned, I often picked him up in

Bagsværd and often drove him back again. Apart from at the beginning of this process, he was never drunk or even half drunk. How he managed in between these times I don't know. It could be two weeks at a stretch before we would see each other. That's why I can't tell you if he stopped drinking, but I can say definitely that he changed. He stopped being indifferent and became present, much more present."

She searched for the right words.

"And . . . what shall I say? . . . very clear. Per could be an exceptionally . . . electrifying person, almost dominating. No, not almost dominating, very dominating. And very intelligent in his own quiet way. It was as if he managed to be humble and arrogant at the same time. A rare characteristic. For better or for worse, Jeremy was very fascinated by him in the beginning and convinced him to tell his story to the other patients."

"Or was it the other way around?" the Countess asked.

"I don't understand."

She did not have a chance to elaborate, as Simonsen's next question trumped hers: "Did you and Per Clausen have a sexual relationship?"

Only years of training made it possible for the Countess to conceal her amazement. An amorous connection between this woman and the janitor was the last thing she would have imagined and the age difference alone made it rude to ask. And then there was the difference in lifestyle. To her great astonishment, Emilie Mosberg Floyd did not dismiss the thought out of hand, nor was she self-conscious in the least.

"No, not sexual, not in the traditional sense of the word. We have never been to bed with each other. Per would never have agreed to anything like that."

"But you had a relationship?"

"Yes, you could say that. We did."

For the first time during her questioning, the woman was

reticent, and the Countess sent silent thoughts of gratitude to her boss. When he was good, he was very good. The psychiatrist's weak link had obviously been his wife. This was beginning to make sense. She slipped in the next question: "When you drove him home, did you stay with him?"

"In the beginning we talked in the car. Later on we went into his place and talked, sometimes all night. Or I slept while he lay next to me. My marriage was very rocky at that time. My husband was always at work and he expected me to do everything at home. To top it off, he had other women on the side and he often took his vacation by himself. Per helped me. He told me which battles I should take on and when and which I should put aside until later. He consulted Jeremy, I consulted him, and in the end we all won. That is, before these . . . crimes occurred. Per died and the newspaper wrote all kinds of things about him. That was hard. I was frustrated and angry and sad at the same time, and I miss him so terribly, much more than I miss Jeremy, but I couldn't get away to go to his funeral so I had to settle for putting a bouquet on his grave the next day."

The Countess observed quietly, "Perhaps it was also because you had guessed at the connection and didn't wish to get involved."

Emilie Mosberg Floyd glanced at the tape recorder and managed a nod. They let it stay at that.

Simonsen said, "It's hard to imagine that the two of you never talked about how things were going with his therapy. The two of you, as well as your husband and you."

"We did but only a little. Per preferred to keep those two things separate. Jeremy did too. He hated the fact that I was talking with Per but he had no choice but to accept it. When I told him about it he was furious and threatened to stop Per's treatment but then for the first time I stood up for myself. I told him in that case I would take the children and leave. He backed down at that and it was my first victory. Later there were others."

"But from time to time his name must have come up."

"Yes, it did. When the one-on-one sessions between Jeremy and his patients were over he liked to place them in self-help groups. How long it took for a patient to be paired with that kind of group could vary a lot from case to case. It could be anything from six months to a year. Jeremy was very very careful about constructing groups that he thought would be successful, including taking geographic locations into account if he could. His patients often came from far away, some even from Jutland. A group usually consisted of four to six individuals and in the beginning they met with Jeremy under his direction. After a while they were supposed to continue on their own without him; they were—so to speak—kicked out of the nest, a process that took a couple of months but could also vary from group to group."

"And Per Clausen joined this kind of group?"

"That was the problem. I talked with Jeremy a couple of times about it. He had some reservations about ending Per's treatment in that way. For his part, Per very much wanted to join a group. He told me so at several different times and I put a lot of pressure on Jeremy to give him what he wanted."

She stared sadly out into the room, then parted with her last bit of information.

"Yes, I forced him to do it, I'm afraid, and Jeremy probably also wanted to be done with Per. Push him out of our lives, so to speak. It was hard for him to separate the personal and professional in Per's case."

"Why did he have reservations? Was it because Per Clausen had not been abused himself?"

"No, it was something else. In part he was afraid that Per would dominate the group and there was some ground for his apprehension. As I mentioned, Per had an incredible manipulative strength, but that wasn't the problem. It was more that Per . . . Per just hated pedophiles. With a red-hot, glowing hatred. We talked about Helene's stepfather once, that he was seriously ill. Per told me that and was overjoyed. I don't know where he had heard it. Another time there had been one of those terrible cases where a child had been killed. Per's reaction was pathological. Not that he seemed beside himself, it was more the opposite. He was very . . . controlled, and at the same time he managed to frighten me without really saying very much. It's difficult to explain. He was . . . I don't know how to explain so that you will understand. He was . . . creepy. It was a side of him I didn't like but perhaps it was his real self if we have something like that. Jeremy said once that there was not enough coal in the world to paint a true picture of Per's soul, but it was during an argument so he was exaggerating."

Neither of her listeners was convinced of this detail but both refrained from comment. On the other side of glass, Troulsen shook his head in vexation. Her story was substantially different from the one she had told only a short while ago.

Simonsen asked, "So the result was that Per Clausen joined a group?"

"Yes, he did, and Jeremy gathered together a group of people that he felt could offer Per a certain resistance, who had strong personalities themselves. The whole thing was quite an undertaking for him."

"But you never got the names? Either from your husband or Per Clausen?"

"No, no, I never did."

She hesitated.

There was something else and the Countess gave her the classic opening: "But . . ."

"But . . . there were some . . . some episodes. Per commented one time that one could say a lot about pedophiles but their victims spanned the social spectrum. Something like that, and then he added, *a nurse, a farmer, an advertising executive, a janitor, and a climber.* That was right after his group was formed."

"A climber. What did he mean by that?"

"I don't know. I wondered that myself when I had time to think it over. In that situation I figured he meant Jeremy, who was a mountain climber in his spare time, but he probably meant someone else. Per would hardly refer to Jeremy as a climber but paradoxically enough I think that that's the reason I can recall the phrase at all, indeed, that I can remember the order. Of course, I have no idea if he mentioned all of them."

"You never saw them?"

"Never, none of them, apart from Per, of course. He always came a little early and sat with me in the kitchen and had a cup of coffee. That is to say, those times when I didn't pick him up. After that he would go down to Jeremy. The others used the basement entrance."

The Countess let her arms fall helplessly to her side. The woman misunderstood this gesture and preassumed it indicated a lack of respect for the patient's right to anonymity. She suddenly sounded sharp and professional.

"A violation of anonymity at the wrong time can often mean the difference between success and failure in this kind of therapy. I don't think you really understand what sexual abuse in childhood does to people and how deeply it scars their souls. Did you know that some victims have to go to special dentists for the rest of their lives because they have such an intractable resistance to opening their mouths for others?"

This was a side of her they had not yet seen. It was the cardiologist commanding the nurse. The Countess didn't bother to explain herself, she simply apologized. That was the easiest. Simonsen brought the conversation back to the matter at hand.

"Is there anything else you can tell us about Per Clausen's group? Anything at all, regardless of what you think it means. You must understand that we are very interested in these five people."

"Yes, I do. There is one other thing. One of the members of the group was called Helle."

"The nurse?"

It was the Countess who made her second misstep in less than a minute.

"I guess that would be a rational choice, if you don't believe a woman can be a farmer or a climber, for that matter."

Simonsen hid a smile. The Countess did not try to cover her mistake.

"I'm sorry. Why don't you just go on and tell us."

"She had left a sweater in the basement and I was about to drive Per home. We were sitting in the kitchen when she rang the main doorbell. My oldest son opened the door and he couldn't have been more than three years old. I remember that he came to me proudly and said, *That one's name is Helle and it forgot its sweater.* Per and I smiled a bit at his words even though the meaning was clear. Jeremy may have heard it because he took over and so I never saw her."

She made one of her long pauses. They waited, but this time in vain as it turned out.

"Unfortunately there isn't anything else. At least nothing else that I can think of."

Simonsen shifted the conversation to more practical matters: "Your husband's archives?"

"I destroyed them after Jeremy died. I burned the files in our fireplace without looking at a single one. There were a couple hundred and it took several evenings. Before I did it I talked with some of his colleagues and they agreed it was the right thing to do."

"What about the accounts? How did your husband get paid by his patients?"

"Always cash, and always at the time of each appointment. He made a big production about the act of handing over physical bills. He felt it motivated his clients to make more of their sessions."

"You don't sound like someone who shares that view."

"It was his department, his practice, not mine. Personally, I suspect that part of this conviction stems to tax considerations or rather tax-avoidance considerations. At any rate we always had a lot of cash lying around. Sometimes Jeremy bought me expensive jewelry without any regard for the fact that I hate fussy accessories like that, and when he died I found almost six hundred thousand tucked away. Some of this was in our safe, but other packets of bills were spread in all kinds of places all around the house. It isn't very long since I found an envelope and I don't hesitate to call it pathological even though he was my husband. But before you get any ideas, I want you to know that I went to the tax authorities myself and after a long investigation they decided that I could keep the money."

The Countess and Simonsen nodded approvingly, although they didn't have the slightest intention of reporting her for tax evasion. Then they asked her half a dozen other questions without getting anywhere. The name Stig Åge Thorsen didn't mean anything to her and a picture of the man also got no response. They did learn that all of Jeremy Floyd's appointments were handled through the National Hospital, so any telephone records would be difficult to trace.

And that was that. They did not get further in this round. The interrogation had lasted for more than two hours and all three wished it would end. It fell to Konrad Simonsen to make that decision. After digging in vain into the woman's relationship with her younger sister and having ignored the Countess's pleading looks, he finally decided that enough was enough. He glanced at his watch, read the time aloud to the tape recorder, and formally concluded the session. The two detectives stood up. Emilie Mosberg Floyd remained seated.

"Have you stopped the tape?" The question was directed at Simonsen, who answered in the affirmative. "I have something that I'd like to tell you but that I don't want to have recorded."

They sat back down again.

"First I want to say—as strongly as I can—that I absolutely do not belong to the camp that claims it is a legitimate act to murder pedophiles. It isn't right either legally, morally, or in any other way, and I feel betrayed by Per even though I still love him. It's strange and it confuses me and I don't understand it, but there it is. And this even though I believe he was behind the burglary that took place in our house last March, and who may have planted the idea of Aconcagua with Jeremy. A mountain he was definitely not ready for, as I see in retrospect."

She struggled with her emotions and said straight out into the air, "Cerebral edema." Then she explained, "Acute mountain sickness."

Simonsen injected a soft, "The burglary."

"Yes, of course. I'll get there. So we were in Canada with Jeremy's brother when someone broke in and rifled through his files. The basement window and the filing cabinet had been forced open but there was nothing missing and we didn't report it, even though it weighed on Jeremy's mind. He talked about moving the files into his office but didn't get to it before he died. Per knew that we were going to Canada and as I said, I believe he was the one who was behind it."

"What do you think he wanted with the information?"

"What do you think yourself? It would have been an excellent place to start if he wanted to find followers—if I can put it that way—and remember that Jeremy had already introduced him to some of them. He wouldn't arrive as an unknowing stranger when he one day looked them up."

This time she was the one who stood up first. On the other side of the glass, Troulsen followed her example. He had an urgent need to go to the bathroom. On his way there he pounded his fist angrily against the doorframe. This time, however, his outburst was not directed to the woman but to her late husband. For careless, stupid, idiotic oversight of the storage of confidential materials.

CHAPTER 55

Like all nurses at the nursing home, Helle Smidt Jørgensen was an expert in counting pills. She had lined up all ten kinds in front of her: seven were taken out of bottles with screw tops, the three others were popped out of foil packets.

She pointed to the last three and explained to her student, "You're going to hate these. They'll cause permanent damage to the right thumb." The student looked down at her thumb as if she wanted to say goodbye to it. Helle Smidt Jørgensen added wearily, "It'll take a while. But now listen. First you take the tops off the dosing cases that are for fourteen days. Then you order them systematically with the morning pills first, then lunch, then dinner, then the sleep aids. That comes to twenty-two pills per day for Signe Petersen, so as you can see, if she isn't already sick the pills will do their best to make sure she does."

While she explained all this she herself started to feel ill.

She of all people shouldn't talk about substance abuse. The room grew fuzzy at the edges and her speech became incoherent.

". . . Sleeping aids and psychopharmaceuticals are alarmingly prevalent and have been so for years. It is dangerous to drink at the same time but I can't get through the day otherwise. Before it was only at night, but now it is also the voices in the hallways—that is if there is any police."

She focused on the student, who looked like she was far away and didn't quite understand. They never did. She explained patiently, "The pulse quickens and the hands shake. That is the stress hormone adrenaline that affects the sympathetic nervous system when you are hunted around the clock. All day, every day. Uncle at night and the police by day, you see. A little pick-me-up and an extra Stesolid takes the edge off. Around and around."

Something was wrong but she didn't know what. She left her office and walked unsteadily down the corridor and sat down on the back-entrance steps of the nursing home. Here she could get some fresh air and recover. The cool wind felt good on her forehead and a single ray of sun braved the gray weather and shone down on her. She inhaled deeply a couple of times and noticed that the world immediately grew smaller, as if anything other than sitting there were of no importance. An unfamiliar feeling came over her, a feeling that was faraway and now close-by. She was a child, she was playing ball, and it was important. *Karen, Maren, Mette bam, Anni, Anne, Anette bam, Kylle, Pylle, Rylle bam, Bente bam.* The rhymes were easy, also the new one: *Alekto, Megaira, Tisifone bam, Nemesis bam,* but it was hard to aim the balls. Especially overhand. From time to time she dropped one and had to start from the beginning. That was the rule. She did so, determined to get as good as the big girls. A ball fell from her hands and she had to make every effort to find it, so she opened her eyes and looked. There were people around her, people who wished her well.

She explained that they shouldn't worry and that everything was going to be all right. They understood. Of course they did, it was easy to understand. It was also easy to swim once you had learned how. She could swim without water wings, proudly, alongside her mother. She loved it when they were at the Østerbro pool just the two of them and of course a whole lot of other people that they didn't know. She ventured away but lost her courage when a big boy of about ten came swimming toward her. It was hard to turn but she managed it. Then she heard the voice ring out across the hall: all the yellow bands out! That was them. They had yellow bands on, a yellow piece of elastic with a key to the locker around her ankle. She made an angry face at her mother, then they kissed and smiled because as they did this they had to struggle to stay afloat. Then they slowly swam to the edge.

CHAPTER 56

In the Homicide Division at police headquarters in Copenhagen, the mood was bleak.

The minister of justice was speaking on the radio. He was well known for his flamboyant expressions and airy turns of phrase but this Monday he set a new record. Among other things because his interviewer served mainly to offer helpful cues for his monologue. Malte Borup looked around in vain for a translation. When he didn't get one, he found a pencil and paper and disappeared into his own world of cryptic characters and signs. The interview ended not long after that and the host announced the next program.

Pedersen turned off the radio while Troulsen most eloquently gave voice to the general attitude in the room: "Populist asshole."

Konrad Simonsen's cell phone rang; it was Helmer Hammer. Simonsen withdrew to the most remote corner of the room. At the same time, Pedersen felt compelled to make derogatory comments about the minister of justice.

"Sentence by sentence it's nothing but hot air, but the under-lying message is clear enough. *Govern by public taste. Tighten the laws to prevent the general public's justifiable anger. Return to a familiar chain of command so that ordinary people can get their police back.* What a bastard, is all I have to say."

Troulsen added, sneering, "*Children who are bought as if they were laundry detergent. We have all seen it and we are horrified.* He really knows how to talk, that swine. And not a word about the five murders that followed. Someone needs to get him to shut up."

The Countess and Pedersen shook their heads helplessly and Berg stared down at the floor.

Simonsen returned and related the details of his conversation with the chief.

"The minister of justice is speaking for himself, and his suggestion that we should return to the usual chain of command is completely without any foundation. If it were to happen, it would have no impact anyway. I have reported to both the police director and the national chief of police as I want to. The idea behind a special group isn't ours and will be viewed as a political stunt to signal to the public that extraordinary measures are being applied in this case. Mass murders are not an everyday event after all, and thank goodness for that."

Pedersen asked skeptically, "Did Helmer Hammer really say that?"

"No, it's my elaboration. He did, however, say that lawmakers have launched into debates regarding the current sentences for child abuse and that these may become more severe. The minister of justice and some of his cronies have put feelers out and this idea has been well received in the other parties. Most shy away from a quick-fix approach. At this time. But this doesn't really concern us. We are going to continue our work and under no conditions comment on the political dimension. This applies mainly to myself. I was under a de facto muzzle, and now that is doubly the case."

The Countess shook her head. "I don't like working for such a fair-weather man." These were strong words coming from her. She mostly only spoke well of people.

Simonsen stopped and stood in the middle of the group, broad-legged and powerful. "And you don't. You work for me, and for democracy. If you are unhappy with the composition of our government, you can join a political party."

He would have liked his words to be more carefully chosen. Touch on something that united them, but he didn't know what that would be. And for that matter, how much did they even have the right to expect? He was neither a politician nor a minister. He stayed with what was down-to-earth, throwing his arms up in an awkward gesture and saying, "And we shouldn't forget that it has been quite a productive day. We have definitely gotten new solid information to dive into. Especially with regard to our interrogation of Stig Åge Thorsen tomorrow. I don't yet know who is going to do it, probably it will be the Countess and me, but I want all of you to be extremely well prepared. In return, Arne and I will finish the television work by ourselves. We spent too long on it last time. I'll be a little late tomorrow morning by the way, as I have a meeting. I may be able to secure an alternative and more reliable supplier for telecommunications data, which might be a good thing considering how maddeningly slow our official sources are right now. And then finally one last thing . . ."

He made short pause before he went on.

"As something tells me that our favorable resource situation will not last forever, I would like to invite all present to a fine and thunderingly expensive dinner with the state as the host, while I still can. And it will be a pleasure for me to send a copy of the check to the iron lady at the *Dagbladet*. Is anyone interested?"

The Countess accepted. Troulsen said no; he had been ignoring a flu with the end result that he was deadly tired and just wanted to go home and rest. Pedersen also had to pass. The following evening, he and Simonsen were to have dinner with Kasper Planck, which could not be mentioned in current company, but to spend two evenings that were not a professional necessity away from his family was simply not possible. A single event was hard enough to defend. Then there was Pauline Berg and Malte Borup, but for once Berg turned out to be quick on the uptake.

"Not us either. Malte has promised to take a look at my home computer. It's been acting up and I need to have it fixed."

Borup glanced up briefly from his formulas when he heard his name. As usual he didn't understand anything. Not even enough to make him blush.

CHAPTER 57

The girl was sitting on a chair in the middle of the studio and looked like an angel. She was dressed in a simple peasant blouse of light-colored linen. She wore no jewelry except for an amber necklace that gleamed like summer on her white throat. Golden curls floated around her picture-perfect face but her clear eyes shone with life and were entrancing at first gaze. Natural as a dream, clean and pure, perfect, if one remembered to disregard her fashionably worn, tight jeans and sexy black leather boots. As the camera did.

Erik Mørk couldn't look away, she drew his gaze like a dew-kissed flower.

The director was giving orders. Without looking directly at the girl, he focused on an oversize TV monitor on the back wall, where her upper half appeared. He gave instructions to the cameraman and interviewer: "We'll run through that part about the abuse again."

The girl grumbled, "It's at least the tenth time."

"It's only the sixth and you are good, really good, but you can be even better. It only needs to be the beginning. The rest of it is fantastic. Are you ready?"

"Okay, okay, but that will be it."

Her face changed in an instant from raw to sweet. The director said, "Start from: 'You were yourself abused as a child.'"

The interviewer echoed this, but with the appropriately emotional tone: "You were yourself abused as a child?"

She looked down and did not answer. Two tears ran down her cheeks but she still did not say anything and her silence screamed into the camera. Then she straightened her head and wiped her face. Her first sentence was hesitant. Searching and unsure.

"Yes, I was abused when I was a child."

Thereafter her voice grew clearer and steadier and took on a slightly questioning tone.

"Abused—abused is what you call it. It sounds like I was forced to deliver newspapers without getting paid. That is what adults call it."

She now sounded loud and clear. Accusatory but not hysterical or aggressive.

"I was raped. From when I was nine until I was fourteen I was raped. A lot—it was a good week if I was raped less than three times and it went on month after month, year after year. That is why I have agreed to do this today and it is because the fate of the victims interests me far more than the perpetrators."

"And you think this will help?"

She overheard the question. It was the third time Mørk had heard the passage but it was as effective and strong as the first. Despair and helplessness passed over her pretty face.

"You should see my brother. He couldn't manage it, he's very sick today and they don't have space for him at the clinic."

The desire to hold her came over him. Just to hold her close for a moment, to comfort and protect her. He rejected the thought as absurd but unconsciously advanced a couple of steps.

The interviewer let her take a moment without injecting a new question. When she spoke again she was more collected and her voice was lower.

"Where were the grown-ups when I needed them most? Where was my mother? My family? My teachers? The counselors? All of the people who were supposed to be watching out for me . . ."

She jerked her head around and spoke directly into the camera.

The director jumped in: "Okay, cut. We're going to have to practice that turn a couple of times before it looks spontaneous. It's too quick."

The girl said sourly, "It was too slow before."

"Yes, and now, as I said, it is too fast. And I'd like it if you would be a tad less accusatory, perhaps with a note of uncertainty. Give yourself more time, so you don't sound as if you're reciting. Can you manage all that at once?"

Mørk had trouble imagining what he meant. Until he watched the girl and then he saw it. She came through that part with bravado and was allowed to keep going.

"Where were you then? And where are you now? Why do you allow pedophilic associations? Why is there a more severe punishment for adult rape than for the rape of a minor? Why—"

"Thanks, thanks, that was great," the director interrupted her.

The girl straightened and her expression changed to nothing. "What do I do if I'm interrupted?"

"You won't be, but there's a little detail . . ."

"Damn, you go on and on."

"I'd like you to seem a little bit more upset when you talk about your brother."

"I can blubber when I talk about him."

There was a pause. The interviewer left the studio. The girl, the cameraman, and the director walked over to Mørk.

The director said, "She's the most phenomenal talent I've ever worked with. She can blush like virtue itself, she can cry and touch the heart of a debt collector, her smile can coax the sun out of a winter night, her phrasing, her tone, her appearance—she has the whole package, and then on top of that she's a quick study." He spoke as if the girl weren't there.

Mørk agreed: her media potential was world class. In spite of this he felt a twinge of concern.

"But what she's saying, is that also, is that . . . what happened to her?"

"Happened? I don't know what you mean."

"Did it happen in reality?"

The director walked away. Mørk stared after him in bewilderment and then he asked the cameraman, "Why did he leave? Is he upset about something?"

"Don't worry about him, he's a little eccentric. There are words he can't tolerate, but we're lucky to have someone of his caliber. He's fabulous."

Mørk nodded, as if he understood.

The man went on: "You should read his book sometime. *In the global village, the camera is god*, or, *Everyone steps on beetles, not ladybugs*. Those are two of his most famous sayings."

"Well, there might be something in that."

"Something in that—you don't get it, do you?"

"No, probably not."

The man held out a packet of cigarettes. He offered them to the girl, who shook her head without answering, then he took out a single cigarette and tucked it behind his ear while he searched his pockets for a lighter.

"Did you see that mother yesterday? In the ruins of the housing block? It was on CNN."

Mørk nodded, he had seen some of that segment.

"She was completely fucked up. Her getup alone was a disaster. Black coveralls, neglected skin, and eyebrows like a pony's mane, and maybe you remember how much she howled? She complained so much the subtitles had trouble keeping up, rocking back and forth, waving her arms and legs and rolling her eyes like a wounded chimney sweep. The truth is she messed up her only chance. People have embarrassed themselves by the million, and where do you think her dead children are now? Zapped all the way into oblivion."

He lit his cigarette and went on: "You asked about what had happened, but what's happened is about the future, not about the past. That's why we practice."

Mørk could see the logic of this. Of course the cameraman was right.

"I understand. It just felt . . . I don't know . . . a bit underhanded."

"Aren't you in advertising?"

"Yes, I am."

"Then what's the problem? She was already fantastic and we make her brilliant. She'll be styled so it doesn't look like she's wearing any makeup but that'll happen the day after tomorrow, when it's for real. You'll get a couple of exclusive shots for your Web site. Black-and-white, I think, she likes that most. And then just wait until you see the final product. You're going to love it."

The girl stood at their side and looked bored stiff. Suddenly she said, "Tell me, did you leave your brain at home? Per Clausen told me you were smart. Of course I have to practice. Didn't you practice the part about your dead sister?"

"How do you know about that?"

"What do you think? Because I was there when you talked about her. Well, did you practice or not?"

"Yes, but . . . that was different."

She gave up on him with a shrug and tossed an impatient question into the studio.

"Can't we get on with it, I'm about to go crazy with this Stone Age talk."

CHAPTER 58

Konrad Simonsen stopped in Østerport Station, bought a cup of coffee, and retreated to one of the tables at the very back of the cafeteria. The morning had started well and ended terribly. The evening with the Countess had been fantastic. They had promised each other to go out again soon, and he had woken up in a great mood with a delicious feeling in his body. He had even sung in his bath, which he had not done for years. Then, just as he was about to walk out the door, the mail arrived and his world was shattered.

The letter was from Per Clausen: a yellow A4-size envelope, postmarked in Fredericia yesterday and containing six fuzzy pictures of Anna Mia. One where she was seen leaving her building, a second where she was unlocking her bicycle, and a third, where she was biking toward the photographer. Then there were two lines of a psalm, the contents of which Simonsen knew all too well: *Though death may enter in the night, you come with the morning light.* A thousand thoughts jostled in his mind while fear churned in his stomach and sweat beaded his brow. The papers fell out of his hand and he sat down on the floor in their midst, gradually starting to overcome his panic attack and forcing his thoughts in a more realistic direction. The day before, Anna Mia had gone to Bornholm to visit a friend who had just had a baby, so she was not in any immediate danger. Common sense also told him that the letter's thinly veiled threat was meant to trouble him rather than to be taken literally. A cool and measured conclusion that his body had initially refused to accept. Only slowly did he regain enough control to order his thoughts. How could Per Clausen know that Anna Mia was his daughter? Or where she lived? Was he being watched? Had the newspapers last Tuesday written about his and Anna Mia's interrupted holiday? Was there another explanation? These questions could not be answered as he sat there, and that added to his feeling of impotence. But he managed to quell them until another emotion slowly took over and got him back on his feet. Then he was able to muster the strength to compartmentalize the incident and put it aside. When he finally managed to pull himself together to leave, his exterior showed no signs of turmoil but inside he experienced a white-hot personal hatred with an intensity he had never before felt.

Simonsen's thoughts about the morning's events meant that he did not notice the person he was waiting for before he turned up at his side. He locked up his foul mood inside and greeted him in a friendly way.

"Good morning."

The man was well dressed in a conservative way. His tie testified to his managerial position. He was middle-aged but his almost-bald head and his slightly stooped posture made him appear older than he was. His voice was toneless.

"Good morning, Inspector, or whatever it is that you are now."

"It was nice of you to come."

The man flashed a sarcastic smile. "Did I have a choice?"

"This isn't an interrogation. In fact, I want to ask you a favor."

"When the police ask for a favor they usually have a solid threat in their back pocket."

"Not this time. What I want to ask you pushes at the limits of the law, so if you don't want to help me our friendship won't suffer."

"So we're friends?"

It was a reasonable question. To call their loose connection "friendship" was to take liberties with the meaning of that word. He had on several occasions played chess with the man in a couple of open tournaments but had not seen him other than that after he had interrogated him and later witnessed against him in court some twelve years ago now. Simonsen said thoughtfully, "No, of course we are not. That came out wrong and you'll have to excuse it. We are not *friends*."

He drank some of his coffee. It was already cold. For a split second he considered divulging his frustration with the social stigma that clung to those who had served time. That only created more criminality and was unreasonable. If you asked him, the slate ought to be wiped clean when a person had served his sentence, but he kept this to himself and said, "Perhaps you could tell me how things are going for you?"

The man answered haltingly and with some reluctance, "Things are as they are. I go to my treatments, I take my medicine, I never interact with children, I don't look at pictures, I don't watch movies, and I don't like magazines."

"I know that. I've checked up on you as much as I've been able but that wasn't what I meant. I meant, how things are going in a more general sense."

The man looked at him in surprise. Then he answered, "Well, in general things aren't going particularly well now that you've put it so directly. I mostly keep to myself, watch some television, sometimes go to the theater, read books to get the time to pass. The weekends are long, as are holidays. Weekdays are better. I do have my work." He stared down at the table. "I miss my boys terribly. Every single day. They are both adults now but I never see them, and that's understandable."

Simonsen found it hard to answer. "It is understandable," he said.

"Yes, yes, of course it is." The man looked up. His pain was fully apparent. "Thank you for asking. Tell me, what is it that I can help you with?"

"Tell me first what you think about the current pedophilia debate."

"*Debate.* Well, I guess that's one way to put it."

"I couldn't find a better word."

"The truth is that I am afraid but there isn't much I can do except keep my head down and wait until it dies down."

Simonsen nodded sympathetically and then explained his errand: "I don't have a good alternative channel for quick information about telephone calls. You know, who is calling whom, where and for how long—but I have no warrants, and if I did, the risk in the current climate is that one or another unfortunate error will end up affecting the very data that I am after. So I don't dare to put pressure on our official sources and my unofficial ones have dried up."

He had the Countess's word for that last part. Under normal circumstances, she was able to find telecommunications information in the wave of a hand.

"That doesn't surprise me."

"It can end up being quite a lot. Will you help me? And are you able to help me?"

"I think I can, yes. I have a colleague who has security responsibility for our switches and he has free access to all of our databases including the old backup tapes. I have to speak with him first, but I'm fairly certain that he will agree. Even if my past would end up . . . coming out."

"Are you nervous about that?"

"Tell me, weren't you even listening?"

Simonsen thought that it was starting to be a pattern that people asked him that question. He didn't answer. Instead he took an envelope out of his pocket and fished a card out of his wallet. He wrote on it.

"Here, take this. My private number is written on the back. The envelope contains a list of things that we would like to have cleared up, and the truth is that time is of the essence, but I understand that you can't perform magic. Call me when you have spoken with your friend and also call if you run into any problems."

The man took the materials. He stuck the card into his inner pocket and put the envelope in his briefcase.

"Will you find the one who slaughtered those people?"

"Oh yes, I will. I shall find them. Each and every one. If not today then tomorrow or next week or next year, but at some point I will find them and with a little luck it'll go fast."

"I'm hoping it'll be sooner than later, so this hatred dies down a little." He didn't sound particularly confident, more like he was saying an incantation.

They walked together for a while and then shook hands before they parted.

CHAPTER 59

Pauline Berg argued enthusiastically for her case and Simonsen let her speak her mind. Only when she started to repeat herself did he stop her and summarize her points without indicating if he agreed or not.

"You claim that Stig Åge Thorsen is afraid of women, or more precisely of intimate contact with women of his own age group, and you are suggesting that we should take advantage of this presumed aversion during his interrogation, which can only mean that you yourself should be the interrogator even though objectively speaking you are the least qualified of us all. And your suggestion comes less than two hours before we are planning to start, based on a ten-minute conversation with someone who got to know the man during a cruise to Greece. Is this correct?"

The youngest member of the Homicide Division stuck to her guns: "Yes, it is."

"The woman from the cruise called of her own accord, so we have no basis from which to judge the truthfulness of her information. Is that also correct?"

"Yes, we don't know anything for certain."

"Go on."

"Me and the Countess should handle the interrogation and we should also move the furniture around in the room so that it is more intimate. All of us should sit closer together."

Arne Pedersen stared up at the ceiling. Simonsen, however, nodded approvingly. Not in favor of the suggestion—he had not yet formed his final opinion on that—but over her determination. He said, "Am I also shut out?"

Berg became vague and answered indirectly: "The woman from his vacation told me about the same signs that I have often noticed in men who have been nervous—or even afraid—of me. These reactions are particularly typical of men who had an insecure childhood, or so I've read. Which fits nicely with the fact that Stig Åge Thorsen sought help from Dr. Jeremy Floyd."

Pedersen looked at her with some astonishment. This was truly a new side of Berg that he did not know. She did not return his gaze but kept her focus on Simonsen, while he watched the irregular path of the raindrops down the outside of the office windows. Her self-confidence was at its peak.

Last night she had turned up—unannounced and

sobbing—at Kasper Planck's home. Her bad conscience about having lied to the Countess about her conversation at the Gudme Sport Complex café tore at her insides. Finally she couldn't stand it anymore and went to see the former head of the Homicide Division, who she thought was the only person who could understand her.

The old man gave her a handkerchief and listened calmly. Afterward he laid a wrinkled hand on her head and said softly, "I think you will be forgiven. Why would you go unaffected when so many have been drawn into this madness? There are many people who don't even want us to find the killers, if one is to believe the media."

"But what about Frank Ditlevsen's friend? One of his old boys. That is an important piece of information. I should have shared that a long time ago."

"Let Simon figure it out for himself. He should have done so already anyway."

"How could he do that? He can't know about it."

"Of course he can. The murder of the brothers was personal. Frank Ditlevsen was hanged in the middle of the event and Allan Ditlevsen was Mr. Extra—an excellent and meaningful choice of words. And the personal always comes from somewhere."

Berg gaped. "How long have you known this?"

"Known—bah. It's still a kind of thought-play but I have a meeting later this week that should cast some light on the situation. So we shall see. Time will tell. But come over here. There's something I want to give you."

The old man drew a box out of the deep interior of a mahogany bureau. He held up a necklace, a fish of gold, very pretty, the chain simple and light.

"It belonged to my wife. Now it is yours."

"But . . ."

312

He held a finger up to his mouth, and she stopped. Then she put it on. It fell elegantly over her throat and was hardly noticeable. As if she had always worn it.

"This is wonderful, but . . ."

The finger across the mouth again. Her spirit felt relieved and lightened and her tears this time were of joy. She borrowed the handkerchief a second time and when she composed herself she asked, "You give and give—isn't there anything I can do for you?"

Planck's face lit up. "You can water my flowers, they need it so badly."

Berg smiled at the thought of her round with the watering can under the direction of the old man, and that clinched the matter. Simonsen decided that when it came to the matter of men's nervousness, he was sitting across from an expert.

"The Countess is the primary driver in this and your role is to assist. I will only make the final decision when the Countess has also talked to this vacation flirtation and agreed with your suggestion. And then one more thing, Pauline."

He looked directly into her eyes.

"If you make one wrong move, or if the Countess needs more help, you will immediately be replaced and I don't want to hear any griping about it afterwards. Understood?"

"Completely, and I appreciate this vote of confidence. I think it is a reasonable decision."

"It's not a decision yet. You only have two hours with the Countess, use the time wisely."

She did. She was out before Pedersen had time to stand up.

Stig Åge Thorsen and his lawyer arrived on time and that Berg had interpreted the situation correctly was revealed early on. The witness apparently did not appreciate being in close proximity to two women, and especially the close contact with the younger woman appeared to embarrass him. He basically whipped his hand back when Berg warmly and kindly laid her hand on his as she greeted him. Simonsen and Pedersen were sitting behind the mirror. Simonsen said, "She's right. Did you see that? It's obvious if you're looking for it. See how he pulls back. He may not even be aware of it himself. His lawyer is not, at any rate."

In the interrogation room, the Countess was gesturing and explaining something to the lawyer.

"Please have a seat. As you can see, we have had to rearrange the furniture in here temporarily but I think we can manage."

They had in all haste managed to get hold of a relatively small square table with a chair placed on each of the four sides so that Berg would be able to sit close to Stig Åge Thorsen regardless of which chair the lawyer chose.

Simonsen commented with enthusiasm, "It's brilliant."

Arne Pedersen asked half sulkily, "What happened with the television program anyway? Weren't they going to come today?"

"It's been postponed for the moment, whatever consequences that may have. There was apparently some other programming that was more important but hold your peace for a moment and we'll follow this."

The next half hour was tough for Stig Åge Thorsen. His well-rehearsed defensive postures were of only marginal help and the Countess drove him around the ring with strikes from all angles.

"Your car was in an accident on the eighteenth of November 2003, when someone drove into it parked on Lille Strandvej in Gentofte. What were you doing there?"

He had never been in Gentofte. He pushed back a copy of the accident report. It must be a misunderstanding.

"Who paid for your cruise to Greece? Was it the same stranger?"

He wavered, could not recall, refused to answer, and finally claimed that he had been saving up for the trip for many years.

"In April you turned to Frederiksværk Stålvalseværk and bought a pile of coal that the factory had lying around in the old commercial port. What were you going to do with it?"

It was nice to have on hand. He had ended up using it to burn the minivan, but that had not been planned.

"How was your childhood? Your old teacher from the Kregme School said that you had a difficult childhood. Is that true?"

He had had a normal childhood, a perfectly one-hundred-percent-normal childhood, and the teacher was crazy, a demented old fool.

"You attacked a woman on the beach in Saloniki. What happened there?"

The lawyer jumped in at this point but the accusation had effect. Stig Åge Thorsen looked like a whipped dog.

The Countess went on and on, jumping from subject to subject, poking here, then there, bringing up things that had him on the ropes only to return to them ten minutes later with double the intensity, and soon the farmer started to show small signs of mental fatigue. Tripping over a sentence, a finger rubbing an eye, a twitch at his temple, anger, irritation, and then carelessness. After the dress rehearsal she drove it home.

"Do you know Jeremy Floyd?"

"I've never heard of him."

"I can get him in and pick you out of a lineup. Is that what you want?"

Berg stepped in. She had said nothing to this point. Now she carefully opposed the Countess: "But, but he is . . ."

The Countess waved her away. "I know that he is a

315

psychiatrist, but his professional vows of silence don't mean anything in a homicide case such as this one. So, Mr. Thorsen, should I arrange a face-to-face meeting?"

Berg insisted, "But, but . . ."

"Not now," the Countess snapped. The lawyer was perplexed, and Stig Åge Thorsen took the bite.

"He's dead, so you can't arrange anything."

"Hm, well, I guess that changes things a bit. It surprises me that . . ."

Simonsen's smile was wide and self-congratulatory. "He didn't even realize he was contradicting himself."

Pedersen answered, "Nor his lawyer. He's just sitting there like a sphinx. He's not much help."

"Don't be fooled by his posture. He's good. I know him. But you are right, it seems as if he doesn't want to do more than he absolutely has to."

A quarter of an hour later, the Countess decided that the time was right. She leaned forward and placed her arms on the table.

"The twenty thousand kroner that you were given by your stranger—you in turn donated them via the Internet to an Indian help organization called Sanlaap. Why that particular organization?"

Stig Åge Thorsen had apparently been expecting this question.

"I think I had seen it advertised on TV but I am not sure. Maybe it was a coincidence, I don't know." He crossed his arms. The subject was finished as far as he was concerned.

But not as far as Berg was concerned. She leaned toward him.

"Sanlaap operates out of Bombay or, to be more specific, the world's largest bordello neighborhood, Kamthipura. There are two hundred thousand women and children for sale there.

Down to seven years of age. The children are kept as sex slaves in dilapidated whorehouses and typically they have to serve fifteen to twenty customers a day. A large number of them come from Kathmandu, in Nepal, where they were kidnapped by various means by slave traders and brought across the border to India, where they are sold for use in bordellos. The first couple of weeks the children are beaten to shreds or outright tortured until they break down and cooperate in their new profession. When they are not being raped, they are hidden away by madams in small, dark places like crawl spaces or lofts so that the police won't find them. Or else the police will demand to get their share of the profits. Most of the girls are HIV positive. They receive no treatment and develop AIDS. Many also get pregnant and raise their babies under unspeakably horrible conditions."

She spoke slowly and clearly, directly to Stig Åge Thorsen. He had pushed himself as far away from her as the chair allowed but could not escape her gaze. When she finished, he answered her without taking into account that she had not asked him anything.

"Yes, it is terrible, and the world couldn't care less."

The Countess cut him off. Her tone was accusatory and as sharp as a razor.

"You give money to Sanlaap in order to relieve your conscience, don't you? You were treated by Jeremy Floyd because you can't keep your fingers away from little children. Isn't that right?"

The lawyer reacted angrily: "What is this?"

But Stig Åge Thorsen's reaction was even more violent. His outburst was loud, almost screaming: "No, no, it's the opposite. I was the one. They hurt me."

Berg also raised her voice, also infuriated with the Countess. "You completely misunderstand. He doesn't do children any harm. Haven't you understood a single thing?" She laid a protective hand on the man's arm.

The Countess did not attempt to hide her disagreement with her colleague.

"For heaven's sake, he was in the behavioral-treatment group with the janitor Per Clausen and with the nurse, Helle . . . Helle . . . oh, what was her name again?"

She snapped her fingers a couple of times, happening also to turn briefly to Stig Åge Thorsen in her search for the name, and then the miracle occurred.

"Jørgensen, Helle Smidt Jørgensen, but we were the ones who had been . . ." But he did not get any further. The lawyer had finally realized what was going on and he effectively stopped the session by placing a hand over his client's mouth.

"This has gone far enough, ladies, more than far enough. I don't even have words to describe what this is."

He was furious. He said into the room in a loud, formal voice, "Let it be known that I am holding my hand over my client's mouth and also strongly advising him to discontinue this interrogation."

Then he stood and more or less heaved up Stig Åge Thorsen with him while shielding him from the two women. He turned to the mirror and said, "This is psychological terror, Simon. Get in here."

Simonsen got up heavily to his feet. "I guess I'll have to go in and pour oil on the water. Did you catch that name, Arne?"

"Nurse Helle Smidt Jørgensen."

"Find her. It can't be done quickly enough."

CHAPTER 60

The Countess caught up with her boss after the interrogation of Stig Åge Thorsen, waiting patiently for fifteen minutes so that he would not slip past her. She pounced on him as soon as he had said goodbye to the lawyer.

"Simon, we have to talk."

Simonsen turned, somewhat perplexed. Her tone was insistent, not to say sharp. He brushed her off as gently as he could: "I'm sorry, Countess, but it will have to wait. I'm on my way to a briefing with the chiefs and after that . . ."

She grabbed his hand and drew him into his own office. To his amazement, he followed without protest and obeyed when she commanded, "Sit down."

She remained standing at his side. He glanced up at her and asked, "What in the world?"

"It's not about me, it's about you."

"What do you mean?"

"I mean that as soon as you have ten seconds of respite you are a hundred miles away. Don't try to talk your way out of this. Just tell me what's happened."

It was more her hand on his shoulder than her words that made him give way. He opened his desk drawer and handed her the envelope from the morning. Then he got up and went up to the window with his back to her. After a while he heard her sit down in his chair, then there was silence for an eternity, until her arm was suddenly around him.

She said quietly but clearly, "What have you done about this?"

Simonsen didn't answer. His words died in his mouth, as he became acutely aware of a sweet-and-sour taste in his mouth. It came without warning and reminded him of the sour hard candy from his childhood, the kind that you could buy from the shop woman on the main street for five øre apiece, or was it two? He couldn't quite remember the price, only that strong, clear taste of lemon and sugar that filled the entire mouth and lingered long after the candy was gone. Like now.

The taste memory frightened him but the images that followed were worse. For a short moment he saw Anna Mia hanging from the end of a long rope. Her arms and legs twitching uncontrollably in death throes and her eyes on him, pleading in vain. The vision lasted no more than a second, then hatred took over and he nodded in time to the devilish impulses that crowded into his brain in order to be tasted one by one. A smashed knee cap or a couple of broken thumbs or, even better—a sharp kick to the back of the head while his victim lay on his stomach and had to howl into the curb. That's how it should be. No one was going to threaten his daughter. . . . He made a fist and hit it against the flat of the other hand. Once, twice, many times in small movements so as not to shake off the Countess's arm.

She repeated her question and brought him back to reality: "Simon, what have you done about this?"

"Anna Mia is with her mother in Bornholm. Don't you have any licorice? You usually have those Gojler. Perhaps you could give me some. Or water."

"How long will she be there?"

"Who?"

"How long will Anna Mia be in Bornholm?"

"Until Friday, I think."

"Have you talked to her?"

"No."

"Or with anyone else?"

"Only with you."

They stood there awhile longer until Simonsen's phone rang and he reluctantly broke away. The Countess sat down across from him and listened approvingly as he delayed his meeting by fifteen minutes, without apology or excuses.

He pointed to the envelope she was holding and asked, "What would you do?"

She answered casually, as if the question were not of great significance; "Only the regular precautions, Simon."

"I can do those myself."

"No, I'll do it. But there's nothing to be nervous about. It's clear the letter was only sent to unnerve you."

"Yes, isn't it? I have also received all kinds of threats."

"Of course. You shouldn't put any stock in those."

"I think it's because I took Pauline with me to his interrogation. That is, Per Clausen's, you know, in relation to his daughter. So it may be a kind of revenge for that. Well, you know what I mean."

"Yes, of course I do. But now you should get along to your briefing and stop worrying about this anymore."

Simonsen nodded and the Countess hurried out of the office with the envelope. When the door closed behind her, he at once felt sleepy.

CHAPTER 61

Anita Dahlgren was no virtuoso in the kitchen so she kept to what was tried and true. An appetizer of shrimp cocktail with garlic bread, for the main course filet mignon accompanied by baked potatoes and parsley butter, served with a pitcher of béarnaise sauce as well as a mixed salad with feta and olives. Dessert was simply vanilla ice cream. Even she could not go wrong with this menu.

Simonsen praised her for at least the fifth time: "This tastes fantastic."

Pedersen added smilingly, "Yes, well done, Planck."

Planck ignored this comment and said seriously, "I haven't just invited you for the pleasant company. I've been thinking about an idea that I want us to talk about, but first you should know that I won't be coming in to HS anymore. I haven't been doing so well as of late and I don't have the strength to visit you anymore."

The atmosphere deflated somewhat. The old man looked around briefly at everyone in the room.

"Don't look so glum. I never planned to get a hundred years old and don't you dare start crying. Anita, dry your eyes—I'm not going to pop off tomorrow."

"Sorry, I'll stop. I've just grown so fond of you."

"As I have of you, my girl. Let's clear the table together while these two gifted gentlemen ponder a little riddle. Our friend with the chainsaw—what was it we were calling him, Simon?"

Simonsen did not reply immediately. He was looking at Anita. Planck noticed this.

"Tonight Anita is part of the discussion."

"Hmm, if you say so. We're calling him *Climber*."

"Climber. An excellent name. What is this Climber's greatest weakness?"

The old man and the young woman stood up and went out to the kitchen together. Anita started to wash the dishes and Planck passed her a new stack from time to time. After a while he said, "Do you also want to guess?"

"No, but I really want to hear the answer."

"The answer is his image. It's very banal of course, but also very important."

She reflected on this and said, "Yes, that's true. The part about his image. Do you think that they'll get it?"

"Simon will, Arne won't. He doesn't think simply enough. And he expends his mental energy on things that he can't control. This whole evening he hasn't talked about anything other than that nurse, so he won't come up with it."

"You're always so sure of yourself."

"Wait and see."

Planck was right. They came back into the room with coffee and cups, and while Anita was still passing them around, Pedersen threw in the towel.

"I'm coming up with nothing. I want to say his childhood but in part I don't really know if that's true and if it is, it hasn't shown itself as a weakness so far, that is, in relation to what he has done. Then I was thinking that we believe that he knew the Ditlevsen brothers back when they lived in Sjælland, but that also isn't a weakness, or is that the connection that you had in mind?"

His contribution was kindly overlooked. Everyone was looking at Simonsen, who was smiling and taking his own sweet time. He wasn't experiencing his usual sweat attack after dinner and he had already answered Planck's question, so what more could an overweight, slightly arrogant former homicide chief ask for? He said, cheerfully, "You mean his statement to the media, don't you?"

"Bingo, Simon, that's exactly what I mean. And what happens if we threaten him with a couple of solid blows to his public image? Don't worry about what exactly, just assume that we can. What would happen then?"

Pedersen improved his own image somewhat by reacting quickly: "He would answer back as well as he could; respond to us even, to the extent that is possible."

Simonsen nodded in agreement. "Someone has at least made some strenuous attempts to hammer unpleasant impressions and images into people's minds. And very successfully, no less."

Anita joined in: "So in the interview with the hardliner from the Folketingets Retsudvalg who oh, was busy with the posters of Thor Gran as a background?" She glanced around to get the others' reactions. They shook their heads, and she explained, "The posters are simply close-ups of Thor Gran from the minivan, you know, where he talks about selecting the numbered delicacies, and underneath it just says, 'No, you won't!' so the message is clear. But if I was going to pick one simple thing in the propaganda circulating in the media, one simple thing that really has grabbed the attention of Danes, then it's Thor Gran when he's . . . selecting the children. The posters were shown for a minute, maybe one and a half, and the interview was probably just an excuse to show it. It's like the subliminal messaging with the image of the Coke bottle that was edited into movies in the 1950s to increase sales of Coca-Cola in the intermissions; someone manipulates our subconscious and no one wants to step in."

Simonsen shot down her last story: "It's called subliminal perception and it is basically a myth. The concept has never been proven and no one has ever manipulated a film in that way. But it's a good story."

"As opposed to the Thor Gran poster," Pedersen added sarcastically. "That's what you gain from hearing that story."

Simonsen immediately stiffened. For a second or two he closed his eyes, then he took a bag of licorice from his inside pocket, helped himself, and offered it to the others. No one wanted any.

Pedersen said, "You usually hate this stuff. What happened?"

"Nothing."

He still didn't like licorice, but Piratos licorice was an excellent antidote to a sour mouth. What could he say? That the photos of Anna Mia that he had been sent occasionally invaded his mouth? Who would understand it when he didn't even himself? And what business was it of the others? It had no meaning, he had it under control. That was exactly what he had—control. As soon as he got his fingers on those assholes who had threatened his daughter he would show them that he had it under control. Psychopathic bastards.

Planck managed to get the conversation back on track. "Now listen up and stop wasting time on that nonsense. I have an idea for how to tell an alternative truth but I'll need help from all three of you. It will also demand a small sacrifice from each. Do you want to hear it?"

It was a theatrical tactic and Anita was the one who told him what they were all thinking: "Sometimes you are so smug. Of course we want to hear it."

Planck did not address the criticism. Instead he turned to his guests, starting with the first: "Anita, you have to forget everything about your journalist ethics, not to speak of your loyalty to your employer. I'm going to force a boyfriend on you, if only temporarily. Arne, you'll have to be prepared to lead astray that voluptuous girlfriend of yours from the *Dagbladet*.

And while I'm at it, I'm going to give you some good advice from an old man. You should get some professional help with your gambling before it gets out of control and you would also do well to get your private life in order."

Pedersen's face went beet red; he said nothing, but wiped his forehead with his tie. They had never seen that before.

Planck turned to Simonsen. "Simon, you get the hard part. First, you can't take the rules too seriously the next couple of days. Many of the methods that I will suggest are illegal. Second, you're going to give an interview with Anni Staal, and third, you're going to have to keep Helmer Hammer and everyone at HS in the dark about our plans."

Simonsen nodded cautiously.

Planck addressed them all: "Perhaps you should take a couple of minutes to think it over before I proceed. If you want to hear my proposition."

Anita did not need to think it over.

"Fuck my workplace, and as far as my reporter ethics go, they're pretty much nonexistent. I think it sounds exciting. Is my boyfriend cute?"

The two men also agreed but with a little less enthusiasm.

CHAPTER 62

Planck's dinner party ended abruptly and unpleasantly for Simonsen. As soon as the arrangements for a media campaign had been discussed and everyone was able to relax and enjoy himself, he received a call from Herlev Hospital, where a nurse in the orthopedic-surgery division had found his card. He excused himself and left at once.

A good half hour later he arrived there. The patient, who was not a friend of his, was sleeping fitfully. Simonsen studied him and shook his head as his eyes slowly adjusted to the dim light in the room. The light-blue duvet was pulled up over the sleeping man's body and the upper part of the bed was raised so that the upper body was slightly elevated. A set of tubes had been inserted into the man's nose and were connected to an electrical outlet in the wall, from which a faint sighing sound bore witness to a connection. He had a turban of white gauze around his forehead and a thick bandage across his broken nose, giving him a macabre appearance.

"Do you want to hear what happened?"

Simonsen turned in astonishment. A man was sitting on a chair pushed away from the bed. Without waiting for an answer, the man launched into the story.

"There were seven or eight of them, waiting for him in the stairwell. Some of them had clubs, all of them with boots. They held me back and went after him. He didn't have a chance. They kicked and hit without stopping and in under a minute he had collapsed bleeding and unconscious on the floor."

Simonsen answered in a low voice, "That's terrible, and he isn't the only one. The same thing has happened in several places all over the country."

"You haven't heard the worst of it. One of them cut his forehead with a penknife. *For your abominable desires, for the childhood you ruined, for the pain you caused,* he said. Like a perverted ritual. The others even seemed like they thought it was too much but did nothing to stop it."

"What are those phrases? I don't understand."

"It's from a grandiloquent hate poem on one of

those antipedophilia sites. I can't remember which one but I remember the stanzas. They were recited six times, corresponding to five numbers and an ellipsis: five, six . . . seven, ten, twenty! His whole forehead is carved up." The man's voice broke. "I can't bear to think about it. Let me sit for a moment."

Simonsen turned his back to the voice. Some time went by, then the man said out of the dark, "I'm okay again."

"Would you remember the one who did the cutting?"

"It was a woman. Well, she wasn't more than a girl. I've never seen anything so terrible, not even in a movie, and the men just stood there. They seemed to think she was going overboard and it was almost as if they were afraid of her."

The man stared helplessly into the dark room. The faint light from the night-light fell over his face, which was set in a kind of bleak melancholy. Then he added in wonderment, "There have been women all day. When he was sacked, the knife, and now here."

"Oh no, has he also been fired?"

"He was let go this afternoon. That was why I took him home. I didn't want him to be alone. They called it a restructuring, but everyone knew that was a lie. A young bitch from human resources had the pleasure and I promise you she enjoyed it. Good God, she was awful. Like hatched from the business school in their brand-new fall collection of polished arrogance and powdery morals. She even brought flowers with her, and do you know what she talked about?"

Simonsen shook his head.

"Envy."

"Envy?"

"In a long, self-indulgent monologue. She was envious of the new freedom he was getting, envious of all the possibilities he had for choosing a new life, envious of the fact that he would now be able to sleep in in the mornings, envious of his severance pay, envious of all kinds of other things, all the time as her victim abased himself. He talked about his Androcur treatment, about how he sends most of his salary to his sons each month without ever hearing from them, about his remorse, yes he pleaded and cried but that didn't help in the least. The witch was oh so sympathetic and also envious of his courage to show emotions. People enjoyed and smiled at her scornful remarks. He had known some of them for fifteen years. I don't know what to say other than that those people . . ."

He came to a halt, at a loss for words. Simonsen also said nothing, and only the soft hum of the electricity could be heard. After a while he tried again.

"Those people and the ones who started this . . . it's just wrong. Evil and horrible, I can't find any other words for it."

The patient moaned, as if he wanted to indicate his agreement. The man didn't reply.

Simonsen felt exhaustion creep over him. If he sat there much longer he would fall asleep. He said, "What did you mean by 'now here'? Are there more?"

"You'll experience her soon enough. She's almost the worst."

Simonsen did not have to wait long. Suddenly, hair-raising laughter filled the room and a woman's voice screeched through the loudspeakers, like high-pitched screams from another world. The patient woke up and began to sob briefly but soon fell asleep again, as full of medicine as he was. Simonsen had jerked up like a spring and calm returned only slowly. He felt a nauseating disgust.

"What in the world was that?"

"A devil who doesn't think that he deserves to sleep, I think."

"What is she shouting?"

"I don't know exactly. Something about being the daughter of the night, the one who never rests, and that she has an eternal rage. I don't understand the rest."

"That's madness. Why don't the hospital staff put an end to it?"

"I've been to see the nurse on duty and told her off four times but no one knows where the voice is coming from or else they don't care. Maybe they're even in on it, I don't know, but it's hard to take."

Simonsen noticed an unfamiliar—even foreign—desire to hit not something but someone. To go after the nurse with a couple of jabs first to one and then the other side of the head and to see her flee down the corridor in her ugly dust-yellow clogs. This only for starters. At once he realized that he was afraid. Afraid of the hidden society he was unable to uncover. The conspiracy without a face, the public mood, which followed its own unwritten laws—frightening in its hatred and worse in its indifference. In the absence of anything better, he kicked the wall in frustration and banged a heating pipe so that it rang out through the room. The man on the bed shivered nervously.

"Dammit."

He didn't even know himself if he was lamenting the situation or the noise that he had caused. Then he tried with all his mental efforts to turn to something more constructive.

"Are you the one who can help me with the telecommunications information?"

"Yes, that's me, and I got your message. This morning I was a bit lukewarm, but definitely not anymore, so you'll get the help you're looking for."

"What about the other companies, that is, your competitors. Can you help me there as well?"

"There's no database in the telecommunications sector that I don't have access to. Us security people work together and we cooperate, but I'll need a contact person on your end to get into the citizen registry and the like. We can make further arrangements tomorrow."

"I'm glad, but I thought of another thing that I'm not even sure can be done."

"Tell me what it is."

Simonsen told him. The man didn't seem surprised.

"What telephone number did you have in mind?"

Simonsen told him and the man took a cell phone out of his pocket. The blue light of the display lit up his face. Simonsen was able to get a good look at him for the first time and thought that he didn't even know his name yet. The man's thumbs were working with a teenager's speed, and when he was done, he nodded a couple of times.

"The police starting to spy on our free press—such times, such times."

His voice had taken on a somewhat inappropriately humorous tone, and Simonsen understood it well. It was a way to keep the beastliness at bay. Overcome despair and smile the three women back to the kind of hell where they belonged. In the half darkness he gestured theatrically, with relief.

"Yes, we've reached a new low."

CHAPTER 63

Anni Staal was waiting for Konrad Simonsen.

Only a few minutes earlier, Anita had called and said that her earlier efforts had yielded results.

"The kilometer stone at City Hall Plaza at two o'clock, and Simonsen only has five minutes."

Anita had hung up before Anni managed to get a word out, so she couldn't do much other than go to the meeting, and privately she wondered whether she had misunderstood the message before she noticed the chief inspector heading her way. He looked exhausted and wasted no time with unnecessary pleasantries.

"I'm sorry about the location but I have an errand nearby and this is what I was able to think of in a hurry, but let's skip all that. I hear you want an interview and a long one at that."

Anni smiled, pleased. This was a promising beginning.

"Yes, I'd like that, and I hope that you will. We are useful to each other."

"Maybe you are right, even though I admit that it took me a while before I saw the sense in this alliance. And I should clarify that I can't stand your line of work in general and that I despise your treatment of my investigation in particular."

She circumvented his disapproval with a short, cloying laugh and said, "But you have concluded that the police have an image problem?"

"That you have played a part in creating."

"So it will be good to get your angle out there."

"I guess so, but I have a few conditions and it is a take-it-or-leave-it situation. There will be no negotiating."

"Let's hear it."

"I want a formal, legal document signed by both you and me, your editor in chief, and someone from the executive level, that says that you can't publish a single line of the interview before I have read through it and given you my written permission. You may also not print any of the information that I will give you whether directly or indirectly, and if you do, it will cost you a five-million-kroner donation to the Red Cross."

Anni did not have to reflect on his proposition very long before she said, "You don't have much faith in us."

"I think that the only thing you have respect for is money, especially money out of your own pocket."

"You'll have your document to your home address by courier by the end of the day."

"That's great, push it through the mail slot, I'll be out. Tomorrow at ten at the *Dagbladet*?"

"What about at your home? That's more private."

"You are sick."

"Not completely. If you want to reach the people you have to invite them to your home. That gives me a better opportunity to present you in a more human way—that is, not just brains but also heart. Believe me, I know what I'm talking about."

Anni crossed her fingers. The thought was apparently appalling to him but her arguments had struck a chord. It took a long time before he answered.

"At my home, ten o'clock, no photographers."

"Wonderful. Ten o'clock at your place, and the photographer will simply take a single picture of the two of us as we are talking and then he'll leave. I swear on my mother's grave."

Simonsen waved his hand in an irritated gesture, which she took as his assent. They parted without warmth.

No one could accuse Anni Staal of resting on her laurels. The solo interview with Konrad Simonsen was an enormous triumph but back at the office she pushed the thought aside and the following hours she concentrated on the next day's edition, rejecting a proposal for an article from her intern and paying her back for her lack of telephone manners earlier in the day. She smoothed a folded piece of paper on her desk.

"You can throw this away."

Anita Dahlgren looked up furiously. The rejection did not come as a surprise. "Did you even read it? His forehead was carved up while he was unconscious."

Anni Staal's voice was cold and her choice of words more

cynical and provocative than she actually felt. She'd had her interview now so there was no reason to thank the girl more.

"I don't care if they cut his dick off. What you have written is not our line and you know that very well. It's not what people want to read and, my sweet . . . it is not getting into print."

Anita stood up and her voice was shrill. "I am not your *sweet* and you should pay better attention too. Things are not always as they appear. If it turns out that the motive of your poison pen is a little less noble than hanging pedophiles up as a deterrent— well then, this whole thing will blow up in your face. Just wait until your beloved people go looking for another scapegoat. I know at least one who will have to eat crow."

Anni Staal stiffened but her warning bells were going off and several colleagues were watching. Even in a workplace where the language was direct and salty, her intern's speech exceeded the acceptable limits. But it was not the insult that bothered the star journalist.

"What do you mean? Try to explain yourself."

That was not something that Anita wanted to do. "I'm protecting my sources." She took her bag and left.

Anni Staal kept working, but Anita's comments proved difficult to shake off and it gnawed at her the rest of the day. For a while it bothered her so much that she seriously thought about contacting her police source even though she knew he would be furious. But it never went further than a thought because that evening he called of his own accord, with a message that felt like a déjà vu from the morning.

"The parking lot by the civic building in Nansensgade in half an hour and make sure you have some cash on you."

She hardly had time to confirm before he hung up.

When she arrived, Arne Pedersen was dozing in his car. She got in and sat down next to him.

"Good evening, my little songbird. You're out late. Are your personal finances squeezing you again?"

Her words stung and Pedersen thought that he hated her more than was reasonable.

"Hello, Anni. I wish you wouldn't call me that. I find it embarrassing."

She apologized, clear over the fact that she had made a mistake: "That wasn't my intention, you'll have to forgive me. But do tell . . . what do you have for me?"

"It's going to cost you five thousand and you have to clear it with Simon before you print anything. My boss has started keeping his cards close to his chest. He doesn't seem to trust anyone, even me, only Kasper Planck. It's totally paranoid. This case is about to crack him and the mood at HS is at a new low."

He thought that the description was not completely off. "Five thousand is a lot of money."

"Maybe, but I'll tell you what's worth even more. Five vacation trips to Thailand at twenty-four thousand a pop, plus five times twenty thousand in pocket money, that's only two hundred fifty thousand. Add to that three cash cards where the original owner was more than willing to share the pin codes when they got going with the chainsaw—another one hundred ten thousand. Furthermore, Frank Ditlevsen's account in Zurich has been tapped for around two million, so the total sum is about two-point-three million, and these are only preliminary findings. New information is coming in all the time. I have account statements from two of the victims with me going back three weeks so that you can see for yourself. Remember that they died fourteen days ago and look closely at the dates from the last withdrawals, but then give the documents back to me. If you put this in the paper I'll be nailed quicker than quick."

Anni Staal looked through the bank statements. Her voice sounded excited when she was done.

"What does this mean?"

"It was a murder-heist."

"What are you talking about? A heist?"

"Forget everything about a noble revenge and all the commotion, that's just a blind alley and smoke. The motive was simply greed."

"But that's terrible. Are you sure?"

"No, only about eighty percent, but yes, that's what I'm saying. You can try to have Simon confirm it but I can give you another piece of information for free. He is going to give you an interview. He told me just a little while ago."

"He's already been in touch. I'm going to meet him tomorrow morning."

"Well then, that's arranged. Do you also know that he's going to Riga this weekend? The traffickers who were working with the hot-dog vendor are from the Baltic mafia, but he tried to double-cross them. The Latvian police nabbed one of them yesterday and I don't think it'll take them long to get him to talk. Their police methods are somewhat more robust than ours."

Anni Staal frowned. She was far from stupid. "Why keep it secret?"

"Simon is quietly gathering evidence while everyone else thinks the motive is . . . shall we say, about sexual politics. Not even Helmer Hammer has been informed about this, I know that for sure. I think that Simon wants to give the country a lesson. Nothing less. Let the beast step in its own shit. That's a direct quote. That's what he told Kasper Planck the other day, but I didn't get it when he first said it. I think I do now. And of course he wants to be one-hundred-percent sure before he goes public since our credibility is so low and half of the country believes that we're concealing information about the victims being pedophiles."

"But, but . . . I have a hundred questions. Per Clausen, the janitor, how does he fit in?"

Pedersen had been waiting for this question. He answered calmly, "He was a useful idiot but he finally understood the truth. At that point it was too late. The corpses were on the stretchers and the traffickers were gone. Why do you think he committed suicide?"

Anni Staal nodded grudgingly. "What about the hot-dog man? He killed his own brother?"

"They hated each other with all their hearts and were both equally emotionally stunted."

"But then why did the hot-dog guy get killed? I mean . . . the whole business with the tree—what was that good for? Everyone's been wondering about that."

He smiled slyly and thought until his head hurt. It had been an oversight. "You may not be familiar with the Latvian proverb but those who are understand that message. *A flower is bestowed upon the steadfast, the branch waylays the traitor.* The original source comes from the Russian Orthodox tradition, but tell me—isn't this worth five thousand?"

She didn't answer at once. Tried thoughtfully to gather up the threads. Finally she said, "My goodness, heads are going to roll. Yes, it's worth five thousand."

Pedersen smiled quietly.

CHAPTER 64

The Countess sat deep in thought and studied the white-board. It hung right next to her desk and she had pushed her chair to the side, the better to see the four names that she had written in her neat, somewhat impersonal, schoolgirl handwriting: *Per Clausen, Stig Åge Thorsen, Helle Smidt Jørgensen, Erik Mørk.*

"Are you sure, Countess?"

She turned around, flabbergasted. Konrad Simonsen had come in without her hearing him. He looked incredibly exhausted. She didn't give a thought to the fact that one could easily have said the same of her.

"Yes, I'm sure. For several reasons but first and foremost due to Helle Smidt Jørgensen's diaries that she has kept for twenty years. The Mayland calendar, the same one year after year, with only a variation in the color. Poul has gone through them in great detail."

"It was a bit of a blow that she was dead. Are we sure it was from natural causes?"

"Yes, completely sure. It was a heart attack, probably brought on by stress, alcohol, and pills. We arrived two days too late. But there's no question that she played a part in the murders, and Poul agrees."

"I heard he went home."

"*Crawled* would be a better word for it. He looked like a corpse; he should have stayed in bed yesterday. But what about you? You look tired. Are you going to make sure you get something proper to eat?"

Simonsen shrugged. He had been to dinner at Planck's yesterday but the last time he'd eaten at home there had been frozen pizza on the menu, which he had forgotten about after it went in the oven with the result that it tasted like cardboard.

He pointed to the names and said, "Can you settle for giving me the conclusions? I have a meeting in the city in less than twenty minutes but I'll be back again tonight so I can read your report."

"You'll have to forgive me, Simon, but I have trouble imagining what could be more important than this. And while we're on the topic, what's happened to our investigation meetings? At the moment you're the only person who has an overview of the situation. All the rest of us can only see a piece of it. Is that your new leadership style? Because if it is, I don't much care for it."

Her words were sharper than her voice, which was closer to sounding a little sad. When he didn't answer right away and instead pulled up a chair and sat down, she regretted that she had talked to him in that way.

"It's really only partially true, this fragmentation," he said. "But you are right. There is something I haven't told you yet and it's because I know you would be totally against it. You'll find out about it shortly, but since you're asking, this might as well be the moment. Can you come in again this evening? Late, say around twelve. You can bring Pauline, if she wants to come."

The Countess decided to back off. Whatever it was, it could wait. It was more important that he get some sleep. He wasn't getting too much of that these days.

"I could, but tomorrow would be just as good, so you're free to take back your offer."

Simonsen frowned, somewhat bewildered by the sweet-and-sour exchange in which he didn't know if he was being criticized or defended.

"It doesn't matter to me. I'm coming back here anyway."

"The anonymous computer expert who has taken over for Malte? And who has special permission from you to run around more or less alone?"

It was a pointed question.

"Not really. He and Malte keep to themselves, but I'm going to read reports."

"I think I'll resume the investigation a little later."

He dropped the subject and pointed to the whiteboard.

"Give me the main points before I leave. You've included Erik Mørk in the vigilante group, I see."

The Countess smiled at his choice of words. It was reasonably inclusive. Then she grabbed one of Helle Smidt Jørgensen's pocket calendars and looked at a couple of the pages that Poul Troulsen had flagged with yellow Post-its.

"May sixth 2005, *at Per's, eight P.M.* October eleventh, 2005, *at Per's, 7 thirty P.M.* November second, 2005, *at Erik's eight P.M.*, and so on and so on. There are sixty-three such notations, about one a week apart from the vacation periods. The first is from February third, 2005, and the last is September twenty-sixth of this year, and since the summer the meetings increased in frequency. She only ever records the first name and it changes. At Per's, at Erik's, and at Stig's. If the meeting takes place at her home she only writes in a star, which happened nine times. There are of course many other evenings with arrangements and first names but nothing else of this regularity. Then there is the matter of Jeremy Floyd. His name is recorded twenty-two times, just eighteen months before the meeting notations begin— that is, from the spring of 2003 until the first part of 2004. She always writes him in as 'PF.' It fits perfectly. I've made a list."

"Last names, addresses, telephone numbers, e-mails?"

"Nothing, unfortunately. Poul has been through all the calendars four times and I've been through them twice. Here and there a page has been torn out. It could be covering her tracks."

"What about the one we're calling Climber? No meetings at his place? Or references?"

"No, nothing, which could either mean that he didn't have a place of his own or that he lived too far away. Stig Åge Thorsen in Kregme has only hosted three times, possibly because of the distance. But there are two notations of particular interest. The weekend of September eighth through tenth of this year: *digging at Stig's, cooking,* and December tenth, 2005, *Christmas dinner (Erik paying) reserve table for five seven P.M. at Hjørnekroen,*

Nørrebrogade 23. I thought that the fifth participant might have been the doctor so I called and spoke with Emilie Mosberg Floyd. It was a little embarrassing. He would apparently never have participated in a private event with his clients, which was something I was hoping and assuming she would say, but he had also been dead for several months at that point."

Simonsen waved his right hand as if he had singed his fingers. Then he checked his watch and the Countess speeded up.

"Erik Mørk is the one who took out the ad about being sexually abused as a child and his company runs WeHateThem.dk, which they do with supreme professionalism. Almost a quarter of a million visitors to this point and the portal is constantly being updated, though the tone is very aggressive. *You shouldn't be embarrassed, they should be embarrassed. You shouldn't hide, they should hide. You shouldn't be afraid, they should be afraid,* and so on and so on. Among other things they have uncovered the advertisement for the victims' sex vacation to Chiang Mai in Thailand that we found in Thor Gran's secret bag and it is probably worth checking carefully into where they got it. My guess is that Erik Mørk had it beforehand and has made it himself."

"Exciting. Anything else?"

"Mørk has restructured his whole company into a hate group with a mission to incite the public against pedophiles."

"We've known that for a while."

"Yes, it's nothing new. What is new is that Poul and I can link him to the crime, and one of the most important ways is this, take a look. This is a list of customers of child pornography that we found on Frank Ditlevsen's hard drive. The three other ones are lists that Mørk's company has allegedly sent to particularly active members who support his mission. Supporters who appear to know exactly what to do with pedophiles in their area when they receive names and addresses. This is the main reason for the violence. But take note of the spelling errors."

Simonsen scrutinized the list while the Countess explained, "Bjarne Anton *Adersen* instead of *Andersen*. Hans *Orne* Nielsen instead of Hans *Arne* Nielsen. *Pale* Henriksen instead of *Palle* Henriksen. These are the same lists, Simon, and what's even better is that it is hard to explain away in a court of law."

"You're right. It seems convincing."

"You should also know that WeHateThem.dk is doing all it can to publicize Stig Åge Thorsen's online appearance tomorrow evening. It wouldn't surprise me if it became a national event."

"It may be an opportunity. He may have joined the . . . movement."

"Yes, but there's more. We have a printout of the telephone numbers from which calls have been made to the Langebæk School in the past week—that is to say, when people were still willing to help us, so it's valid. Mørk called Per Clausen's work phone twice and Stig Åge Thorsen once. They are also an advertising executive and a farmer respectively so they both fit perfectly with the list of occupations that Emilie Mosberg Floyd got from Per Clausen."

"Okay, I believe you. This is well done both by you and Poul. Make sure that you inform Arne and maybe have him assist you in writing up the report."

"I've already talked to Arne but I can't find Planck, so I've left an update on his answering machine. Where is he anyway?"

"Sorry, I forgot to tell you. He's sick. Or rather, tired. He doesn't have the energy to come in anymore and there's not much I can say about that."

"No, of course not. But what do you think—should we bring in Erik Mørk?"

Simonsen did not answer immediately. He wanted to stay awhile and chat with her about this and that, if for no other reason than to break up his tight schedule, which was his own fault. Perhaps a function of pride, a manager's classic overinflation of his own importance. He glanced at his watch again and let go of the illusion. And how could he know that she would be up for it? She had her own affairs to manage.

"Sorry, I dropped the thread," he said.

"I'm wondering if we should have Mørk brought in?"

The thought of physically getting his hands on one of the people who had photographed his daughter left its trace. Simonsen's mouth longed for licorice. He took out his Piratos. The bag was almost empty. He took the last three and concealed his enraged gaze from her by looking down. Then he answered, "No, I don't want anyone else brought in unless I have a charge that holds. Next time they won't be able to go home for a long, long time. But I do want you to send Pauline to Hjørnekroen pub on Nørrebrogade and say a little prayer that our advertising executive paid with a credit card."

"Hm, all right. that's exactly what I'll do."

The Countess stared after him for a long time. Maybe he was overwhelmed, maybe he was getting involved more deeply than was good for him, but his head was certainly screwed on right.

CHAPTER 65

A young woman was sneaking around at the plaza in front of city hall in downtown Copenhagen, taking cover behind passing pedestrians, billboards, and parked cars. She finally managed to slink into a doorway quite close to the man that she wanted to surprise, and when he turned his head and looked away, she sprinted the last ten meters behind him. She placed a finger on his neck.

"Bang! You're dead."

Malte Borup twirled around. "Hello, Anita. Where did you come from?"

"I dropped down from the heavens. You are a terrible police spy, you know, given how I can sneak up on you like that without any trouble."

"I'm not a police spy."

"Whatever. You wouldn't last many hours. But come on, and remember that we're a couple." She put an arm around his waist and dragged him along.

It was a good eight hours since they'd been introduced to each other and it seemed to Anita that she had known him for years. She had had this feeling from the first time she laid eyes on him. That had happened at the McDonald's at Strøget in Copenhagen.

She had already been seated when Arne Pedersen and Malte Borup turned up. As soon as she saw them she stood up and greeted them. Pedersen received a hug, much to his astonishment, then she turned to her new partner. He was cute.

She curtseyed coquettishly as she held her hand out. "I'm Anita Dahlgren, a newspaper intern. You must be the computer-spy genius."

Malte Borup returned her greeting and appeared to accept this title: "Yes, that's me. My name is Malte."

They sat down and shared the three colas that the men had brought with them.

Pedersen prefaced his remarks with a warning: "You should both be clear about the fact that what you are doing is both illegal and done of your own initiative. That's another way of saying that if you are caught then all hell will break loose and you should know that we will simply deny any involvement. It's not fair, but that's the way it is."

The two young people nodded and Malte underscored this with a short "yes." Anita sat with her hands under her chin and stared deeply into his eyes.

"How long will it take to do the installation?" she asked.

"One minute on the remote computer, ten minutes on your computer, and about one to five minutes for you to learn the program."

"Probably more like thirty seconds. I'm quick."

Pedersen had to poke her on the shoulder to regain eye contact. He asked, "How will you get in?"

"The plan is to use the door. That's why we're boyfriend and girlfriend. Can't you remember what Kasper Planck said?"

Malte looked uncertainly at Pedersen. "Uh, boyfriend and girlfriend?"

Anita asked sharply, "Didn't you tell him about it?"

"No, not really, I thought it would be better if you explained that part yourself. It would seem more real, but I can tell that you're going to manage well on your own so I may as well push off right now. I was really only here to introduce the two of you to each other. You can split my cola—I haven't touched it."

He got up quickly and hurried away while Anita's gaze bored through his jacket and burned him alive.

Malte tried again: "Uh, boyfriend and girlfriend?"

"Yes, you know—the kind that walk hand in hand and are all cutesy to each other. Do you have a girlfriend?"

"A girlfriend? No, I don't."

"That's good. I don't have one either. Now we're a couple."

"Uh, well. Yes. I mean, thanks . . ."

She smiled at him.

* * *

The doorman greeted them.

"Hello, Anita. It's late, did you forget something?"

"Yes, I need to print a couple of files. You don't happen to have an old guest card so that my boyfriend can come with me? I'm pretty fond of him and if he has to stay down here and freeze I might lose him."

"You don't need it, no worries. You can go right in."

They strolled over to the elevators without hurrying. On the way up, Malte asked, "You don't like your boss?"

"Not a bit. She's just so . . . ugh, so bad, so obnoxious."

"Ugh, so bad, so obnoxious?"

"Exactly."

A short while later she added, "I'm hard core when it comes to language reform. You have to be if you're going to be a journalist."

He nodded seriously and she hit him in the side.

"That was a joke, stupid. Didn't you get it?"

"No, I'm pretty slow on the uptake, apart from with technology."

The next few minutes confirmed Malte's claim and in only a few minutes his programs were installed on Anni Staal's and Anita's computers.

"It's ready now, you'll see. If you go into your browser and write 'Garfield' in the URL field—no WWW or HTTP or anything—just 'Garfield,' then the browser will show you the other computer's screen and you'll be able to see what she's doing. If anyone comes by and you want to get out quickly, just hit the space bar. Are you following this?"

"Yes, absolutely. Garfield and space bar."

"Exactly. If you write 'Garfield dash code' you'll be able to see her ID and password but only after she's logged in the next time. Remember that it is a dash and not a backslash. After that you'll be able to log in as her. On your own machine and even

346

when she's on hers if you want to. Then you'll be able to read her e-mail. Or send e-mails in her name."

"Garfield dash-and-not-backslash code and I steal her ID and password."

"Yes, that's right. If you want to connect as her, you'll shut down your own machine and restart while you have this CD in your drive. You won't notice any difference but it will make sure that afterwards no one can tell which computer you used."

"Boot up on the spy CD if I want to connect as her."

"Yes, and then the last thing. If you hit Control Alt Escape, then my applications are erased and no one knows what you've been doing but of course that also means you can't use the programs any longer. And you can't undo it."

"Control Alt Escape and I'll be as pure as the driven snow."

"Uh, that's it."

"That was quick."

Anita jumped down from the desk and gave him a kiss that was not particularly quick.

"Why did you do that? There's no one here."

"Best to be on the safe side."

She smiled sweetly at him and he returned it bashfully.

The clock at city hall rang out the bells for midnight over the city roofs and a new day began.

CHAPTER 66

Simonsen was vacuum cleaning. The meeting with Anni Staal was coming at as unlucky a time as possible as far as the appearance of his home. He had a housecleaner who came every other Sunday, which left him here and now with almost two weeks' worth of clutter and dust, so if he wanted to appear decent to the many thousands of *Dagbladet* readers, the vacuum cleaner was the only option. The activity was abruptly interrupted when a sock invaded the mouthpiece and blocked the air intake, which he took as a clear sign from the higher authorities that all good things could be taken to excess. He stopped. There was no reason to go to the other extreme and end up being portrayed as pathologically clean.

Shortly after this the doorbell rang and the man from the hospital was outside.

"Good morning, Mr. Simonsen. Yes, things went more quickly than I thought. Your young co-worker is talented and with the right experience he will be very good in future but at this time you should let him finish his education."

Simonsen stepped aside. The man walked in but stopped in the hall without making any gestures toward removing his outer clothing. He held out an envelope.

"We have found forty-one men who all more than once have contacted the National Hospital switchboard in the period from 2002 to 2005 and have lived in Trundholm County from 1965 to 1980. If we assume it is the same man, around the age of twenty-five to forty and that he has not been admitted to the National Hospital, the list can be reduced to four, of which one emigrated out of the country in the fall of 2005, so you may be able to eliminate him. But we included him because he has lived in the same village as your two murdered brothers. He is the first on the list."

Simonsen took the envelope and expressed his thanks.

The man continued, "And then there's this one, which reminds me that your guest from the *Dagbladet* is running late. She's got problems with her photographer. He overslept so she hasn't left home yet." He held out the phone.

Simonsen said, "Seems like your technical tricks are working."

"Of course they are. It is easier than you would think, as long as you have the right knowledge and access. And it is easy to use. It rings every time her cell phone makes a connection with another phone, regardless of who is contacting whom, and then you pick it up and listen in on the conversation. She or the one she is talking to can't hear you and when the call is over or if you don't want to hear any more you just hang up. But you can't use it as a real phone. It simply won't work."

"Is there any risk of you being found out?"

"Not on my end. In that case I would find myself. In terms of risk, you are the weak link so when you're done I'll get this contraption."

Simonsen grinned. "Of course, it would make my work much easier to have a thing like that around."

The man answered dryly, "Come on, you've got to think big. It would be much smarter to insert a citizen's chip into all of us so the state could keep an eye on us."

Despite the exaggeration, his words emphasized the path they were embarking on and neither one of them made any further comment.

At that moment, Anni Staal's copy phone rang and the man

held it out to Simonsen, who carried off his debut with aplomb. He listened and an unfamiliar concern for decency made him turn his back to his guest. It was a short call. The photographer had been replaced by a healthier one and the reporter was now on her way.

Simonsen's initial interactions with the *Dagbladet* crime reporter, Anni Staal, were marked by palpable tension. The photographer quickly went about his task, then took his leave. The two antagonists were left behind, feeling somewhat self-conscious. But it soon turned out that they found many of the same topics of interest—albeit from their own points of view—and the first quarter of an hour was spent in chitchat. The strained atmosphere gave way to a kind of guarded amiability and from time to time they even found themselves smiling.

Then they got to work. Anni Staal suggested a dialogue divided into two parts.

"We'll start with gathering material for your profile. I ask, you answer, and later I write up the whole thing. Afterward we'll do a classic interview about your current homicide case and I'll quote you directly and without editing."

Simonsen agreed and the following hour they spoke freely about him and his work. Her questions were informed by a substantial insight into his work, and even though her focus was banal and gossipy, her professionalism demanded respect, just as her knowledge of individual cases was impressive. Simonsen never relaxed, however: in part he had his own secret agenda to pursue and in part he sensed that behind her friendly facade he was continually being put to the test.

There were only two times that her questions made him uncomfortable.

"You sometimes employ parapsychological consultants. Do you believe in ghosts and poltergeists?"

The subject was a mine field but he managed to get through it more or less unscathed. He discussed the use of clairvoyants in a sober and balanced way, providing a couple of general examples of where their assistance had been helpful.

The second topic that made him sit up was when they touched on his relationship to the media.

"In media circles you are known as being arrogant and uncooperative. Always dismissive and often coarse. Why is that?"

Instead of launching into a long explanation of his view of crime, entertainment, newspaper sales, and audience numbers, he frankly confessed, "That is one of my weaknesses. I'm a better investigator than communications officer."

And then there was no more meat on that bone.

Suddenly there was an incident that could have been fatal. Anni Staal's cell phone rang; she apologized and picked up. Shortly thereafter, the copy phone on the windowsill rang, echoing its master. He hurriedly turned it off. Anni Staal had not noticed anything, and when she was ready he had been out to the kitchen and regrouped. He finished the sentence he had been in the middle of before the interruption.

"But, as I said, a couple of times a sloppy investigation will lead to prosecution and conviction while a skillfully conducted one won't. You learn to accept it or quickly forget that the work is unfair. And in a while you'll get fresh coffee."

Anni Staal nodded thoughtfully. "That sounds good. I for one need to cut back, of course. I have about twenty cups a day. Well, this went wonderfully. I think I have enough now. Is there anything you'd like to add? Or is there anything you think is missing?"

"I don't want you to give the name of my daughter and ideally I'd like you to leave her out altogether."

Anni Staal nodded, stuck out her hand, and stopped her tape recording.

"I can understand that, all things considered. All right, I'll drop her."

He took a Piratos from a bowl and let it swirl around in his mouth. Then he snarled, "You can never know what kind of perverted animals are on the loose out there."

"Excuse me, what was that?"

The words had leaped out of his mouth. He cleared his throat and started over: "It was nothing. Thank you for leaving out my daughter."

"You're welcome, but it's not much to thank me for. You're the one who's done all the work."

He smiled, with more confidence than he really felt. "I guess."

"Let's go on to the current case—that is, your high-profile murder case. As I said, I imagine that it will be handled as a normal interview, that is to say with your answers to my questions. Direct quotes."

"And as I said, that's fine with me."

"Smashing, then we're in agreement on this point. I'll switch tapes."

She found a new tape in her bag and removed the plastic film. Normally she used her digital recorder for her interviews but a tape recorder afforded more natural pauses, and that was what she needed. She wrote a couple of lines on the cardboard container before she inserted the tape. Then she explained, "I'm using a good old-fashioned tape recorder today. My digital wonder is scratched up to the point that none of the IT folks can repair it."

"I know that well. Most of my people prefer the old tape recorders to the unreliable digital versions."

Simonsen's tone was conversational, as was hers, but inside he felt his tension increase and he leaned back in the sofa with an assumed calm. In his thoughts he had spent considerable time rehearsing how he would approach various things. Especially in relation to the financial motives for the pedophile murders that had been planted with her. And what he should do if she didn't even bring it up. Finally he had tried to push the thoughts away, which was easier said than done since they went around in circles without generating anything fruitful.

But perhaps it was because he had twisted and turned every hypothesis countless times that he managed her initial, seemingly innocent questions with ease. It started casually, before she had even turned on the tape recorder, but when he later thought back on it he was in no doubt that the questions had been carefully formulated and that his answers were far from inconsequential

"Tell me, was it your idea to agree to an interview with me?"

She had landed on the greatest illogical crack in Kasper Planck's scheme. If he knew that the motive to the crime was money and that everyone else—specifically the tabloid press, which he hated—was chasing in the wrong direction, he had no reason to improve his relationship to the public and particularly not with her. In fact it would have been smarter to let the *Dagbladet* lie in its bed until his prosecutor could raise a couple of solid charges of burglary-murder.

He was able to clench his teeth as if repressing some bitterness. "No, not completely."

"Helmer Hammer?"

He shrugged. What could he do except parry her words? Then he added, "If you ask me on tape then I will tell you it was all me. Your little handshake, however, was one hundred percent my idea but my boss approved it later without problems."

Anni Staal smiled understandingly. She also had bosses who had to be obeyed. He stood up, fetched the coffee, filled up both of their cups, and sat back down again. His guest thanked him and started the tape.

"Let's just jump straight into things. If there is a question you don't understand then we'll talk about it before you answer."

He nodded. "That's great."

353

"Let me begin by getting right to the heart of the matter. Is it true that the motive for the pedophilia killings is money and that we are simply talking about murder on purely financial grounds?"

Simonsen spilled half his coffee down his pant leg. It was convincing, but hurt like hell.

CHAPTER 67

Arne Pedersen was in trouble. The two women he was explaining himself to were not listening very carefully. With sarcastic attitudes and skeptical little remarks, they more than hinted that his words were not having the intended effect. *Bastard* and *shithead* were not expressions that had a positive influence on the conversation. He went on as well as he was able and no one faulted him for not trying to defend the precarious position his boss had assigned him. He concluded his explanation with additional detail, giving the reasons why it had been necessary to keep the women in the dark for over a day and, in certain contexts, even longer.

The Countess's eyes glowed with rage and he focused on Pauline Berg, until she poked her tongue out at him. Then he trained his eyes on the ceiling. When he finally fell silent, neither of his listeners said anything immediately, and for a brief moment he hoped that the conversation was over and that he would perhaps be able to slip unscathed back into his own office. But this optimism was not grounded in reality.

The Countess's voice took on an exaggerated tone, as if she were talking to a child: "Is Simon the one who has sent you out with this drivel? Isn't he man enough to tell us himself? Why hasn't he turned up? That interview can't take all day."

"He won't come in, he's going to be at home for the rest of the day. . . . Dammit, Pauline, stop that."

Berg had poured a handful of paperclips out of their container and was tossing them one by one at his head. Since the distance was relatively short she could hardly fail to miss her mark, and the last one had struck him in the forehead.

The Countess ignored his exclamation and said, "At home? Is he sick?"

"No, he isn't sick, he's just staying home. Maybe he wants to think things over. And drop the injured tone. Simon knows what he's doing."

"That's not the problem. The problem is that *we* don't know what he's doing. And what about you? Do you know what he's up to?"

Pedersen had to admit the truth. He had been wondering the same thing. "No, I don't."

Berg took over. "Tell me again why you haven't informed us of this before now, but spare me all your superfluous concerns. If you don't trust us, just say so. Why weren't we at the meeting on Tuesday?"

"You know, that wasn't a real meeting. It was a dinner. And there are no guarantees that our plan is going to succeed—oh stop it for God's sake, Pauline—a lot of things have to line up first. But of course we trust you. Until now you've been doing really brilliant work."

"Idiot."

The Countess chimed in, "Knucklehead."

"I need to take a break."

"Get in line."

Pedersen turned to the Countess. Despite the fact that their relationship was often somewhat lukewarm, he felt unsettled by the situation. Pauline he could more easily tackle once they were alone.

"Listen, I'm not the one who wanted to keep you out of this."

"Now you're being pathetic, Arne, but we'll let it go. Tell me who got the idea. Was it Simon himself? And who found the intern reporter?"

"It was Kasper Planck. Both of them, Kasper Planck."

"Hm, I should have guessed. Then there is another thing. I don't understand why Anni Staal trusts you."

"Well, that's not so easy . . . but . . . I have a relationship with her."

Berg exploded, "You have a relationship with that sack of blubber?"

"No, dammit, not that kind of relationship. That is . . . well, I guess I should tell you how it is."

He told them how he had been selected by Anni Staal as a potential source because of his gambling, and, compelled by his guilt, he laid it on thick in order to improve the mood. It worked. Berg poured the rest of the clips back into the container. The Countess nodded and returned to the subject at hand.

"So let me see if I understand this correctly. You have planted the traces for the robbery-murder—or whatever we should call it—ahead of time with Anni Staal, and Simon will be forced to corroborate it today in the interview. She will go back to her office and finish her article, but before she gets it printed on the front page she has to have his written permission. Ergo, she sends a copy of the article to Simonsen and the intern reporter will supply a copy of this to Mørk, after which we hope to shake the Climber out of the trees. How that will happen is as yet unclear. And in order to follow our progress we have installed listening devices in the editorial offices of the country's largest newspaper. In addition, we are unlawfully tapping a journalist's telephone because a friendly, completely unknown man has fiddled with her connection. Does this cover the situation more or less?"

Pedersen did not like her sober take on the situation but he could not say it was wrong.

"Yes, I guess it does. That part about the phone has only come in later. And Simon also said that you might be against it."

She heard his comment and stared for a moment out the window, after which she shocked them both: "Damage control, yes, that isn't completely misguided, and other than an interview with the killer himself, the vigilante group most likely has nothing that could trump this kind of news, but even with source protection they are taking a huge chance."

"Hardly bigger than the murderer, who assumed that the Langebæk School lay empty during the vacation. Much could have gone wrong there. And the burglary-murder motive will strike them hard, yes, will devastate them. They will lose support everywhere so they'll have to try something. Simon gives the chance of success for this plan as fifty percent but I think it's more than that."

"What about us? How do we enter the picture?" Berg was trying to connect to the more forward-thinking direction that the conversation was taking.

Pedersen explained, "When the intern reporter—her name by the way is Anita Dahlgren—has delivered Anni Staal's manuscript at Erik Mørk's company, Simonsen wants her and Malte out of the way. We're going to send them away for the weekend and you'll be going along to look after them. Together with a couple of other colleagues."

He went over the practical details and ignored Berg's sour expression. Afterward he turned to the Countess to instruct her, but here he was constantly stopped.

"Just drop it. If Simon wants me to take part in this agent setup, then he can come talk to me himself. I should refuse of course, on the other hand I am probably the only one who can live without my salary, now that we will soon all be suspended."

It stung. Pedersen went pale, as if he had used up his last lottery ticket, and it got worse when the Countess, after a brief nod to Pauline, went to her office while Berg stood up in front of him. Much too close.

"There's something you should know, Arne. Something I've been wanting to tell you for a while."

He simply nodded.

"You and me, it's almost too much fun for you."

"No, absolutely not. You shouldn't think that." His denial was genuine, and he stretched a hand out for her.

"Be still and listen. You have your children. Your wife, your house, your regular mealtimes."

Again he simply nodded, without knowing what he should say. She grasped his head and looked him in the eyes.

"From now on it will be on my terms. When I want, if I want it, that is. Do you understand?"

He nodded a third time. She kissed him on the mouth, then pushed him away, then changed tack and suddenly sounded like a pouty schoolgirl.

"I don't like the idea of playing governess to Malte and whatever that little chit is who has turned his head. A weekend away, God help me. Why can't I be with the rest of you? Can't you talk to Simon?"

CHAPTER 68

The drive to Ullerløse, four kilometers northeast of Vig in Odsherred, took a good hour and a quarter and Konrad Simonsen took pleasure in the trip. The sky cleared up the farther east he went and soon the Danish countryside was smiling at him in sunshine, which elevated his good mood even more.

The interview with Anni Staal had exceeded his expectations and he was sure that she was headed back to her office convinced that she had a new sensation on her hands that would shake the nation and generate record sales. He had confirmed the robbery-murder angle and then given her a series of additional details that were lies from beginning to end, but carefully formulated so as to be impossible to corroborate. He had also forced her to turn off the tape recorder and rely on her rusty stenography so that she would not be able to pin him to his words later. If her article was enough to shake the vigilante group, and perhaps draw Climber into the light through Erik Mørk, remained to be seen. There was reason to hope.

He had no problems finding the village, which turned out to be a collection of houses clustered around a supermarket and a church. He slowed down and drove slowly down the main street to gain an impression of the place. There was no sign of any industry or other places of employment and—apart from an elderly woman on a bicycle—no people. Soon he was out on the other side and surrounded by fields, so he turned the car around and headed back and stopped by the supermarket, which he assumed was the village gathering place. He was received in a friendly manner by an overweight storekeeper with an infectious, joyous laugh.

"If this is about the past here in Ullerløse, you'll have to get a hold of old Severinsen, and it would be smart of you to take a couple of those cans with you. They help jog his memory."

She smiled as she handed him a couple of beers. Then she followed him out of the store and pointed, smiling, at the house where the man lived.

Shortly thereafter he stepped into old Severinsen's backyard, where he heard someone chopping firewood. Severinsen was a weather-beaten and sinewy old man. He was dressed in worn, dirty green work clothes and his thin white hair fluttered in the wind around a beautifully furrowed face. He laid his ax down when he saw that he had a visitor. A dog of uncertain extraction raised its head and stared at Simonsen before it lay back down to sleep. After having shaken hands, the old man led him to a moldy bench along the side of the house. Simonsen sat down and hoped for the best. The bench held up, and he opened the beers.

"They say you've lived here a long time."

"My whole life."

"I've come from Copenhagen to hear something about the brothers Allan and Frank Ditlevsen. Can you remember them?"

The old man drank some of his beer and Simonsen followed suit. Then the man spit contemptuously. Simonsen copied him. The beer tasted like a disaster.

"You didn't like them?"

"No, they were pieces of shit. They spent more time at the pub than on honest work and if there was anything they could get away with, they did." A peculiar expression came into his face. "They are both dead. Someone hung them in the capital city. It's nothing less than they deserved."

The information was not completely accurate but Simonsen did not correct him.

"I beat up their dad one time when we were young. He is of course also dead and has been for a long time, but no one around here misses them. They were rotten bastards, all three of them, if you ask me."

"I have some names that I wonder if they mean anything to you."

"Let's hear them."

He started with the first name on his short list: "Andreas Linke?"

The old man reflected on this. Then he said, "Andreas. Well, I don't know exactly . . . I can remember dates and see faces, but I forget names."

"So you don't know him?"

"Maybe. Andreas—it could be the son, that is, the grand-son, but Linke I know of course. That's the German. Yes, we never called him anything but the German even though Linke was his name. He lived here for many years, right next to the brothers for that matter."

Simonsen felt triumph rush through him, the beginning of an intense relief in his body, swelling to a boastful pride and culminating in an inner roar of victory that felt as if it separated everything around him into a before and after. He had found Climber!

What he wanted most of all was to take a little walk around the garden and savor the moment but, of course, that wouldn't help anything. He continued the conversation.

"They were neighbors?"

"Yes, they were, but the addresses are different. The German lived on the side of the road down by the church, and the road there stretches into a curve so the last two houses toward the forest lie directly behind the brothers, who lived on the main road. A Copenhager lives there now but he's never there."

"Do you want to tell me about the German?"

The old man nodded. For a while he just sat and thought himself back in time, then he started to tell.

"The German, well that's a long story. After the war, in the summer of 1945, he moved in together with his wife. They wanted to get off the main road a bit because the missus had been through a little of everything—had her hair cropped, that kind of thing—and back then there weren't many who wanted anything to do with that kind of folk. Later they came and took him away. He wasn't a real German, he was from Tønder, part of a minority population, but he had fought for Hitler so he had to sit on the inside for a couple of years while the wife had a baby and everything. Well, she was hardly a tender mother and there were all manner of things that people said that he had done even though most of it was just idle rumor. Otherwise he wouldn't have been let out after three years."

"And the wife had a child?"

"Yes, it was a girl, and then she had another while he was still in prison but that one disappeared. Well, she brought shame on herself, but on the other hand . . . things weren't completely easy for her, to manage the everyday and such. And they reconciled when he got out in 1949 and then there were two of them to get things to work. He hired himself out locally as a farmhand. He was strong and as time passed people thought less often of the war so in the end he was an appreciated commodity. But then the girl grew up. She was quite pretty. She went to study in Nykøbing, that must have been in 1960 or 1961, but it wasn't long before she moved back home again knocked up, as it were. Well, well—she was a chip off the old block, and then they had to start over, the old couple."

"So she had a baby as well."

"She certainly did, and she couldn't have been more than sixteen. The old couple never complained. They were used to it.

Back then the German had gotten a secure position at the automobile factory in Vig and the mother and daughter kept a kitchen garden, some chickens and such and that yielded a trifle. And they looked after the little boy. But then came the fire. It was in 1964, October 1964, I remember it well. It was a tragic story."

"Their house burned down?"

"Yes. It was the electricity, some old stuff, and a fire started at night. The German got the grandchild out. The two others perished inside."

"So he was left alone with the child?"

"Yes, and a burned home. The insurance paid a little but he had to build most of it up himself, even though we helped a little. He became strange then too. It was as if he no longer understood what was going on. The eastern front he managed, but not the fire."

"So the boy lived alone with his grandfather."

"Yes, until 1975 or 1976 and then he died. The German, that is, and then the county took the boy but at that point he was basically grown. Or, wait a little now, he went down to some relatives in Germany."

Simonsen forced himself to take a sip of the beer. The old man noticed his aversion.

"If you don't like it, let it be. I'll give it to Klods-Hans. He knows what's good."

He pointed to the dog, who looked up lazily without getting to his feet. Simonsen put the bottle down on the bench. Then he said, "If I wanted to look up Andreas Linke in the church records, who should I go to?"

"Go back to Brugs-Katrine. You talked to her when you were buying beer. She is the reserve deacon, church servant, gardener, choir, and whatever else she can get hold of. She'll be happy to help you when she gets back. Right now she's busy helping the retired officer in the forest."

"The retired officer?"

"Yes, he was also here yesterday. Nice man. They just walked past along the road. For a chief detective inspector you don't seem very observant. Didn't you see them? He must be persuasive because she's not one to take walks." The old man grinned and his tone was teasing, but not mean-spirited. Then he added, "Out here in the country, we read papers too, you know, Mr. Simonsen."

Simonsen stood up. The man gave him directions to get up to the forest. The church records could wait. The dog also got to his feet. There was beer waiting for him.

Simonsen weaved in among the beech trees of Ullerløse forest. The terrain sloped up and the forest floor was soft with fallen wet leaves that were heavy to walk in, and after only a short while he was panting like a bellows. He slowed his pace. In front of him to the left in a glade he caught sight of a person with his back to him; he changed his direction and walked toward him. When he was a few meters away, he loudly made his presence known so that he wouldn't cause any unnecessary shock.

Kasper Planck straightened up without turning around. "Quit your shouting, I'm not deaf."

"No, and you look better all around, actually. What happened to your fatigue and your failing health?"

"God's nature does an old man good."

Planck kicked a tree stump and pointed his toe at two others close-by. "It was here it started. Or almost here. Frank had been the first, but it took place in the barn. Allan joined later and he was a real outdoorsman. But you must know that. I saw you talking with the old man."

"Apparently not thoroughly enough."

"No, that has always been your problem. You don't give yourself the necessary amount of time, and you never learn."

Simonsen felt a sting of irritation.

"I'm here, aren't I?"

Planck didn't comment on this. He said, "They were felled in the winter of 1984 and later nicely cut up and everything. Four large beech trees in their prime. The whole countryside heard about it, but apparently no one felt it necessary to alert the police or forest ranger. An outhouse was set on fire and that was also not reported."

"It must have been terrible for him. How long did it go on, do you think?"

"Five–six years. The grandfather couldn't really watch him. They say he was strange."

"Everyone knew and no one did anything about it?"

It was a question. Planck was apparently more familiar with the reaction patterns of the village and their small hidden secrets.

"*Knew* is maybe too strange a word, but in such a small town you can't so much as fart in a storm without your neighbor holding his nose, so some of them have surely guessed. I mean, there were times that the poor boy couldn't even walk normally but it took several beers before the old man was willing to talk about it. By the way, that beer tastes awful, don't you think?"

"Yes, it's unusually bad, but the poor boy—I mean, Climber—he returned to revenge himself on the past? At least physically, you could say."

Simonsen pointed to the tree stumps all around. "Well, what's strange is that he didn't, if the old man is to be believed. He paid others to do it. They brought a map where the trees were marked. He couldn't stand to come back himself."

Simonsen stared thoughtfully out into the air. Then he said, "What brought you up here?"

"The killing of the brothers was personal. That was the starting point, and with a lot of hard thinking you can get far. Suddenly the truth shines through. Like a falling angel that stands on your doorstep one night and illuminates your mind. And when the puzzle has been laid it gives meaning to many other things."

This was a little too lofty for Simonsen's taste, not to say incomprehensible.

"Can't you be a little more down-to-earth?"

"It was because the hot-dog vendor absolutely had to have five tons of copper beech in the head after all life had been beaten out of him. Our good man Andreas had to raise himself back up by the tree where he had been taken down. And his big brother had to dangle in the middle and witness the executions of his traveling companions."

"Andreas Linke, you know the name. Have you been in the church records?"

Planck patted his coat pocket. "Brugs-Katrine gave me a photocopy but I'm assuming that all your electronic brains also have spit out the name. Where does he live now? You're bringing him in, aren't you?"

Simonsen hesitated. They started to walk back to the village. Then he said, "There are certain problems. In the citizen's registry he is down as having emigrated about half a year ago, and if I put out a search for him I risk having the public work against me. I think I'll keep him to myself for a couple of days and see if your idea with the *Dagbladet* bears any fruit. If it does, I may be able to pick him up quietly."

Planck stopped and looked suspiciously at his former employee. "Be careful, Simon. We've both seen this before and it's thin ice you're stepping on. He isn't yours and your explanations sound a bit thin."

"Only a couple of days."

Planck shook his head. "It's always only a couple of days."

"I *will* get him. He's not going to get away with killing six people and the others won't either."

"No, they won't."

"If I can't get a confession with some information that only he and we know, I risk ending up empty-handed. The prosecutor almost laughed in my face when I talked about eventual charges filed against Stig Åge Thorsen, and Erik Mørk is nowhere near an arrest."

"Yes, it's not easy living in a constitutional state, but we should be able to pin those two and it is just a question of time and you know that very well."

"Climber also has to be put away. He can't be allowed to go free."

"Of course he can't, that's not what I'm saying. This is not about him. This is about you."

Simonsen filled his mouth with Piratos. They walked for a little while, then Planck said, "If I was your boss I would take you off this case and send you home."

He received no answer, just a shake of the head.

"You're not like them, Simon."

"No, of course not. Why do you say that?"

"Oh, stop with this nonsense. Do you really think that you can repair fourteen years of neglect of Anna Mia by behaving like Popeye?"

"How the hell do you know why I'm behaving like this?"

"You have always been an open book, even if you try to convince yourself otherwise. But that's of no consequence. The important thing is that you realize that you aren't like them. It's that simple. Think it over."

Simonsen stopped and spit his half-dissolved piece of licorice into the forest. Then he looked back at his old boss and shook his head. What did he know about being a father, childless as he was?

Planck changed the subject: "How did your interview go?"

"Above our expectations. Anni Staal swallowed the whole

thing and Anita Dahlgren has already been out to get the article from me that she will take to Erik Mørk's business tonight. In the middle of their so-called online program with Stig Åge Thorsen. Wait and see, this is going to stir things up in the duck pond."

"Keep an eye on her. Remember that they are killers."

"She is diligently guarded until she's back at the *Dagbladet*, and then when she is ready, she and Malte Borup will go on a state-sponsored vacation. I have three officers looking after them. Pauline Berg is one of the three, but that's mainly to get her out of the way. There's no point in her putting her career on the line. It's enough that the rest of us are."

Planck nodded, satisfied, and asked, "Do you think it's a coincidence that Andreas 'the Climber' Linke—or whatever we're calling him—has devoted his adult life to felling trees?"

"Is that what he does?"

"Yes, he attended a forestry school in Germany. Brugs-Katrine's son met him once in Odense, where he said so."

"I'm no psychologist."

"What is that supposed to mean? Didn't I approve your request to attend a course in criminality and the psyche? You should have learnt a thing or two in there, or was that money also wasted?"

Planck laughed excessively at his own joke and refused help in crossing the ditch that separated the woods from the path down to the village.

Simonsen did not smile.

CHAPTER 69

Stig Åge Thorsen was at Erik Mørk's business location in Rødovre, south of Copenhagen, and he was getting more and more irritated. As arranged, he arrived almost three hours before the online broadcast was set to begin, but after a tedious tour among countless unfamiliar people whose names he very quickly stopped keeping track of, he was parked in a conference room, where the bombardment of information gave way to a period of long, passive waiting. The room was decorated with a trendy minimalism. His irritation grew.

An additional amount of time passed before his friend finally turned up. He had a plate with six sandwiches and looked stressed.

"Sorry, Stig Åge, I apologize for the wait, but something came up."

Thorsen mumbled something incomprehensible and managed a thin, polite smile. Mørk sat down and helped himself to a sandwich. He did not look calm or collected.

"Maybe you just need to relax a little, Erik."

Mørk loosened his tie and tried to follow this advice.

"You're right, things are pretty hectic. I've never worked this hard. But have you been following the media these past couple of days?"

"If you mean her, that high-school girl—I thought she was utterly convincing; she almost made me cry."

"She was helpful, no doubt about it, but I was actually

thinking more about you. Everyone is looking forward to your interview. Five local TV channels are going to broadcast it live from their Web sites—if you can call that live—but with commentary from the studio, if you follow. That's one of the things we've been working hard on the past couple of days."

"What will happen after the interview?"

"After the interview?" Erik Mørk sounded surprised. "Well, there's a demonstration outside the Christiansborg parliamentary building tomorrow and in selected places in the provinces. In the middle of your program we'll put up a screen in the reader's face along with our demands, our slogan as well as times and locations. That's the whole point, of course. We're making use of your media attention to kick start our mobilization of the public and securing maximal dissemination, which is what we want. So tomorrow we'll follow up with a full-page ad in all the big daily papers. Incidentally, with the high-school girl to catch people's eye. I'll show you a copy of the proofs in a bit and it's really come out well, if I do say so myself."

"Hold on, hold on, slow down for a minute. Our demands—"

But Mørk was hard to stop. Too little sleep and too much adrenaline had left its imprint of mania.

"We have been conducting massive election campaigns directed against close to one hundred members of parliament, so the parties are boiling, and my last political report says that there is now open discussion of a pedophile deal. Pressure from voters, Thor Gran's beastliness, the violence, and not least this high school girl who blew through from cottage to castle, has laid the groundwork. By the way, do you know what *half a USA* is?"

"No idea, but I know that you go over there—"

"Sentences half as severe as the USA, which back home means a quantum leap forward. And our support on the Net has been completely fantastic. It takes less than—"

Stig Åge Thorsen slapped his hand onto the table. "Stop it, Erik. And listen up for a change."

Mørk stopped. And listened.

"First up, what do you mean by 'our demands'? As far as I'm concerned, we unanimously established our demands a couple of months ago. Don't tell me you've changed them."

"No, I've just systematized them a bit."

"Go on."

"They fall into three areas. Judicial, where we demand severer sentences and a stop to parental protections. Preventative, where we want more money set aside for county resources and training for all teachers and educators. And finally, if the damage is done, we want subsidized psychological assistance."

Thorsen accepted this. It was in large strokes what they had agreed on.

"Slogan, what slogan?"

"*Stop the violence, tighten the law.* It is the only slogan until tomorrow and there won't be a speech or any other activity. In fact, the idea is for people to stay there—in dignified silence—until the politicians produce a bill."

"Good, now you suddenly sound normal again, that's nice. All that's left is for you to brief me on the interview, nice and slow."

"We've brought in a media consultant. She will read the questions to you and you answer verbally and she'll write to those who are online. That will be faster than if you type yourself. Those people who get through with questions will usually be allowed to ask one or two follow-up questions so that a small dialogue develops but you and she will decide how many and for how long. Everything works more or less as it would in a radio program. Apart from a certain filter."

"That sounds simple enough."

"It is simple, and you will of course decide yourself which

questions to answer, but the consultant will help you as best she can and she'll warn you if she thinks you're getting off track."

"Excellent."

"I'll be the only other person in the room but I won't get involved. It'll only be you and her who are directly involved and I'm there mainly as a kind of backup. Is there anything you're wondering about?"

"No, that was very thorough."

Erik Mørk smiled. "Should I go and get the proof for our ad?"

"Yes, please."

He stood up and left. And Stig Åge Thorsen was left alone again.

A couple of hours later it was time and the online interview started well. Stig Åge Thorsen was nervous at the first questions but after a while he and the media consultant established a good collaboration. From time to time, Mørk informed them how many people were following the event. His voice was triumphant: they had around 280,000 hits.

The media consultant read from her screen: "A follow-up: do you approve of the fact that he killed five people? Suggestion: do you approve of the fact that he killed five pedophiles?"

Stig Åge Thorsen nodded. "Yes, I do."

"My suggestion: I approve of his struggle against pedophilia."

"That's good."

The consultant quickly typed the answer. Then the door to the room opened with a bang and all three turned. A handful of employees filtered into the room. A woman who appeared to be in charge approached Mørk and did nothing to hide the seriousness of the situation.

"Erik, you have to come with us right away. We have a big problem."

Mørk went with her, convinced that it was the police that had come to arrest him. He was led into this office, where a young woman was waiting. The woman in charge introduced them.

"This is Anita Dahlgren. She is a student intern at the *Dagbladet*. Read this."

A packet was thrust into his hands, the logo of the newspaper on the top of each page. He started to read. Already after the first two paragraphs he started to sweat and had to sit down. After he was finished, he had the presence of mind to gaze down at the text for a little longer as he tried to gather his thoughts. When he looked up and met the accusing gazes of those present, he was not completely unprepared. He took the lead and turned to the girl.

"Where did you get this? And why have you come here with them?"

Anita Dahlgren explained her sympathy for his cause. She also told him how Anni Staal had scored an unexpected interview with Detective Inspector Konrad Simonsen.

"But since you are telling us this in advance, you don't believe this, do you?"

"I came here to give you a piece of my mind. When I heard about the interview I didn't know what it revealed. Anni Staal has kept that to herself. But then I thought, that if I . . . made sure that you could see it in advance, that might be able to help you and when I got the chance I copied it. But now that I've read it . . . well, it made me angry and I still am. On my way out here I thought all kinds of things that made me want to cry, but I didn't. That is, when I saw the place . . . I don't know, it was hard to cry but I wish I could have."

The woman broke in, "It was nice of you to come and I understand your anger. I'm angry too."

Mørk decided to believe the girl. She was a naïve little thing, but credible nonetheless.

"When is it coming out?"

"No idea. Tomorrow or over the weekend, I think, but I certainly hope that there's some explanation for this or I'm not sure I support you any longer."

The woman spoke again. She gave Mørk a hard look. "I hope so too. I don't know what kind of wagon you've been hitched to but I'll be getting off if this is true."

He ignored her and focused on the girl. "Do you have a phone number for Anni Staal?"

The answer came hesitantly, although Anita Dahlgren was jubilant inside: "I don't really know . . . of course I have it, it's just that if you tell her that I—"

"Of course I won't," he interrupted. "I wouldn't under any circumstances, but the police have concocted a bunch of lies and it's in both her and my interest to correct it."

The skepticism of his co-worker was only minimally altered. He continued, as persuasively as he could: "This is bullshit, nothing more or less."

"Why would the police lie? That makes no sense."

It was the woman.

"It makes a lot of sense. They want the public's help to solve the crime and as soon as this web of lies is publicized they're sure to get some information."

He pointed at her. "You can draw your own conclusions. I know that you have been a fantastic help but if you can't support me completely it's better for you to go home. I need you more than ever, just not halfhearted."

The woman did not conceal the fact that she considered this option. His pulse was throbbing in his temples as he waited. Not because of her—he was indifferent to her personally—but she could be the first pebble in what could become an avalanche.

After what seemed like half an eternity she had made up her mind.

"If this is published, I'll leave. There have also been some other things as of late that I don't care for. People who have been beaten up and such. But this . . ." she pointed at the pages, "I can't live with."

Many others indicated that they shared this opinion.

Mørk did not have a lot of options, but with as much confidence as he could muster, he said, "It won't be published."

That promise would not be easy to keep, Mørk realized a couple of hours later. He was at the bar at the restaurant Andrikken in the center of town and Anni Staal's mistrust was almost tangible.

"I'm not impressed that you know about *Chelsea*. You could have found this out from any number of places and there's nothing that proves that you were the one who mailed me the videos, and not even your supposed outtakes change my mind."

She held up the flash drive that he had given her.

"And it's for the same reason. Because you could have been sent these by your supporters, but naturally I want to peek at this material. To be honest, I also have to say I couldn't care less about your talk of a police conspiracy. The bottom line, Erik: I don't believe you. You may have been misled yourself, who knows. I can't be sure of your role in all of this. The only thing I know is that you haven't said a single thing that would make me pull my article."

Anni Staal was enjoying the situation. It was eminently clear that she held all the aces and it was equally clear that the man did not know about Konrad Simonsen's clause. Maybe this could be used to her advantage, in case he actually had something to contribute.

"But I'm a busy woman. We have a deadline soon and it won't help either of us to sit here and waste any more time. If we do, the decisions will be made for us. You can start by telling me who gave you a copy of my interview. That much I want to know."

Mørk resembled the hard-pressed man that he was. The only reason he did not give Anita Dahlgren away was that he had forgotten what her name was. He did, however, remember the name of the secretary from the *Dagbladet* who had contacted him about the matter. Without having a copy of the interview itself. Anni Staal listened to the name.

"What do you know. Well, the next and last question on the agenda—what can you give me? You tell me that I've been tricked, but you have no way to prove it. For my part I've confirmed this information from a number of different sources. Try to see the situation from my side. Do you or do you not have anything? To put it bluntly, Erik, shit or get off the pot."

Somewhere inside him he had known that what followed would be the eventual outcome.

"If I arrange an interview with the man who did these things, then will you wait to hear what he has to say before printing your conversation with the chief inspector? He knows what happened to the money and he'll be able to prove it."

"An interview with the killer himself. Not bad."

He didn't reply, or consider that she might be frightened.

"One day. I'll wait one day. I want a confirmation later this evening and the interview has to be tomorrow. And one more thing. It would be best if he contacts me himself and I'm going to test him to make sure it's him. Agreed?"

Mørk agreed. The bartender brought them a couple of drinks that they hadn't ordered. It was a gift from a customer who had recognized Staal. She took a sip and then raised her glass to a bald older man a little farther down the bar. He smiled back at her, half drunk. Mørk toasted him as well, foolishly, then he said, "He'll only talk to you. No cops."

"Well what do you know. Killers are often like that. Let's say that I'll hear from him around eleven on my cell phone."

She finished her drink and put her cigarettes away in her purse, then slid elegantly down from the stool and started to leave the restaurant. On her way out she gave the bald man a kiss on the forehead. Her lipstick left a mark. Mørk found it grotesque but the man smiled happily and looked very much like a pig.

CHAPTER 70

On his way back from Odsherred, Simonsen called his inner circle to a nighttime meeting in his apartment. The exception was Poul Troulsen, who according to his own account was lying on his deathbed, hoping that death would come quickly and spare him from further pain. His wife, on the other hand, had downplayed the illness and described him as being just a little under the weather, so Simonsen pressumed that the truth lay somewhere between these two extremes, but in any case he had to proceed without him. The others promised to be there at ten o'clock. Only Pauline Berg objected and Simonsen had to use capital letters on the phone with her.

"This is not under discussion, Pauline. You will get Anita Dahlgren at eleven o'clock at the *Dagbladet* and drive her to Søllerød pub. On the way you'll collect Malte Borup and all three of you will sit tight at HS until you hear from me. You are there to keep an eye on them, and that is an order."

Unbelievably, Berg remained obstinate and Simonsen had to tighten the screws.

"You will also be allowed to join us, at least in the beginning, and I shall keep you informed, but this is how it is going to be. Make sure you understand that."

Kasper Planck, who was sitting in the passenger seat, grabbed the cell phone from him and said quietly, "Hi, Pauline. You really should do what Simon is asking. It's important."

Then he hung up. Simonsen commented, "How in the world did you do that? She was all worked up."

"You should speak slowly and give clear directives. They accept that. That goes for all women."

Simonsen reflected on this most of the way in to Copenhagen.

At home, he got out the chessboard but the old man was clearly tired and this time it was unfeigned. Simonsen meaningfully cleared his throat a couple of times when his opponent suddenly thought for an unreasonably long time over a relatively banal move. But it didn't help. One could clear one's throat as much as one wanted—he had fallen asleep. Simonsen maneuvered him into bed and took his shoes off, slightly irritated over the situation since in his view he had been winning. But perhaps the interruption wasn't so bad because shortly thereafter the Countess arrived. Half an hour too early and clearly worked up.

She had hardly hung up her coat before she started laying into him.

"I feel left out, Simon, left out and underrated. And I get particularly upset when I think about Monday evening. I had a wonderful time, but if I see it in the light of your faltering will to share your knowledge, I don't hesitate to call it false, not to say an outright betrayal. And you can say however many times you like that we should keep our work and personal lives separate but you, if anyone, do the opposite and keep me out of the loop on top of it all . . ."

She continued in the same vein for a while. A couple of

times he tried to follow Planck's advice but it didn't help and actually seemed to make things worse. Finally he couldn't think of anything but to tell her she was right and hope that she would eventually run out of ammunition. Which did in fact occur, but in a highly unpleasant way.

"I've been thinking a lot about whether or not I even want to be part of this. Risk my job and my career for an idea that is as illegal as it is personal, and *personal* being the operative word. The question now is why I would help you, Simon, when you don't even help yourself."

He didn't follow, but quickly caught up. She dismissed his objections.

"I've been on the phone with Anna Mia many times. She hardly knows what to think and is very worried, which I understand very well. She loves you and maybe I do too, I think. So now the conditions. I am together with you and Arne in this, wherever this leads. You have to give your word to obey the following starting Monday: one—take your diabetes medication regularly; two—go to a dietician and follow the directives you are given; three—stop smoking. The choice is up to you, Simon, but don't bother telling me that your personal life doesn't concern me. You opened the bag and you're eating the sweets."

It was a lot at one time, even for a mature man in his best years. Perhaps love was blind, but definitely not mute, at least in her case, and the romantic element was not immediately apparent in her carefully numbered conditions. Simonsen looked away and chose escape. At least an attempt.

"Kasper Planck and I established the Climber's identity today. His name is Andreas Linke. But we don't know his present whereabouts so we have to see if we can't coax him out. Exactly like before we knew his name."

The Countess's surprise was marked. "You've found him? Why haven't you said so? Where was he?"

The retired homicide chief's voice cut dryly through from the bedroom and was impossible to ignore: "He's throwing out jewels in order to escape, just like Rolf Krake of ancient lore."

Simonsen peered bewildered toward the sound of the voice. He had thought that the old man was sleeping. Then he drew his finger in a circle at his temple to indicate to the Countess that his predecessor was mentally unstable. It didn't help matters much because Planck's next sentence was not lost in the mists of fairy tales.

"He's sleeping. Hold him steady, you batty woman."

Simonsen threw his arms in the air with irritation. He shouted back, "Express yourself like a normal person. We don't talk to each other like that."

He glanced apologetically at the Countess, but his third attempt to circumvent the issue didn't work.

"I asked you a question, Simon. Please be so kind as to answer it."

A couple of hours later, Kasper Planck, Arne Pedersen, Pauline Berg, and the Countess were sitting around Simonsen's sofa table as their host was out on the balcony, smoking. Arne Pedersen was holding a telephone line open to Anita Dahlgren, who was at the *Dagbladet* office.

He recounted to the rest, "She is wearing a headset and can speak more or less freely. Her computer is hooked up to reflect Anni Staal's screen but right now that is just blank because Anni Staal hasn't arrived yet. It's worrying her that the place is starting to empty out. Most people have gone home."

Simonsen tossed the cigarette aside and closed the door. Then he said, "Anni Staal is on her way there. Erik Mørk has just called her and he said that she would be contacted in the space of half an hour. Now you can begin to hope."

No one talked for a while and everyone waited tensely until the Countess broke the silence: "I have some good news. Simon will stop smoking as of Monday."

The others nodded approvingly and praised him, apart from Planck, who chuckled.

At the same moment, something started to happen. Arne Pedersen related in a running commentary, "Anni Staal has arrived."

Some time went by until his next sentence. The others sat on pins and needles.

"She's turning on her computer and inserting the flash drive . . . one moment, it takes a second . . . she is maybe starting a movie. Anita is not completely sure, but yes, now she's sure and it's from the hangings. Anita has no sound but the man in the film is crying, she says it's Thor Gran. Yes, it is *Gran*. It's horrible, absolutely horrible, Anita says. Anni Staal has stopped the film. She's making a call on her landline phone."

He held up for a moment. "She doesn't seem to be making a connection." Suddenly he called out, "Dammit, Anita, hang up! I'll call you back."

Then he ended the call and took the next one. It had been indicated in the background of his mobile phone's call-waiting plan. The others were impressed by his complete transformation: he sounded like thunder.

"What the hell is this, Anni? Can't you get it into your pea brain that you can never call me? Last time you promised me that it would never happen again, so what is your pathetic excuse this time?"

He listened, then he sneered, "Now I don't *believe* anymore, I'm just sure, but if you have doubts you should get yourself a better source."

Again he listened and then answered, "No, that was right. The sequence in the films was different. The first one who was killed was Jens Allan Karlsen, he was at the very front and to the left, and the last one was Frank Ditlevsen, who was in the middle. Tell me, why in the world would you want to know that?"

Again a pause. Then he wrapped things up: "Yes, do that, and you can add a thousand to my fee and don't contact me again. Do you understand?"

He hung up and then called Anita Dahlgren back. The connection was reestablished.

The next twenty minutes were uneventful, aside from the fact that Pauline Berg left, which she did without fuss. At the *Dagbladet*, Anni Staal was writing an e-mail about how her interview with Konrad Simonsen had found its way to an unauthorized individual. She suspected a certain secretary.

Then suddenly there was action again. Arne Pedersen narrated, "Her cell phone is ringing."

At the same time, the copy phone rang. Simonsen picked it up and listened. At one point he wrote something down and when he stopped, everyone was starting intensely at him.

"He passed her test with the order of the hangings, and they are going to meet tomorrow."

Cheering followed this news. Even Kasper Planck made a fist.

"Kongens Kringle at Hindstrup Hovedgade, eight kilometers east of Middelford at exactly twelve o'clock."

The Countess gently squeezed his arm. Then she asked, "Did he give her a name?"

Simonsen purred like a hungry cat.

"He did, in fact. He said that she could call him the Climber."

CHAPTER 71

Stenholm Castle dated back to the middle of the 1500s, when the county's baroness Lydike Rantzau had the Renaissance water fort built. At that time, Skipper Clement and his peasant mob's abuses of the Jutlandish gentry under Count Fejde was still fresh in people's minds and so the new home of the baroness was fortified to withstand a rebellious horde—strong and formidable, with thick double walls, countless embrasures, machicolations, and a moat and a drawbridge. The most attractive feature of the castle was without a doubt the old rhododendron garden in the month of May and the castle park, which was maintained in a natural English style with winding paths and superfluous little bridges arched over artificial ponds. The property stretched all the way down to Gamborg Fjord and continued into the Hind fir-tree nursery.

Below the castle lay Hindstrup, a smaller province town that had an excellent yacht marina, a number of small niche industries, and a central square and adjoining pedestrian zone where a handful of stores struggled for survival. To call it a bustling town would be an exaggeration but people managed to get by, and although most of them were employed in Middelford or Odense, the village was far from dead. Mainly because the house prices were reasonable and the stream of tourists in the summer was substantial.

In Hindstrup, Konrad Simonsen added "trespassing on private property" to the long row of sins he had compiled over the past few days. Luckily he was simply invading a woodshed and luckily the house it belonged to was currently for sale and unoccupied, but he really had no legitimate grounds for his presence there whatsoever. On the other hand, the spot was almost perfect.

He had arrived at night and begun by surveying the main street, a luminous white autumn moon making this possible. Diagonally across from the bakery Kongens Kringle was a library with an informational poster that promised access at eight o'clock the next day. He called the Countess and recounted this to her. She confirmed it groggily. Shortly afterward he found the shed behind a house on a side road off the main street. It was unlocked and filled with firewood, nylon packets with wooden blocks of irregular size piled from floor to ceiling, against one whole wall. Only the long sides of the shed were made of brick. The other two were made with horizontal lathing fitted with wide spaces so that the firewood could dry out in the wind. He made his way past the wood by laboriously moving bag after bag to the opposite wall and realized, once part of the wall had been freed, that this was the place he had been searching for.

To the right he had an excellent view out to the bakery and straight ahead up the hill he saw the outline of the castle. The woods at the end of the castle grounds lay a few degrees to the left, and even with the naked eye in the moonlight one could see most of the edge of the forest. It didn't get better than this. He fetched blankets and his travel bag from the car. He made himself as comfortable as possible on top of the woodpile and set his alarm. Right before he shut his eyes he shot a last, long look up at the forest and said quietly, "Good night, Climber. I'm going to get you tomorrow."

Then he fell asleep.

Five hours later, his alarm clock chimed and he started his day as he had finished it the day before, by peeking out between the slats up toward the forest and the castle. In the dark the grade had appeared steeper but the scene was not much different from what he had imagined back home when the Countess—with the aid of some scissors, tape, and a printout from the Internet—had created an excellent map of Hindstrup and its environs. They had placed it on the dining-room table and studied it as intensely as a general's map before a battle. After a while, Arne Pedersen had suggested a systematized approach, slapping the flat of his hand over different areas of the map as he spoke.

"Okay. Village, castle, castle grounds that run up against the woods, the water, and tree nursery. The woods and the castle are high up, the village below. Let's imagine that we're the Climber. Where will he have the best overview of the situation? It's almost a given."

He let his finger run along the edge of the woods.

"Here he has an unobstructed view down to the main street. At least on the one side and I'll bet five rum balls that that's where Kongens Kringle is."

The Countess agreed: "Apart from the fact that betting no longer has a place in your repertoire, that fits very well. The building over here is probably the nursing home and it has an odd number. The bakery is probably opposite but he may also live in the village or have access to the castle. The view from there is even better. What is it being used for?"

"A school for children with learning disabilities. I don't think the possibility is very likely. His retreat would be hampered if—"

Simonsen had been looking at the map for a long time. Now he broke in. "It's the woods. He feels safe among the trees. He sets up in there and lurks around until the coast is clear. I can feel it. He's probably already there before it gets light. Remember that he waited half the night by the hot-dog stand in Allerslev."

Planck shook his head. The Countess gave him an anxious glance and Pedersen said, "I suggest eight to ten plainclothes officers in the village, ideally from PET, and then thirty to forty men in the woods and the nursery. That will create an iron ring that he doesn't have the chance to escape."

He went on, turned directly toward Simonsen: "Call in the special forces if you can. Those boys are supertalented and we have enough time to organize it."

Simonsen shook his head. "How many people want him to get away? Half of the population? Twenty percent? Ten percent? Give me a guess."

The Countess answered reluctantly, understanding where he was headed, "It is hard to say. Public sentiment is about to swing again, I think, but for the moment we have what is almost a media war. The press coverage is unpredictable and much of the so-called news reporting is manipulative or strongly biased."

"A speech, Countess. You may want to write it down. Is it ten percent?"

"No, that is too optimistic. Much too optimistic, unfortunately."

Simonsen turned to Pedersen. "Arne, you're good at estimating. To assume a low estimate, let us say five percent. What are the chances of selecting seventy people where no one—not a single one—divulges the plans before they are under way?"

It was an irrefutable point and neither Pedersen nor the Countess made any objections when their boss concluded, "Our task force tomorrow consists of the three of us. I'll take off soon and you, Countess, will turn up at eight A.M. At that time I will have scouted out a place for us both. Arne, you follow Anni Staal, but in a car other than your own."

No one had any reasonable alternatives to offer Not even Kasper Planck. Pedersen asked, "What if he calls back and changes the location? That's something I would do."

"You'll take the copy phone and we'll have to improvise, but I know that he will be hiding in that forest until they meet. That's how he is. The woods are his best friend and his worst enemy."

This time even Pedersen grew worried.

But Simonsen, in the woodshed, was not worried. Without any sense of urgency, he ate his liverwurst sandwiches and washed them down with a big gulp of water from his water bottle. Coffee and a morning smoke would have to wait, which turned out to be easier than he had feared. A pleasant tingle of anticipation went through his body and made him at once relaxed and restless. He took out his weapon from his service bag. It was years since he had been armed, and he had to spend a little time adjusting the straps of the shoulder holster to accommodate his current size. Immediately thereafter, his cell phone rang.

It was half past eight and Pedersen had arranged a phone meeting. His voice came through clearly: "I've pulled over at a rest stop outside Korsør. There's nothing of interest from Anni Staal's telephone, apart from the fact that she hasn't left yet. I hope they haven't changed the meeting place to Valby, for example, because in that case we'll be screwed. I've rented an Audi, by the way, a sweet car. I'm going to switch now and am anxious to see if you can hear me."

The Countess answered. She was whispering, but also came through clearly: "Bookworm here, and I can hear you loud and clear, Audi. I'm reading the paper and have an excellent view of the café but not much else. My only problem is the head librarian, so I'm going to limit my communication to what is absolutely necessary—as long as she is in the reading room."

It was Simonsen's turn. He had wedged his cell phone between two of the sacks of firewood close to his head so that he had his hands free. His message was brief: "I hear you, but let's concentrate."

Arne Pedersen answered, "Audi here. I have nothing to

concentrate on except a half-empty freeway. What are you doing, Simon? Shouldn't you have a code name as well?" He grinned.

It was the Countess who answered, still whispering, "I think we should call him Nimrod."

She was not smiling. Nor was Simonsen.

"I'm working, so stop with the nonsense."

They were silent.

Simonsen hunted. Slowly, methodically, and with the utmost concentration he searched for his prey by scouring the edge of the forest. The fall colors made it easy to differentiate among the trees. The sun was behind him and its pale light filled his sight with clear red, yellow, orange, and green shades. Here and there were trees that had lost all their leaves and broke the palette with their black branches and naked twigs. Like witches' fingers. From time to time a cloud obscured the sun and the woods changed character to an inscrutable mass, uniform and compact. But hardly a minute would go by before the sun came out again. He used these pauses to train the binoculars down on the main street or on the freestanding trees of the castle grounds. He did not bother to look at the castle itself.

Not much happened. At one point, a gardener came to a halt on one of the many small white bridges in the garden. He stared out in front of him for almost ten minutes, unmoving, as if he were sucking up groundwater. The man was over fifty and presumably of no interest. Nonetheless, Simonsen drew a sigh of relief when he finally decided to continue with his life and slowly shuffled off down to the village, where he disappeared. Two men appeared, occupied with surveying, but they also disappeared after a while. No other human activity was discernible.

"I hope you're inside somewhere, Simon."

It was the Countess and her voice was normal. The head librarian must have left.

"Why? What do you mean?"

"The weather, of course. We're going to get a real shower in a little while, or what do you think? You are the one who has the better view, unless there's something I've misunderstood."

There was nothing she had misunderstood but Simonsen had a view only of half the sky. He put the binoculars down, crawled down from his seat, and made his way to the door of the shed.

Out over the water, the sky was covered with leaden thunder-clouds and lightning flashed at the horizon. He watched the storm with fascination. Turbulent air flow and currents on the underside of the weather system tore off gray wisps of clouds and hurled them toward the water. Darkness won out and approached. Suddenly there was a waterspout, then another and, a little farther, a third. Curved, thicker at the top and slender at the bottom, the three giant fangs drifted toward the coast in an uncertain dance. But the phenomenon lasted only a short while. Immediately upon reaching land, the three columns were consumed by the earth, while a rumble rolled in over the village like a casual burp. Then the rain started to fall.

A quarter of an hour later the front had passed and the light returned. Simonsen resumed his post. Everything was as before, the same irregular shapes and outlines, the same nuances of decaying green, the same concentrated lack of activity. And yet not. The rain shower had drenched the area and now the sun was reflected in a myriad of drops so that each leaf glittered and each branch gleamed while little creatures carefully ventured forth from the many hiding places of the forest in order to reconquer their wet, reborn world. Even Simonsen was aware of the change and he whispered to himself, "You are there, Climber, and I'm going to nab you. At some point you're going to make a mistake, a simple little mistake, and then I will get you. I'm at the top of the food chain and I am very, very hungry."

At that moment Pedersen called in to report some

developments: "She just drove past. I'm about one hundred meters behind her."

A little while later he added, "Nothing new about Steel-Anni. I've just gone over the bridge and I'm on her tail. We're going to reach you in about an hour but I've heard some news on the radio. Do you want to know what's going on?"

The Countess was quickest. "Of course we do."

Pedersen continued: "The lead story was a long piece from outside the Christiansborg parliamentary building where people have started to gather for a protest, and apparently there is a strange kind of muteness over the whole thing. There are no speeches, songs, or chants. Apart from a banner that urges tightening the law and stopping the violence. The reporter found the expression *dignified* and couldn't get past it, whatever that means. And the report came from the same place where there is hectic activity right now. An antipedophile gang is on its way and the politicians are grappling with the three main demands that were listed in today's newspapers but there are other things in play. Great increases in the severity of punishments and abolishing the limitations protecting parents in relation to sexual abuse of children. Support for the victims in the form of state-subsidized psychological or psychiatric help as long and as much as is necessary. Abolishment of pedophile associations and strengthened abilities for us to trace child pornography on the Internet. In this capacity an upgrade of our resources as well as the possibility of, certain cases, punishing the monetary bodies that allow for the payment of the material. Also travel agents whose customers who go after foreign children."

Simonsen interrupted, "Keep to the point. I have a highly developed sense of smell."

Pedersen was bewildered. "The point, sure. I didn't get that last part."

"I understood it very well," the Countess commented. "You frighten me, Simon."

There was a pause. No one knew who should speak next, so everyone was silent. After a while, Pedersen wrapped it up: "Some say it is the nation's constitution that's the problem. The freedom of association applies to everyone, as we know, and the responsibilities of banks and travel agents are under discussion. Those are business interests and, well . . . thus somewhat tricky."

The Countess took over. "I can't say I don't agree, but I would definitely have wished that the organizers had found a more orthodox way of breaking into the public stream of information."

Neither of the men answered. It was clear that she was speaking mainly because Simonsen had asked for silence. Shortly thereafter she was more direct.

"Oh, I don't care for this. Are you armed, Simon?"

"No."

"I'm glad to hear it."

Support for Simonsen came from an unexpected source—an unfamiliar voice interjected itself. It came through clearly and needed no further explanation.

"Please, this is a reading room, not a fish seller's market."

The Countess stopped speaking and Simon patiently continued his vigil. After a while he recognized each silhouette and all the trees in his line of vision and knew what would come into his binoculars before it appeared. The relentless repetition, where he scrutinized the same hundred meters of tree line again and again, destroyed his sense of time, and Pedersen's sporadic reports about his position struck Simon as unreal. Only the hunt carried meaning—the narrow cone of his field of vision, which panned systematically across the terrain, back and forth, again and again, without deviation. A battle of stamina and concentration in which he never doubted his superiority or allowed the least bit of uncertainty to shake his confidence that the Climber was hiding somewhere in the faded damp foliage.

Suddenly a flock of blackbirds took flight over a collection of treetops, the outline of which resembled a fist. They circled over the forest for a while before they landed again. They looked like rooks. He could not see what had startled them but it had to have been something so he kept his gaze trained on that place for a long time, without discovering anything. Finally he gave up and again resumed his scanning in the old familiar pattern.

And then disaster struck.

The Countess was the first to comment and this time in a full voice, without giving any consideration to the library rules.

"Oh no, this isn't true!"

Simonsen turned his binoculars to the main street and his exclamation was of a different order. In front of the bakery was a patrol car and three uniformed officers were on their way inside. Shortly thereafter, a cacophony of voices streamed through the cell phone like a ridiculous radio play.

"You can blame the neighbor, the bank, the merchant, it's all the same because debtor's prison has been abolished, but don't blame the government and if you do, at least communicate with them. You can't ignore their requests however wrong it's gone and you should know that, Bolette."

"I want all of you out," the Countess shouted. "Now!"

No one took any notice of her. A woman's voice came through: "So listen to this. I don't have a television. The same day that Anders died it blew out and that was four years ago. Four years and they keep asking me to pay the license however many times I write or call. It's simply impossible to register as having no television. They don't believe me, those crazy Copenhagen apes. Just imagine if I demanded money for bread that my clients did not recieve."

"You are interfering with an incredibly important mission

and you have to leave. Your pickup will have to wait until tomorrow."

The bakery woman continued: "And then you turn up here, three officers strong. Don't the police have anything better to do?"

A couple of customers supported her but a young voice countered, "She could have been brought to the hearing on Monday when I was here alone."

The Countess tried again with the full strength of her lungs: "Out with you. I am from the Homicide Division."

"The Homicide Division? Because she's been lax about paying her license? That's just too much."

"I haven't been lax. I don't own a television, I don't have a television. I don't want a television. Don't you get it?"

"Can I buy four focaccia buns before you take her in?"

And then suddenly Pedersen broke in with a message that did not leave much room for interpretation: "Anni Staal has received an SMS. It says *dumb pigs*."

Simonsen turned off his cell phone and turned one last time to the forest edge. For more than three hours he had been staring at the place with no results before he packed up and left. But his optimism had suffered a blow, he no longer thought about luck, and then he got some just the same—the first time he panned the area with his binoculars a rope dropped down into his line of vision from one of the trees that the birds had circled a while ago. Immediately thereafter, a boot followed.

Simonsen had a reputation for handling himself rationally in situations that required quick decisions, and what he now did was in large part without error. First he thought for about ten seconds without moving from the spot, then he took a map out of his bag and again studied the area behind the castle and out toward the water and the nursery. It was clear that it would have been senseless to sprint up to the castle gardens, partly because it would have taken him too long and partly because his chances of catching the man when he finally made it were minimal. The Climber was faster than he was and was on his home turf. The odds would be more in Simonsen's favor if he drove up behind the park and tried to find him on one of the nursery roads. He tossed his things into his bag and half ran to his car.

As soon as he was out on the highway and the coast was clear, he increased his speed as much as possible and in only a few minutes he was racing down the long, straight forest road that cut through the Hind tree nursery and divided the area into easterly and westerly parts. About halfway through he turned down a side road, parked his car about ten meters down, and continued on foot. Without hurrying, he walked as quietly as he could toward the next intersection. Soon he would come out to the right at the back of the castle, and a quick calculation in his head told him that if the Climber had not run—which he had no reason to do—there was a good possibility that he was still in the area.

The vegetation along both sides of the road consisted of tall spruce trees and a person wishing to hide himself would have only to take a few steps behind the tree trunks and stand still. The most important thing was therefore to be neither seen nor heard. From time to time he stopped and listened without perceiving anything other than birdsong. At one point he surprised a couple of pheasants, who flew away noisily, flapping. He crouched down next to a tree and waited a little while until peace had returned. Then he went on noiselessly. He reached the intersection after twenty meters. He kept well to the left along the trees and when he turned he therefore spotted the man walking toward him a couple of seconds before the other. At that time he had long since managed to get out his pistol. The distance was exemplary: the other man was too far away to go to attack and too close to avoid a bullet. Their eyes met and each knew who the other was.

"Get down on your stomach."

The man did not react and his eyes flitted between the gun

and the woods. Simonsen released the safety. The little metallic click sounded ominous and full of foreboding.

"Don't get any ideas. If you run, I'll shoot you in the legs and I'll do it now if you don't lie down. You'll get your shin shattered for no reason, especially if I choose to shoot you in the mouth a few times so I get the joy of seeing you die and the result will be the same, namely that you'll lie down. Please go ahead and make your choice before I do it for you."

The man put his bag aside and lay down. He showed no signs of any emotion, neither anger nor resignation. Simonsen walked behind him, bent down, and clasped his handcuffs around the man's wrists in an experienced way. Without hurrying, he put the safety back on the gun and put it back in its holster, then lit a cigarette. He inhaled greedily and gazed at his catch. The man was lean and well proportioned, clearly used to physical work, his hair blond and wild and his face weathered. The clear blue eyes were watchful and hostile and over his right eyebrow he had an irregular red scar. Simonsen pulled the man up onto his legs, searched him for weapons, and—as expected—found nothing. In the side pocket of his sturdy shell was a cell phone with a missing SIM card. The bag contained professional climbing gear as well as ropes, harness, and a pair of specially constructed boots with iron spikes at the front. There was also a thermos flask made of aluminum. Simonsen placed the bag under a fir tree and covered it with branches. Then he checked his watch.

"Andreas Linke, the time is eleven thirty-seven and you are under arrest. I also want to inform you that I hate you with all my heart and that you are going to cry blood over the pictures that you sent me of my daughter. I bid you a very hearty hello."

As expected, he received no answer.

They walked side by side to the car. Simonsen took a chain out of the trunk. He carefully nudged the man into the passenger seat and secured the chain around the handcuff on the right side and the other end to the safety belt security catch that was mounted in floor of the car, where beforehand he had attached a small padlock. Then he locked the door, walked around to the driver's seat, put his coat on the roof, and unfastened his shoulder gun holster. He tossed it into the backseat before putting his coat back on and getting into the car. Before he drove off, he freed his passenger a little more by unlocking his left hand. This gave the man a reasonable amount of mobility, but constrained by a radius of action where it was possible to hit him with a forceful strike of his fist.

"If you touch me or the steering wheel, I'm going to hit you in the face. Hard. Understand?"

The Climber did not respond. Simonsen jabbed him with his fingers and repeated his question: "Understand?"

A curt, angry nod indicated that the man had understood, and Simonsen smiled, pleased. This was contact.

A couple of kilometers after he had left the tree nursery, he neared the highway to Odense. He turned to the right and some ten or so kilometers farther up he came to the E20 freeway toward Copenhagen. He slipped into the fast lane and kept a steady speed of a little over a hundred. Traffic was moderate but did not demand attention. At twelve o'clock he turned on the car radio to hear the news. Without commenting on it, he noticed that his passenger followed the announcements carefully. Many people were apparently gathering outside Christiansborg Palace. At least, if one was to believe the speaker—and he was not one hundred percent convinced that one could. At any rate, the reporter sounded far from objective as she melodramatically described the people that quietly but deliberately waited for their legislators. There was nothing new from Parliament itself. He turned off the radio and drove a dozen kilometers as he rehearsed in his head for his coming telephone conversation. Then he called Pedersen.

"Hi, Arne, my battery is about to run out so listen without

interrupting. I've got him and I'm on my way to HS. You and the Countess should ask for a couple of canine units."

He told him quickly about the tree, the bag, and the SIM card, then added, "There won't be a problem with evidence. He talks like a frightened child and admits to everything."

Then he hung up.

The Climber appeared strangely unaffected by the situation. Apart from a brief, slightly astonished look when he heard himself described as a frightened child, he stared blankly out the window. But Simonsen perceived—with satisfaction—a certain tension in him. He had trouble finding a comfortable position and kept shifting in his seat. Not much, but enough to reveal his restlessness. They drove south of Odense and Simonsen broke the silence.

"Did you know that you killed your victims on the day of the Eleven Thousand virgins? That is what the eighteenth of October was called in the Middle Ages, or the Day of Ursula. Take your pick. Both names come from the same legend."

He glanced at the man. The Climber did not answer, but he turned his head slightly and shot him a look of irritation. Simonsen continued in a cheerful and casual voice.

"Yes, it was a terrible story. Very sad and unfortunately very bloody. Ursula was a Breton princess back in the fourth century. Extraordinarily beautiful, as they are, the princesses of legend. She was also extremely pious. The English king, however, was not. He was a heathen. Still, he proposed to Ursula, who accepted but on the condition that she first had to undertake a pilgrimage to Rome in order to satisfy her deep desire for a spiritual union with Christ."

He stopped abruptly. There was an accident ahead of him and traffic was starting to build up. He drove by slowly without staring at the ambulance or the damaged car at the side of the road. The Climber did not look either. When they had resumed their cruising speed he continued his story—sure that it embarrassed and confused his passenger.

"Now, where was I? Oh yes—Ursula took off for Rome but not alone. She took eleven thousand maidens with her, and you have to admit that is an overwhelming, colossal, and extremely large number of maidens. Don't you think?"

The Climber did not appear to think anything. He had turned his face away.

"Okay, we'll wait to hear your opinion, but anyway, I think it was a lot. In any case, the whole horde came to Rome, and the Pope—his name was Cyriacus, by the way—was besotted, to say the least, which is actually a bit strange because one would think he would become extremely irritated. I mean, it's an imposition of the worst order. Imagine eleven thousand uninvited guests. The cost of food would have been enormous so he was clearly a very hospitable man, that pope. Anyway, they left eventually. Ursula had to go home and get married. But the journey home did not go as well as the way there. Not by a long shot. They bumped into Attila the Hun and presumably a number of Huns, and they were killed—all of them. No one quite knows why. Maybe Attila was having a bad day or perhaps they had taunted him, who knows? The point is, little Andreas, that in this context your deed doesn't really hold muster. You only killed six, and five of those on the same day that the maidens died only some seventeen hundred years earlier."

He could see the Storebælts bridge ahead of him and decided to wait with the conclusion. His audience said nothing anyway so he would most likely get no complaints. When they were nearing Slagelse, he went on.

"My story from the past . . . oh, that's right. I didn't quite finish. Almost, but not quite. That is, all those maidens. Do you know where they were killed?"

As usual he received no answer, but Simonsen noticed that the man tightened his right fist, looked down and away.

"You know, I do believe you know where it is. They all suffered the martyr's death in the middle of Cologne, and even if the facts remain a bit hazy they built an entire basilica in memory of the bloodbath. The Basilica of Saint Ursula, Ursulaplatz 24—to be precise. You must know it, I mean, you've lived only two streets away on Weidengasse 8. Actually, formally you still live there. A rented room on the third floor right under the roof, so of course you know the church. I think you may also have noticed that I've shifted the dates around a little to get my story to fit. I'm like that. Can't always be trusted. The day of the virgins is on the twenty-first and not the eighteenth of October, but you knew that well because Ursula's Day is well known in Cologne."

The Climber's ears had grown redder. He did not care about the conclusion. He maintained his silence but there was no great poker player in the man.

When they reached Sorø, Simonsen left the interstate and continued along the highway toward Holbæk. He could see that the Climber was confused. The most sensible thing would have been to continue in over Ringsted and Køge, and hit Copenhagen from the south. But it was not completely misguided. At some point they would hit the Holbæk motor-way, from which they could reach the capital over Roskilde and Glostrup. It was already one o'clock and he turned the radio on again. The timing was impeccable. The triumphant voice of the reporter filled the car:

"It has become worse to be a child abuser in Denmark. The Pedophile Packet has been negotiated here in a broad coalition between the government and the opposition. Initial treatment of the proposals will take place as soon as later this afternoon. Sentences for the sexual abuse of children will more than double and the parental protective clause will be removed. Rape in general becomes a more severe crime. In addition, close to eighty million kroner will be set aside in the budget each year for a series of actions to counter child abuse, including victim assistance, expanded police services, Internet surveillance, and psychological research. In the plaza in front of the parliamentary building here at Christiansborg, a huge celebration is under way. We now go to the ministry of justice, where the minister is preparing to make a comment."

Simonsen turned it off. The Climber had a tight little smile on his face.

"I guess you won. Now all that's left is settling the bill, and you especially have run up quite a debt to be repaid. Even though I might wish that it was Per Clausen and not you sitting beside me. I'm just a bit worried that after I get you to talk it'll turn out that you aren't more than a pathetically engineered copy of the real thing. Annoyingly enough."

The words did not fall on deaf ears; the smile disappeared. Simonsen added aggressively, "There's a personal dimension as well that we two have to work through. You sent me some pictures of my daughter and that's something you shouldn't have done. You're going to cry over that one, but I guess I already told you that."

They drove on in silence again. Simonsen's lower back had started to ache and he wanted to stop and take a rest. He tried to help the situation by shifting his weight from one side to the other. Halfway to Holbæk, in the village of Ugerløse, he left the main road and turned left, toward Mørkøv and Svinninge. They were now driving west, in the opposite direction of Copenhagen, and it didn't take long for the Climber to get nervous. He looked around with obvious bewilderment and became more and more restless.

Simonsen debated with himself. Reason told him that he should give up his plan and turn around. What he was doing was wrong, even though he was in control of himself and the situation. He decided to abandon it. But only after a final little theatrical gesture.

He opened the container between the seats, grabbed a couple of bags of Piratos candy, and tossed them onto the dashboard. Then he growled, "You're the one who hooked me on this shit."

Up to this point he had been calm and calculating. It felt good to let loose. He shouted, "Soon I'm going to shove this entire bag down your throat."

His prisoner gave him a frightened look, which Simonsen enjoyed. Then he rolled down the window and threw the candy away. He didn't want to use it anymore. Nor did he have any use for the original reason. That could go to hell, too, it could.

Once they had passed Mørkøv, the Climber could no longer hold back his questions.

"Where are we going?"

It was the first time that Simonsen had heard him speak. He had a nice, slightly husky voice that was marred by an undertone of panic.

"Haven't you guessed yet? You're not particularly quick on the uptake. If you were a little smarter you would already have started to beg for mercy."

He reduced his speed, uncertain if the man would think to grab the steering wheel, and they slowly made their way through the autumn landscape. It had gradually become more overcast the farther east they had gone, but now the sun broke through the clouds and lit up the rolling terrain. Simonsen looked around, smiling slightly, as if he were sightseeing. There was nothing particularly noteworthy to see. A farm here, an approaching car there, mostly harvested fields with hay bales strewn hither and thither as if a giant had thrown a handful of dice.

Without looking at his passenger he said, "It's funny how the mind works. You can go back and forth for months at a time for your old tormentors Frank and Allan while you nurse your own private agenda that will tempt them to their deaths. You have reached adulthood and no longer need to fear them. But the place where they abused you, you still avoid. The shed and the woods. You spend almost no time there and all your strength doesn't help. At least you yourself couldn't manage to fell the trees and set fire to the place. You needed help for that. On the other hand, it was clearly a long time ago and things change. We'll see, we'll see. What do you prefer to be called, anyway, Climber or Andreas?"

The question came without warning.

"Tell me where we're going, dammit." The voice was almost shrill.

"I asked you a question."

"Here in Denmark everyone calls me Climber, so that's what I prefer. Where are you taking me?"

"Good. Then I'll call you Andreas, because I can't stand you, Andreas. In fact, I hate you, if truth be told. You should have let my daughter be, you scum."

The man twisted his hands and jerked his body restlessly from side to side. Simonsen kept driving. They passed Svinninge and then Hørve. The Climber started to sweat. Tiny beads appeared at his hairline and along his nose, and from time to time he rubbed his sleeve across his forehead.

"You have no right to take me there."

The tone of aggression was gone, and was closer to pleading. Simonsen answered cheerfully, "Right, that's an interesting word. If we were all to go out and hit each other in the head with what we have and don't have a right to do, then we wouldn't get anywhere, would we?"

"Can't you just let it go? I can't . . . I don't think I can bear it."

"No, I assure you, I won't. It suits me perfectly to take a detour to the place where it all began. To the shed, where Frank raped you, and the trees, where it was Allan's turn. Were they all cut down or just the ones that were most commonly used—if I can put it that way?"

The man had put his hands over his ears in order not to hear, and he banged his head against the back of the seat. The color of his face drained away—apart from the scar, which was a deep red. As soon as he removed his hands, Simonsen was on him, mean and merciless.

"The old people in the village tell me that you could hardly walk when the brothers had had a go at you. You waddled around as if you had shit your pants."

The Climber turned his head as if he could shield himself from the words.

"Okay, you piece of shit, if you tell me where you live in Germany and where you live in Denmark, I'll turn the car around."

It wasn't quite that easy. At first, the Climber chose to put up with his discomfort, but the closer they got to their destination, the harder it got. Finally, he gave in.

"In Germany, I live where you said. Weidengasse 8, in Cologne. Here in Denmark I have a garden-level apartment in Fredericia, Ivertsgade 42, and it's under the table. The owner doesn't care who I am as long as I pay the rent. Take me back to Copenhagen. I want a lawyer."

The rage in his voice had returned as he spoke. His gaze filled with aversion and the restlessness disappeared.

"You want, and you want. You can get a kick to the head for all I care. Tell me about the pictures I received."

The answer came after a short pause.

"That was Per Clausen. He sent me the envelope with the message to wait a week before mailing it. I didn't even know what was in it until now."

"How did he know my daughter?"

"I don't know. He was prepared for you, I think. Turn around.

I want to get back to Copenhagen like you promised. We have nothing against your family."

"Then you shouldn't have dragged them into this, because it has really made me mad, more than you can imagine. And now for the fun. I lied to you before but it's your own fault that you believed me. I told you once that I'm not to be trusted. You should listen more carefully another time."

The Climber stared at him without comprehension. Then his panic returned and this time it was worse than before. Now he trembled uncontrollably as if he was cold. He whimpered from time to time and after a couple of kilometers he started to beg. It sounded pathetic and he got no reply. Simonsen turned right by Fåreveijle, and soon they had a view over Sejerø bay on the left, so there wasn't far to go. The Climber alternated between crying and pleading. In between, he rambled incoherently about everything between heaven and earth, big and small, and it was not uninteresting but worthless as evidence from a judicial standpoint.

Suddenly Simonsen stopped the car. He took a map out of the glove compartment, then got out of the car and lit a cigarette. He let the door stay open so that they could talk, although the Climber's ability to speak was greatly reduced.

"You still don't understand, Andreas, that this is not about your confession. That will come later. This is about revenge. Revenge for the people whose lives you took. They probably pleaded for theirs but you killed them without mercy. You are up against a life sentence and deserve it as much as anyone. But first your worst nightmare will be realized. Do you dream of the place? Despite all the psychiatric treatment and your glorious crusade. I think you do, and in a bit you'll experience it again, regardless of whether you peep, sing, or scream."

Scream was basically what he did do, but not loudly, more high and squeaky like a kitten being squeezed. Then he started to pull on the chains, but with no result other than to cause a red mark on his right wrist. Simonsen continued to smoke, unconcerned, until the man suddenly threw himself in between the seats and caught sight of the pistol that Simonsen had carelessly tossed into the backseat. He yanked it desperately toward himself and grabbed the gun out of the holster, at first only to drop it in his lap. He quickly picked it up again, unsecured the weapon, and pointed it at his captor's face with an uncertain, shaking hand.

Simonsen calmly flicked away his cigarette. Then he sat down in the driver's seat and irritatedly pushed both the gun and the man away with the flat of his hand, as if they were an annoying insect, and the Climber pulled back as far away as he could.

"I don't believe it, Andreas. And I don't think you would hit me, the way you're shaking, and anyway it wouldn't help you one bit. You and I are still going to Ullerløse."

He turned the key and started the engine. The Climber stared at him for a long time in confoundment, then he pointed the gun into his mouth and pulled the trigger. It clicked. He tried again, with the same result. Then he slid down, as powerless as a tuft of cloud, into his seat, his gaze empty. Simonsen could tell by the smell that he had peed his pants. He turned off the engine and stepped out. He placed his hands on the roof of the car, rested his hands in them, and stayed like that for a long time. Then he straightened up and shouted at the top of his lungs, "It should have been you, Per, you devil, not this pathetic wreck."

He stared measuringly down the road, then back where they had come from, and said straight out into the air, "But I'm not like you, Per. You would have liked it, if I had been. A nice little bonus on top of the victory. But you won't get it, not on any terms."

Then he walked around the car, freed the Climber from his chains, pulled him up, and helped him mop of the worst of the urine with the help of some paper towels. Then it was time to head home.

They were greeted at the HS in Copenhagen by an agitated Pauline Berg. He had interrupted her at the inn and commandeered her back to work, where she had to make sure that an interrogation room was made available. In addition, she would be the one conducting the interrogation. She had done what he had asked her, but she had also spoken several times with the Countess and Arne Pedersen.

"They want you to call them at once. Both of them are . . . worried about these developments, and they don't understand why you have turned up alone with . . ." She searched in vain for the right words and pointed to the Climber, who was self-consciously huddled behind Simonsen, as weak and pliable as child in Sunday school.

"Andreas Linke, his name is Andreas Linke, and there's nothing strange about the fact that I took off with him alone. He is completely harmless. As it happens he is also nice and cooperative."

The Climber nodded softly as if he wanted to confirm the statement. Berg stared at him, frowning, while Simonsen went on.

"Now let's go in and have a chat with Andreas, so it will have to wait. We can sort it out later. Are you ready?"

That she was not. Clear over the fact that she could not do anything other than obey, she excused herself and went to the bathroom, where—like a schoolgirl in trouble—she called the Countess. When she entered the interrogation chamber a little while later, her boss had already dispatched the initial steps and she heard him tell the tape recorder that she had arrived. Andreas Linke sat on his chair with the legs pulled up under him and his arms wound around his body. As submissive as a beaten dog, he followed each movement and each word that came from Simonsen. His face was unnaturally pale, and when he gave an answer he sounded like a son who wanted to say whatever it took to placate a strict father. Simonsen's communications were simple and direct.

"It's not enough to shake your head. You have to tell the tape that you don't want a lawyer."

"I don't. I want nothing to do with any lawyer."

Then came a long strong of questions that had to do with the Climber's life and a systematic investigation of his relationship to the others in his self-help group. Then finally Simonsen arrived at the murders.

"Did you kill five people in the gymnasium at the Langebæk School in Bagsværd?"

"Yes, I did. I was the one who killed them."

"Tell me how."

"They were hanged. I hanged them." He smiled apologetically.

"Who helped you do this?"

"The others, the ones from the group were also in on it."

"What are they called?"

"Do you mean their names?"

"Yes, Andreas, tell me their names, both first and last names. I want you to repeat their names if they were involved in the murders."

He counted on his fingers. "There was Per Clausen and Stig Åge Thorsen. And Erik—Erik Mørk, that is. And then me."

"No one else?"

"No, no one else."

Simonsen frowned slightly.

"Oh, sorry. Yes, there was Helle Jørgensen—Smidt Jørgensen, I mean. I forgot about her. You have to excuse me, but she's dead anyway. And Per Clausen. Per is also dead." He giggled and added, "Helle did not try to die, it just happened.

Berg finally pulled herself together. They had the confession, that was enough. She pushed back her chair noisily and stood up. "I don't want to be party to this anymore."

But Simonsen also stood up, and his voice was hard and commanding: "Sit down, young lady, and do your work."

She sat down again, flushed, while he stopped and rewound the tape. It gave him some trouble and a couple of minutes went by before they could continue.

"There's one thing that is important to me, Andreas, something that only you and we know and that I would very much like for you to tell me."

The Climber nodded accommodatingly.

"How did you get the five men from the minivan into the gymnasium?"

"Some of them walked on their own, but I took the ones that were unconscious on a wheelbarrow. I tied them to it. They were heavy but I'm strong. Was that what you wanted to know?"

"No, not completely. Something happened with one of them, as you were getting him out of the minivan, do remember that? And can you remember who it was?"

The Climber thought back and for a while he said nothing, then suddenly his face cleared up, pleased. "Thor Gran, it was Thor Gran. He fell and started bleeding from his ear. His ear hit the ground and he got a big cut, but that was an accident."

"That was exactly what I was thinking of. Tell me now, who was the first one to have the idea to kill all these people and why they had to die?"

This time the Climber needed no time to think.

"It was Per Clausen, he was a very smart guy. He said that when they were all dead, all kinds of people would want to listen. We would get attention, Per said, and then it would be more difficult for someone to . . . that when someone . . ." He looked down self-consciously and searched in vain for a suitable formulation.

Anna Mia walked into the room, immediately followed by Poul Troulsen. He glanced at the suspect, then shot Pauline an order: "Go call an ambulance, and hurry."

Berg almost ran out the door, while Anna Mia calmly walked over and put her arm around Simonsen.

"You must be tired, Dad. Let's go."

She took his hand and he followed.

"I got them, Anna Mia, did you hear that? I got them."

"Yes, you did. That was wonderful, but it's over now. We're going on a vacation."

Quietly, undramatically, they left the room.

CHAPTER 72

Once back at Simonsen's flat, Anna Mia made her father some food and helped him pack. The Countess joined them a little later, but they didn't talk about the case. The case was closed. Simonsen was placed in an armchair, where he tried to focus on reading a chess book. If they spoke to him he answered politely but in monosyllables, as if he was not one-hundred-percent clear on what was happening around him. The women let him sit. The Countess went to the kitchen two or three times to take a phone call and on one occasion she raised her voice, but when she returned she said nothing about it and neither of the other two asked her any questions. It was none of their business. It was close to eight o'clock in the evening before they were ready to leave.

All three of them traveled in the Countess's car. Simonsen was relegated to the backseat, where he quickly fell asleep. The women took turns driving an hour at a time while they chatted and enjoyed themselves. They arrived at two o'clock and quickly agreed to let the sleeping man in the backseat stay where he was. They helped carry in the luggage and unpacked the essentials, then wrapped up the day with a glass of white wine before turning in. The Countess went to her room; Anna Mia went back to the car.

To her surprise, Anna Mia managed three hours of unbroken slumber, which she put down to the wine. In any case, the sun was rising when she opened her eyes and after a moment of disorientation she realized where she was. Her dad was also awake. He was sitting up and looking out the window. She smiled when she caught sight of him and said quietly, "Good morning and welcome to the North Sea. Want to walk down to the beach?"

Simonsen wanted nothing more. They got out of the car and, hand in hand, wandered over the outermost dunes and down toward the water. Once the sea was within sight, they stopped. Strong foam-topped breakers that shone like silver in the morning sun came roaring toward them, and the wind whipped their faces. Anna Mia rested her head on his shoulder.

"It's beautiful, isn't it, Dad?"

"Yes. Yes, it is."